Gorgeous

Gorgeous

PAUL RUDNICK

 SCHOLASTIC PRESS / NEW YORK

For my mother

Library of Congress Cataloging-in-Publication Data

Rudnick, Paul.
Gorgeous / by Paul Rudnick. — 1st ed.
p. cm.
Summary: When eighteen-year-old Becky Randle's mother dies, she is whisked away from a trailer park to New York City, where fashion designer Tom Kelly offers to transform her into a glamorous Rebecca, a girl fit for a prince — but soon she begins to fear that she will lose touch with her real self.
ISBN 978-0-545-46426-0 (jacketed hardcover) 1. Identity (Psychology) — Juvenile fiction. 2. Beauty, Personal — Juvenile fiction. 3. Princes — Juvenile fiction. [1. Identity — Fiction. 2. Beauty, Personal — Fiction. 3. Princes — Fiction.] I. Title.
PZ7.R8792Gor 2013
813.54 — dc23
2012046062

10 9 8 7 6 5 4 3 2 1   13 14 15 16 17

Printed in the U.S.A.   23
First edition, May 2013

The text was set in Mrs Eaves.
Book design by Elizabeth B. Parisi.

The privileges of beauty are enormous.

— JEAN COCTEAU

BECKY

1.

I grew up in what some people would call a mobile home and what other, snobbier people might call a manufactured home, but I was always fine with calling it a trailer. That's right, I said I grew up in a trailer. Fuck you.

I lived with my mom in East Trawley, Missouri, until I was seventeen. My mom weighed almost four hundred pounds and you're probably thinking that she was lazy or everything that's wrong with America, or that she belonged on one of those stupid cable TV docudramas called stuff like *Jumbo Mama* or *I Weigh More Than My House*, but you're way off base because my mom was the sweetest person and the best mom ever. But she did have a problem, because from as far back as I can remember I only knew one thing for sure: My mom was terrified of something, and as long as she kept eating she'd never have to go outside and face it. Whenever I asked her about my dad or about what she was so scared of she'd just sort of smile and say that I was talking crazy, and so after a while I stopped asking, because I was pretty sure that my dad, whoever he was, and her fear were the same thing.

On the morning of my eighteenth birthday, just as I was about to leave for work, my mom grabbed my hand. She'd been sick for almost a year and she could barely leave our couch, but being my mom, she wouldn't see a doctor.

"Oh, baby," she said, "I know it's your birthday and I can't buy you anything, but I have something to tell you, and that's going to be your present."

"Mom, I don't need presents. . . ."

"Hush, just listen. I know that I haven't been the sort of mom you deserve. . . ."

I rolled my eyes because she knew this wasn't true.

"I just wish that all sorts of things were different. And I know that lots of people think I'm gross, or a freak, or they feel sorry for me. But they shouldn't, and you really shouldn't. Because I've had the best life, because I've had you. But Becky, you have to promise me something."

"I know, I remember, I will pick up more laundry detergent, in the Mountain Spring scent. . . ."

"You have to promise that — you won't be me."

I wasn't sure why she was talking like this but her voice sounded urgent.

"Things have happened to me, all sorts of things, grown-up things and I just, I got overwhelmed. I let myself get overwhelmed. And I don't think that's been fair to you, not one little bit. But something is going to happen to you. And it's going to be magical."

She was gripping my hand very tightly and looking right into my eyes. "And it might be scary and you might not know what it means, not at first. But it's going to change your life, forever. And Becky, I want you to swear to me, because I love you so much, and because you deserve everything, you deserve the whole world, so Becky, when the magic shows up — I want you to say yes."

Later that afternoon when I called to check on her, she didn't answer her phone, so I called 911 and I ran for my car. By the time I got to the trailer a police car and an ambulance were already parked outside but everyone was too late. A policeman asked if I wanted to see my mom's body, instead of just asking did I want to see my mom.

My mom was lying on our couch with her eyes open, and one of her hands was slightly raised, as if she'd just thought of one last thing she wanted to say. I knelt beside her and part of my brain told me to say good-bye, but instead I just touched her hand and said, "Hi." I wondered if her soul had flown upward, grateful to be leaving her difficult body behind. I stayed like that for a while, just watching her. But then my knees started cramping and when I stood up I got dizzy, so the cop dragged me outside for some fresh air.

A bunch of people had gathered from the nearby trailers, and they were discussing the whole deal.

"That poor woman," said Mrs. Stangley, who was wearing a kerchief over her head full of curlers and dropping cigarette ashes onto her nylon housecoat. "She certainly was large."

"Large?" said Emmett, the guy with the gun collection from two trailers down. "Hell, she was huge. If they want to get her out of there, they're gonna have to take that door off its hinges."

"I will pray for you," said Cheryl Gann, clutching my arm. Cheryl weighed about ten pounds and was always handing me pamphlets about abstinence, with drawings of screaming fetuses. "Your mother was such a sad woman, so perhaps this is truly a blessing."

I looked at her. I looked at all of them. "Excuse me," I said. "On her worst day, my mom was still a million times nicer than all of you put together. And if you want to stand here and talk about her body, why don't you take a look at your own. Because, Mrs. Stangley, if you're going to have a fake tan, you should remember to spray your neck. And, Emmett, maybe my mom was fat but at least she never exposed herself to a crossing guard."

"She's possessed!" cried Cheryl, stepping away from me. "Please, Jesus, don't listen to this girl!"

I was about to say something to Cheryl but instead I just howled like a demon and lunged at her, which made her shriek and run back into her trailer, while Mrs. Stangley lit another cigarette and Emmett mumbled something about me being a whore.

Then at least four guys from the volunteer fire department began maneuvering my mom out of the trailer and I yelled at them to be careful and then I apologized for yelling, and then I started crying. Which was when I knew for pretty much 100 percent certain that no matter what my mom had promised me, I was never, ever going to believe in magic.

2.

After my mom was gone, I felt beyond lonely. I felt like there'd been some terrible mistake and that God was going to find me and apologize and bring my mom right back, so we could still do what we always did, which was to read magazines together and watch TV shows about celebrities and Google any details we weren't sure about, like the exact square footage of a celebrity's beachfront Malibu home or the age of another celebrity's much younger third husband or the brand of eco-friendly guest towels made from hemp, which the much younger third husband swore by. It sounds silly and loony but my mom loved all of that gossip and information, and while I was growing up, those stars and their favorite designers and their spa treatments were like my fairy tales, and I memorized the details of every strappy sandal and contested prenup and five-step system for removing eye makeup, because my mom and I could have the best time, just by talking really seriously about ridiculous things. No one could make the world seem sparkling and enchanted the way my mom could.

Three weeks after my mom's funeral while I was getting her clothes together to give to the church, I came across her favorite sweater, which was a Volkswagen-sized cardigan of hot pink acrylic yarn crocheted with powder blue bunnies holding Easter baskets. My mom had loved holiday-themed clothing and the sweater was so neon-bright and cheery that I started crying again because the bunnies reminded me so much of my mom, and of how incredibly hopeful she'd been. I curled up inside the sweater, which became my hot pink acrylic igloo, and I kept sobbing, because while my mom had been obsessed with glamour and romance and magic, she'd never had any of those things in her life, and that was pretty much going to be my life too.

As I was sniffling and nibbling some stale peanut M&M'S I'd found in the sweater's pockets, I heard a few notes of my mom's ringtone, coming from beneath a mound of her Christmas, Thanksgiving and St. Patrick's Day sweaters — we weren't Irish but my mom had fallen hard for a kelly green hoodie with sequined shamrocks. I froze because my mom hadn't had many friends, so I wondered who could be calling. But when I looked under the sweaters for her phone, it wasn't there. Instead there was a pearl gray shoe box. The shoe box said "Tom Kelly" in silvery, almost invisible letters and at first I thought it was empty because it was really light and just filled with crumpled-up tissue paper, but as I was about to toss the whole thing I heard something rattle and so I uncrumpled the tissue paper and found one of those little hinged velvet boxes, like for an engagement ring. Only the little velvet box was empty too but then, tucked under the piece of velvet-covered cardboard where the ring would go, there was a scrap of paper ripped from the flap of an envelope with a phone number scribbled on it in pencil and the phone number had a New York area code.

I didn't call the number for a week because I was afraid. It was like on my mom's death certificate where it said Cause of Death, I felt like instead of saying "complications from diabetes" there might be that phone number. But then I decided that I was being superstitious and besides, that phone number was the closest I'd ever been to New York or anywhere except East Trawley. So I called the number and a lady answered and she asked me my name and then fifteen minutes later the lady called back and offered me a thousand dollars and a plane ticket.

I asked my best friend, Rocher Bargemueller, what I should do. Rocher's mother had named her after a box of imported, gold foil—wrapped chocolates and most people pronounce it *Ro—share*, although when Rocher is being fancy she calls herself Roshay, and when the other kids in first grade were being mean they called her Roach Motel.

"Wait, so you called this number and some lady wants to send you a thousand bucks and a plane ticket to New York?" Rocher asked while we were on our breaks from working checkout at the Super Shop-A-Lot. There were also regular Shop-A-Lots but adding the word "super" meant "we promise to mop the floors at least once a week, especially if a baby throws up in the produce aisle."

"What should I do?" I wondered as we were sitting on top of the Dumpster behind the store, dangling our legs while Rocher chain-smoked and I sucked on a grape slushie. "I mean, what if it's like when they tell those poor girls in, I don't know, China, or the really crappy parts of Russia, they tell 'em they're gonna get married to rich, handsome guys, and they send 'em a plane ticket and then when they get off the plane some creepy guy with gold teeth steals their passports and they end up being like, sex-slave hookers on some rich creep's yacht in like, Vietnam?"

"Becky," said Rocher, "we're checkout chicks, excuse me, Register Associates, at a supermarket which from what I hear, is probably gonna get shut down by the end of the month along with all the other stores in the strip mall. Which means that we'll have to drive fifty miles more each way just to fill out applications to work behind the counter at Kentucky Fried Horse Doodie in Jamesburg. When we were still in high school and that guidance counselor, the sweaty one with the hair plugs, when he asked me what was my dream career, I told him 'sex-slave hooker on some rich creep's yacht in Vietnam,' and I asked him if he had a brochure."

"You did not!"

"Get on the damn fucking plane, shit-for-brains. At least find out. Your mom kept that number for a reason. You should honor her. You know, her last wishes. Like, my mom says that after she dies she wants me to kick my stepdad really hard in the balls."

I got on the plane. I'd never been on a plane and my seat was in something called Premium Ambassador Class, which meant that I sat right up near the front, in a wider seat, and there was a menu and a complimentary headset for watching a movie. I liked all of that fine but all I kept thinking was, I wish I could tell my mom about it.

I got to the New York airport, which looked like the biggest mall I'd ever seen, and I got so scared and confused that I just let myself get swept up with all of the other people from my plane and as we're all swooping along and I have no idea where I'm headed, I hear that music again, my mom's ringtone, and while I'm trying to figure out where it's coming from I see this really good-looking man. I mean he was so good-looking that it was almost silly. He had the square jaw of a marine commando in a video game and these friendly, squinty, Windex-blue eyes and the sort of thick, wavy, dark blond hair you only see on professional surfers or soap opera actors playing heart surgeons. And he's wearing a black uniform, including a stiff-brimmed hat, like he's a chauffeur in an ad for really expensive vodka or one of those body sprays called Mach Noir or Stealth Sport, and then I see that he's holding up a small rectangle of white cardboard with my name printed on it — Rebecca Randle — only no one ever calls me anything except Becky.

"Um, that's me, right?" I said to the good-looking guy in the uniform and when he smiled he got even more ridiculously better looking, to the point where I wanted to kiss him or smack him, and then he said, "Of course, Ms. Randle. Right this way. Is there any checked luggage?"

"Um, no, just carry-on," I said and I only said it because Rocher and I had agreed that I should call my old, stained, lime green nylon backpack, the one I'd used all through high school, we'd decided that if I brought it on the plane with me that I should call it "carry-on."

"If you'll please wait here, Ms. Randle," the driver guy said, showing me where to stand on a curb outside the airport. "I'll bring the car around. I'm Drake, by the way." Then he smiled again and I knew that if I was Rocher I'd be thinking sex-slave-hooker thoughts, so I used my phone to take a picture of the back of Drake's head and I sent it to her.

Pretty soon a black Mercedes pulled up and Drake jumped out from the driver's seat and opened the rear door for me.

"Is this your first time in the city?" asked Drake once we were underway.

"This is my first time anywhere," I said, and that was when I saw the New York City skyline and I felt like I was drunk and like I was about to cry and like I was really far away from East Trawley. Then we began gliding along what Drake said was the West Side Highway and he said that I could see across the river to New Jersey.

Pretty soon we reached a long stretch of high chain-link fence, at least three blocks of it, topped with curls of barbed wire, like it was guarding a top secret military base or a nuclear reactor. Drake pulled up to a checkpoint and we drove through, passing all of this expensive black gravel that had been raked into neat furrows connecting to perfect circles. We drove farther, out onto a mammoth pier set atop hundreds of wooden pilings and jutting out onto the water itself.

The pier was filled by an enormous warehouse, or an airplane hangar, with no windows, just towering walls of rusting, battleship gray steel. A wide, concealed door set into the side of the building yawned open, and Drake drove through. Everything was happening smoothly and automatically, as if the building itself had studied us and made a decision, and I could hear the river lapping and heaving beneath the pier; it was like boarding someone's private ocean liner or aircraft carrier. Even now I can't describe exactly what was inside the outer shell of the building. There was more of that Japanese-style landscaping only with white gravel and gnarled, almost leafless trees, like five-thousand-year-old stick figures, flailing toward an endless, floating dark glass pavilion, a sort of epic, gleaming, ultra-high-end car dealership kept hidden from view, because if regular people ever saw it they'd get too jealous or angry and they'd smudge their fingerprints all over the miles of tinted glass.

Drake stopped the car, and leaped out and opened my door. "Don't worry," he said as a glass panel in the pavilion hissed open. Even though I still hadn't seen a single other person, I clutched my backpack tightly in front of me, like a nice girl in a bad neighborhood.

A woman was waiting, seated behind what I think was a desk, although it was the size of at least two dining room tables. There were no drawers, no wastebasket, and no electrical cords or office equipment of any kind; the glass desk was more like a sketch, or the ghost of some actual object. The woman stood up, smoothing her slim, taut black skirt, which she wore with a crisp white shirt and very high heels. Everything about this woman was classically simple, from her clothing to her hair and makeup, but I knew instantly that even beginning to look like her would cost thousands of dollars.

"Hello," said the woman, smiling. Her voice sounded like cashmere, if cashmere could talk. "I'm Lila."

She studied me with a professional's expertise, as if she were a hairstylist who could be nasty or nice. "I can see it," she concluded, although I had no idea what she was talking about. What could she see?

Lila led me into an elevator where everything, including the ceiling and the floor, was made of black glass. Even though there were no visible buttons, Lila knew just where to lightly tap her forefinger along a wall, and the doors closed and we began to rise. All I could see through the black glass were tiny, distant, flickering lights, as if there was some midnight traffic jam at an airstrip hundreds of miles away. Then the doors opened, and Lila made a small gesture with her hand and her head, to direct me, and I stepped out, into nothing.

When I say nothing, I mean acres and acres of the purest whiteness, as if the elevator had zoomed to the Arctic Circle during a blizzard. At first I went snow blind but as my vision cleared, I could tell that I was in a room, or maybe I should call it an area, or a zone, because it was the size of a football field. The walls were pure white, unveined marble, with no visible seams, and the floor was drenched with super-high-gloss white enamel, and I hesitated to step forward because the floor was so glossy it looked wet. But when I turned to Lila for instructions, she was gone, and I couldn't see where the entrance to the elevator had been.

I shoved off my sneakers and I began walking, in just my little, only slightly grimy, white half socks. I could see that, miles away, at the far end of the room, there was a soaring, completely transparent glass fireplace, an almost invisible cylinder set out from the wall, where pale blue flames leaped twenty feet into the air from a bed of crystals, booming and crackling even higher the closer I came. Around the fireplace was a grouping of long, low, sort-of couches, and a large, blocky, sort-of chair, all covered in that kind of obscenely soft black leather, which a host on one of the home shopping channels is always calling "the finest, unborn, triple-grade-A dee-luxe Italian kidskin."

"Becky," said a voice, and then, as I got closer to all of that black leather furniture-type stuff, I saw that there was a man, not exactly sitting on one of the couches and not exactly lying on it. I'd have to say he was lounging, with one bare foot on the leather, and the other on the floor. Despite the unbelievable self-consciousness of the room and the fireplace and the lack of color scheme, and the fact that the man had clearly arranged everything from the furniture to his feet for maximum effect, he looked comfortable, because he owned all of it.

"I'm Tom Kelly," said the man, and then he stood up. He wasn't being polite; it was more like he wanted me to get a good look at all of him, as a dare. Most guys introduce themselves with a hey and a handshake, but Tom Kelly used his entire body. He was staring at me clinically, as if he could twist or erase or vaporize whatever he didn't like about me with his eyes. I felt like a rabbit, being eyeballed by either a scientist with a syringe, or a master chef with a cleaver. I started to shiver and I almost threw up, but then I remembered something that my third-grade teacher had once said, about how all people are created equal, and so I tried to see if I could believe it and I stared right back.

Tom Kelly was tall and rangy and seriously handsome, but not like Drake, because Tom Kelly wasn't ridiculously, uselessly beautiful. There wasn't anything boyish or innocent or simple about him. He was a great-looking man, and he knew it, but that was only one of his advantages. He was wearing a white T-shirt and cream-colored canvas pants, with the cuffs casually rolled up, and both of us were very aware of his body. He was somewhere in his thirties and proudly athletic. I'd never been so conscious of a guy's neck and ankles and forearms.

"Welcome," he said as he sat back down on the couch and pointed me toward a black leather-upholstered cube. I stumbled and managed to perch on the cube, but then I leaned back, into thin air, which wasn't a good idea. I jerked upright and fumbled with my backpack and finally just let it slump to the floor beside me.

"You look a bit — only a bit — like your mother," Tom continued. His voice was both masculine and insinuating, and everything he said sounded like a compliment, a come-on and a challenge. "Your mother — oh my Lord. She was so gorgeous. Beyond belief."

"I'm sorry," I said, seriously pissed off. "I know she's gone, but I still wish you wouldn't be mean."

"Mean? You really don't know, do you?"

"Know what?"

Tom picked up a bone-like chunk of hammered silver, which turned out to be a custom-made remote control. He pressed a few recessed buttons and the entire room went inky, bottomless black.

Then an enormous photograph was projected across one of the endless white marble walls. It was a picture of a stunningly beautiful nineteen-year-old, with her long dark hair flying around her face. She was looking right at the camera, right at me, and at first I thought, why is this guy showing me a picture of some total knockout, and then I gasped as I made the connection: It was a picture of my mother.

Tom continued to point his silver remote at the walls and at a forest of glass panels that slid from both the floor and the ceiling, and soon I was surrounded by more cascading photos of my mother, hundreds of them, and she was always slim and dazzling and wearing the most out-there fashions of twenty years earlier. Some of the photos were from magazines but others were snapshots of my mother on a grand sailboat or sauntering down the steps of a museum or sitting on a bench in Central Park and hugging a collie.

Then, unbelievably, from a far corner of the room, my mother came walking toward me. She was fresh faced and skinny and she was wearing a black ribbed turtleneck, tight jeans and a floor-length, laser-cut, weightless suede coat that billowed around her, and she was smiling at me, and I'd never seen her so happy. But as I stood and reached out to touch her or hug her, the life-sized, three-dimensional hologram from a fashion show runway flickered and vanished. From another corner, a second hologram, in a wisp of an evening gown, approached me and then countless other catwalking versions of my mom appeared, all in different but equally impossible outfits until I was spinning, but as quickly as they'd filled the room, swirling around me like a theme park exhibit devoted only to my mom, the images left, the gloom lifted and the white glare returned and I felt like my mom had died all over again.

"I met your mother when she was sixteen," said Tom. "I was waiting for my car in Times Square and I looked across the street and there was this girl. Oh, she was a total hick, she was on a field trip to the city, her high school had flown everyone up north to see some godforsaken musical. But I could tell she was dazzled, by the show and the city and by being away from home for the first time. She was wearing tight, acid-washed jeans and a hot pink puffy jacket and all sorts of I LOVE NEW YORK crap, oh, and one of those green foam rubber Statue of Liberty headbands, with the spikes. Her hair was nothing and her makeup was drugstore overdose but I took one look and I said that's it. That's her. That's the next great American face. And so I dodged a few taxis and I ran over and I told her, 'Look, I'm Tom Kelly, and you're going to assume that I want to drug you and fuck you and sell you to an Arab, but I don't. I want to put your face on every public surface, perfume package and magazine cover in the world. Call me.' And I gave her my card."

"And she called you?"

"From her little Midtown Holiday Marriott Best Western hellhole and she said that she knew I was a liar and a fake, because there was no real Tom Kelly."

As Tom said this, I realized that until a few seconds earlier I'd been just like my mother. Because like most people, I'd grown up in a world saturated with the name Tom Kelly but I'd had no idea he actually existed. Tom Kelly was like sugar or TV or God. He wasn't a man, he was a thing, and he'd always been there. His name appeared on the back pockets of both premium and discounted designer jeans, on the waistbands of men's boxer briefs and on the seams of women's black lace thongs. There were perfumes with names like Tom Kelly's Expectations, Arouse by Tom Kelly and TK Surprise. His name was woven into socks and pantyhose and wedding gowns and basic gray eighty-dollar T-shirts with the Tom Kelly logo either almost undetectable along the side or dead center and the size of a hubcap. His name was stamped across frozen dinners and special limited-edition sports cars and sunglasses and shoulder bags and workout gear and sneakers and Designer Collection Barbie Strapless Weekend in Aruba Fantasy Gowns. Tom Kelly, or sometimes just his initials, could be found on barely-there camisoles and the most cuddly, oversized boyfriend sweaters; worked in twenty-four-karat diamonds and glinting gold embedded in the front teeth of rap stars; embroidered over the left nipples of enough polo shirts to prep out mainland China; and often, I'd seen the name all by itself, the silver letters barely visible against the gray background, as if the Tom Kelly brand was so steamy and desirable that it only needed to whisper, showcasing nothing but Tom Kelly—ness and all of the status and sizzle it promised.

The Tom Kelly ad campaigns featured only top-echelon models, both male and female. Becoming the face of Tom Kelly, everyone knew, was the modeling pinnacle, the modeling equivalent of not just an Academy Award but the Nobel Prize for looking unbearably sexy, blank faced, and sluttishly yet elegantly disinterested. The models were always very young and sometimes naked, which led to the ads being protested by parent groups and Christian coalitions and congressional subcommittees on moral decay. One notorious series of ads had used pouting, topless girls barely shielding their exposed breasts while squatting in prison cells, where the Tom Kelly logo had been scratched into the blood-spattered cinder-block walls. This had been declared kiddie porn, terrorist chic, misogynist, satanic and worse. The ads had been pulled but the cologne they'd been promoting, First Offense by Tom Kelly, had sold out instantly in over fifty-eight countries.

"Oh my God," I said and even as the words were leaving my mouth, I knew how idiotic they sounded. "You're Tom Kelly."

"Yes," said Tom, and I could tell that he both understood my confusion and that he was thinking about kicking me into the fireplace and warming his hands with my screams. Then he tapped his remote and, from the darkness, another set of pictures blasted over me as I began to discover that before I was born, Tom Kelly had been the face of Tom Kelly. I saw that for thirty years Tom's handsome, slightly mocking features and his lean, defined body had been a mainstay of the Tom Kelly campaigns. There he was in a tux, leaning against a split-rail fence on a New Mexico prairie and then he was wearing a ripped sweatshirt and ragged jeans, galloping on horseback through some pounding California surf and then he was naked, with his crotch barely covered by the biceps and elbows of a pileup of equally naked, blissed-out male and female models, in the snow, in a grove of evergreens: This last image had been from a holiday campaign and the caption read, SAVIOR BY TOM KELLY.

Everything vanished except for a projected photo of a three-story-high Times Square billboard of Tom standing shirtless on some whitewashed Greek balcony with his arm around the bare, tan shoulders of my stunning young mother, who was wearing only the filmiest white mesh midriff-baring top over a crocheted white string bikini bottom. They made an overwhelmingly beautiful couple; they were Adam and Eve with money, a personal trainer and a great dermatologist.

Tom, the real Tom, stood up, so the billboard image was layered over his face and body. Even though he was now many years older, the faces were almost identical. Maybe this was because he was so rich — was that how he'd managed to either stop, or certainly slow, time? Then, with a click of the remote, the projected image was gone and all of that white marble returned.

I still had no idea why Tom Kelly was showing me all this or why he'd brought me to his — I didn't even know what to call it. His home? His domain? His — maybe compound was the right word, because everything was so industrial and off-limits and well guarded. But before I could even begin to make sense of where I was, there was something I had to know.

"What . . . what happened to my mother?" I demanded. "What did you do to her?"

"What did I do to her?" Tom replied, with an edge of incredulity. "I gave her, I offered her, everything. I found her. I created her."

"But what did she think about all that? About you? And I'm sorry, I know I should shut up, it's just, well, when I was growing up, I loved my mom, and she was so good to me, but she didn't look like that. And I've never seen any of those pictures. And she never told me. She never told me anything."

Tom smiled, and placed his palms together. "Try to understand her," he advised. "You have to think of her back then, at sixteen. I tracked down her teacher, and I gave her some numbers to call, to check me out. And so your mother decided to at least talk to me. And that first morning, when she came here, she was shaking. And I said, look, I will buy you a bus ticket and you can run right back to wherever, to . . ."

"East Trawley. Missouri."

"That's right. East Trawley."

He said the name as if it were a dental procedure or something he'd found on the bottom of his shoe.

"But then I said, or you can stay. And see what happens. You can see who you might become. I told her, you don't look like anyone else. Don't act like them."

I was trying to imagine my mom, or anyone at sixteen, faced with that kind of decision.

"And so she stayed?"

"For three years. And then something happened. Something scared her. Everything changed. And she ran away. And I never saw her again."

"But what happened? What was so horrible? What scared her?"

I was excited and fearful and desperate, because now I understood why I'd come to New York and why I was meeting Tom Kelly. All of my questions about my mother's life, and her fear, and her sadness were about to be answered. I'd been waiting for this moment for eighteen years.

"What made my mother hide for the rest of her life?"

"I can't tell you that. Not yet."

"Why not?"

"Because you wouldn't believe me."

He smiled, which made everything worse, because I didn't just want to wipe the smile off his face, I wanted to shove dynamite up his nose and blast it off.

"Let's talk about you," he said. "You're eighteen years old, you've finished high school and you couldn't be more ordinary. Yes, you have the tiniest hint of your mother, but don't kid yourself. You're nothing. You're no one. And you look like — anyone. You don't exist."

I knew I should punch him or shoot him or at least disagree but I couldn't, for one simple reason. He was right.

"So here's my offer," he said, sitting up straight, as if he was about to conduct serious business. "I will make you three dresses: one red, one white and one black. And if you wear these dresses, and if you do everything I say, then you will become the most beautiful woman on earth. You will become, in fact, the most beautiful woman who has ever lived."

"What?"

"You heard me."

At first I couldn't even process this proposal; I couldn't begin to wrap my brain around what he'd just said. He was a rich and successful man and, in his way, a major force. He'd known my mother. And he'd insulted me and tried to make me feel like shit. But aside from all that, I didn't know what the hell he was talking about.

Or maybe I did know, maybe I'd understood him perfectly and maybe that's why I felt like I was choking and drowning and like I had to get out of there, I had to run, even if it meant bashing myself against the marble walls and scratching to find the elevator or a hidden emergency exit and a staircase.

"I'm leaving," I said, standing. But once I was up, I couldn't move. I couldn't leave. And he knew it.

"And I'm not talking about a makeover, or surgery, or about having you lose some weight and then hauling in a team of hair and makeup people. Because then you'd still look like you, on a good day. Which isn't enough. Which isn't anything. No."

I wanted to kill him and I wanted to nail-gun his mouth shut, but my feet were still refusing to obey me, to run and escape.

"I'm talking about something else. I'm talking about everything. I'm talking about beauty."

"Beauty?"

"Real beauty. Indescribable beauty. Beauty as a gift, and an art, and a superpower. I'm talking about handing you a passport, and the keys, and the credit limit, to everything you could ever conceivably want. To everything that you, or anyone else, might ever dream of. You could rule the world. You could own it. Three dresses."

I was relieved. Tom Kelly was obviously crazy. Completely gone. Certifiable. He was just some hard-up, forgotten pervert, probably trying to get into my pants and assuming that I was the easiest mark ever.

"Does this whole thing," I asked, "this I-can-make-you-the-most-beautiful-woman-in-the-world deal, does it ever work? Are there other girls who fall for it?"

"I've never asked any other girls."

"You're ridiculous. And pathetic. And nuts."

"Then turn around. Walk away. Drake will drive you right back to the airport and East Trawley and your mother's trailer. Or he can take you to a hotel, where you will have twenty-four hours to consider my offer. And after that, the offer will be withdrawn, forever."

3.

Drake brought me to a fancy hotel just off Fifth Avenue. I recognized the main entrance with its brass lampposts, because sometimes my mom had looked at websites for places she'd seen on TV shows. Only now I wondered — had she stayed here?

The hotel dated from the early 1900s and was supposed to look like a French château, only it had boutiques displaying three-thousand-dollar Italian sweaters and even pricier Swiss watches in the lobby, and all I kept thinking was, a few of those watches could buy health insurance, and SUVs, for everyone in East Trawley. The bellman took me up to my room, handed me a plastic key-card and then left me alone with my backpack. I'd never been inside any hotel before, let alone a suite.

At first I didn't touch anything but stood in my down-filled vest in the parlor section. Finally I lowered my backpack very gently onto the desk, which was trimmed with bronze scroll-work, and the desktop was inlaid with scenes of French aristocrats playing cards. Then, tentatively, I sat on the overstuffed, brocade-covered couch and then I tried the matching armchair, which was like curling up in Santa's lap, if Santa were French and tasteful, and then I worked up my courage and tiptoed into the bedroom, where I stuck out my arms like a scarecrow and I fell flat out on my back, onto the bed, which had a quilted brocade headboard, a ton of different-sized cream-colored damask pillows edged with gold rope, and so many layers of airy coverlets that I felt like I was sinking into a king-sized, formally dressed bride or maybe into an entire wedding party.

I got so overwhelmed that I jerked into a quivering ball, and I called Rocher on my cell. I didn't use the hotel phone because I wanted to talk to her on my terms and not Tom Kelly's. It was as if I were sharing a bedtime fairy tale with a five-year-old, because Rocher kept gasping and interrupting and saying, "WHAT? WHAT? He actually SAID THAT? To YOU?" And once I'd finished, I brought the phone even closer to my face and I whispered, "So what should I do?"

Rocher got angrier than I'd ever heard her and I'm talking about her spitting and cursing and making such disgusted, high-pitched yelping noises that sometimes there wasn't any sound at all. "What . . . should . . . you . . . do?" she began in a low, ominous voice. "WHAT SHOULD YOU DO? YOU ASSHOLE! YOU ASSHOLE! Listen to me, you little cracker-headed ass-wipe, and I'm only calling you that because you're my best friend in the whole world, and because I love you so much, but you DUMBASS FUCKING WHOREHEAD!!! Your mom is dead, you're not going to college, you live in a condemned trailer and you work checkout at the most raggedy-assed about-to-close supermarket in three counties. So when some incredibly rich dude whose name I am looking at right now on my bra strap, when that guy asks if you want to be the most beautiful woman on earth, here's what you do: YOU FUCKING SAY YES!!!"

"So you really think I should do it?"

"Can you feel them? Can you feel my fingers reaching millions of miles right through this phone and grabbing your throat and trying to strangle some sense into you? Becky, what do you want to do with your life?"

"I don't know, I was just dealing with graduating and with my mom, and I guess I thought that I'd, I don't know, maybe work really hard and apply myself and get a better job, and maybe become an assistant manager or something."

I was lying and Rocher knew it. I wanted to do so much with my life, but I tried as hard as I could never to think about it. I hadn't been able to talk about my insane ideas with my mom, because I'd never wanted her to feel like she was holding me back or that she should feel guilty because we never had any money. And I couldn't talk about anything with the other kids at school because if I said what I really felt, if I called any attention to myself, I'd become a target. And I never really told Rocher about what I was after because I knew that she'd be totally on my side, and that was the scariest thing of all. Here was the truth: In secret, when I wasn't being careful and gutless, I wanted the biggest life I could possibly get, a life far beyond what East Trawley had to offer. I wasn't sure of the details, but I wanted to see the entire world and meet every possible kind of person and dive headfirst into every possible adventure, because once all of that had happened, I'd have turned into whoever I was meant to be.

But aside from being eighteen and scared of my shadow there was something else stopping me, and an hour later I was staring at it, in the mirror of the hotel bathroom. I know that looks aren't supposed to matter, or to stop you from living your life, but an awful lot of people would disagree. So I decided that before tomorrow, before I gave Tom Kelly my answer, I wanted to determine, once and for all, what I really looked like.

So I stood, in my limp East Trawley Tigers T-shirt and my saggy gray sweatpants with the stains from buttery-flavored microwave popcorn, and I stared not just into my eyes but into my face. The problem was, the harder I searched and focused on my whole face and not any one feature, the more everything became a blur or like the pieces of a jigsaw puzzle tossed on a tabletop, with an eyebrow here, the nose off in a corner, and the lips somewhere on the floor. I knew that I wasn't hideous and Rocher and my mom had sometimes said that I was pretty but they were my mom and my best friend, so they didn't count. Being supportive was part of their job descriptions.

I kept staring, trying to decode how I'd be described to the police, if I went missing: lank brown hair stuck behind mouse-like ears, cautious brown eyes, grudgingly unshaped brows, a not completely straight nose, some lingering forehead acne, okay teeth with one snaggly renegade, chapped lips, not the greatest posture, average height and weight and what? I remembered Nicole Debra Galtrow, a girl from my high school who'd been anorexic. Of course, Rocher had said that any girl from East Trawley who was under two hundred pounds could be considered anorexic, but Nicole had been painfully thin. When I'd researched anorexia online I'd read about something called body dysmorphia. Anorexics have it and also those seriously bulked-up bodybuilders. Dysmorphia is when someone looks in the mirror, and sees something else. While I studied my own whatever I was, I decided that maybe everyone has at least a touch of dysmorphia; maybe it's impossible for anyone to ever truly know what they look like.

I remembered something that Cal Malstrup, this guy in my class, had scribbled under my picture in our yearbook: "I like your smile." So I smiled, but I kept looking goofier and more like a cartoon sketch of myself and that was when I burst out laughing. Which made me catch something in the mirror: When I was laughing, my mouth was huge and gaping, like a hyena's, and my eyes didn't match and my nose got all squinched up so I could see right up my nostrils to where my brain should be, but still, that's how I wished I'd looked in my yearbook photo instead of all stern and stiff with my hair draped over one shoulder like cold, dead spaghetti. When I was laughing I couldn't tell if I was pretty or not, but I looked happy.

That's when a part of me urged, just take off, get yourself out of New York as fast as you can, who gives a shit about being unbelievably beautiful? I had friends and a little bit of money saved up, but then another part of me remembered when Cal Malstrup had hoisted me up on the tailgate of his pickup and talked to me, eye-to-eye, about going to prom, in what he'd termed "a preliminary possibility consultation" and an "availability check." I later found out that he'd had the exact same no-commitment conference with Caroline Getterschmidt and Kristin Cranmere, but the front-runner had been Shanice Morain, who everybody thought was so hot because she'd been voted Miss East Trawley Memorial Day Picnic Corn Queen.

Right after I'd had my conversation with Cal, Shanice and her posse had started a webpage called Pretty Or Shitty? They'd posted pictures of every girl in our school and then everyone got to anonymously critique them.

I'd sworn that I'd never click on the page and Rocher and my mom had warned me not to, but finally trying to ignore the whole thing had been obsessing me even more. At first I'd checked out some other girls' pictures, with comments like "Pig's snout," "Looks like her dad, after his stroke" and "Maybe it would help if she put her head on upside down." Everyone was topping each other in nastiness, which had made me unbend; the page was a joke. So I'd scrolled to Shanice's picture and I'd suspected that most of the comments were from her buddies, because they'd said, "Totally cute, but not stuck-up," "Should go on one of those Top Model shows, cuz she'd win!" and "If I looked like that I'd be so happy and she's also really sweet!" There had been only one negative comment, which I'd known was from Rocher, because it said, "Mutant alien attempting to pass as human, or world's only ugly vampire? You decide."

Without giving myself even a split second to log out, I'd scrolled to my picture. The first comment had clearly been Rocher's: "So cute!!!" Then came everyone else: "Not just uggabug — boring uggabug." "At least she's not an elephant like her mother." "Ugliest girl in our school, no question." There was a final comment and I'd had the feeling it was from Shanice. Because the other comments had been so spiteful, this was her pretending to be a good person: "I don't think Becky is the ugliest. She's not Suellen Sheever, who was in that five-car highway collision thing, so half of her face droops, even after the surgery — that's why Suellen's picture is in profile. Becky just always sits in the back of the class, all hunched over in her hoodie and her jumbo T-shirt, so that no one can see her fat rolls. And she has her hair in her face to cover the zits. Becky just looks like she's somebody's sad cousin, the one who never got married and maybe is a lesbo, if she's lucky. I'm not saying she should kill herself, but it would be cheaper than lipo. She's just nada special."

I'd slouched back from my computer, as if the page had ejected an iron cannonball at full force right into my gut.

The next day, Cal had asked Shanice to prom and they'd strolled through the halls together with his arm protectively around her shoulders and their foreheads touching as they shared intimate stuff that the uggabugs would never understand, because Cal and Shanice didn't speak Uggabug.

Back at the hotel I looked myself in the eye and I said, Becky, don't do this. Don't buy into it. Don't let Shanice and all of the Shanices and the fraction of you, okay, maybe more than a fraction, that agrees with them be right.

I thought about how sometimes, after my mom had gotten really big, she'd fall asleep on our couch and I'd watch her, I'd analyze her face and I'd try to decide if she hated her life and felt trapped in the folds and heft of her body, and if she watched the pretty, skinny girls on TV and wished she could be just like them. But my mom had never complained, and I wished more than anything that she was still here, so she could tell me what to do. But since she'd left me that phone number maybe she already had.

Because what if, and I was just throwing it out there, just for shits and giggles, and because I couldn't not think about it, what if I called Tom Kelly and said yes, and what if I could become the most beautiful woman in the whole goddamned world.

Beautiful.

The most beautiful.

Me.

4.

"Take off your clothes," said Tom Kelly.

I was standing on a round platform at one end of a workroom in the compound, encircled by eight full-length mirrors. I felt like a miniature plastic ballerina, her arms curved over her head, in a little girl's music box. The workroom was long, narrow and painted laboratory white and it held rows of rectangular worktables with their surfaces upholstered in smooth, flat, white linen. There were sewing machines and every possible dressmaker's tool set out on the tables, and a silent workforce of mostly Chinese women stood beside their stations, all wearing crisp white lab coats over their black T-shirts, black slacks and black low-heeled shoes.

I'd called Tom from my hotel at 2:00 A.M., before I could lose my nerve.

"Okay, I don't trust you," I'd told him, "and I don't believe for a second that this is going to work, not in one million, trillion years, and I know that this is all going to end up on one of those tabloid TV shows on a segment called 'Becky Randle Has the Brain of a Sea Monkey,' but let's do it." I could hear him smile as he said, "Oh, my sweet girl, this will be fun." And then, just as I was about to ask for more details and whether I should talk to a lawyer or a priest or a psychiatrist, he hung up, and a few seconds later Lila called and began to schedule my fittings.

I had stripped to my underwear, which was tidy but not especially new, as Tom and Lila stood on opposite sides of me, managing to surgically assess me while ignoring me completely. My body was, well, it was my body, and I waited for Tom and Lila to pick up Magic Markers and outline problem areas on my thighs and lower back, as if they were planning a rump roast and a loin of pork. Tom glanced up and a Chinese woman in a lab coat approached. Her hair was cropped into a shining pageboy and she wore her lab coat as if it were a Chanel suit, the kind which I later learned have tiny silver chains tucked into the hems of the jacket and skirt so that the garment will hang properly.

"Becky, this is Mrs. Chen," said Tom.

"Good morning, Miss Randle," said Mrs. Chen, briskly unfurling a fabric tape measure with a sharp snap, as if it were a lion tamer's whip. I tried not to squirm as she efficiently measured every inch of my body but I begged her, "Please don't say the numbers out loud," so she murmured them to Lila, who inscribed them into a small leather-bound journal. Once this torture was completed, Mrs. Chen told me, "One more item. Give me your hand."

As I held out my palm, Mrs. Chen swiftly removed a needle from the small round pincushion she wore on an elastic band around her wrist, and gripping my forearm, she pricked my forefinger. She used a small spool of silken white thread to absorb the blood and the thread was instantly soaked through.

"But why do you need my blood?" I asked, yanking my hand back.

"This is couture," explained Mrs. Chen, depositing the spool in a test tube. "Every garment will be custom made, only for you. You will become a part of each dress."

Then Lila and Mrs. Chen retreated as Tom sat backward on a white metal chair, still staring at me.

"Fine, I'm a lump," I admitted as I gratefully tugged on my T-shirt, jeans and down-filled vest. "I like potato chips and rocky road ice cream and chocolate-covered pretzels, the kind that look like doggie treats. And I know I should eat healthy and exercise, but as my friend Rocher says, I could get hit by a bus tomorrow and refined sugar is good for healing."

"You're not a lump," said Tom. "But I just want to remember what you looked like, before. It's like alchemy, when scientists in the Middle Ages struggled to turn lead into gold. They tried to find the formula."

"I'm *lead*?"

"In a way. You're raw material. Cookie dough. Sand. With a very few helpful characteristics, thanks to your mother."

Tom's insults, which I knew were going to continue, made me bold.

"Can I ask you something? I know I said yes and I'll wear the dresses and I'll do what you tell me but, huh? Three dresses? And I'm suddenly gonna be the most beautiful woman in the world? What makes you think you can do it? I know that you're rich and you were a big deal and all, but do you really believe that you have some sort of power?"

Tom had flinched when I'd used the past tense about his having been a big deal but when I asked about his power he sat bolt upright and said, "I'm Tom Kelly," and then he swung one of his long legs over the chair and strode out of the room.

There was a pause as all of the Chinese seamstresses eyeballed me, as if my WANTED poster had just been downloaded onto all of their phones for a crime involving schoolchildren, or worse, the destruction of blouses. To appease the seamstresses, I ran after Tom calling out, "I'm sorry!"

The hallway from the workroom kept taking sharp turns and the white walls, ceilings and floors became dizzying, as if I were chasing someone through an abandoned Swiss clinic or a maze constructed from freshly bleached laundry, but then I turned a corner into an interior garden, open to the sky but enclosed on all sides by unclimbably high whitewashed brick walls, which were densely layered with the darkest black-purple ivy. The garden itself was a perfect square, but I couldn't figure out how large it was because it kept seeming to expand and contract around me. There were white gravel pathways, and the plantings were severely manicured and blooming exclusively with white flowers set against more gleamingly near-black foliage. There were the deepest green boxwood topiaries, pruned into spheres taller than me, hosting trembling camellias, beside black-enameled trellises tumbling with fat white roses, falling toward beds of white freesia and white tulips and lilies that resembled beckoning hands or exotic sex organs. There were ebony-burgundy Japanese maples frosted with white moss and there was a central, round, black slate reflecting pool darting with especially snotty piranhas. The garden was alive yet so artificial that it had to be the hothouse, where the top-of-the-line Tom Kelly fragrances began. And here was the creepiest part: I felt like I'd stumbled into the most haughty, vicious cocktail party because all of the black-and-white blossoms and leaves and vines were undeniably listening.

Tom was standing with his back to me. He turned abruptly and said, "Look at this lily." He bent to caress a flawless white flower, which craned upward, anticipating Tom's touch. "This flower is at the peak of its beauty. Which means that, in an ordinary garden, it would have begun to die. In perhaps an hour, its petals would begin to curl and yellow, invisibly at first, but it would inevitably droop and brown and rot."

"Because that's what flowers do," I said to inject a note of, if not Botany 101, then at least common sense.

"Not here. These flowers, my flowers, everything you see here, and not just the original plantings, but each bloom is over twenty years old. And yet they remain perfect. Unblemished. Eternal. Always beautiful."

Tom inhaled again, and the full garden leaned toward him. I knew it was a mechanical trick, a super-refined Disney attraction, and that if I looked hard enough or started to grab and rip the various stems and roots, I'd find bundled cable and buried electrical boxes. At least that's what I wanted to believe because otherwise, if Tom Kelly was telling the truth, if he could keep a lily obediently alive and perfect for decades, if he could truly create beauty from his fingertips, then . . . what could he do to me?

I glanced at my own fingertip and saw that despite Mrs. Chen's having just taken a blood sample, the wound was already not merely healed, but gone.

5.

Drake arrived at 9:00 A.M. the next morning with Tom in the car's backseat.

"We're off to see the wizards," Tom explained as I climbed in beside him.

"What wizards? I thought you were the wizard."

"I am, but if we're going to do this we need expert assistance."

The car made its way through the backed-up, honking streets of what Tom said was the Diamond District in Midtown. "On any given day," he explained, "over three billion dollars' worth of precious gems are cut, polished and sold within a four-block radius. If you look out your window you'll see men and women wearing brown polyester, as if they worked preparing tax returns at walk-in storefronts. But they've got Peruvian amethysts and fistfuls of fire opals tucked away in the softest flannel pouches strapped to their inner thighs."

We left the car and entered a shop where the dusty windows showcased, on faded velvet display stands, thin gold electroplate chains, sometimes dangling with cheeseball pendants of flat, gaudy intertwined hearts. Tom kept moving past the bored clerks until we reached a small, airless back room where the walls were lined with tiny oak drawers, and there was a woman bent almost double over a metal table as if she'd just dropped a contact lens.

"Madame Ponelle," said Tom, with a surprising amount of respect.

The woman looked up, and I saw that she had a magnifying device like a small telescope, comfortably wedged, or maybe implanted, in her right eye.

"Thomas," said the woman, and I knew that she was the only person on earth who could ever get away with using his full name. "You're back."

"And this is Becky," said Tom. "Becky, this is Madame Helena Ponelle, who deals in only the very finest gemstones. Madame Ponelle, we'll be needing all sorts of things, in red, white and black. Because Becky is about to become the most beautiful woman in the world."

"Of course," said Madame Ponelle, who resembled an especially regal basset hound, in a pale pink smock. "Rubies, diamonds and perhaps black pearls, a single strand, I think — more youthful."

"I agree," said Tom. "And what are you working on?"

"Since you last visited, I've retired completely from cutting the stones myself. But when this arrived, from a bed of volcanic ash in the Maldives, I couldn't resist."

She stepped back, revealing that at the center of the table, mounted in a vise, was the largest diamond I'd ever seen, even in a photograph. It was the size of a multifaceted softball, and I thought it was a joke and that Madame Ponelle was about to squeeze a hidden rubber sausage so her bogus diamond would squirt me.

"Is that . . . real?" I asked.

"Indeed," said Madame Ponelle, "and I've only just sold it. It's being used to ransom an extremely wealthy family who are currently being held hostage by Somali pirates." Then she sighed and brought her lips very close to the diamond, whispering, "I'll miss you."

"You can't do better than Madame Ponelle," Tom told me once we were back in the car. "Her inventory is so comprehensive that it can't be insured. The premiums would be impossible."

"And she just keeps everything in those little wooden drawers?"

"Yes. Although I should mention that all of those yawning clerks, in the outer showroom? They were all once either presidential bodyguards or Mossad agents, and they're armed to the teeth. If you had tried to even touch that diamond, well, what was left of you could've easily fit into one of those little drawers."

"Oh my God . . ."

"But let's talk about something infinitely more serious."

"Like what?"

"Shoes."

We were soon in Brooklyn and Drake pulled up in front of a five-story-high brick building that was painted with ancient, barely legible advertisements reading HEEL-TO-TOE INTERNATIONAL and FINE FOOTWEAR FOR GENTLEFOLK OF THE UTMOST DISTINCTION.

"Heel-to-Toe has been here for almost two hundred years," said Tom. "The company was founded by Italian immigrants, who left for America after the king of Naples had insulted them."

"How? What did he do?"

"On a whim, he'd worn a pair of French shoes, which Napoleon had provided, as an act of diplomacy. The Neapolitan king had quickly realized his mistake but it was too late. The far superior Italian shoemakers had taken all of their equipment, their awls and their needles and their glues, and left the country. They make all my shoes."

Tom angled his foot and his black lace-ups gleamed, although not too brightly. "The simplest design," he said, "requires the most skilled workmanship, because you can't hide your mistakes.

I've had these shoes for over twenty years and they only look better."

A small reception area was lined with pegs that held hundreds of carved wooden forms shaped like streamlined feet and calves. "They're called lasts," said Tom, "and they've been whittled for the company's most cherished clientele. If you look closely, each last is stenciled with a coded series of letters and numerals, to protect everyone's privacy." The lasts were made from a golden pearwood and they reminded me of artificial limbs, or the feet of those posable artists' mannequins.

As Tom led me into the factory itself I could hear Italian curses overlaid with snatches of laughter and the tapping of hammers. "Each floor of the building houses one step of the process," said Tom. "There are the rooms where the hides are tanned and dyed, and the rooms for cutting, stitching and molding. One pair of shoes can take three months of labor, by twelve separate artisans. But the main floor is reserved for the final adjustments. This is where the world's finest shoes are born."

This area was open, with brick walls, pitted plank floors and crude wooden farm tables. There was a single Italian dwarf seated on a high stool at each table, and each dwarf was wearing a dark suit and tie, and most of the dwarves had thick heads of hair and handsomely trimmed and oiled mustaches. The dwarves were all very good-looking, and while they kept working, each one managed a sideways glance at me, followed by a facial expression that didn't look very impressed.

"Anselmo," said Tom warmly as an older, silver-haired dwarf using a gold-topped cane approached us.

"Tom! Where have you been?" said the dwarf as Tom knelt slightly and the men embraced. "And this must be Becky."

"I had Lila warn him," Tom told me.

"I'm the Before," I told Anselmo.

"You will be beautiful," said Anselmo, taking my hand as his eyes swept to my feet, which were wearing my most comfortable shoes, which were a discount store knockoff of those lumpy suede Australian booties that, I admit, do make your feet look like blobs of chocolate pudding.

"I hope we are not too late," murmured Anselmo.

"But why are they all, you know, little people?" I asked Tom, back in the car.

"Because their shoemaking secrets are so precious that the original Heel-to-Toe families intermarried. Once you've worn their product, you'll understand. And approve."

An hour later, we were outside the penthouse on the one-hundred-twenty-eighth floor of a glass-and-steel skyscraper on the Upper East Side, where, as Tom informed me, "We are about to meet with the most gifted perfumer alive today. He lives all the way up here because the air is the coldest and the cleanest, and doesn't compete with his work."

An assistant brought us into a room that made Tom's compound look like a festering garbage dump. Everything was so white and hypoallergenically sterilized that I worried about depositing grime, just by exhaling. There was laboratory equipment, including glass canisters holding samples of everything from freshly mown grass to just-ironed linen to clippings of recently shampooed blond hair, along with some camellias I recognized from Tom's garden. Assistants were measuring and sifting and recording results on touch screens, and while each man and woman sprouted an extremely large nose, when Tom said, "Archie!" I wasn't prepared for what swung around to greet us.

Archie was the biggest nose I'd ever seen, with a man attached to it lagging far behind, maybe within shouting distance. Archie's nose was like one of those huge modern sculptures that fill the entire plaza in front of an office building, where people have to squeeze around it to get to work in the morning. His nose was arched and curved, and while his nostrils were finely molded, they were so deep that I expected to see an ENTRANCE sign on one and an EXIT sign on the other. I loved Archie's nose because it made me get what Tom had been talking about when it came to expertise. If Archie's nose couldn't detect and classify and judge a scent, that scent didn't exist.

Tom and Archie couldn't hug or shake hands because there was too much nose in between them. Instead, Tom nodded as Archie stayed still, because if Archie moved his head too abruptly, people could get hurt.

"Becky is going to need fragrances for day, evening and all sorts of special events," said Tom.

Archie slowly moved his nose in my direction and when he inhaled I felt a definite suction and the ends of my hair were lifted and tugged in Archie's direction.

"Missouri trailer park," Archie deduced, although his voice, coming from far beneath and behind his nose, had an echo. "I'd say you lived near the recycling bins, and about fifteen yards from . . . from . . ."

As Archie continued to sniff, I helped him out: "An alcoholic named Emmett."

By late afternoon we were on a balcony overlooking the bustling main floor of a Tom Kelly manufacturing and distribution plant in central New Jersey. There were conveyor belts snaking around stainless steel vats and the machinery that was being used to mix, solidify and package Tom's many lines of cosmetics.

"I just wanted you to see this place," said Tom. We were both wearing hard hats and protective goggles with the Tom Kelly logo.

"I'm having a batch of products custom-blended for your particular and extraordinary needs."

I wasn't sure if Tom was insulting me again by implying that in order to make me beautiful, he'd need the whole factory's worth of wet-look mascara and barely there pore-minimizing foundation. I watched employees in white jumpsuits pouring buckets of additives into the larger vats of creams and powders. The additive buckets were labeled in silvery gray letters, with terms including "Renewal," "Tenderness" and "Firmness," like campaign promises.

By dusk we'd returned to the compound for my next fitting. I still didn't know what I'd be wearing, because my red dress now only existed as a stiff, cream-colored muslin mock-up, held together with tape and straight pins, and covered with markings in grease pencil. I looked like a not very appetizing rag doll, as Tom, Mrs. Chen and Lila circled me, exchanging a shorthand of frowns, fluttering hand gestures and tongue clicks.

"What?" I finally said. "Do I look that bad? Are you all that worried? Is it that impossible?"

Tom, Mrs. Chen and Lila all glanced at each other and, in instant agreement, joined in a massive tongue click.

"SHUT UP!" I yelled as they all continued to shake their heads in sorrow.

6.

The next day I left my hotel and moved into the compound. Lila brought me to my room, or my cell, which was down another long, twisting hallway on a lower floor. It was an L-shaped chamber with Tom's mandatory white walls and the furniture included Tom's favorite black leather armchairs nestled in chrome tubing.

Once I was alone I picked up a remote control, which activated a wall of what I thought was solid black leather but which turned out to be drapes, which were dramatically swooshed into a corner, revealing a wall of glass overlooking the Hudson. I was practically walking on water and strolling out to greet the tugboats, ferries, kayaks and a trio of mega-yachts. I staggered backward, both drawn to the river and terrified of crashing through the glass and drowning.

"Come on," said Lila, who'd reappeared. "The red dress. It's done. They're ready for you."

Two of Mrs. Chen's assistants helped me into the dress, lowering it over my head, and then adjusting the intricate boning and mesh. The whisper-light, concealed corset and stiffened bodice were both confining and necessary; they were Tom Kelly's hands, insistently compressing and shaping my flesh. The dress itself floated over this gently rigid core and there were at least three layers of fabric. First came a mist, or maybe a rumor, of the most caressing, liquid satin, which was covered by a haze of something iridescently sheer, followed by a swirl of the airiest pure silk chiffon, a fabric so transparent and alive that it became a delicate force field.

Before I go any further, I just have to say one thing: Until that moment, I hated dresses. Dresses were girly and impractical, so I stuck to oversized T-shirts, sweats and jeans, which didn't cost much or get in my way. When I had sidled past them in the halls, even when I'd kept my head down, Shanice Morain and her clique had cackled and asked me if I was the new school janitor. They'd always dressed alike, in tight, micro-short white denim skirts, with sherbet-colored skimpy ribbed tank tops, worn in layers to emphasize the girls' thinness, and they'd flipped and stroked their yards of shiny, flat hair which they'd spent hours shampooing and conditioning and most likely deep-kissing because they loved it so much.

One of the only fights I'd ever had with my mom revolved around what I'd intended to wear to my middle school graduation. The school had forbidden pants so I'd bought the plainest, most shapeless navy blue polyester dress I could find. "Becky!" my mother had said as I was leaving the trailer for the ceremony. "What are you wearing? You look like a nun. No, I take that back — you look like a depressed nun."

"It's fine," I'd insisted. "It's no big deal."

"Oh, sweetie," my mom had said, sitting me down. "I know that, because you don't want me to feel bad about getting so big, you never want to dress up. You sort of hide out inside your clothes. But you don't have to. I've worn some pretty clothes, and I loved them and I don't want you to miss out on that."

"But this won't show any stains if I spill something. I don't need anything fancy. . . ."

"It doesn't have to be fancy. But you should wear something

that makes you feel wonderful. That's what a really good dress can do, if it's the right color and it fits well. It can make you feel like — like nothing can stop you. Like you can rule the world."

I'd remained doubtful but because my mom had insisted, I'd worn the navy blue dress with a narrow red leather belt and some red glass beads. "You see?" my mom had reassured me. "It's a start. Now you look like — like a nun going on a date."

But now, at Tom Kelly's compound, in a dress designed by Tom and painstakingly stitched by Mrs. Chen and her seamstresses, maybe everything would be different. I shut my eyes and held my breath. I decided that, for once in my life, I wouldn't be nervous or skeptical, and I wouldn't make a wisecrack and try to automatically lower my expectations. I decided that maybe, for the first time ever, something amazing was going to happen. My mom had sent me to Tom Kelly for a good reason and when I opened my eyes I was going to be someone completely new, someone who'd never be afraid and someone who could do anything. I was going to believe in magic, and I could feel the magic working: My blood was pumping and my skin was tingling because the red dress was changing me, and the atoms of my face and my body were being reborn and rearranged, as a totally fresh human being, or maybe a superhero, bursting out of my old, useless lumpiness, just the way Tom Kelly had promised, and I got so giddy and excited that I made a mistake. I opened my eyes.

All I saw was me, the same old awkward, slouching, pigeon-toed, a-diet-wouldn't-kill-you, not-pretty girl with the drab brown hair and the plain brown eyes and a little too much chin. I was a hapless teenager on a misbegotten prom night packed into an overblown disaster loaned to me by one of those church organizations that try to cheer up the poor kids. My dress could've been donated from long-unsold stock by Karol-Amber's

Ultimate Bridal Experience Plus Dressy Dresses Boutique-on-the-Square.

Tom and Mrs. Chen were smiling, and I'd never hated anyone so much. This whole three-dresses deal was obviously a rich people's prank to humiliate the imported trailer trash, and there were most likely hidden cameras, and the footage would be aired on one of those *America's Most Gullible Morons* compilation shows. My face was hot with shame and embarrassment and I only blamed myself: Why had I agreed to this bullshit? What did I think was going to happen?

I was about to rip off the dress and throw it on the floor and spit on it, but then I remembered my mom and I knew that I had to demonstrate at least minimal good manners because I hadn't been raised by wolves.

"So what do you think?" asked Tom, goading me, seeing how far he could push me.

"I think it looks . . . fine," I said, probably with steam blasting from my ears.

"Good," said Tom. "Very good. So I'll go get dressed, and then we'll be on our way."

On our way? To where? Was Tom going to drive me down a lonely highway to a swamp and dump me into the muck, giggling as he told Drake to floor it, or, even worse, so much worse, was Tom going to drag me to a happening restaurant or to someone's twelve-million-dollar penthouse loft and exhibit me to his friends, asking everyone, can you believe this pathetic blob is Roberta Randle's daughter?

"Becky," said Lila, who sat with me at her desk while Tom was getting ready. "I can only imagine what you're feeling. And yes, New York City, and people like Tom, can do more damage than a flamethrower at full blast. But there's only one word you need to remember, as your mantra. . . ."

"My what?"

"A mantra is something that centers you. And prepares you. And it pays off."

"Fine," I said as I slumped on a curved glass bench. I didn't care if I was creasing my dress, in fact, I hoped I was. I hoped that people would say, sure, that girl is a hopeless, butt-faced, stoop-shouldered uggabug, but her Tom Kelly dress sucks too. "So what's my mantra?"

"Your mantra," said Lila, "is 'wait.'"

Tom appeared a few seconds later in his hand-tailored tuxedo, which he wore with a careless ease as if he were still hanging out in his T-shirt and jeans. Tom looked like a man in an advertisement, ambling barefoot along a St. Croix beach at dawn, still in his formalwear but with his tie undone and his pleated shirt hanging open, with one arm draped around some blond hottie and a bottle of champagne dangling from his other hand. The ad could be for anything, from Tom Kelly cufflinks to a chain of exclusive Tom Kelly gated resort communities to a prescription-only Tom Kelly cure-all for erectile dysfunction.

"How do I look?" asked Tom.

"Fuck you," I replied, and Tom laughed.

As Drake opened the limo door for me, he gave a low, appreciative whistle, which convinced me that he was in on Tom's diabolical scam.

"Eat shit," I told Drake helplessly. "Eat shit and die."

As we drove uptown, Tom rolled down his window to take in the city. Through my furious tomboy funk I asked, "What are you looking at?"

"New York City."

"But you live here. Don't you see it all the time?"

"Not at night. Not like this. You see, I haven't really gone out."

"In how long?"

"Almost twenty years."

Then, as the car rounded a curve, Tom turned his face toward me, without meaning to, and I saw that his eyes were wet with tears. And even though I was still busy hating him, I wanted to touch his hand, to comfort him in some blundering, small-town way, but I didn't dare. He wouldn't allow it.

After a few more blocks, Tom told me that we were headed to Lincoln Center "because there's a lot going on. Multiple events. There's a film festival tribute to someone and a ballet premiere starring a French someone else and some absurd benefit for the rain forests, where all sorts of people are going to pretend, not just that they care, but that they even know where the rain forests are. But we're not going to any of that. I just needed a circus."

The car pulled up to a block-long row of marble steps climbing to an open-air plaza bounded on three sides by buildings that could've either been museums or airline terminals. The whole place was a coliseum, as if people were going to be seated along the balconies, judging us and providing a thumbs-up or thumbs-down, before starving lions would be released.

"Do we really have to do this?" I asked.

"We made a deal. And this is only your first dress."

Drake ran around and opened the car's rear door, and Tom stepped out and offered me his hand, as if I were a child being coaxed toward her first morning at preschool or maybe an electroshock treatment for early-onset depression. Tom smiled at me, but we both knew that support and understanding weren't his strong points, so he began tugging me along, like an arthritic donkey, up the wide marble steps, along a red carpet probably soaking in gallons of just-spilled blood.

"I hate you," I told him. "I really, seriously hate you."

"I know."

As we climbed the steps, inch by agonizing inch, I heard the notes of my mom's ringtone again, and I thought they were coming from Tom's phone, in his breast pocket, but he didn't answer it and then the plaza came into view. Through my Goodyear blimp—load of self-pity, I took in an enormous, weirdly silent, expectant crowd. Tom yanked me up a final step and then we were facing them, easily more than a thousand people, all staring directly at us. I wished I were blind so I'd never have to know, under any circumstances, that people were looking at me.

As I stood beside Tom, a murmur rippled through the mob and built furiously as so many people repeated Tom's name. No one had seen him, not just in public, but anywhere, for almost twenty years. Tom's expression combined amusement with something like endless regret.

As I tried to enter the thoughts of someone like Tom, someone so forbiddingly private, a fireball the size of Manhattan burst from the sky and filled my eyes and the plaza and the world with the most impossibly blinding yellow-white light, as if we were stranded at ground zero during a nuclear blast, in the eerie pause before your skin begins to melt from your bones, when the glow is pure and alive and beckoning, like the heavenly tunnel you're supposed to see just before you die. But I wasn't incinerated, or going anywhere: The blindness and the dazzling whiteness only continued and intensified, backed by a chattering thunderclap of clicks and whirs and beeps along with a hollering chorus of insistent voices, which, as far as I could tell, weren't shouting but shooting the words "Tom!" "Over here!" and "WHO IS SHE?"

As we were bathed in, and almost raised off the pavement by, the shrieking glare of the flash attachments and the pulsing strobes and the bobbing TV lights attached to high aluminum poles, and as the voices slammed out questions that Tom and I couldn't even begin to answer, I wondered if this was fame: the total loss of your senses. I couldn't see, hear or identify anyone, or smell anything except the mechanical smoke and the crisp October air. I felt adored, for absolutely no reason, and erased, by all of that sound and light and attention. As my brain rebooted its most primal functions, its notions of left and right and right and wrong, a fresh mantra took hold: WHAT THE FUCK IS GOING ON?

The clamoring focus had to be all about Tom — everyone must want to know why he'd retired and why he'd returned and there'd be a premium on photos of this rare and haughty creature who hadn't aged an instant. And while there was plenty of interest in Tom, he took a half step to one side, as if he was presenting me, but out of what? A smidgen of good manners? Gracious superiority? Or was he just hoping to calm everything down?

Instead, the media cataclysm just expanded into the uncontrollable photo-lust that only descends on a sexy new president waving at his inauguration, or a shackled serial killer during his perp walk into a federal courthouse, or — me.

As Tom withdrew, I stood alone and unprotected as the flashbulbs became an X-ray device, recording and exploring and exposing every ounce of my body. As I tried to comprehend why anyone would want a picture of a dumpy, barely post-adolescent zilch from a Missouri trailer park, Tom reached for my hand. A platoon of burly men in dark suits, barking into their earpieces, cemented themselves around us and became a human wedge, allowing us to make our way through the mob without getting torn to bits, or giving autographs. As we were hustled along we passed a wall of darkened windows, and I caught sight of someone's reflection. She was gliding along beside Tom, gleefully and professionally bodysurfing the tsunami of press. And although I only saw a fraction of her face, a flash of eye and a quarter inch of cheekbone, for less than a second, I could tell that she was staggeringly beautiful, someone undeniably worthy of all the frenzy and fuss. I jerked my head around to see who she was, and how she'd joined us without squeezing through our wall of human defense, but there was no one. The only people within the wedge of black-suited brawn were Tom, and me.

The security team hoisted us past the glass doors and into the soaring lobby of the opera house at the far end of the plaza; there was more red carpeting along with a double coil of winding staircases and crystal chandeliers swinging overhead. The lobby was ringed with additional guards, so we were momentarily safe among an entirely different throng of well-dressed people who were all strenuously involved with their handheld devices, as if they'd just overheard an illegal stock tip and needed to text their brokers. Then, from everyone's defensive, furtive glances, I knew that their texts were about me.

We passed a large framed poster, under glass, announcing the schedule for upcoming operas and concerts, and I was inches away from the glimmering reflection of a woman who was not only unthinkably beautiful, but at ease with herself and entertained by my gaping. And that was when I first suspected that the reflection, and the woman, and the miracle, might be me.

My instantaneous response was a screaming brainload of panic. I pulled my arm away from Tom and I ran down the nearest available hallway, to the ladies' room. The room was deserted, so I all but long-jumped past the stalls to the row of mirrors over the sinks, where I saw Becky Randle. I'm not sure if I was relieved or crushed or more confused than ever, but I steadied my hands on the countertop and took a deep breath, peering at that ordinary, panting, discombobulated girl, shifting uncomfortably in her way-too-luxurious dress. Then the door opened and I turned to see a woman in her forties with wild, choppily cropped hair, like drunken platinum toothpicks. She was wearing extremely high black satin spike heels and a narrowly cut tuxedo with an open, formal shirt, revealing a hint of tattoos. She could've been the jaded maître d' of a members-only, all-lesbian nightclub in Berlin.

"Who are you?" the woman asked, blocking any possible exit and making sure I knew she'd deliberately followed me.

"I'm . . . nobody," I said, and as I went back to the mirror to verify my statement, I saw that I'd just lied, big-time, the biggest, because smiling back at me was the image of a woman so beautiful that my first response was, oh my fucking holy shit, I think I want to be a lesbian too.

I was in shock. I was euphoric. I was scared beyond death. I jerked away from the mirror, my stomach churning as if I'd had a rifle pointed right at me and I was going to will it away and run. But the woman in the tux was staring at me with such breathless wonder that I turned slowly back to the mirror, pretending I was a bystander who just wanted to see what all the gawking was about. And once I caught sight of my reflection I was riveted, hopelessly enraptured, as if I were watching the most impossibly glamorous car accident, or the birth of the baby Jesus, if Jesus had been the world's first supermodel, or something even more unbelievably alluring, something which used to be and might still be — no. No. No fucking way.

I flapped my hand up and down, cautiously, as if I were a marionette working my own strings, or as if the mirror might actually be a window and I needed to see if the woman trapped behind the glass would copy my gestures, which she did. But no matter how quickly I moved or turned my head, she followed me so precisely that I knew, that I had to accept, that I had to somehow internalize the fact that I wasn't looking at someone else, someone imprisoned and imitating my movements. I was looking at — no. It couldn't be. It didn't make any sense. NO.

I raised my right hand, which had once been square and stubby and scrubbed raw, and saw that it was now slim and graceful, with each aerodynamically tapered fingernail glossy with Tom Kelly's Savagely Scarlet polish. I gingerly touched my new, ungodly perfect cheek with a fingertip to see if my face had become a fragile porcelain mask that might crack or crumble, or be removed, so I could sleep and wash my real face, which must be lurking underneath. But my face wasn't cold or kiln-glazed or removable; all I grazed was flesh. The creamiest, most petal-soft, flawless complexion I'd ever seen, let alone touched, let alone owned. I saw amused, almond-shaped, emerald green eyes, and when I say emerald green, I mean that my eyes glistened like precious gems and were many karats more valuable than most people's eyes. I saw a nose that wasn't coy and unbreathably small, or honkerishly bold. It was a nose, perfected. My lips were not only sublimely outlined in Tom Kelly's Lip Lust and bright with Tom Kelly's The Only Red You'll Ever Need, they were the lips used in an ad for a concert or a movie, where all you see are the lips of the star because her lips alone are more than enough to identify her and sell out every available ticket at indefensibly jacked-up prices.

And this was the most unexpected and chilling detail: I saw me. While I was unrecognizable, I hadn't been leveled and demolished and replaced, I hadn't become an opposite, alien being. I was, I guess I'd have to call it, an impossible version of myself. It was as if God had taken a time-out from guiding the fate of humankind and had dedicated Himself only to me, until we were both completely satisfied, no, not just satisfied, but dumbfounded, at what we'd accomplished.

But how had this happened? What had been attached onto or stirred into or sprinkled across my DNA? I remembered what Tom had said when we'd first met, about how he was going to change me. So I was now — what? A supernatural science experiment? Was I Cinderella, or Dr. Frankenstein's monster, and were both of those creatures equally freakish? And why did I feel so unbearably exhilarated, and also like I'd just dropped acid and jumped happily off the tallest building I could find?

Whatever had occurred, whatever had been done to me, whatever or whoever that phenomenon was looking right back at me, for the very first time in my life, I was absolutely certain about something. There was no back-and-forth, no second-guessing and no need to consult with Rocher or Shanice Morain and her cafeteria coven or the Pope or the Joint Chiefs of Staff or even Tom Kelly. Without bragging or exaggerating or deluding myself, I was now, I had become, I inhabited, the most beautiful woman in the world.

I turned to the woman in the tuxedo and I said, "I'm Rebecca Randle."

As the short-haired woman was about to ask me another question, the lights flickered, indicating that the evening's entertainment, aside from what I'd just seen in the mirror, was about to begin. The woman continued to study me, as if she were a private detective and I were her favorite sort of person: a murder suspect. Then she left and I pivoted back to the mirror, only to find Becky. Old Becky. Real Becky. Me.

I was getting handed the rules of my new life. It seemed that when I was with at least one other person I would become Rebecca, but when I was alone, I would remain, I would dwindle into, I'd be back to Becky.

The rest of the evening was a blur as I sat in a box seat beside Tom, high above the crowd. I could barely concentrate on the stage, where a plump, older woman, in an elaborately sausage-curled wig and a floor-length, stiff-collared velvet gown, was singing. I'd never seen an opera before but from what I could tell the woman was supposed to be a beautiful young girl, a courtesan, which Tom told me was a French term for a fancy hooker.

I couldn't pay attention to any of this because my mind was careening. And when I shook my head, to clear my tumbling, ricocheting thoughts, I saw that almost no one in the opera house was facing the stage. People were craning their necks and nudging their seatmates and passing around pairs of miniature brass-and-mother-of-pearl binoculars, all for a closer view of me. I felt terrible for the singers because there was now an audible buzz of feverish gossip as theatergoers held up their phones to take my picture and transmit my face all over the world. People were kneeling or standing backward on their seats and others were streaming down the aisles and up the stairs toward where Tom and I were sitting. And strangely, I felt both insanely exposed and completely anonymous. I was the center of everything, and yet I was entirely hidden.

"That's enough for tonight," Tom told me, and we stood and left our seats. The bodyguards were waiting in the hall to ferry us to our limo. As we fled the opera house with half of the mesmerized, jibbering audience in our wake, I heard the singer unleash a piercing high note, which sounded like music and a scream. This was followed by an actual scream as the singer demanded, "WHO WAS THAT BITCH?"

Once we were in the car heading downtown, Drake asked, "So how did it go?"

"Let's ask the lady," said Tom, turning to me. "How do you feel?"

"I have no idea," I said, bobbing my head to sneak a look at myself in the rearview mirror. I didn't want to say anything else because I knew I'd stutter.

"Things went quite nicely," said Tom. "Let's just say that — people noticed. And, Becky — or is it Rebecca?"

I could see that Drake was watching me in the rearview mirror and that he was deeply impressed, because he was no longer the prettiest person in the car.

Tom continued: "I'm only getting started."

One of Mrs. Chen's assistants came to my bedroom and helped me out of the red dress, which she draped over her outstretched arms as if she were returning it to a lead-lined crypt, or some mystical dry cleaner. I wondered if once the dress came off, my beauty would leave with it, if I'd become the ultimate advertisement for Tom Kelly since I wouldn't exist without his label. But before the assistant went out the mirror confirmed that Rebecca was still in place and looking right back at me.

As the door shut, my cell phone rang. It was Rocher, who'd seen footage of someone on both a late-night entertainment news show and all over the Internet.

"Oh my God, Becky," she said, "that woman, that person, with that Tom Kelly guy, in all of those pictures is that, Jesus, I can't believe I'm even asking this, but, was that — you?"

"Why can't you believe it?" I asked. "Because on some level she looked like me or because I'm usually so gross and hideous that we could never possibly be anywhere near the same person?"

"No! Of course not! I mean, the captions on all the pictures say Rebecca Randle and the pictures do almost remind me of you, I mean, if you sort of . . ."

"If I sort of what? If God came down and said eat shit to Cal Malstrup and Shanice Morain and anyone who ever made fun of my mom? If some wizard from another planet waved his wand over my life? If you took all of my bones and eyeballs and blood and mixed them all up in a blender and put the setting on 'Most Beautiful Woman Who Ever Lived'?"

"Yes."

"Rocher, I'm freaking out. I have no idea what's happening. I know that I wore the first dress, the red one, and I know that Tom Kelly thinks he can do anything but Rocher, tonight, at that opera thing, there were all these people and they wouldn't leave me alone and when I looked in the mirror, I mean, as long as someone else was in the room — that woman, the unbelievably beautiful one, the most beautiful woman in the whatever, she was me. We're me. I think."

"Jesus holy motherfucking fuck me until I bite off my own head and eat it with canned frosting Christ Almighty."

"Rocher, please, I'm not being a bitch or a snob, but there's something I have to do, right now. And I can't even really explain it but can I call you back?"

"Okay, but first you just have to answer me one thing and you have to swear to tell me the God's honest motherfucking truth."

"What?"

"Where can I fucking buy that dress?"

Once I was off the phone I calculated how I could do what I needed to do, which was to get a hard, specific look at Rebecca. I was alone, so I couldn't use a mirror because all I'd see would be Becky. So instead, I found some footage of Rebecca on a cable show, on the huge flat screen TV that filled the wall opposite my bed, and I waited for a close-up and I froze the image. And I sat on the bed in my T-shirt and sweatpants, hugging my knees, and then, just like everybody else, I stared at Rebecca's face. At my face. At it.

Tom had more than kept his promise. I was watching a movie star, in her very first role, in the movie where everyone in the audience asks, "Who is that?" or maybe in the movie that makes her a reigning international star, the sort of star where people all over the world copy her hairstyle and eye makeup and the way she laughs, when the handsome hero tells her he loves her. Rebecca Randle was confident and magnetic and irresistible, and she made all of this feel as easy as taking a breath or tucking a wayward curl of hair behind her ear, in a way that would make all of the women in the audience unconsciously reach toward their own faces and do the same thing. Rebecca was a revenge, a gob of well-aimed spit right in the eye of every rejection I'd ever known, from other people or from my own lowest and most indefensible judgments of myself, which are the only judgments anyone ever trusts.

I tried to decide if Tom had created an exact replica of my mother, but this wasn't the case. If anything, Rebecca was, like me, my mother's daughter — my mother, continued.

My hold on reality was in serious danger. Maybe I was like a character in one of those movies where a girl gets tossed down a flight of stairs, lands on her head and imagines the whole film, or she dreams it and in the movie's last scene she either wakes up back in her own familiar bed, or she dies, because the entire story was a hallucination caused by a fatal gunshot. But I was pretty sure that I wasn't asleep because my dreams were usually more hazy and featured edible Christmas trees made out of Mallomars and typhoons that swept through the Super Shop-A-Lot, sending Rocher and me surfing toward Arkansas.

So, if my life wasn't a dream or a delusion or a drug reaction, I had to make a decision. I could track down Tom and insist that he undo his enchantment, or his curse. I could tell him that I'd changed my mind and that I hoped he'd understand, but that being so beautiful wasn't a good fit. And then I could torch the red dress or knot it around a cinderblock and heave it to the bottom of the Hudson to be colonized by what would become the world's most beautiful algae.

I could scrounge for bus fare and hightail it home to East Trawley to face Rocher's understandable scorn and to live out my expected life, my real life, my pre–Tom Kelly life, as Becky, and no one else.

But running away, with two dresses to go, wasn't just timid and cowardly. A fast exit would be an insult to my mom. Because, when she didn't shred that phone number, my mother had held out this possibility. She'd handed me that plane ticket, or maybe a pair of iridescent couture wings, and now I was flying, or at least cleared for takeoff.

Locking eyes with the woman on the TV screen, I knew that I had to find out where Rebecca might take me. Maybe Rebecca was more than a shell; maybe she was an amazing means of transportation, a surreal, hypersonic, goddess-shaped rocket ship, blasting out of East Trawley. And because Rebecca could do anything, maybe I could finally learn what had happened to my mother, and what had destroyed her.

I decided to believe in some version of God, just possibly in Tom Kelly, and definitely in how much I'd loved my mom. I would believe in magic. I would say yes.

"By the way," said Tom Kelly; he was leaning into the room with both hands braced against the door frame, like a warm-hearted Christmas Eve dad, ·checking that I was tucked in and that sweet dreams were on their way.

"I should mention something. You have one year to fall in love and get married. One year, or all of this, by which I mean Rebecca, all of it disappears forever."

REBECCA

7.

I chased Tom down the hall, yelling, "Hey! Wait up! Hold on!"

"Yes?" said Tom, barely pausing.

"What are you talking about? I've only been beautiful for about ten seconds and now I have to fall in love and get married? That's ridiculous and it's not much time and it's not fair!"

"And you've just answered all of your own questions. Because there's a clock attached to every beautiful woman. From the second she comes into her own, she begins to decline, because she begins to age. Aging is every beautiful woman's kryptonite. And so, yes, it's ridiculous and no, you don't have much time and of course it's not fair. Those three statements are the essence of beauty."

"But . . . but . . . ," I protested as I slumped to the floor, with my back against the wall. Just a moment earlier I'd been giddy, riding the delirious crest of my new beauty and now here I was, back at square one.

"But — how am I supposed to meet someone? Where am I supposed to go? A bar? The Internet? Or do I just stand near an exit ramp and hold up a cardboard sign that says, MOST BEAUTIFUL WOMAN BEFORE THE TURNPIKE — MARRY ME?"

"Oh, please," said Tom. "Have some faith. And get some sleep. You've got a big day tomorrow."

"Why? What am I going to do?"

I shivered, unconsciously holding my hands in front of my endangered new face. What did Tom have planned? Speed dating? A singles cruise? A slave auction?

"What's the first and most important rule of successful marketing?"

I waited for it.

"If you want to sell the goods, you've got to put them in the window. So tomorrow you're going to be photographed. For the cover of *Vogue*."

8.

*V*ogue had been my mom's favorite magazine. Every month she'd sit and
slowly turn the pages, as if she were searching for an especially meaningful biblical passage. She'd be absorbed for hours
and sometimes she'd point out a photo of a particular model and
say, "She knows what she's doing" or "She's almost it, but not
quite, which is heartbreaking," and once she'd scowled at a model
and commented, "She's a total slut, and she doesn't bathe, ever.
Trust me."

The next morning as Drake drove us to the photo shoot I asked
Tom, "But — *Vogue*? Isn't that aiming a little high? Like the highest? Isn't that dangerous?"

"Not for Rebecca."

As we entered the industrial building where the photo session was going to take place, I saw that there was a gaggle of
models lounging in the lobby area, slumped sideways over vinyl-
upholstered chairs, their feet paddling in midair, or crouching
in corners like injured sparrows, ignoring the NO SMOKING signs.
They were all at least six feet tall and weighed less than their outfits, which were very tribal. When they were off duty the models
all wore the sloppiest, most ill-fitting clothes, like a man's oversized button-down dress shirt with a partially torn pocket, baggy
khakis hacked into shorts with manicure scissors and heavy,

battered work boots with the laces missing. My mom had once explained to me why models dressed like this: "It's because they spend all day getting shoved and stapled into fancy clothes, but they also do it because they're models. When a model wears something that looks like she found it in a Dumpster, everyone says, 'See? She can look good in anything.'"

"I can't go in there," I told Tom, grabbing his arm. "Those girls will laugh at me, they'll eat me alive. Those are . . ." I whispered the word, because I didn't want to draw their fire. ". . . those girls are *models*."

Tom shot me one of his looks, the one that meant "Becky, do you have the IQ of a folding chair," and he put his hand in the small of my back and shoved me forward.

"Um, hey," I said to the models, ducking my head. There was a pause as the models scrutinized me. This took a bit, because the models weren't used to looking at other people.

"Jesus fucking Christ," said one of the models, "it's so not fair."

"I hate you so much," said another model.

"Oh my God," said a third model, both numb and startled as if she'd just been beaned with a frying pan. "I'm having, like, it's sort of, like, a breakthrough. It's like, I finally understand something."

"What, Smura?" another model asked her, and as I was processing the idea that someone could be named Smura, which sounded like a sexually transmitted disease, Smura walked over and stood right beside me. "See," she said to everyone, "for the very first time, standing next to her, I'm the uggabug."

This struck the models as a significant insight and they joined hands.

"Now, when I'm walking down the street and I see an uggabug, I'm not just gonna avoid them," said Smura. "I'm gonna tell them, 'I *know*,' and give them money."

Tom ushered me through the modeling circle as some of the girls reached out to touch me, and he opened a heavy steel door into a large, shadowy room with bare concrete walls and rusting iron beams.

A batch of assistants was buzzing around someone in a fitted, untucked white shirt and tight black jeans, and when she turned around I saw that she was the woman I'd encountered the night before in the ladies' room at the opera house.

"Tom," said the woman, running her hand through her spiky, Norwegian-bleached hair and pinching a few strands upright as she inspected me. "I know what happened. I know exactly where you've been all these years."

"Where?" asked Tom.

"Well, from what I'd heard, from extremely reliable sources, you had an inoperable brain tumor, which led to a spiritual rebirth and a trip to Calcutta where you fed lepers, and then once you'd achieved a state of perfect tranquility you were hit by a cab and got institutionalized as a hopeless vegetable."

"Really?" said Tom.

"But you still looked good," said the woman.

"Thank you," said Tom, relieved.

"But here's what really happened," the woman continued, still not taking her eyes off me. "You went away, because you were waiting for her. For this creature. For Rebecca."

"So was it worth it?" Tom asked teasingly. "All those years?"

"Seeley Burckhardt," the woman told me, not bothering to answer Tom's question directly. I'd arrived in the red dress, and there was a squad of hair and makeup people at the ready. Seeley looked at them, looked at me, and said, "Why?" Then she said, "There," and motioned for me to move onto a swoop of thick, seamless white paper, which fell from a roll anchored to a beam and stretched many yards along the floor. I stepped gingerly onto the paper because I didn't want to scuff or rip it and then I stood there, facing Seeley, with my arms hanging lifelessly and my feet skewed at ungainly angles.

"The Chromo-Flex," said Seeley, and as an assistant passed her a complicated, boxy German camera, I yelled, "Stop!"

"What?" asked Seeley. "What's wrong?"

"She's new," Tom explained. "She's never done this before."

I was having a massive anxiety attack. I couldn't have my picture taken. It was the thing I hated most in the world, whether my photo was being snapped for my driver's license or for a laminated fake-wood plaque when I'd been chosen the Super Shop-A-Lot Employee of the Month. I'd looked beyond terrible in both of those pictures. Even Rocher had agreed that the combination of bad lighting, my blotchy skin and my unwashed hair had made me look like I'd been arrested after a meth lab explosion. There was nothing more humiliating than having my picture taken because when someone takes your picture, there's no argument. That's what you look like. That's who you are.

Except now — I was someone else.

"I need to check on something," I said. "I need a mirror."

"Of course," said Seeley. "Get me the half-pint," she ordered an assistant, who wheeled over a truncated mirror, reflecting my body only from the neck down.

"Take a look," said Seeley.

I saw red. Even last night, I'd been so caught up in Rebecca's face that I'd barely considered the first dress, which, of course, fit superbly, but now I saw that its color kept shifting, from the most gloriously blaring, hussified crimson, to a richer, moodier claret, to everything from sunny tomato to severe Chinese lacquer to the thousand reds of a forest fire. I never wore red, because red was sexy and brave and out there, and I wasn't. And could it be, had the dress mutated since its debut only last night? The dress had been floaty and effervescent but now it was sleeker, more form fitting, more on the prowl.

With my face, with Rebecca's face, gone, out of the frame, I was free to acknowledge that for the first time in my life, I had a body. No, that wasn't it. I had a bod. I had what Rocher would call a smokin' bod. I had what every guy in East Trawley, and in all of the East Trawleys everywhere, would growl or pant or howl was a rockin' bod. And I was turning myself on.

From the half mirror at Seeley's studio, here's what I found out: Rebecca was at least five inches taller than Becky, among other things. I gaped at my long, elegant neck, my sculpted but not overly muscled shoulders and at my staggeringly amazing breasts, which were doing what breasts ordinarily only do in the comic books hoarded by the most slobbering teenage boys. They were high and firm and while not Playboy humongous, not shy either. Even more shockingly, I realized that I was wearing very high heels and that they didn't hurt and I wasn't falling over.

"Rebecca?" said Seeley, and I blushed because I'd been doing everything but feeling myself up. As an assistant wheeled the half-pint into a corner I almost followed it, as if I were chasing a wartime lover through a packed train station.

"Wait," said Tom. "One more thing." Anselmo, the dapper owner of Heel-to-Toe Footwear, elbowed his way through the clustered assistants, carrying a Tom Kelly shoe box, just like the one I'd found in my mom's trailer.

"To your exact specifications," Anselmo told Tom. "Our entire staff worked through the night. We hope you will be pleased."

The box contained a pair of red spike heels that were at least six inches higher than the stilettos I was already wearing. I dragged Tom aside because I didn't want to hurt Anselmo's feelings.

"Are you crazy?" I hissed. "I can't wear those shoes! No one could wear them! They're designed for the Jolly Green Hooker!"

"They're perfect," said Seeley, eavesdropping.

"Rebecca," said Tom, and I reluctantly kicked off my previous shoes and contemplated the twin skyscrapers, which had the cherry red candyflake glimmer of a souped-up Corvette hardtop.

Grimacing, I slid first one foot and then the next into these blocks of fashionable cement, praying that I wouldn't hit the floor face-first.

"You know Superman's cape and Batman's utility belt and Captain America's shield?" said Tom. "Those are just accessories. Those guys wish they had these shoes."

Tom was miraculously right. Instead of feeling crunched and crippled, I had just grown even taller and more powerful and, well, even more Rebecca. The shoes strode onto the swoop of white paper as if they meant business and as if they couldn't wait.

Someone flipped a switch and the room was in darkness except for a bank of lighting instruments aimed directly at me. There was a muffled mechanical click as Seeley took a test shot. Then an assistant switched on something that was like music, only hotter and really filthy. It was a gut-busting bass line using the notes of my mom's ringtone remixed as a throbbing beat, growing tougher and more demanding, like a boyfriend you'd be ashamed of but could never resist. When I heard that sound I experienced my most staggering revelation to date. Because thanks to Rebecca's red dress and her hips and her heels, I wanted to dance.

As Becky, I could barely walk. At the few dances I'd ever been to I'd either sat on the sidelines or I'd hidden in a dark corner, shuffling my feet and never raising my rigid arms. I'd been way too self-conscious about my face and my body and my lack of rhythm and I never wanted to be like one of those girls who thinks she's hot stuff and who gloms onto the center of the dance floor, chugging away in a wild-and-free spaz attack while everyone else imitates her and falls all over themselves laughing.

Rocher was a decent dancer but still careful. Shanice and her friends usually danced together, doing choreographed gestures copied from videos. As long as they all did the same few moves, and as long as Shanice did them the best, everyone was safe.

I remembered something else. One afternoon when I was thirteen, I'd come home early from school and I'd heard music blasting from inside our trailer. Through a window, I'd seen my mom, all by herself, dancing to a song on the radio, an earlier, disco song. Her eyes were shut and she was really moving. She'd already gained a lot of weight but it didn't matter, because I'd seen that she loved to dance.

"Oh my God," she'd said when I'd opened the front door.

"Mom?"

"I'm sorry, I'm so sorry," she'd said, shutting off the music. "I shouldn't be doing that, there is nothing worse than an old person dancing."

"But — you were really good."

"No, maybe once upon a time. I just heard that one song and I remembered it, from a long time ago."

I'd tried to get her to tell me about when she'd first heard the song but she changed the subject and she started asking me about school and I never saw her dance ever again. But I had the feeling that she was here with me right now, at the *Vogue* shoot.

I began to move my pelvis, just a few inches from side to side, finding the beat. My shoulders joined in because they couldn't resist. My head started to sway and then my arms got on board and then I just balls-out erupted; I shimmied and shook and howled, because I was wearing a sizzling red dress and killer red shoes, and because for the first time in my life I felt absolutely liberated from any embarrassment or clumsiness or doubt. Some beautiful women can't dance; their beauty paralyzes them. They're like opera divas trying to sing pop hits or ballerinas trying to get down. But, as I was learning, Rebecca could do anything and now she was driving the entire room into a frenzy. She was having such a good time that pretty soon everyone, including the assistants and even the burly union guys who'd been hired to move the heaviest equipment, was joining in and Anselmo had tossed aside his gold-topped cane and was boogying on a tabletop. Rebecca wasn't just perfect, she was a party and she was teaching me what it was like to love every inch of my body and everything it could do.

The only people who weren't going wild were Tom, who was leaning against a cast-iron column with his arms crossed in satisfaction and Seeley, who was busy taking hundreds of pictures. As the music boomed and everyone began peeling off their sweat-soaked clothing and the waiting models from the outer lobby began wailing, every fuse in the building blew and there were sparks spewing everywhere and then darkness.

"Fuck," said Seeley admiringly from the gloom, lit only by the glow of her cigarette. I was exhausted but still vibrating, as if I'd just competed in a triathlon and set three new world records. As I tried to regain some control of my body and my personality, like a cowboy settling a snorting bronco, I remembered something else about my mother. Every month, after examining each page of *Vogue*, she would carry the magazine outside atop her flattened hands, as if it were radioactive, to the tag-sale barbecue rusting behind our trailer. She'd douse the magazine with lighter fluid and burn it to a crisp.

When Tom and I left Seeley's studio the limo was waiting but our exit had been stalled by a second gas-guzzling land yacht, a Mercedes so lustrous that it must've been coated with a custom blend of moonlight and melted Rolexes. Drake was standing beside our car, just about to head-butt the driver of the Mercedes.

He said to Tom, "He pulled up right after you guys went inside and he won't move. He says that his passenger needs to talk to Tom."

"Who's his passenger?" asked Tom.

"I am," said a forceful, tough guy's voice.

The passenger was standing a few feet away, balancing a cigar and a cup of take-out coffee in one hand. I'd expected a construction worker or a police sergeant but this guy had the burnished Ivy League polish of a man's man in an ad for Canadian scotch or serious leather luggage. He was tall and well into his sixties, with creased flesh, a strong jaw and thick silver hair, which was probably trimmed every other day by a personal, old-school barber. His tan could have been acquired on the ski slopes, or in the Kalahari while he was digging the grave of the bandit he'd just stabbed to death.

"Hello, Tom," said the passenger, although he didn't offer a handshake.

"Brant," said Tom warily.

I knew, because I'd Googled Tom, that this was Brant Coffield. He was a major player in Tom's life. Years ago he'd provided the start-up money for Tom's company.

"How long has it been?" asked Brant, who knew to the second how long it had been.

"Too long," said Tom, and then, taking a step closer to Brant, he opened his arms and the two men embraced. Brant was taken by surprise, which meant that Tom was winning.

"What are you doing here? I heard that people saw you and I couldn't believe it," said Brant. "What's going on? What in God's name . . ."

"Brant," said Tom, cutting him off. "This is Rebecca Randle."

"My God," said Brant. He was stunned and there were tears in his eyes and I knew that when he saw me, he was seeing my mother.

I wanted to ask him what he remembered about my mom but something else was happening. Brant kept looking at Tom and then at me, in disbelief. And I wondered: Unlike Tom and Drake and Lila, why didn't Brant look unnaturally young?

"You can't do this," said Brant, with a rising agitation. "It's not possible."

"I can do anything I want," Tom replied evenly.

"But you can't!" Brant insisted, and I wanted to slap both men or kick them and ask why no one was bothering to fill me in about their past or my future. But all of my borrowed courage had fled in the daylight. Even after my performance at the *Vogue* shoot, I'd shrunk to the practically invisible size of Becky Randle from Missouri. I was a pathetic fraud and I knew it. As I was about to howl that I wasn't and I could never be my mother, and that the Most Beautiful Woman Who Ever Lived was the Biggest Dishrag on the Block, I heard the roar of a Harley-Davidson without a muffler, and a third man's voice — a voice that belonged to the only guy I'd ever loved — told me, "Get on."

9.

Of course, I recognized the voice, but when the guy on the motorcycle tugged off his helmet and shook out his swirling tousle of expertly highlighted, fetchingly matted, exquisitely wayward hair, I forgot that I was standing on a street corner in a dress that had transformed me and that I was being fought over by two dashing and possibly homicidal men. Because the guy on the motorcycle, with the tortured hair and the disgruntled, bruised, dreamable lips, not to mention the unholy cheekbones and the eyes, oh my dear God, the eyes that had taught me everything I knew about love — those eyes, both of them, they were a Beverly Hills swimming pool filled with that blue-colored sports drink and stocked with diamonds — those eyes could only belong in the sockets of Jate Mallow.

As a little kid, I'd never developed goony celebrity crushes or overflowed my hard drive and phone and locker with visions of some lip-synching boy-band member or the mop-topped surfer dude on some Malibu kid-com. I'd sneered at the girls who couldn't shut up about Togger or Danny or Steeve and who'd texted their favorite hottie five times an hour and truly believed that he'd personally responded when they'd received generic mass emails promoting a new CD along with machine-autographed photos signed "To someone really, really special in my life."

But this was totally and completely different. This had nothing to do with all of those other manufactured, prepubescent, girly-man skeeve monsters who the other, pathetic girls had liked. This was something they couldn't even begin to worship or even see, because if they so much as looked at him, his beauty and their evil would make them go blind. This was something beyond sacred, this was something real and true and for all time, and anyone who didn't get it should just drink drain opener and die gurgling but even with their last ammonia-scented breaths they shouldn't even be allowed to say his name, because this was JATE MALLOW.

Since I was eleven years old I had known, and it hadn't been a shooting-star wish or a trigonometry-test daydream, I'm telling you, I *knew*, because there are some things, like that the sky is blue and the earth is round and love is real, that you just know, that Jate and I would be married. I'd prepared myself by learning every conceivable factoid about my husband-to-be. I knew that Jate was Jate's real legal name because his parents had wanted to mix the earthiness of "Jake" with an antidote to "hate" and a gesture toward his future when he would "create."

Jate had been born into a religious cult with twenty-three members, led by his wild-eyed, shaggy-haired dad, who'd worn a clerical collar over his limp, tie-dyed T-shirts and the long vests that Jate's saintly mother had stitched from Guatemalan souvenir placemats. The cult's primary belief system had demanded moving Jate's family, in a dented, decal-smothered van, out of Illinois to Los Angeles, where the twelve Mallow kids had sought the glory of Jehovah by acting on television. Jate and his siblings had been homeschooled so they'd been available round the clock for auditions, underage pageants and go-sees. Jate's dad had forced Jate to pretend to be a twin so his two selves could work longer hours.

I'd first seen, and loved, and become engaged to, and secretly married to Jate when he'd been cast as one of the title characters on a syndicated kids' show called *Jackie + Jate*, where he'd played Jate, the whimsically rebellious, electric-guitar-strumming, tank-top-wearing brother of Jackie, a studious, by-the-rules girl played by his real-life sister, who later became a radical lesbian and had then renounced lesbianism for evangelical Christianity and had then died of a heroin overdose. She'd been played in the eventual TV movie of her short, sad life by her own younger sibling, Juliet. Jate's father had given all of his children names starting with *J* for Jesus, and because, as the family's manager had advised, "It's catchy."

Every week on *Jackie + Jate*, Jackie had hit the homework and tried to lure Jate into a trip to an art museum or a science fair but the pair always wound up at a beachfront tiki shack or a dance contest or a mall talent nite — anywhere that Jate could shake his unruly locks, which were soon insured for millions, and grin his unruly grin.

Rocher and I had been wedged onto our couch on either side of my mom, who'd shared our Jate-ism. Jate had conquered every demographic, so around the world entire families had solemnly repeated Jate's all-occasion catchphrase at car washes and tea ceremonies and child-custody hearings: "Well, that's just Jate!" Rocher, my mom and I had spent at least two-thirds of our waking hours gathering and collating Jateiana and analyzing Jate's favorite foods ("I like to eat healthy, but man, I love chocolate"), colors ("something about blue just gets me"), dog breeds ("I love my mutt, because he needs my love"), first-date preferences ("I like to just talk and really get to know someone"), and, most especially, what he hankered for in a girlfriend. Jate's tireless publicists had reported that Jate's "must-haves" were "a sense of humor," "someone who just likes to hang and have fun" and "someone who's not stuck on herself."

Rocher, my mom and I had each privately known that we were the only person alive who met every requirement but to keep the peace we'd agreed that when Jate showed up at my mom's trailer, we'd each chat with him for five minutes and then he'd make his final and irrevocable choice. I had no doubts about Jate's decision because I had planned on underlining the fact that I didn't have a dad, which would position me as brave and needy. I'd rehearsed in the bathroom mirror, admitting, "I've never met my father, and I don't even know who he is," with a wavering, don't-you-worry-about-me smile and a single tear running down my cheek, a tear I'd applied with clear nail polish, so I'd never be caught tearless. I hadn't told Rocher or my mom that they were out of the running because I'd pitied them and because after Jate and I were married, on a Very Special Episode of *Jackie + Jate*, costarring Jate's real-life mutt, who'd be wearing a gingham bow tie as Jate's best man, I'd fully intended to let Rocher and my mom walk the many additional dogs that Jate and I would rescue from the pound and they could also supervise the Midwestern branches of our fan club.

Jate had known early on that his teen idol bubble, while lucrative, wasn't the key to career longevity. He'd sued his parents at age sixteen to become an Emancipated Minor and then he'd quit his TV show after five seasons to buy a loft in Manhattan and study his craft. He'd appeared in one Off-Broadway play for a sold-out limited run of twelve performances, playing a charismatic, self-destructive, inarticulate college dropout squatting on a friend's couch and then he'd nabbed the romantic lead in what had proved to be the most successful movie of all time, a tragic yet uplifting story, set against the sweeping canvas of early air travel. Jate had played Orville Wright, the hunkier and more nakedly sensitive of the two pioneering brothers, who'd fought his attraction to Emily, his brother Wilbur's lovely young blond fiancée, who'd also been, in many ways, the world's first flight attendant. Immediately following her wedding to Wilbur, Orville and Emily had escaped on an epic flight around the globe and while their love was true and strong and kept their spindly aircraft soaring, they soon accepted that they'd betrayed Wilbur and right after some gorgeously photographed sex, partially blurred for PG-13 purposes by puffs of mist, they'd plunged intertwined into an active volcano. The final words of the film, which received a record twenty-eight Academy Awards, belonged to Wilbur, who, as an eagle perched on his shoulder, told the proud bird, "I can never hate them. Because they loved, all over the sky."

I'd seen *Cloudborne* eighteen times and whenever Jate had taken Emily in his long-john-clad arms and murmured, "You're my propeller," I'd felt he was sending me, and only me, a coded message which read, "I really hate Emily and after she gets killed in the volcano I'm going to crawl back out, without being disfigured in any way, although the molten lava may have seared my sleeves off, and I'm going to find you, Becky Randle, and kiss you and hug you and talk about your life and then let you call Rocher and your mom so you can tell them all about it." The movie had been historically demented and Jate's greatest accomplishment had rested in his saying his lines without laughing, but I hadn't cared. Jate had done what only the greatest movie stars could do: He'd let me love him. And when Cal Malstrup, with his arm around Shanice, had said that "nothing in that movie was even true, it was all, like, a movie," I'd replied, under my breath, "I guess you know everything, Cal. Except about love."

Which is why, without another word or an instant's thought or anxiety, I tucked myself onto the back of that motorcycle, linked my hands around Jate's waist and left Tom and Brant yapping at each other. I didn't care. I didn't run through a checklist of pluses and minuses, I didn't worry about offending Tom or losing a chance to learn more about my mom. All I knew was that the wind was playing photogenic havoc with my red dress, that I could feel Jate breathing through his battered leather jacket, and that I was completely happy.

We sped out of the city with Jate winding heedlessly in and out of traffic, which was thrilling, especially because I'd been cooped up in Tom's compound. We reached a small private airport where the security guards recognized Jate and opened the chain-link fence and soon Jate was steering directly onto the tarmac, coming to a halt beside a sleek private jet. Of course he has his own plane, I thought, because if he boarded a commercial flight he'd be hounded by people like me. Removing his helmet, Jate said, "Man, I think that having your own jet is disgusting. It eats up money and fuel and fucks up the environment." Then he grinned and added, "So that's why I borrowed one."

Jate helped me off the motorcycle, slung my helmet onto the handlebars and asked, "Are you cool with this?"

"Where are we going?" I asked and immediately wished I hadn't, because needing a destination was so wussy and nice-girl and non-Jate.

"You'll see," said Jate as his arm swept chivalrously toward the mechanical stairway that was descending from the plane's forward hatch.

Just a week earlier I'd been overwhelmed by a hotel duvet, and here I was on a private jet, which was exotic and unnerving on a whole new scale. This was the first moment when I told myself: Becky, remember everything. Not just because it's Jate but because it's the world. You're not looking at a picture of a private plane in a magazine, it's the real thing. And who knows what's going to happen next, so be your own scrapbook.

The jet's interior was an open lounge, with the curving walls paneled in a rich mahogany set off by deep, beige wool carpeting and honey-colored leather banquettes. There was a fully stocked bar and behind touch panels, all sorts of flat screens, audio equipment and a candy store's worth of treat-filled apothecary jars.

"Welcome aboard, Ms. Randle," said a pretty, uniformed flight attendant. "I'm Kyla. And, Mr. Mallow, what can I get you?"

"Rebecca?" asked Jate, and from hearing him say my name, I inwardly screamed and cheered and recorded his saying Rebecca for use as the greeting on my voicemail.

"Oh, just some water, please," I said, because I'd read somewhere that you should stay hydrated during a flight.

"Good to go, Jate?" asked the captain's voice via the sound system.

"Roger that," said Jate, raising his voice slightly, and then, to me, "I'm such an asshole."

Then Jate grinned at me and acted like a guy and ran his hand through his hair and shrugged off his leather jacket, which I knew, from the website Fashion Freekz, that one of his stylists must've tracked down for him at a vintage leather jacket source in the East Village, the kind of place that supplies clothing poor people have broken in so that rich people can feel cool. Between Jate and his jacket and the plane I was getting so overstimulated that there was only one thing I could do. I dug my phone out of the slouchy red Italian goatskin shoulder bag that Tom had made for me, and I stood beside Jate and I sent the picture to Rocher. Two seconds later I only skimmed Rocher's text message, because I didn't want to be rude but I registered the following words: "Jate," "JATE," "love," "marry," "ME," "hate you forever," "tell everything" and "mmm . . . rubbing photo of Jate against a part of me."

"I'm sorry," I said to Jate. "I'm a much bigger asshole."

"Here we go," said Jate as we buckled ourselves in using the custom-stitched leather seat belts that matched our armchairs. As the plane taxied and picked up speed I clutched my armrests and shut my eyes, pretending that this was my longtime takeoff ritual, knowing full well that sooner or later I'd have to open my eyes and when I actually did, a few seconds later, Jate was looking right at me, in the same way as Seeley, Drake and so many others, with a thunderstruck, scientific awe. "You are so beautiful," Jate said.

"I am not," I insisted.

"You are the most beautiful woman in the world. And I'm not blowing smoke or trying to get into your pants, because if I was, I wouldn't say something that corny and useless. And I'm not even being nice. I'm just being accurate."

"Stop it, right now, shut up. I'm not the most beautiful woman in the world, I'm not what you or everyone else thinks I am, I'm just . . . a girl from out of town."

"Don't. Don't do that. It's tacky. And beneath you. And you don't have to do it, at least not with me. You don't have to do it with anyone."

"Do what?"

"Go through the motions. Put yourself down. Talk about how gawky and ugly you were in high school and how you couldn't get a date and how the guy you had a crush on blew you off and took someone else to the prom."

"But he did, he went with Shanice Morain. . . ."

"I don't care. It's bull. And it's ridiculous. Especially on you."

"So what should I say? When you tell me I'm the most beautiful woman in the world?"

Jate smiled. "You could say thank you. And then you might

return the favor, and say something nice about me. Maybe about my hair."

"Excuse me," I said as I unbuckled my seat belt and ran for the bathroom, closing the accordion doors behind me once I was inside. Even though the bathroom was fitted with marble and brushed steel fixtures, it was still small and when I looked at myself in the mirror over the sink I saw Becky, just the way she'd appeared in my mom's trailer in our claustrophobic, molded pink fiberglass bathroom to which my mom had added way too many of what she'd called "decorator accents," including a hanging white wicker basket of trailing, pink polyester silk petunias and a doll whose crocheted skirt had concealed an extra roll of toilet paper as if the doll were a cunning midget shoplifter.

What are you doing here, you dweeb, you imposter, you total fake? I asked my reflection. Who the hell do you think you are? You can't handle this, you can't talk to Jate Mallow on a private jet, you could barely manage to say hello to Cal Malstrup in the East Trawley High School hallway between classes, when you'd dip your head and manage a sort of half wave while muttering "hey."

I heard my mom's muffled ringtone coming from my shoulder bag but when I reached inside, my hand closed around another surprise gift from Tom Kelly. It was a velvet pouch from Madame Ponelle's gem shop, containing a pair of square-cut ruby earrings which looked like the world's most expensive sore throat lozenges. As I slid them into my earlobes I could hear Shanice comment, "Becky, you look like your ears are bleeding." My mom had forced me to get my ears pierced but I only wore the most insignificant, almost nonexistent gold hoops. I owned almost no jewelry because I never wanted to call attention to my head or my neck or my wrists or any other part of me.

"You okay in there?" I heard Jate call out, and with my rubies clanking against the sides of my head I stepped out of the bathroom, even though I'd been seriously considering washing my hands for the rest of the flight.

Before I could sit down I caught sight of my reflection, of Rebecca, in the glass of a large, framed black-and-white photo of the Chrysler Building hanging on the wall behind Jate's head, and I saw that my rubies' sparkle only enhanced Rebecca's phenomenal head of hair.

I'd gotten so flustered, and so hopelessly Becky, over meeting Jate that I had totally forgotten — I was Rebecca Randle.

"So," I began, "you're an actor?"

As I spoke I overheard myself and I didn't sound like Becky, whose voice was usually a please-don't-call-on-me-even-if-I-know-the-answer mumble. Rebecca sounded years older, or at least more experienced, as if no matter what she was saying what she meant was, "In your dreams, baby" or "Does your mama know you're here?"

"I think you were on some sort of TV show?" I asked.

"A while ago," said Jate, refusing to be riled. "Lately, I've been into movies."

"What would I have seen?"

He named a batch of films, all of them mega-blockbusters, including, of course, *Cloudborne*.

"*Cloudborne*?" I repeated vaguely, as if the title were something caught in my teeth.

"It was about the Wright brothers?"

"You're kidding."

That did it.

"Oh, come on!" said Jate, laughing. "You've at least heard of it! It's the biggest movie of all time, even if you hated it, even if you got bored and walked out, you know about *Cloudborne*!"

"Of course," I said gently, making it clear that I was still just being polite, to spare his ego. "It's . . . a wonderful title."

"And what do you do?" Jate asked, trying not to sound patronizing but not trying all that hard.

This was a good question: What exactly did I do? Was I a recent high school graduate or a Super Shop-A-Lot Employee of the Month from two Septembers ago, or as of today, was I a sort-of cover girl? What was I going to print on my tax return where it said "Occupation"?

"I'm the most beautiful woman in the world."

I said this with serene, immaculate confidence, as a simple statement of fact. And as my remark lingered in the air I added calmly, "There was a vote."

Jate and I both burst out laughing because what else could you do? What I'd said was completely true but it was also nuts.

"When I saw those pictures of you online," said Jate, "at first I thought they were Photoshopped. But then Seeley sent me some stuff from the *Vogue* shoot."

"While she was taking them?"

"We're buds. She said you were so gorgeous that putting you on the cover of *Vogue* was redundant. She said that she's been taking pictures for thirty years and she's never seen anyone even close to you. And she said that she knew I'd be interested."

"Why?"

"Because that's how it works. Because for the moment, and maybe only until we land, I'm the biggest star out there. Name a continent. And so I get first pick."

"First pick? Of what?"

"Women. Planes. Projects. Leather jackets. If I see something online about a guy who's just invented the next step in wireless digital whatever, I call him up, I say my name, and suddenly he's at my door, hand-delivering the prototype. If I hear that some

Pulitzer-winning novelist has written the first chapter of a book that might have a role for me, I text him, and he makes the character hotter and younger and American. And if I have a pet cause, Slovakian orphans or Icelandic voter registration or bipolar baby ocelots, I don't give anonymously to the appropriate organization. I call the president, and we have lunch."

"Good to know."

"But all of that access and the influence and the perks, they're the least of it. They're nothing, compared to the sex."

Sex. I was now talking about sex with Jate Mallow. OMG. OMFG. Or as Rocher would say, OMF-My-Head-Just-Exploded-G.

"And I'm not just talking about stalkers or lonely First Ladies or God knows, actresses."

"And do you take advantage? Of your options?"

Rebecca was coming off as equally experienced; she was raising the sexual ante. But Becky was growing more and more anxious because I could tell where things were headed. And while no one was hotter, or better in bed, or more worthy of Jate than Rebecca, Becky was a virgin.

And yeah, I know, I was eighteen, what was my problem? If Cal Malstrup had asked me, would I have done it, in his parents' house while they were over at that ribs joint for their anniversary, or in the back of Cal's pickup where he kept a folded-up stack of those grungy, quilted blanket—type things he used for moving furniture? Yes, I would've had sex with Cal because he was nice looking and because I wanted him and because I knew I should have sex with somebody, because it would've proved something, it would've proved that I was cute enough or at least available enough, for someone to want to have sex with me. But Cal hadn't asked. And now Jate was about to.

"It's crazy," said Jate, leaning forward. "But I can pretty much have anything and anyone I want. And I'm not saying I deserve any of it, but I'm not going to say no."

"Of course not."

"Are you?"

Oh my God. OH MY GOD!!! No that's not right, that's not nearly enough because right now even God must be tweeting everyone in heaven and asking, "Did U hear what Jate just said???" Somebody pinch me, somebody stop the blood from pounding in my ears, somebody scrape me off the ceiling and shove what's left of me into a keepsake locket. Because this was it, this was everything I'd thought I wanted since I was eleven years old. This was my destiny. This was why my mom had left me that phone number and this could be my first step to satisfying every one of Tom Kelly's conditions, because I was already more than in love with Jate Mallow and sex with Rebecca could only lead to marriage because how could Jate ever improve on Rebecca?

Beyond all that, this was the moment that every beautiful woman knew all about but which I'd never been anywhere near. This was when beauty became a bargaining chip, something you traded for something else. Jate was watching me, and he wasn't about to let me squirm off the hook, claiming that I was exhausted or seeing someone or just not into it. I was Rebecca Randle and now I had to decide: What was I worth?

"Look at you," said Jate. "You're so unbelievably gorgeous and you're shaking like a little kid. You're about to burst into tears. Because you think that I've kidnapped you and cornered you and that I won't let you off this plane until we have sex. Because I'm Jate Mallow and I get whatever I want. And right now I want you."

"But — isn't that what we're talking about?"

"Yeah, maybe. If I was a total prick. If I believed any of that bullshit I just told you about getting first pick. Oh, and if I wasn't gay."

10.

W hat? WHAT? Jate was WHAT?

    I'd tracked all of Jate's romances. When he was seventeen he'd been linked to Madison Maystock, the teen star of *Too Much Madison*, another hit syndicated show, where Madison had played a girl who was secretly a witch but who'd also just wanted to be a cheerleader and have fun. After two years together, which had included the platinum-selling duet "We Could Be Us," Jate and Madison had broken up and Jate had moved on to much publicized relationships with a Venezuelan supermodel, a Broadway dancer and then someone whom Jate had told the press was just "a regular girl from back home in Illinois who likes to stay out of the spotlight." Of course, I'd been jealous of all those girls but Jate had left each of them because, I'd assumed, they hadn't been me.

"Rebecca? Hello?" Jate was saying.

"Uhm, what, um, what did you say?"

"I said I was gay. And yes, I'm careful about it and I'm gonna assume that you'll protect my privacy, because we have so much else to talk about."

"What? What? I'm sorry, what?"

"Okay," said Jate, "let's go over this, so we can get it out of the way. And don't lie and pretend that you never saw my show, because I am so onto you. When you first saw me, on *Jackie + Jate*, what did you think?"

"I thought . . . that you had the most beautiful hair I'd ever seen. I loved the way it swept sideways across your forehead and then curled under your ears. My mom and Rocher and I always had fights about how long it took you to get it like that and whether you had to spray it rock hard to keep it that way. And I would always defend you, I would say, I bet Jate's hair just grows like that naturally. And that it was because you wrote such beautiful songs so that your hair was like music growing out of your head."

"You said that?"

"I was eleven."

"And while you were thinking about me and my incredible musical hair what were your fantasies?"

"I always dreamed that I'd be in a nightclub, just like the one on *Jackie + Jate*, which looked like a preschool classroom with a disco ball. And I would be sitting by myself at one of the little round tables up front and you'd put my name in a song except the only words I could think of that rhymed with Becky were necky and wrecky. . . ."

"And did you ever picture the two of us having sex?"

"No! Of course not!"

"So all you wanted was an imaginary boyfriend with great hair who could fake playing the guitar."

"But you're gay!"

"Which is pretty much what I just described."

I was coming off as forlorn so Jate came over and knelt beside me and took my face in his hands, just the way I always thought he would do on the first episode of our imaginary reality show about our wacky hijinks as young newlyweds.

"But if you're gay, if you didn't want to . . . I mean, if we weren't going to . . . if there wasn't even a chance, goddamnit — then why did you come and get me, on your motorcycle? And what am I doing on this plane? And why are you being so nice to me?"

"Because you're gorgeous. And because even though you think you're such a tough cookie, you're also incredibly sweet. And because, I hope — you're Elyssa."

"Elyssa?"

11.

Elyssa, it turned out, was the female lead in *High Profile*, which was the action movie Jate was about to begin shooting in our flight's destination, which turned out to be Paris.

"So what do you think?" Jate asked after he'd described the movie and my role. "You're perfect for it. We'll have a blast. Are you on board?"

My head was spinning, like one of those carnival wheels that could stop at all sorts of different outcomes. I was Becky, no, I was Rebecca. I was miles up, with Jate Mallow, who was gay. And now he wanted me to become a movie star. My phone rang. It was Tom.

"Is this Elyssa?"

"How did you know about that? Jate only asked me five seconds ago!"

"I know everything."

"So — should I do it?"

"Of course. You're not getting any younger. Eyes on the prize, Rebecca. It's an easy yes, because tell me, who falls in love more passionately, and gets married more frequently than any other group of people in the world?"

Of course. Movie stars.

Once we'd landed in Paris, I stayed with Jate at The Ritz and I was amazed, not just because we were occupying half of an entire floor but because I had to get used to telling cabdrivers, as if it was something I tossed off every day, "The Ritz." By the time that *High Profile* began shooting two weeks later, paparazzi photos had cropped up all over the world of Jate and me getting out of cars and being hustled into restaurants, and having stores cordoned off so we could browse undisturbed. The headlines blared, "JATE'S MYSTERY CRUSH!" "TOM KELLY DISCOVERY NOW JATE-BAIT!" and, just as I'd always dreamed, "REBECCA: SHE'S JUST JATE!" I began to suspect that everyone, from a chambermaid pushing her laundry cart to a gendarme directing traffic, was going to surreptitiously photograph me and I was always right.

I met with the movie's director, Billy Seth Bellowitch, who reminded me of a gangly, middle-aged, slump-shouldered eleven-year-old because he offset his thinning hair and pot belly with baseball caps, high-topped sneakers and baggy, prewashed jeans; he bristled with sports logos while being too out of shape to move very quickly. He had trouble remembering my name because, as Jate explained, "It's a two-hundred-seventy-five-million-dollar movie, so he spends most of his time storyboarding the action sequences, like when we're hang gliding over the Amazon, and a tribe of angry pygmies shoots flaming arrows at us."

"Why are the pygmies angry?" I asked.

"Because they work for the Soviet mobsters," Jate replied impatiently.

When Jate had introduced me to Billy Seth, Billy Seth had looked me up and down and given Jate an enthusiastic thumbs-up but without a trace of lust. This was because Billy Seth was emotionally stunted and he hadn't discovered girls yet. I was a necessary element in his movie and I seemed every bit as promising as the night-vision headgear he'd just inspected.

I read the movie's script, which Jate told me was just a blueprint and was being continually rewritten by tag teams of writers.

Jate would be playing Renn Hightower, a renegade American CIA operative, while my character was described as "a high-class international call girl, a total uber-hottie, with extreme martial arts moves." I told Jate that I'd never acted before except for performing as a dancing pumpkin pie in my second-grade Thanksgiving pageant. "That's more than enough training," Jate assured me.

Before the actual filming began, Jate and I spent a week with J. P. Drayer, whom everyone said was the greatest stunt director who'd ever lived. J.P. was in his sixties and he looked like a grizzled, chain-smoking cigar-store wooden Indian or a taciturn cowpoke who'd beaten lung cancer by lassoing it and dragging it out of town.

I loved the stunt rehearsals because I felt grounded. I got to wear sweats and get grimy and knee people in the groin. As Becky, I'd been okay at soccer and the balance beam so I had something to offer Rebecca; in a way, I became her stunt double. When J.P. taught me how to block a punch or get my foot high enough to pierce someone's throat with my spike heel, I was focused, and when I got it right, proud of myself, maybe because I was doing something that didn't depend on what I looked like.

I'd never been anywhere near a movie set so on the first day of shooting I didn't expect there to be so many people. There were over one hundred crew members gulping 5:00 A.M. bagels outside a warehouse in a nondescript neighborhood. Inside the warehouse was a set built to resemble an exclusive private gambling club atop the Eiffel Tower. The action of the movie took place over a single weekend so I'd be in my Tom Kelly red dress for most of the film. Tom had flown in with Mrs. Chen and her assistants to maintain the dress and to provide red silk lingerie, a red bikini and a clinging red Hazmat suit, which I'd be wearing in the scene where Jate and I were exposed to high-grade antimatter.

I had been granted my own trailer parked outside the warehouse. As I waited, I felt even more at odds than usual. The trailer was brand-new and twice the size of the ramshackle home where I'd grown up. This trailer was bright and outfitted with countless TVs, a spacious bedroom and a full kitchen with a dishwasher and a yogurt maker. There was thick, clear vinyl protecting the upholstery, a pleasingly chemical new-trailer smell and a full-sized fridge stocked only with bottled water, carrot sticks and little sealed cups of Jell-O, because as a production assistant had whispered to me, "the camera adds ten pounds."

On that first morning, at 6:00 A.M., I sat before the vanity table and the large mirror outlined with lightbulbs, which had been set up in my trailer's living room area. Mrs. Chen had already helped me into my dress and departed so for a moment I was alone, watching Becky in the mirror. Becky's hair and face were, of course, familiar and ordinary. Like everyone else on the set I was waiting for Rebecca to appear.

I was about to star in a movie and my life had already surpassed every dream I'd ever had, but something was missing. Could it be that becoming so beautiful and meeting celebrities and seeing the world from the tinted window of a limousine still wasn't enough? Was that why my mom had run away? Tom Kelly wanted me to fall in love and get married but those goals felt impossibly distant. I was caught, hovering midway between Becky and Rebecca, between whoever I used to be and whoever was about to go before the cameras, and add another layer to the deceit.

An assistant with a walkie-talkie appeared and escorted me to the set, reporting along the way, "Randle on the move . . . Randle in sixty seconds . . . Randle approaching . . ."

The set was a satisfyingly stupendous casino in the sky. There were roulette wheels, blackjack tables and, standing or seated in clusters, at least seventy-five extras dressed as oily, jaded, tuxedo-clad high rollers and their bored, bejeweled trophy wives.

I was brought to the elevated VIP balcony of the casino, guarded by hydrant-necked goons with black mock turtlenecks, ski-goggle sunglasses and greasy ponytails.

I was seated beside my on-screen mobster boyfriend, a man-mountain of tapioca-colored fat squeezed into a bulging black suit and an open-collared black satin shirt, with a neckload of gold chains. He looked like what would happen if you went into a pancake house and ordered a triple stack of jowls. I recognized this actor from the movies where he'd played every nationality of dictator and drug kingpin and once, to win his Oscar, a crusty French villager who against his better judgment had hidden an adorable Jewish child from the Gestapo.

"Hello, so good to meet you," said the actor, in his real-life English accent. "I'm Colin Swetland-Jane and I'm going to treat you horribly, because I'm the most dreadful Soviet mobster." Then he grinned happily, which made me love him.

I only had one line in the scene. The camera would spot me as Colin was snarling into his cell phone. He would warn me to "Stay!" and lumber off. As I sat, moody and restless, I was supposed to ignore all of Paree as Jate sauntered over. He would ask, "Is this seat taken?" And I would reply, "Can you afford it?"

Billy Seth was crouching many yards away deep within a fortress of video monitors and sound equipment, with a set of bulbous headphones clamped around his skull as if he were back in his childhood New Hampshire basement playing a maximum-mayhem video game.

"Lights!" cried the assistant director and the soundstage was flooded with artificial moonbeams and the dapple from twenty chandeliers.

"Quiet!" yelled another assistant as the crew's jabbering voices, planning the menus for their lunch breaks, ceased, and everyone began watching the scene unfurl.

"Rolling!" shouted a final assistant and from inside his humming hideout of moviemaking wizardry Billy Seth said, "Action!"

"Screw ju, American schvine!" Colin sneered into his phone, with a guttural Russian accent. "I vill tek jour eyes, and de eyes of jour cheeldrens!" He glared at me as if he could barely remember where he'd bought me, barked "Stay!" and, breathing heavily, heaved himself to his surprisingly tiny, alligator-loafered feet. He nodded to his goons and angled himself toward his hair and makeup people, waiting just off camera and eager to begin touch-ups. Then Jate came toward me, rugged and suave, with one hand tucked into the pocket of his white dinner jacket, as if he might remove a diamond bracelet as a gift, or a revolver. He caught sight of me, cocked his head an eighth of an inch and asked, "Is this seat taken?" After scrambling for what felt like three lifetimes to remember my line I blurted out, "I don't know!"

"Cut!" yelped an assistant and Jate assured Billy Seth and the hundreds of other crew members that this was my first time on a movie set and that I was a tiny bit nervous and that I was going to be great. Then he added, "I mean, if only she didn't look like a baboon," and everyone laughed. There was a second call for quiet, a second "Rolling!" a second "Action!" and a second "Is this seat taken?" to which I answered, in a trembling whisper, "I can't afford it!"

"Cut!"

There were many, many more takes, as I said, among other things, "It's the mobster guy's seat!" "Wait, what was the question?" and "Hi, I'm a call girl!" I was shaking and shivering and about to crack when Jate asked for a time-out and guided me swiftly into my trailer.

"Are you okay? What's wrong?" asked Jate once we were inside.

"I don't know!"

"You're gonna be terrific. And you look, okay, I'm just gonna say it, you look even better than me."

Jate wanted to lighten things and I almost smiled but I didn't know what to tell him. Something in me, in Rebecca, had stalled and I was lost. Was it the pressure of living too many lies, of Becky trying to be Rebecca who was aiming to become Elyssa? Were my triple personalities short-circuiting?

"What can I do to help you?" asked Jate.

There was a knock on the door and Tom Kelly stepped inside, making it known, with a glance, that as far as he was concerned, even the fanciest trailer was still just a trailer.

"Tom Kelly," he said. Tom and Jate had never met but they instantly sized each other up as rival brand names.

"Jate Mallow," said Jate.

"Could I have a minute with Rebecca?" asked Tom.

"Please?" I begged Jate. "Maybe he can help."

"I am so disappointed in you," said Tom after Jate had left. "What is your problem?"

"I just — I feel like the biggest phony who's ever lived! And when people see this movie, everyone's going to know that I'm not beautiful and I'm not sexy and I have no idea what I'm doing!"

"Which is precisely how just about every human being in the world feels, every morning," said Tom. "Including the movie stars. Especially the movie stars. They're the most frightened, insecure people of all because they know the world is watching. That's why they go crazy and take drugs and shave their heads. In fact, your having a breakdown and running off the set practically proves that you're a movie star."

"But how do they get past it? The real movie stars? How do they deal with the pressure and the stage fright and the expectations?"

"They use this," Tom explained as he reached inside his jacket and removed, from a pocket, a silvery tube of Tom Kelly lipstick.

"Lipstick?" I asked doubtfully.

"Not just lipstick. Confidence. Raw courage. Stardom in a tube."

Tom tilted the lipstick so that I could see the circular label on the bottom of this prized Hollywood secret. The color was called Icon by Tom Kelly.

Tom rotated the outer tube so the lipstick itself appeared. It was a clear cylinder, more like crystal than wax or whatever lipstick is ordinarily made of. As I watched, tiny veins of red began to appear in the lipstick, creeping and expanding and intertwining until the lipstick was the exact color of my dress. The lipstick was glowing and pulsing, as if it were either sexually aroused or radioactive; either way, it seemed eager and alive.

Tom took my chin in his hand.

"Hold still."

As Tom deftly applied the lipstick to my mouth, something occurred to me.

"Was my mom ever in a movie?"

"She was going to be. Right before she vanished. She was going to be the lead and she was out of her mind with excitement. And, of course, she was scared to death."

"Which movie?"

"It was called *Under the Tree*."

I was stunned, not just because my mom had almost appeared on-screen but because of the title.

"That was my mom's all-time favorite movie. We would watch it every Christmas and she'd cry her eyes out."

Under the Tree was a Christmas classic about a young girl from Iowa who arrives in New York on Christmas Eve and meets a handsome guy as they both admire the towering Christmas tree in Rockefeller Center. They spend the night together and arrange to meet again the next evening under the tree but the guy gets in a car accident and doesn't show up and it takes the rest of the movie for the couple to find each other, on the next Christmas Eve, under the tree.

"She would've been sensational," said Tom, but he wasn't taunting me. This was hard to believe, but he sounded wistful.

I knew what I had to do. The lipstick would help but if I really wanted confidence, my performance couldn't be just about me. I had to become a star, because my mom had never gotten the chance.

"Lights!"

"Quiet!"

"Rolling!"

"Action!"

"Is this seat taken?"

I took a strategic pause, allowing everyone on the set to wonder if I was going to blow it again, if I was beyond hopeless.

I crossed my legs at the knee, rustling the graceful layers of red chiffon and revealing a swath of sleek long leg and a fetishist's dream of a foot in my red high-heeled shoe. I licked my lips, just lightly, tasting my Icon by Tom Kelly. As I was about to speak, I heard my mom's ringtone coming from a deluxe red phone that the props person had set on the table in front of me beside my red satin evening bag. As the ringtone continued, I instantly knew that the sexiest thing I could do would be to ignore Renn Hightower completely, and take the call. As I lifted the phone to my ear I glanced at Jate disdainfully, because he was interrupting my evening. "Can you afford it?" I asked.

"Oh my God, cut! Cut! Shit! CUT!" yelled Billy Seth, and for the first time in his career he left his video village and dropped his headset onto the floor, the wires trailing. He was staring at me in helpless, distracted bewilderment and there's no polite way to put this: There was a stain, from seconds earlier, spreading across the front of his pale blue jeans. Thanks to Rebecca, Billy Seth had finally hit puberty.

As Jate beamed, I asked, "Billy Seth, would you like me to do it again?"

"Yes! No! I don't know!" Billy Seth wailed and, clutching his crotch, he ran off, into the darkest recesses of the soundstage.

"That was perfect," Jate whispered to me.

"Thanks," I said, just to Jate. "Still gay?"

12.

The rest of the filming went smoothly as the cast and crew were shipped from Paris to Berlin and then to Cairo. And more than ever I was learning just what it meant to travel first class or, as I was starting to think of it, Triple Premium Platinum Elite Everything. And I kept reminding myself, Becky, take notes.

I became aware of urgent debates held just out of Jate's and my earshot, which would clear hallways and lobbies and screening rooms for our use. I never needed tickets or keys or cash as such things were handled by skilled personal assistants walking briskly a few feet ahead of me and murmuring into their headpieces. I'd once seen a study online where an anthropologist had charted how attractive people get better jobs, bigger and more frequent raises, faster and more attentive service in restaurants and, in general, have an easier time of things than their less attractive counterparts because, as Tom Kelly loved pointing out, life isn't fair. But as Rebecca I could get apprehensive about taking advantage of, well, my advantages. Yet when Jate and I were automatically ushered past long lines and behind the velvet ropes of the most exclusive clubs and hangouts, I noticed that the otherwise bristling and impatient crowds didn't complain, because the presence of Jate and Rebecca, or Jatecca, as we were sometimes known, assured them that, even if they were never ultimately allowed inside, they were wasting their hours and their flashiest outfits

on exactly the right quest. Some waiters would yawn conspicu-
ously and pretend they didn't know who we were but I'd always
catch them in a corner, texting all their friends about who they'd
just ignored.

Jate and I were regarded as a couple, and he became, in a way,
the fantasy boyfriend that my childhood self had pined for.
He was wry and generous and always available for gossip; at
times he would literally take my hand and steer me through the
tricky stuff. Jate knew all about navigating interviews with communist journalists ("Just compliment the interviewer's terrible
hairstyle — they get confused."), appearances on non-English-
speaking Japanese talk shows ("Learn three words of Japanese
and keep repeating them — they'll appreciate the effort, and they'll
think your accent is hilarious."), and our audience with the Pope
("Just cover your hair, smile and check out his little red shoes.").

During these unnatural days of filming shoot-outs atop the
Sphinx's forehead and sharing a lavish multicourse breakfast
with one of the film's backers, a Saudi billionaire and his eight
burka-shrouded wives, I wore either my red dress or an additional and extensive wardrobe that Tom Kelly had provided.
Many of these clothes weren't red but each piece held some hint
or layer of the first dress's signature shade. The collar of a silk
blouse was trimmed in a millimeter of red silk ribbon and a
pair of navy blue linen pants concealed red pockets. All of these
clothes fit with the identical perfection of the original dress
and soon Tom and I were being ranked alongside other legendary masters and muses such as Audrey Hepburn and Givenchy,
and Catherine Deneuve and Yves St. Laurent. I'd never heard of
most of the stars and designers people were talking about so I'd
look them up online and gasp. The designers all shared Tom's air
of I'm-the-best-and-I-know-it disdain and the women were
always impeccably lovely. It was as if each couturier had taken a

beautiful woman and made her distinctive, someone whom other women, and drag queens, could imitate. And when I saw photos of myself dressed by Tom I could understand the comparisons. There I was, chatting with a Parisian shopkeeper or feeding a baby elephant and laughing at a Berlin zoo. My clothes could've been designed at any time during the past fifty years and no matter what I was doing or wearing, I looked like an ad for Tom Kelly.

Tom explained to me that, "Beautiful people exist to be photographed. You're like a rare natural resource and pictures of you allow the world access, for fantasizing. You're a glamour machine."

"But that sounds creepy," I'd protested, "and exhausting."

"Which is why the truly great beauties are like athletes or dancers or mathematicians. At their peaks, they're glorious to behold, but their gifts can't be sustained."

"So what happens to them? To all of those people?"

"They have two choices: They can either develop an exit strategy, or they can die young and become legendary. Both choices work."

When Tom said this, I felt a chill, especially because shooting Jate's movie had taken over two months and I still hadn't fallen in love and gotten married.

But here was the most shocking development of all: I was actually getting used to being Rebecca Randle. The line between Becky and Rebecca had begun to dissolve. Inhabiting Rebecca, and accepting her beauty and the opportunities and adulation, was like learning a foreign language; at some point even the most die-hard American patriot can begin to think and even dream in French or Farsi or Portuguese. When someone gaped at me or tried to speak and stuttered or silently handed me a rose or a room key, or the deed to their family's ancestral manor house, I'd almost stopped wondering why and I'd begun to think, of course.

The filming ended in London, with a Lamborghini, hover-craft and Jet Ski chase along the Thames. I had to sit or stand behind Jate in most of these vehicles looking impassive and mildly annoyed as the wind rippled my hair, and sometimes I fired an automatic weapon to prove that, even in a Tom Kelly dress, Elyssa was a feminist. The shooting days could last till four in the morning and I knew that I was starting to think like a movie star when I caught myself telling Jate, "This is really hard work."

Jate patted my face and agreed, "It's tragic. People just don't understand."

While we were in town, Jate and I were invited to visit a local children's hospital to help raise funds for a badly needed expansion of the burn unit. At the last minute Jate was called away for a day of reshoots so I went to the hospital alone. I was met by body-guards and two members of Parliament and was introduced to Dr. Imogen Barry, a sturdy older woman whose silver hair was tugged into a Swedish prison matron's bun and who'd founded the burn unit twenty-three years earlier.

"You have extraordinary skin," said Dr. Barry, whose eyes were quickly only a few inches from my face. Dr. Barry was like Seeley Burckhardt, because both women's professions involved staring at people up close. "It's completely poreless, it almost seems . . . not possible. This is the sort of skin we've been trying to grow under laboratory conditions, combining donor DNA and artificial polymers, for use in grafts. What are your parents?"

"Just regular people."

"You're like some sort of next-stage android."

I wasn't sure if I should be offended and then Dr. Barry couldn't resist and she ran a fingertip across my cheek. "May I?" she murmured, although her hand was already rubbing my skin, as if testing its resilience and harvesting a microscopic sample.

"That's enough," I said as I had a pang of sympathy for the celebrity mannequins in wax museums, those life-sized replicas that are always being groped and kissed and occasionally beheaded by aggressively devoted fans. Rocher had once asked if the Jate Mallow mannequin was anatomically complete, for dating purposes. "I mean, it would be almost as good as the real thing," she'd theorized. "Or maybe even better because it couldn't leave."

"So sorry," said Dr. Barry, reluctantly withdrawing her hand as I wondered if there was any way she could detect what had happened to me.

"As you know," said Dr. Barry, "Mr. Mallow has been unable to join us. So to compensate, we've been lucky enough to recruit someone of perhaps a more useful renown."

"Who?" I asked as I heard a babble of voices and then the all-out blast of a paparazzi assault from nearby. The front doors of the hospital were flung open and at least ten English police officers from Scotland Yard marched rapidly toward us, all of them managing that elite surveillance trick of seeming to stare straight ahead while sweeping the room for terrorists or overzealous admirers.

"Miss Randle," said Dr. Barry, "I would like to present His Royal Highness, Prince Gregory of Wales."

The twin flanks of officers parted, like Vegas showgirls or a team of synchronized swimmers, revealing their hidden treasure, their precious cargo, their prize.

Prince Gregory was a teeteringly tall, amiably shambling, pink-cheeked twenty-five-year-old wearing a moss green tweed three-piece suit that was lovingly cut yet still at odds with the prince's lanky frame. He wore the suit as if he were a top-ranked contortionist and could wriggle out of it at any second or as if his body were racing a few yards ahead of his wardrobe. The prince's thatch of reddish gold hair was recently chopped and barely tamed, like glinting crabgrass. There was something breathless and awry about the prince, as if he'd just struggled into his grown-up clothing after a spontaneous rugby match or a quick skinny-dip in some royal pond or pool. He was all elbows and knees and craning neck, with each sector of his anatomy insisting on a separate destination.

"Good morning," he blurted out. "Hello, so sorry to be late, Prince Gregory, and please don't anyone bow or faint or fall to their knees, oh, all right, you may all grovel just a bit, if it will make you happy."

I laughed, because I'd been about to opt for a deep curtsy, a respectful nod and maybe a military salute, all at the same time. Instead I just stood there, giggling and wondering if because we were both celebrities, I should hug the prince and complete an air-kiss. Jate had once told me that, "When you meet another famous person, you have to do an instant star-check. If the person is less famous than you, you can shake their hand and be very warm, to show that you're such a good person, but never air-kiss a less famous person, because that's what they want, they hope that your more-famousness will rub off on them. If you meet someone who's exactly as famous as you, a hug and a kiss are just right, because that way you can both pretend that you're normal people, who've happened to run into each other at the local Famous People's coffee bar, or the Kennedy Center Honors. But if you meet someone more famous than you, and that almost never happens, you have to behave like a fan. You have to face the truth and say, 'Hi, you're you and I'm just me, so you win.' And so they get to make the rules."

Prince Gregory stuck out his hand vigorously, proving that just because he was a young prince, he didn't have delicate, over-bred, forbidden hands, and he said, "Good God, you really are that beautiful, especially here in England, where everyone is simply hideous. You're completely out of place. You have no business here, children will point at you and start to sob, asking, 'Mummy, I thought you told me that attractive people were extinct. By decree.' You're just appalling."

Of course because I'd stood behind the Super Shop-A-Lot register for hours at a time, I'd memorized Prince Gregory's features from the covers of all the celebrity weeklies. He was especially known for his mother, Princess Alicia, who'd died horribly in a plane crash on her return from a humanitarian visit to an earthquake site in Africa. In the last known photograph of her, Princess Alicia had been wearing a fitted safari jacket and kneeling beside a bereft Kenyan woman who was cradling a dead infant. The princess had her hand on the woman's shoulder and was absorbed in their conversation, through a nearby translator. The princess was young and tall and unbearably beautiful but despite all that, you didn't want to smack her.

Princess Alicia had used her looks and her title to both dazzle and improve the world and she'd concentrated on riskier, less immediately popular causes. She'd had herself photographed cuddling babies with infectious diseases and she'd blackmailed unscrupulous corporations into providing flour, rice and basic sanitation for sprawling, crime-ridden refugee camps. She'd auctioned off her most memorable gowns to establish schools for little girls in fundamentalist strongholds and she'd attended the birthday blowouts of rock stars, provided that the rock stars appear at concerts benefiting rape victims from countries bordering on more civilized regions, where the rock stars had enjoyed five-star safaris and burbled on their blogs about receiving spiritual wisdom from cheetahs.

Princess Alicia had died the year I was born and my mother had idolized her. She'd kept scrapbooks of the princess's life and accomplishments and she'd page through them, chatting about

Alicia as if they'd been buddies. "Oh look," she'd say, "this was when Al went to Moscow, I love her in purple. And see how she's smiling at that prime minister, you can tell that she hates him."

While I'd known what Prince Gregory looked like, this was still the first time I'd ever met royalty in person. When I was little, I'd never been obsessed with princesses like Cinderella and Snow White and the rest of the Disney chicklets, with their bulging hair and their tinkling voices. I'd thought they were all simpering and drippy, running around with teeny noses and warbling about how they couldn't live without their dopey, strong-jawed boyfriends who were always off in the forest. Rocher, on the other hand, had dressed up in her highly flammable budget Halloween princess costume as often as she could and she'd been known to sleep in it. This outfit had a shiny polyester ice blue satin bodice crisscrossed with thick, drooping black bands, grimy white puff sleeves and a limp, dead-salmon-colored satin skirt with an increasingly ragged hem. Rocher had worn this sad dresslike thing over a long-sleeved T-shirt and thick pink tights with blackened knees, along with a golden plastic crown that she'd nabbed by telling the counter girl at Burger King that it was her birthday. The crown's golden finish had soon chipped and its large plastic ruby had only lasted a week until Rocher's dog had eaten it and gotten diarrhea.

Rocher had worn her princess getup on every possible holiday, including Martin Luther King Jr. Day and the Fourth of July, because, as she would explain, "It's a special day, so there has to be a princess, to proclaim things." If Rocher hadn't wanted to finish her beets, she'd announced, "Beets are not princess food. Beets are for common folk." And when her cousin Cortney-Brianna wore an identical, only brand-new princess costume, Rocher had decreed, "Cortney-Brianna is not a princess. She's a turd." From Rocher's example all I'd learned was that royal people are flighty and bossy and allowed to make everything up as they go along.

"His Royal Highness has been with us before," said Dr. Barry. "But, Miss Randle, have you ever visited a burn unit?"

"No, I don't think so."

"Oh, I believe you'd remember. We'll begin gradually, with some of our less extreme patients and then progress. If you're having any difficulties, please let me know."

When I said, "I'll be fine," I noticed that Dr. Barry and the prince exchanged a glance but I was determined to prove myself brave and unflappable. I was becoming protective of Rebecca; just because she was beautiful, I didn't want her to be underestimated.

We were all issued stiff white nylon smocks, headgear fitted with elastic like a shower cap and fabric face masks because, according to Dr. Barry, "All of this isn't for our sake, but to protect the children. We can easily endanger them, by bringing in outside bacteria. Their wounds make them extremely vulnerable to infection."

Dr. Barry led our group through a well-sealed, thick metal door and into the unit itself, which was a large, almost circular space with beds set at intervals around a central nursing station. Each bed was encased in walls of thick, clear, shimmering plastic, hanging from tracks on the ceiling.

"This is Devlin," said Dr. Barry, parting a set of plastic curtains and bringing the prince and me to the bedside of a little boy whose arms and legs were wrapped in layers of gauze. "Devlin is seven, and he's been with us for almost a month. Devlin, I've brought some new friends to see you. This is Prince Gregory and Rebecca Randle, who, I'm told, is a kind of actress."

"Hello," said Devlin, smiling. "I'm sorry, but I can't shake your hands." Devlin moved his limbs a fraction, to prove they weren't only bandaged but immobilized.

"That's perfectly all right," said Prince Gregory, tugging a small metal chair up to the bed so he could speak to Devlin face-to-face. "Does all this drive you mad, when you get an itch?"

"It's awful," Devlin admitted. "Sometimes I have to wait for a nurse and then she scratches the wrong side of my nose or the itch is underneath my bandages, where no one can reach and I just want to tear them off."

"Which, as Devlin and I have discussed, would not be a good idea," said Dr. Barry. "Devlin is extremely brave and we're very proud of him. When his home caught on fire, he saved his younger sister."

"Your parents must be so proud of you," I said, following Dr. Barry's lead.

"My parents died in the fire," said Devlin. He didn't say this as an accusation or with a trace of self-pity, but as information, as if he were telling me, "I have a new bicycle."

"I'm so sorry," I said, and I was about to add, "My mom died too," but I didn't want the conversation to become a contest. I had no idea what to say next, what possible comfort to offer, so I just asked, "Do you need any scratching?"

"My left ear," said Devlin and as I leaned across his body, Dr. Barry began to object and then Devlin screamed, as I'd accidentally brushed against the bandages on his arm.

"Take care," Dr. Barry admonished me as I jerked my hand away from Devlin's ear.

"I'm sorry," said Devlin, now taking short, deep breaths, to quiet the pain. "I shouldn't have screamed."

"It's quite all right," said Prince Gregory. "In fact, that's the great advantage of being in hospital, and being all banged up. You're allowed to scream whenever you like."

Devlin smiled at the notion of such royal permission and while I was feeling clumsy and stupid for needlessly increasing Devlin's torment, I was grateful for everything the prince had said. Unlike me, he hadn't forgotten what it was like to be seven, and he knew that little boys are big on loud noises.

"And now let's have a visit with Angus," said Dr. Barry, holding open the plastic panels that led to the next bed. "Angus is ten," she continued, "and he's been with us for almost a year."

At first Angus resembled a pastry, a pillowy white cream puff nestled against his bedding. His head, except for his small pink mouth, was completely swathed in bandages, along with his chest and the stumps of his arms, which ended at the elbows. Both of his legs were also gone, from just above the knees. I struggled not to gasp. I didn't know if Angus had been permanently blinded or how aware he was of his ravaged body. I'd also heard about phantom pain, where people can experience agony in parts of their bodies that aren't there anymore. As I tried to figure out where to look I knew that both Dr. Barry and Prince Gregory had begun chatting with Angus, but I hadn't registered anything they'd been saying.

"Miss Randle?" Dr. Barry repeated.

"Yes?" I said, trying to sound cheerful, as if I'd just rushed in from a nearby ward.

"This is Angus, and he has a question for you."

"Of course. Hi, Angus."

"Hello, I can't see."

"Because of all the bandages."

"So when people come by, I always ask them, what do you look like?"

I froze, because I had no idea what to say. Should I describe what Rebecca looked like, or Becky, or would it be enough to say, "I have brown hair"? Everything about me was a lie and while I'd grown comfortable with fooling everyone else, misrepresenting myself to Angus would be unforgivable.

"Miss Randle is very pretty," supplied Prince Gregory. "She has dark hair and green eyes and there's a toad squatting right on her head, pounding on her skull and searching for mosquitoes."

This made Angus laugh, or it made his isolated pink mouth laugh, and he insisted, "There is not! There isn't a toad! Miss Randle, is there a toad on your head?"

"No, there isn't," I said, longing to sound as even-keeled and resourceful as Prince Gregory. "Prince Gregory is lying. It's a pig."

"You have a pig on your head?" asked Angus, both skeptical and hopeful.

"Yes," I said. "It's small, it's more of a piglet, but it goes with me everywhere. Because it likes the taste of my shampoo."

"Is that true, Dr. Barry?" asked Angus "Is there a pig?"

"I'm only a doctor," she replied. "So I'm not qualified to say. But we should remember that Miss Randle is an American."

As Dr. Barry examined the dressing on what was left of one of Angus's arms, I aimed to breathe normally. I was taking my cues from Dr. Barry and Prince Gregory, who were using jokes to put everyone at ease. I felt very young and very scared and very self-ish, because I wished that I were somewhere else, in the hospital cafeteria or on the movie set with Jate, any place without such well-lit, overwhelming tragedy.

"Ah, and here we have Selina," said Dr. Barry, taking the prince and me toward the most substantial enclosure in the unit, which shielded what appeared to be a small inflatable kiddie wading pool being monitored by a skyline of boxy, chest-high cabinets, fitted with rows of blinking lights and round gauges with arrows, all draped in miles of bunched wires and plastic tubing. Even Dr. Barry paused as a nurse unzipped a clear plastic panel; these panels were thicker and included a plastic ceiling as well.

Selina was a twelve-year-old girl who, Dr. Barry told me later, had been tied with clothesline and duct tape and then doused with gasoline and set on fire by a drunken, psychotic uncle because Selina's father hadn't been willing to lend the uncle money for beer and whiskey. The police and ambulance hadn't arrived for almost an hour and Selina hadn't been expected to live. She'd been maintained in a medically induced coma for over a month and fed intravenously and she'd only recently been allowed to regain consciousness.

Selina didn't seem human. Her body had been burned over 90 percent of its surface, and her raw, weeping flesh, or whatever was now exposed underneath where her flesh had once been, was still too tender for any attempt at skin grafts. She was being kept heavily sedated and every inch of her was coated with a gluey antibiotic gel that had to be removed and replaced, as gently as possible, with a trickle of water every twelve hours. What was left of Selina's body lay suspended on a hammock of webbed plastic netting stretched between metal posts, so that air could circulate and begin to promote the most minute, earliest stages of healing.

My eyes refused to focus, darting from a few inches of charred, blistered skin to a set of tubes somehow anchored to a pus-bloated forearm. Without meaning to, I saw what had become of Selina's face. There was a single eye staring from a bare socket and there was a clear breathing tube located near what had once been Selina's nose, above a twisted mouth of bloated, rubbery, scarred lips. These few remaining, distorted features were floating in a mass of wet pink and purple membranes, as if tossed into a bubbling stew.

Without thinking, I ran, away from the draped cube and out of the ward, through many sets of doors and into a restroom, where I vomited into a sink. My thoughts flew, from what had happened to Selina's face, to any notion of her physical pain, to her prospects. What life, what future, could she hope for? Why hadn't the hospital staff let her die? Wouldn't that have been kinder, and the only real way to save her? After trembling, sweating and retching until my stomach was empty, I cupped my hands beneath the cold water faucet to rinse my mouth. I was alone, so when I stood, the mirror revealed Becky, her straggly brown hair damp and smeared across her splotchy cheeks, her eyes blank and her mouth open, trying to grasp — what? Selina's life? My own? How everything, all of my happiness and excitement and adventure had become, not a joke, not a useless irony, but ugliness itself? The sort that has nothing to do with what you look like?

I wiped my mouth with a paper towel and gave a halfhearted tug to what had once been my red silk jacket and skirt and I stepped out into the hall, searching vaguely for a nearby exit, fresh air and a return flight to Missouri. Instead, Prince Gregory was standing nearby. He grabbed my elbow and marched me to a deserted waiting area, where he sat beside me on a pale green vinyl bench. He gave me a second to pull myself together, as he watched me with a certain kindness but far more impatience.

"We are exactly the same," he began. "We are the luckiest idiots. Through no fault of our own, we were both born with certain extreme and unjust natural advantages: I am a prince, and you are the most beautiful woman in the world."

"Who cares? It's disgusting. It doesn't matter. It doesn't help anyone."

"Look at me," the prince continued sharply. "And listen carefully, because I'm one of the very few people who can actually tell you this. No, we're not doctors or nurses or researchers, we don't possess any sort of practical or helpful skills. We can't heal Selina, or lessen her agony, or make certain that her repellent uncle is punished. We couldn't be more ridiculous or more inept, or more of an insult, really. Except for one absolutely absurd and entirely essential fact: We rule the world."

"What?"

"When I was turning six, there was a small party in the family quarters at Buckingham and I was told to invite a few of my little friends from school. And one of my gifts was a small metal fire truck. And David, my first cousin, he wanted that fire truck so very badly, and we fought over it, and I blackened his eye. And then I grabbed the truck and I told David, 'This is mine, because I'm the prince and one day I shall be king. And you are only a duke. A duke. I pity you.' And that was when my mother all but dislocated my arm and dragged me off and hurled me into a chair and she said, 'You are a dreadful little boy. You don't deserve to be a prince, let alone a king.' And I insisted, 'Yes I do!' and I sobbed. And then, for the first and only time, she struck me, quite hard, right across my smug little face."

"She did? Princess Alicia hit you?" I didn't say this because I was shocked at a mother smacking a child who deserved it, but because it was Princess Alicia, the beacon of beauty and goodness everlasting.

"And I was so surprised at how really angry she was that I stopped crying, and she said, 'Gregory, you are a very lucky little boy. People look to you and to me and to your father. And so we must set an example. For the rest of your life, you must always be kinder and more generous and more loving than anyone else. And do you know why?' And I asked, 'Why, Mummy?'"

"You called her Mummy?" I was following his lesson but I was also a fan and I'd always wondered if royal children had to call their parents "Your Highness."

"Yes, I called her Mummy. And when I asked her why I had to be so much better than all of the other children, in the entire world, which really didn't seem fair at all, she said, 'Because that is what a prince does.'"

I thought of that photo, my own mother's favorite, of Princess Alicia kneeling beside the mother of the dead African child. That grieving mother would have been more than justified in telling the princess, "please go away" or even "fuck off." But maybe that woman had sensed through her despair that the princess was there to help, or at least to listen.

"Your mother was wonderful," I said.

"And she packed quite a wallop. I recall thinking, I'm going to ring up all the newspapers and tell them that Mummy has struck me. And then I went further, and I decided that once I got to be king I would stick her in a tower somewhere until she apologized to me on national television. But I was like everyone else — I adored her. And, of course, most people loved her because she was a royal and because she was so pretty. The combination was so unlikely. Although you're far prettier. My mother would've pummeled you, pulled your hair, tossed you down the stairs and said, 'Rebecca, I have two choices. I can hate you, because you're so attractive, and I can have you deported, or you can come with me to Haiti.'"

"What was it like for you? When she died?"

"Hideous, beyond belief. For weeks, I refused to believe that she was gone and I kept telling my father that her plane had gotten lost and that it would be landing shortly. Everyone tried to keep me away from the telly and the papers, but there were windows and I could see the mobs and the hand-lettered placards and the mountains of flowers, and at night there'd be thousands of candles. I hated those people, all of them, because they kept insisting my mother was dead. And finally, because he thought it was important, my father took me and my younger brother and he brought us outside. We weren't surrounded by guards, it was just the three of us. And we walked, directly into the crowds of people. The thousands of people. At first no one was quite sure if we were, you know, who we were. And then all of those people, they grew very quiet. And my dad began introducing himself, and us, one at a time, to this person, and the next person, and the person after that."

"My mother told me about it. She said that no one could believe that your father was doing that."

"But everyone was so . . . I'm not sure what the word might be, because people weren't just kind, or understanding. They were with us. And it wasn't that we were better than anyone else. We were a father and his children, and we'd lost someone. And a little girl came up to me and she offered me a stick of gum. Not the entire pack, mind you, she made that clear. But she said, 'Take this,' and then she said, 'Sorry about your mum.' And I can't say I felt any better but I did feel, let's call it, my mother's presence. Because that stick of gum, and the faces, and the good intentions of all those people, that's what my mother had believed in. And she'd wanted me to be a decent person, just like that little girl."

He stood up.

"So to answer your question, yes, when my mother died, everything went to shit, and I suffered. But it was nothing compared to what has happened to Selina." He held out his hand.

"But I look awful."

"You look like a monkey's rectum."

"A what?"

"You heard me."

I stood and I shook my head, returning every bountiful strand of chestnut hair to its sublimely impossible perfection.

"That's extraordinary," said the prince, regarding my hair. "How that happens."

"And you said I didn't have any skills."

I stood beside Selina, leaning slightly forward so she could see me. She spoke in a hoarse, almost inaudible bleat, as the fire and smoke had severely damaged her lungs and larynx. "You're . . . pretty," she told me.

"I'm not as pretty as Prince Gregory," I said.

"No you're not," the prince, standing beside me, agreed.

"I'm . . . not pretty," Selina wheezed, and the moment was beyond heartbreaking. Selina was using her only superiority, as the victim of such a terrible act. She was challenging us, daring us, to disagree with her, to try to make ourselves feel better at her expense, to lie.

"You're going to be pretty," I said, "because you have the best doctor in London."

"Just London?" murmured Dr. Barry, a bit put out, since she had been, more than once, short-listed for the Nobel Prize in Medicine.

"The best doctor in the world," I said, and I forced myself to look directly at Selina, at my opposite, at someone who'd been so cheated of everything, at someone who, far more than me or anyone else, deserved Tom Kelly's magic. And as I looked at her single, darting eye, I knew only one thing. I knew what I was supposed to do with my life, with the fairy-tale wish I'd been so unexpectedly granted, by the unlikeliest of wizards.

"Rebecca?" said Selina, although continued speech was exhausting her.

"Yes?"

"Can I ask you something?"

"Of course. Anything you want."

"Is . . . is . . ."

I leaned closer, because Selina's voice was now barely an urgent whisper. "Is what?"

"Is . . . is . . . Jate Mallow gay?"

Prince Gregory and Dr. Barry were both watching me, every bit as eager for my answer as Selina. Gossip, I decided, trumps everything, including royal grace, immortal beauty, advanced medicine and unbearable physical pain.

"Excuse me?" I told the prince and Dr. Barry. "But could you please wait outside? This is between me and Selina."

Later that day, back in my hotel suite, I called Rocher, waking her up, because it was 6:00 A.M. in East Trawley, but I knew she wouldn't mind. She'd instructed me, "You're allowed to call me any time, anywhere, if it's about a famous person."

"Roche," I said, "I have to tell you something, because nobody else knows it yet, because I only just figured it out. I know why my mother left me that phone number and why Tom Kelly made me so beautiful and why God put me on this earth."

"What? Why? And please don't tell me it's some spiritual bullshit, that you're like the Golden Child or like right after the aliens made up Scientology they invented you."

"No, it's nothing like that, not really. It's better. It's perfect."

I was thinking about a TV documentary I'd watched with my mom about Princess Alicia. There'd been clips of the princess as a child at Buckingham Palace, in a little blue tailored coat, with a gleam in her eye. Then had come footage of her hell-raising teenage period, when she'd failed to graduate from three different schools, danced drunkenly at a St. Moritz disco with shady, polo-playing Argentinians and been photographed topless, via a paparazzi's zoom lens, at the Barbados retreat of a notorious

Dutch financier. "She was a kid," my mom had said. "People should have left her alone, to grow up."

But then Alicia had traveled to the Sudan, where she'd been introduced to girls her own age who'd suffered from genital mutilation and lives of extreme poverty. For the first time Alicia had been ashamed of her privileged background and she'd vowed to change her life. "At first she thought she should just quit being a princess, and go to medical school or get a job at the UN," my mom had told me. "But then she decided that as a royal, she'd have all sorts of access and she'd still get to go to parties."

The documentary had included a famous clip of Alicia, a few years later, waltzing with the president of the United States in the ballroom at the White House. Alicia was wearing a clinging blue gown, with a tiara secured to her blond upsweep. "She'd gone full princess," my mom had commented. In the clip you could see the president's hand inching toward Alicia's backside and the world had watched as Alicia allowed a few strategic seconds of contact before repositioning the president's grip. Later that week the president had appeared before Congress, speaking in support of Alicia's international effort to prevent childhood blindness in developing nations.

"Alicia knew what she was doing," my mom had told me. "She knew that because of her past and because she was so gorgeous, people would underestimate her. But she used all of that to her advantage and she surprised everyone." Because I'd been only eleven at the time, my focus had wandered and I'd asked my mom to change the channel so we could catch a rerun of *Jackie + Jate*. My mom had refused, and she'd said to me, in a surprisingly tough tone of voice, "Not yet. This is Alicia. Pay attention."

"So what's the deal with your life?" asked Rocher, on the phone. "What's the master plan? What are you gonna do?"

I looked across the hotel room at a mirror and there was Becky, nodding her encouragement. I picked up a magazine, with Rebecca's face filling the cover, and I held it up so that her face appeared in the mirror beside Becky's. Because to make things happen, to achieve what I was after, they'd have to work together.

"I'm going to help people. I'm going to change the world, as much as I can. I'm going to have the biggest life I can get."

"Wait — bigger than your life right now? I mean, come on, everything's been going pretty damn great."

"Yeah, but I can't just keep being the most beautiful everything. It's not enough. I have to use it, just the way my mom would've wanted. It explains everything."

"But how are you going to do all that? I mean, what would make people listen to you? How can you get there?"

I took a deep breath, because when I said what I was about to say out loud, the idea, and the dream, would start to seem real.

"I'm going to marry Prince Gregory."

13.

First there was silence and then an eerie gurgling, as if a goldfish were drowning, if that ever happens.

"Roche? Are you okay?"

There was pitiful whimpering, a puppy with its paw caught in the screen door.

"Roche?"

"You . . . you . . . you are going to marry Prince Gregory? You are going to be . . ."

Thundering dry heaves, from the largest mammal ever, some tyrannosaurus whatever getting dragged into a tar pit and summoning every beast in the jungle.

"A PRINCESS?"

I spoke over Rocher's jubilant screams.

"Rocher, I was at this children's hospital and I met Prince Gregory and he was incredible, he looks like his mom, and it just came to me, that being the most beautiful woman in the world was just the beginning. Because even doing what Tom Kelly said I had to do, if I wanted to keep being Rebecca, you know, finding some guy and falling in love and getting married, that can't be all my mother wanted. And sure, I guess I could try and do good stuff all by myself, but there wouldn't be any reason for people to pay attention and get on board. And I could run for president but I don't think people would vote for Rebecca."

"That's true. Because I don't think the president is supposed to be that hot."

"And so when I thought about Princess Alicia it all came together. I can try and do what she did only maybe I can take it even further. I can try and help everybody everywhere because if I marry Prince Gregory then I can be . . ."

We said it together:

"PRINCESS REBECCA!!!"

My phone went dead and a few seconds later it buzzed.

"Rocher?"

"I'm sorry, I was jumping up and down and screaming and my stepfather came in and told me to shut up so I had to throw a lamp at him."

"But, Roche, here's the problem: I only have nine months left and I don't know anything about royalty and how it all works and the whole princess deal. So I need, like, a princess authority. An expert. A princess person. So, Roche, and I know it's a huge thing to ask, but if I send you a ticket and money and everything, can you get over here and help me do this?"

"Okay. Okay. Let me think about this. Because at the Shop-A-Lot, Chad, remember, that new assistant manager with the one long eyebrow and the stud in his tongue, he asked me if I wanted to see his new nipple ring, before it healed completely, and he said that he was considering me for a position in poultry, which would mean I'd get to wear a hairnet, a bloodstained white coat and rubber gloves, which I could really rock. So I have to decide if I want to smell like chicken parts and E. coli or do I want to take an all-expenses-paid trip to London?"

I heard Rocher's stepfather come back into her room and he told her that he was watching wrestling and that she was going to pay to fix the lamp.

"Excuse me, just a second . . ."

Then I heard Rocher's stepfather start screaming in a really high-pitched voice because something heavy had hit him in the crotch, or in his words, "My dickshooter! You fucking bitch, you aimed right for my dickshooter!"

"I think I'm free," said Rocher.

Before I'd called Rocher, I'd already had a text from Lila telling me what time I was expected to meet Tom Kelly. I'd assumed that Tom already knew about my introduction to Prince Gregory and I wanted his blessing because I'd need his full arsenal of couture magic to burrow my way into the Royal Family.

Drake had been imported and he picked me up a few hours later outside my hotel. "So now you're a movie star," he said, grinning as he adjusted to steering from the opposite side of the front seat. "And I hear you've got other plans as well."

"So what does Tom think, about the prince? Does he approve?"

"Oh, sweetheart," said Drake, "I am not about to speak for Tom."

"Can I ask you something? You knew my mom, right?"

"Sure. Such a great girl. The best."

"Was she scared of Tom?"

Drake thought for a moment. He was about to answer but he stopped himself.

"Ask Tom."

Tom Kelly owned homes throughout the world and they were all kept in perfect order and fully staffed even though Tom hadn't visited any of these locations since he'd retired. His London place was a granite town house on a secluded, pristine block where the street curved and all the buildings were carved from the same severe stone and I could tell that only the very richest people lived there, the Taiwanese tech magnates and the Australian media barons and the occasional deposed dictator, the folks who might spend only five days per year in any of their multiple outposts.

The street was forbidding, without children, nannies, sightseers with guidebooks or any signs of life beyond the idling, bullet-proofed black limousines.

Lila let me in, saying, "We've been expecting you. It's the top floor." Then she added, under her breath, "I love the whole princess idea. Go for it."

Tom's town house wasn't furnished in his trademark surgically stylish mode but with hunter green flannel walls, gleaming mahogany woodwork and carefully edited, masculine antiques with the seating upholstered in a woolen tartan. It was like entering a gentlemen's club so exclusive that Tom was the only member.

There was an airless, coffin-sized elevator paneled in burgundy velvet with nail-head trim. Tom was waiting for me in his parlor, sitting in a carved mahogany armchair beside a black marble fireplace with an open fire, which was weird, because I knew that working fireplaces had been outlawed in London due to air pollution, but, of course, this was Tom Kelly. He was wearing a black T-shirt, a skinny black velvet blazer, dark stovepipe jeans and riding boots. On anyone else this would've come off as a costume but in Tom's house, on his terms, it worked. Today he was a semiretired rock star, living obscenely well off his royalties and reissues, endorsing a men's cologne sold in a deliberately tarnished silver flask, called Perverse by Tom Kelly, or maybe Tom Kelly's Cyanide Pour Homme.

"Rebecca," he said, standing to greet me. Tom being polite was scarier than Tom being arrogant.

"Hi?" I began, because even after my months of stardom and luxury, when I was near Tom, I became Becky, dragging my backpack across the floor.

Tom walked toward the fireplace, leaning against the mantel for a country squire effect. All he needed was a snifter of brandy, a riding crop and his accountant crouched at his feet.

"So you'd like your white dress."

I hadn't thought about it but Tom was right. We were talking about my next dress. My second dress of the three. My wedding dress.

"Yes?" I said, half asking and half hoping that I could muster an ounce of Rebecca's oomph.

"You'd like to marry Prince Gregory."

"I know I only met him yesterday but he's so terrific, I think you would really like him. . . ."

"I've met him," said Tom, cutting me off. "When he was a child. I knew his mother. I dressed her."

No matter how hard I tried, Tom was always so many steps ahead of me. Of course he'd known Princess Alicia. He knew everyone. I wanted details but I knew not to ask.

"And you want to become a princess."

"Yes. Because that way I'd be able to use everything you've given me and I know that it's what my mom would've wanted. I'd be taking Rebecca and positioning her to do the most possible good."

"Why do I feel like you're trying to sell me a used car?"

"No! It's just that I need to know if you think it's the right idea and if you'll help me."

"If you pursue Prince Gregory, if you aim that high, there can be consequences. Look what happened to his mother."

"She died in a plane crash. It was an accident."

"Which has never been entirely proven. What I'm saying is, when a beautiful person attempts to become a very powerful person, things can happen."

"Like what?"

"The people in charge of things, especially the men, they like to stay in charge. Would you like to know what happened to Drake?"

Tom was offering personal information. If he'd let me know about Drake he might someday fill me in about my mother.

"If you'd like to tell me."

"Drake was from California, upstate, somewhere near Big Sur. He was a good kid, a surfer, and one day he bummed a few rides and ended up in New York, at nineteen. And when I met him he was a bartender at a dive in the East Village. Where one day he fell in love, with exactly the wrong person."

"Who?"

"She was a southern girl, a real honeybunch, rich and pretty and bored out of her mind at junior college after, as she put it, 'Almost an entire whole semester!' And she'd headed north for a friend's bachelorette weekend and she was out slumming and when she came across Drake, she fell hard and so did he."

"So what happened?"

"So Miss Carole Ann Basnight Shelburne, she extends her stay for two weeks and on her last night in town, Drake proposes and she accepts. And I met her, she wasn't a bad person, she was just greeting-card romantic and chronically impulsive and not really spoiled, not a ninny, but a touch helpless. And Drake had no idea what he was getting into."

"Which was . . ."

"Carole Ann was a senator's daughter from South Carolina and the senator wasn't about to have his presumably untouched debutante sweet pea shacking up with a bartender and a Yankee at that. Not when the senator had his eye on the White House."

"And?"

"And so first the senator goes behind his daughter's back and he offers Drake a bundle, his own bar, to bow out. And Drake says no. The senator gets angry, he forbids Carole Ann to marry Drake. She says no, she's convinced that she and Drake will be deliriously content in a fifth-floor walk-up on St. Mark's Place and Second Avenue. And she might've been absolutely right. Who knows?"

"Until . . ."

"Well, the senator, as such men will, had contacts within organized crime. And he arranged for certain men to wait outside Drake's bar one night until the 4:00 A.M. closing time. And they followed Drake and they dragged him into an alley and they went to work, with their fists, their feet and a baseball bat."

"Oh my God . . ."

"They broke almost every bone in his body. He was unrecognizable. And he didn't have a penny or any health insurance, so all he could do was languish in the stifling back ward of a truly repulsive petri dish of a hospital and receive only the most basic, inept care possible."

"But what about Carole Ann? Didn't she help him?"

"Oh, she tried, she promised she'd never leave him. But she didn't have any money of her own and she'd always planned on a full-tilt, banjos-on-the-verandah wedding and she really wasn't equipped for nursing a poverty case. And her daddy swore that he'd had nothing to do with Drake's beating and the thugs were never caught and six months later, Carole Ann was engaged, again. To someone else."

"Who?"

"A young Republican tax attorney from back home, although are Republicans ever really young? But he was a suitable choice from a suitable family and as a wedding gift, Daddy gave the lucky couple a suitably colonnaded and weeping-willowed home on three hundred and eighty acres and he offered the young man a job with his campaign. And within two years Daddy became the vice president of the United States. So I suppose, in a way, he was punished."

"But — what happened to Drake?"

"When I heard what had happened I took him in. I paid for some top-of-the-line Brazilian cosmetic surgery and I pushed him through rehab. And I offered him a job as my driver."

As with so much of what Tom accomplished, his actions at first appeared unselfish and then took a turn. He'd discovered my mom but I knew how her life had ended. And if I could believe him, he'd pretty much rescued Drake but now Drake was another fiercely loyal, vigilantly secretive, possibly imprisoned employee. I was Tom Kelly's most recent acquisition: Where was I headed? If I couldn't meet his deadline, if I didn't marry the prince, where would I be a year from now?

"Would you like to see a sketch? Of your wedding dress?"

I knew better than to answer. Instead I waited, as Tom went to a mahogany library table and removed a large sheet of white parchment from beneath a stack of art books. He held the sketch at arm's length, admiring it.

"A royal bride. Just imagine."

As he began to flip the sketch so I could share his design and grab a glimpse of my possible future, the sketch burst into flames and became smoke. This was a lounge act gimmick, a pick-a-card-any-card, first-day-of-Junior-Houdini-school fizzle, until the ashes from the parchment began to rise and multiply and coalesce and become a life-sized replica of a truly stunning wedding gown, comprised entirely of floating ash, like the most well-drilled army of fluttering moths. As I reached out to touch the hovering, ghostly gown, the ashes fell to the floor.

"Earn it," Tom advised.

I arranged to meet Rocher at the airport and I waited just outside a secluded VIP lounge requisitioned through the movie studio. I stood at one end of a long hallway as Rocher stomped toward me.

She had slung a sports equipment—sized duffel bag over her shoulder, packed with her entire wardrobe, and clutched in her fists and spilling from her pockets were a sleep mask, felt slippers, an in-flight magazine and a thankfully unused air-sickness bag. As she drew nearer, Rocher griped, "It takes too fucking long to get here, why can't people just get beamed places, like on *Star Trek*; I smell like airplane air, and they took back my headset, what're they gonna do, sterilize it and pass it along?"

She was now close enough to see, for the first time ever, full-on and in person, not me, but Rebecca.

"Oh my God, oh my Jesus holy fucking pee-on-me God."

"Roche, it's so good to see you. . . ."

"No. No. Don't touch me, not yet. Just stay right there. Oh my God, oh my sweet Jesus in the motherfucking manger, no. No. Fuck me. NO."

"I know it's going to take some time for you to get used to —"

"NO! NO! I mean, I've seen you, on TV and online and in the magazines but WHO ARE YOU? WHAT ARE YOU?"

Rocher looked as if she'd seen the ghost of someone she'd killed in cold blood. Then sheer curiosity got the best of her and she inched forward, still with hesitation, as if I were foaming at the mouth or might spew fireballs from my eyes.

"Becky?" she finally asked, as she tiptoed within a foot of me and peered into my face, seeking anything familiar, some trace of Becky, as if she were incredibly nearsighted and was trying to read the fine print on my forehead.

"Becky? Is that really you? Are you in there?"

"It's me. Ask me something. I'll prove it."

"What's my favorite ice cream flavor?"

"Butter pecan with little frozen marshmallows, chopped-up graham crackers and stale cashews."

"What does my stepdad do for a living?"

"Irritates your mom. Except lately he's been pretending to be laid off from never having worked at the post office, which was an idea he got when he once had to mail a letter."

"What do I have tattooed and where?"

"You have a picture of Jate Mallow right under your left butt cheek because his love for you is a special private thing just between the two of you and because it's your lucky butt cheek."

"Becky! It is you!" she yelped and then she flung herself into my arms where, after a meaningfully suffocating hug, we both, still holding each other, jumped up and down on an invisible trampoline.

"Roche! I can't believe you're here!"

"Princess Becky!"

And from both of us: "YAYYYY!!!!"

Back in my hotel suite Rocher sat cross-legged on my bed, amid the crumbs and the smeared plates of the room-service desserts which she'd mainlined and a few that she was still considering: "I'm gonna hold on to the weird little pancakes, what do you call 'em, the crepes, for later, because they look kinda light or maybe I'll just roll 'em up and smoke 'em like joints. And you gotta tell me, is this all part of the package, I mean, can you eat like this, all of this amazing crap, and still look like that? And answer carefully because if you say yes, then on behalf of women everywhere, I'm gonna come at you with this butter knife and do as much damage as I can."

"Well, at first I scarfed down everything I could, just to test it out and I have to tell you, I didn't gain an ounce. I can eat, like, fifteen bags of real potato chips, not the baked or the reduced fat, or the Olestra. . . ."

"Ewww!!!" we both said, acknowledging that the label on the fat-free, fried-in-Olestra variety warned about stomach cramps and anal leakage.

"And I can eat ten boxes of Mallomars and drink a gallon jug of Coke, real Coke. . . ."

"Real Coke?"

"And I still look exactly like this."

"Fuck you. Fuck you. Just fuck you."

"Except for one thing — when I'm alone, and I look in the mirror, it all shows up on Becky."

"Oh my God. Oh my God. That's just wrong. That's just evil. That's like if when the Prince finally met Cinderella and she tried on the glass slipper, she had bunions."

"But today is a special occasion so we can both eat whatever we want."

"Damn right," said Rocher, plowing another chocolate-dipped strawberry into her mouth.

"Okay, Project Princess."

"Okay," said Rocher, wadding up her napkin and wiping her lips. "I know what you told me on the phone, about the burn unit and everything, which was a good beginning, because there you were, looking like Rebecca and then you were a mess and he helped you. But here's my question: Since then, have you heard from him?"

I pointed to a three-foot-tall cut-crystal urn packed with fifty red roses in full bloom and I read the attached card aloud, "To Rebecca, who must be so tired of roses. Your Prince."

As I was reading Rocher had begun emitting high-pitched squeaking noises, like one of those ceiling smoke alarms. I thought she was reacting to the prince's note but when I looked up I knew that she hadn't heard a word I'd said, because she was staring past me, with her eyes wide and a thread of drool spilling from her lower lip. I turned to find the object of Rocher's stupefied ecstasy: Jate had let himself into the room via the door to his adjoining suite.

"Hey," said Jate, moving carefully. Jate knew that whenever he was within a few yards of any female, age seven through senility, he had to permit her time and space to catch her breath, to sob softly and to acknowledge or at least pretend to acknowledge, that the two of them were both human beings. For a girl like Rocher — okay, for almost any girl — catching first sight of Jate was like becoming a French peasant child, hurrying home across a barren, rocky field and slamming right into the Virgin Mary floating atop a golden cloud. Even if your family and the townspeople and the local nuns never believed you, your life would still be changed forever.

"I'm Jate. And you're, it's Rocher, right?"

"He . . . he . . . you . . . you . . . you said my name. With your mouth. With your Jate mouth." Rocher held up a hand, warning Jate to remain a few feet away, so she could settle her internal organs and prevent herself from vaulting right onto him, knocking him flat and then kissing him until she'd swallowed at least one of his lips.

"I told Jate about Prince Gregory," I said to Rocher, ignoring the fact that she'd now stuffed a hefty chunk of the bedspread into her mouth, inadvertently sending the room-service platters clattering to the floor.

"Going for the prince is cool," said Jate. "It's the right move."

Aside from my newfound desire to help others on a global scale, I'd also explained to Jate that I wasn't really an actress. He'd been disappointed, but then he'd agreed that a crown and a kingdom could be "a sort of Euro-version of an Academy Award, like for Best Princess in a Country That Could Really Use One."

"I've been thinking about the whole situation," said Jate. "And the first step is, Rebecca, you and me, we have to break up. It can go two ways. First, we can go messy, like you catch me with some other girl, like my makeup artist or some babe from a TV show who could use the coverage, or even better, some hot girl who doesn't speak English, so she can't answer any questions. And then you and me, we have a vicious fight in a restaurant parking lot, close enough to the cameras so that we can make big arm gestures to show how upset we are but far enough away so that they can't hear us. Then you go off to a spa in Arizona and I do a charity golf tournament in Vegas and we both have our people issue statements about how we'd like the media to respect our privacy at a time of great personal loss. And we both refuse to talk about each other until right before the Renn Hightower movie comes out and then you can tell *Vogue* that our breakup has left you feeling hurt and betrayed but that it helped you to grow as a person, and if *People* puts me on the cover, I can tell them that we're both so young and we just grew apart but that we'll always love each other."

Rocher was on the floor, crawling on her stomach toward Jate's feet. "I love you . . . ," she kept repeating, in a demonic whisper. "I have to show you . . . my butt."

"Or," Jate continued, since Rocher was still a few yards off, "we can do the ultra-classy, romantically mysterious, only-the-two-of-us-can-ever-know-what-we-meant-to-each-other deal, which is probably the better route, and we can ask the press why a man and a woman can't just be friends. Because if the whole story gets too trashy then you turn into this trampy little supermodel/actress/ho and I turn into a bastard with no feelings. But if the three of us, you and me and Prince Gregory, if we all hang out at the children's hospital or if we cohost something in Monaco for famine relief, then we're all best buddies and we're mature and smiling for a worthy cause and everybody wins."

"Look . . . ," Rocher was pleading on her hands and knees, facing away from Jate as she demurely lowered her jeans and her underwear to reveal her tattoo of Jate's face.

"That is unbelievably and totally mad sweet," said Jate to Rocher. Jate, over the years, had been called upon to admire and autograph similar, even more detailed tributes, inked across women's breasts, on their shoulders and across their backs.

"And there were these three sisters," Jate had once told me, "and one had me as a baby, tattooed on her shin, the second sister had me as a teen idol, on her neck, and on the third sister's stomach I was being sworn in as a Supreme Court justice."

Rocher pulled up her clothing and faced Jate as she rose to her knees. "I'm glad you're gay," she said solemnly, "because that way, if I can't have you, no one can."

"Um, Rocher," I mentioned, "like, a dude could have him."

This had never occurred to Rocher because she'd thought that Jate being gay translated as, "I love Rocher Bargemueller so much but I don't deserve her so I'll never have sex again." The concept of Jate with a guy was fresh turf and Rocher regarded him with an especially deranged sparkle in her eyes.

"I could be a dude," she said.

As a favor to me, Jate took Rocher into his adjoining suite and gave her a signed *Cloudborne* poster, a vintage *Jackie + Jate* lunch box and thermos and a rare bottle of the discontinued Mallowrinse Shampoo and Conditioner in One, while convincing her that "even though we're never going to be, like, together, I really respect you and please don't force me to put you on any of those no-fly lists."

By the time Rocher returned, definitely more centered, Prince Gregory's secretary had called and invited me to accompany His Royal Highness to the British Museum the next night, for the opening of an exhibit entitled *The Female Ideal*.

"Okay, this is a really good sign," Rocher said. "But there's something I have to say, if we want this whole thing to work. I know that Prince Gregory is so cute and smart and nice, he's the total package, but you cannot, under any circumstances, no matter what he says, even if he promises you, like, a castle or a golden fleece or Ireland, you cannot fuck him."

"What?"

"Just listen to me, because it's a rule, it's like the biggest princess rule of all. It's like, what if Cinderella is at the ball and she's waltzing with Prince Charming but she's keeping one eye on the clock because it's 11:15, and she knows that, if she's still there at midnight, boom, everything vanishes, the carriage turns back into a pumpkin, the footmen are all mice and the Prince finds out that she's just some skank from the suburbs.

"But because the Prince is so hot," she continued, "and because Cinderella, she's been cooped up with her stepsisters for so long, and her dress is so amazing, so what if she drags the Prince into the royal cloakroom and gives him a blow job. You know, just as a way of saying, 'I really like you and it's such a great night and I just want to prove that you're special.'"

"I am not going to do that!"

"I know, because it would ruin everything, because the next day no decent prince is going to knock on every door in town going, 'I'm looking for the beautiful young lady who fits this glass slipper and who also gives the most righteous head in the kingdom.'"

"So you mean if I want to marry the prince I should do what, play hard to get?"

"No, I'm not saying you need to be an A-plus, number one, slap-her-silly cocktease like Shanice Morain. Even though that is how she got Cal Malstrup to ask her to prom, she just kept giving him these hand jobs in the equipment shed next to the football field and she kept telling him that she'd love to do more but that she was a good Christian girl and that it says in the Bible that good Christians can only have joyful intercourse in the back of a white stretch limo."

"She did not say that!"

"Uh-huh, I heard it, 'cause I was up on the roof, grabbin' a smoke. And he bought it. But, Becky?"

"Yeah?"

"I have no right to say this but I have to ask you something."

"Of course, anything. What?"

"Could I, just for a second, and I just washed my hands, and I promise that I'll be extra-super-unbelievably careful, but could I — try on your coat?"

I was now wearing Tom Kelly's latest creation, which he'd designed with my new ambition in mind. It had been messengered over in an enormous, glossy, silvery cardboard box, almost a trunk, embossed with a subtle geometric pattern of Tom's initials. The dress had been nestled within hundreds of sheets of lightly crushed, acid-free, archival tissue paper, the kind they use to preserve historic textiles in museums, and the outfit included a high-necked, sleeveless red silk sheath with a matching red coat, a small red hat and red calfskin gloves. Taken as a whole the look was covered up and appropriately modest but the color and curves made it high-voltage Rebecca.

"Could I?" Rocher repeated in a small, straightforward voice. "Just for a second? Please?"

As I slipped off the red silk coat and gestured for Rocher to turn around so I could help her into it, I tried to remember how old I'd been when I'd first noticed not just what people looked like, but which people looked better. I'd always thought that Rocher looked wonderful but she'd hated her bushels of thick, kinky red hair and her generous buckets of freckles and her long, wiry arms. Rocher thought she was a prancing sock monkey or an overgrown shrub but when we were little, I'd never rated her looks because she was Rocher, who I'd talk to a million times every day and who sometimes got overexcited about, say, a new elastic bracelet comprised of miniature baby-doll heads, or who'd gotten royally pissed off when a boy she'd had a crush on called her a creepy caterpillar.

It was only later, when we were around twelve, that we'd started to consult each other about stuff like whether Rocher should get her hair chemically straightened or shaved off completely, or about how soul-slashingly horrible it would be, and about how we'd stab ourselves to death with forks, if either of us sprouted a mustache like Connie-Gwen "El Diablo" Whitby.

My mother had warned me about spending too much time looking in the mirror "because you might fall in." But the real reason I'd begun avoiding the mirror hadn't been my mom's advice, but her size. For years I'd overheard all of the nasty, ignorant names that the other kids, and sometimes the other kids' parents, had aimed at my mother and I never got used to the sting of "lazy cow," "hungry hippo" or "gross fat pig." But the phrase that floored me had been my third-grade teacher's; Ms. Hibble, who was otherwise totally nice, had taken me aside and told me that my mom was "morbidly obese." I'd asked her what that meant and she'd said that my mom was so overweight that she might die.

Anyone who says that looks don't matter or that it's only what's inside that counts never saw Selina, or my mom, or Rocher's face, with her eyes squinched shut and her lips murmuring the most heartfelt prayer, over and over again, as I slid my red coat or Tom Kelly's red coat or, most significantly, Rebecca's red coat, over Rocher's skinny shoulders.

Rocher pulled on the red coat over her favorite shredded jeans, her I HATE YOU MORE T-shirt, her mustard-and-green-striped polyester cardigan and her many clustered strands of beads and chains, from which dangled, among other things, an oversized crucifix that Rocher had hot-glued with rhinestones, a tiny pipe-cleaner giraffe and a large electroplated golden initial R. We were facing the full-length mirror, which had been set up in the middle of the room, and with her eyes still closed, Rocher asked, "So? Tell me the truth. How do I look? No, that's wrong — what do I look like? Do I look like me, or you, or me plus Tom Kelly? Am I the most beautiful red-haired woman who's ever lived? Has anything, you know, happened? Who am I?"

Rocher opened her eyes. She looked exactly the same. No, she looked like Rocher playing rainy-day dress-up in her mother's or her older sister's fancy wardrobe. The coat didn't suit her, and it hadn't changed her, and I felt guilty and disgusting because a part of me was relieved.

"You look great," I said.

Rocher eyed me in silence. She knew everything I'd been thinking, and she understood. She slowly took off the coat, with divided emotions. She loved touching it and sliding the richness of the fabric against her skin, but having tried it on, having made the attempt, she knew for certain that the silk, and Tom Kelly's alchemy, would never be hers. Rocher was really smart and she knew that envying Rebecca was useless; envying Rebecca was tossing darts at the moon. So instead Rocher gently, almost reverently, held the red coat by the shoulders and helped me into it. This was a gesture of both abject surrender and true friendship. Rocher would let me be Rebecca — she could deal with that — but only me.

I started to say something, to offer some syrupy, useless reassurance, but Rocher held up a hand and said, "It's okay."

14.

"There she is," said Prince Gregory as I was presented to him in the huge central hall of the British Museum.

"Your Highness," I said.

"Why are you laughing?"

"I wasn't laughing!"

"Yes you were, although you tried to stop so now you must tell me — what was so amusing?"

I had a choice. I could make up a convenient lie, or just toss my hair, but when I saw the prince smiling at me, I took a risk. At the hospital the prince had valued honesty and he'd had a terrific sense of humor. So I decided that if I was going to spend any amount of time with the guy, let alone marry him within a very few months, I was going to, sort of, be myself. I'd look like Rebecca but I'd dare to behave like Becky.

"I was laughing because where I grew up in the States, every guy dreams of being called Your Highness. My friend Rocher's stepfather sometimes pats his crotch and calls it King Rodney."

The prince glared and then burst out laughing, insisting, "You say the most impossible things!"

"I'm sorry — it's just, I'm still not all that clear on royal protocol. I'm not sure if I should keep my head bowed when I'm around you or stand a few steps behind you or just pretend that you're a person."

"Well, I'm not at all sure how to behave around you. Should I try not to stare or should I keep reminding myself that even if you're so beautiful, you might want to have a conversation or should I simply dissolve into a puddle of adoration at your feet."

"All right, here's what we're going to do. I'm going to pretend that you're a guy and you're going to pretend that I'm a girl."

"Very good. So how are you? Do you live nearby? May I get you a drink?"

"Are you hitting on me?"

"Perhaps."

"Do you have a job?"

We were joined by Ivor St. Hallaby, the museum's director of acquisitions, who would be serving as our protector and tour guide. His slicked hair, prominent nose and ramrod posture lent him the air of a pedigreed greyhound and he spoke with a grand yet unplaceable accent, as if he'd absorbed the native languages of every artwork on the premises.

"Your Highness," Mr. St. Hallaby said as I pictured him grandly unfurling a satin-lined cape. "Thank you so much for joining us this evening and for visiting with our ladies."

He swept a hand toward large, scripted letters on a nearby wall, which read THE FEMALE IDEAL. "We're paying tribute to the most beautiful women who've ever lived. And this must be Ms. Randle, whom I must say, truly completes our exhibition."

I'd learned from Jate to accept such overblown compliments with a nod and a smile, rather than deflecting or denying them. "Don't be a snot," Jate had said. "Let them enjoy you."

"Our signature piece," intoned Mr. St. Hallaby, taking Prince Gregory and me into the first gallery space and introducing a canvas that had an entire wall to itself. "On loan from the Uffizi in Florence, Botticelli's *The Birth of Venus*. We had to have her. She's our hostess."

"She's a bit chunky, wouldn't you say?" commented Prince Gregory and while I resisted kicking him, I had to agree. I'd never been to this sort of world-class museum or any museums at all, outside of a seventh-grade field trip to a restored plantation and the attached Jamesburg Historical Society Collection, which had been a small, clapboard building filled with faded rag rugs and framed ancestral silhouettes. But I recognized *The Birth of Venus* from reproductions in books and parodies in comics and lingerie ads, where the goddess would be wearing a push-up bra or suffering from dry, itchy winter skin.

"You truly are exceptional," the prince told me, "and no, I'm not talking about what you look like. It's just that when most people are at a museum, they're instantly bored and they spend all their time on their phones, searching for some other activity, or they run for the gift shop or the snack bar. But you're actually looking at the paintings."

"Well, it's interesting," I replied. "Because, if you read the label it says that Venus wasn't just the goddess of love and beauty but that she was born from the foam on the waves of the sea and that she arrived all grown-up, but here's my favorite part — she was born laughing."

"I like that," said the prince and when he smiled at me, I smiled right back. The prince was turned in my direction so he didn't notice that the portrait of Venus had altered and that the ancient goddess was now in fact observing us and chortling with delight.

"Hello, Marilyn," said Mr. St. Hallaby, gliding us into the next room and toward a six-foot-square Andy Warhol silk screen of Marilyn Monroe's face, in which the star's complexion had been inked into a flat, sizzling hot pink with acid yellow hair and half-mast eyes, drooping with hormones and mascara; she was a beach towel of herself, a Day-Glo-frosted holiday cookie.

"My mother loved Marilyn Monroe," I told the prince.

"As did mine."

"My mom read all of these trashy books about her."

The prince paused and then admitted, "As did mine."

"Really?" I said, tickled at the thought of my mom and Princess Alicia with the same taste in paperbacks. Over the prince's shoulder Marilyn awoke, offering me a sly, sexy, conspiratorial wink.

"And that Warhol fellow also did a portrait of my mum," the prince told me. "All in bright blue and orange, as if he'd used crayons. If Warhol was still around he'd be after you like mad. The way everyone is. People have been warning me, you know. They claim that you're a gold-digging, predatory Hollywood siren. They say we'll end up in the tabloids, shouting drunken filth at each other across a nightclub dance floor. They say that you'll drag me into a fiendish morass of narcotics and cheap publicity and deviant sexual practices."

"And what do you tell them?"

"I tell them, 'God, I hope so.'"

Then he leaned down and kissed me, as Venus and Marilyn exchanged a knowing glance.

I'd been kissed before, but never as Rebecca and never by a prince and certainly not outside of Missouri. I was caught off guard and I began observing the kiss, through Rebecca's eyes, as Becky. Prince Gregory is kissing her, I thought, he's kissing me, I should kiss him back, Rebecca, do it, kiss him back, that's perfect, that feels lovely, that's just the right, perfect first kiss, and now we're all daring each other, the prince and Rebecca and Becky, to see who'll end the kiss first, to see who's in charge of the kiss. I want it to last forever, but Rebecca is so much smarter than me, she has a master's degree in Advanced Premarital Kissing, and after all, she kissed Jate Mallow, or Renn Hightower, now it's all getting so confusing, and now, without any of us making a conscious decision, we're not kissing anymore. But Prince Gregory is looking at me as if he's still kissing me, or her, he won't let the moment end, he can't bear to, because it's like he's just discovered ice cream and fast cars and great American kisses.

"Good Lord, that was just dreadful," said Prince Gregory, not taking his eyes off me. "It was like kissing my brother."

"That's so strange," I replied. "Because I was going to say the exact same thing. Except your brother's taller."

For a flicker, this outraged the prince. People weren't allowed to speak to him this way. Then he grinned.

"If we're ever going to get this kissing business in order," he decided, "we're really going to have to work at it. Because right now it's hopeless. Embarrassing. We'll need hours. Days. Full semesters. Exams."

"Moving on," I said to Mr. St. Hallaby, remembering Rocher's instructions about keeping the prince at a constant, desperate simmer. Was I a girl on a date or a monster on a mission? Was there a difference? Was I bewitching the prince into falling in love with me so I could remain Rebecca and help the world, or was I getting way too attracted to a seriously dreamy guy?

The answer to all of these questions, especially after the rest of the evening went even better, was yes.

Everything went straight to hell the next day when two photos raced their way across every English website, tabloid and TV show. The first photo commemorated what became known as That Kiss, which every columnist, commentator and citizen insisted had occurred too early and too publicly. In the words of Mrs. Beryl Slasger, "a homemaker and volunteer for the elderly and the sadly infirm in the extended Hastely-on-Snegs area," as quoted in the *Daily Monitor*, "When I saw that pic of our Greg snogging that American harlot, I became physically ill, and since that moment I have only been able to ingest two small almond crackers, one of which immediately repeated." Cheryl Meers-Trambley, an entertainment correspondent for the BBC, reported that "Once again, an imperialist American force invades a foreign land, as Rebecca Randle all but consumes a helpless Prince Gregory." From the floor of Parliament, Lord Charles Benderley announced that "The photo in question can justly be termed pornographic. When my dear wife, Clairesse, viewed this explicit embrace, she became disoriented and incontinent. Are there no limits?"

The second and more seriously offensive photograph had been snapped literally behind my back. After our tour had finished, Mr. St. Hallaby had whisked Prince Gregory off for some additional pictures posed beside the museum's most deep-pocketed benefactors. Left on my own I'd wandered into a nearby gallery which hadn't been associated with *The Female Ideal* exhibit. I'd stood before *Portia*, a life-sized, full-length portrait of a raven-haired woman whose alabaster shoulders rose proudly from her wasp-waisted, strapless, black satin gown, accented with glinting opal earrings and a brooch shaped like a crescent moon, nestled in her powdered and impressive cleavage. The woman in the portrait was being deliberately flirtatious, daring the viewer to disapprove of her lusciously exposed flesh, her lavender-tinted eyelids and a star-shaped beauty mark applied just to the left of her knowing half smile. Even though the portrait had been completed almost two hundred years earlier, the woman was a do-me-now centerfold, or an early ad for, say, Infidelity by Tom Kelly. Portia had only increased her allure by raising her slender fingertips to her champagne-moistened lips and blowing me a kiss.

I heard my mom's ringtone and I saw that, in Portia's other hand, she was now holding a cell phone.

I'd thought that Venus and Marilyn and Portia had been welcoming me to an ongoing parade of portrait-worthy femme fatales but it turned out that they'd been warning me about the collateral damage of beauty. Venus, through her meddling, had kicked off the Trojan War, while Marilyn, at thirty-six, had died alone in a shabby Los Angeles bedroom and it seemed that Portia had been a married American who'd been the long-time mistress of Prince Gregory's great-great-grandfather King Stanley. She had borne the king two bastard sons and after her divorce, she'd been exiled to Pennsylvania, where she'd supported herself by publishing a bestselling and scandalous memoir, revealing, among many erotic details, that the king had enjoyed being spanked while dressed as a Catholic schoolgirl called Little Naughty Nancy. In England, it had been the Catholic angle that had caused the greatest outrage.

In the photo that filled the entire front pages of the *Monitor*, *Early Examiner*, *National Notation* and *Spinning Globe*, I was standing with my back to the camera and my head tilted upward, considering Portia and offering, according to the *Morning Spectacle*, "A WHORE'S SALUTE!" The *Evening Express*, in a three-column editorial, accused me of demonstrating "the grossest and most malign insensitivity, along with a shocking and near-inconceivable lack of even the most primitive moral code." The television coverage snowballed, as various Concerned Persons Speaking on the Street called me "an insult to the crown," "a cheap and steaming little slice of American popular culture" and something termed "a naff and a half." There were constantly updated online polls, in which I was rated as either A Blundering Moron (15 percent), An Ignorant Strumpet (37 percent) or The Most Vile American Import Since Cold Milk (48 percent).

"What were you thinking?" asked Tom Kelly as I tried to disappear into his town house couch later that day, already on my second box of Kleenex. "How could you be such an idiot?"

"I don't know!" I wailed. "All I did was kiss him! And it was such a nice night!"

"Excuse me," said Tom, who was wearing a gray cashmere sweatshirt, Tom Kelly jeans and bare feet. "But haven't you heard of Tall Poppy Syndrome?"

"What?"

"Jesus! What do they teach you in those East Trawley schools?"

"Math! Biology! Maybe I was absent the day they covered how to marry a prince!"

"Years ago, centuries ago, England owned everything. America, India, Canada, Australia, South Africa, half the planet. But there were wars and uprisings and tiffs and gradually, it all went away. And now the English have nothing. They've even lost their shoulders, their chins and their ability to carry a tune."

"But why are they mad at me?"

"They're mad at everyone. They're festering and bitter because all they have left are non-folding umbrellas, decent skin and their pride. Which they take very seriously. So if anyone, on their home turf, attempts to achieve anything, let alone succeeds, they become extremely irate. If someone paints a masterpiece, or becomes a pop star, or even bakes a decent pie, England declares that person vain and self-important and vulgar — a tall poppy. And a tall poppy gets its head chopped off. To teach it a lesson."

"So I'm a tall poppy?"

"You're a sequoia. A space needle. A moon landing. You're the most beautiful woman in the world."

"Oh no . . ."

"And you've plunked yourself down at the brutally frigid heart of the only country where that's a hanging offense. And yes, there are, through the sheer law of averages, good-looking English people."

"Princess Alicia was gorgeous!"

"And she was loved and hated. The English remained deeply and lastingly suspicious. Only her death made her truly acceptable."

"But how can I fix this? How can I make all of the English people decide that I'm ugly?"

"Seven months and twenty-eight days, Rebecca. Or is it Becky?"

"Open it," said Rocher. We were back in my suite, and Rocher was holding out a heavy cream-colored envelope, imprinted with the royal crest.

"What do you think it is?" I asked, weighing the envelope in my hand. "Do you think it's a note from Prince Gregory, calling the whole thing off? Telling Rebecca to get lost?"

"No!" Rocher crowed. "I already opened it! It's good news! The best! You're saved! 'Cause you've been invited to Ladies' Day, at Ascot!"

"To what?"

"It's huge. And it's exactly how you're going to publicly apologize for the whole museum shit show, and make everybody love you. Especially Prince Gregory."

"How?"

Ascot, Rocher taught me, was a racetrack just outside of London and once a year, the Royal Family invited a few hundred guests to join them for five days of racing. Ladies' Day was the third and most anticipated occasion, when the Queen attended, and all of the female guests were expected to look their very best. For research Rocher had bought a DVD of *My Fair Lady*, which was a movie musical where Audrey Hepburn plays a guttersnipe, a cockney girl who's been selling flowers on a street corner until a professor named Henry Higgins takes her in and trains her to speak and behave as an upper-crust lady of quality.

"See, you're sort of like Audrey," said Rocher as we watched the movie, "because you're this normal person who gets turned into this total knockout and Tom Kelly is sort of like Henry Higgins, 'cause he's a real prick."

We fast-forwarded to the Ascot scene, which was amazing. Ascot, at least in the movie, didn't look like any racetrack I'd ever been to, because it wasn't carpeted with empty plastic cups of beer and thrown-away, losing tickets and half of the people weren't drunk out of their minds, having just blown their kids' college funds after betting on a long shot. Ascot was a Victorian ginger-bread gazebo and everyone in the Royal Enclosure was wearing only black and white. Audrey Hepburn was gowned in spun-sugar lace with a sinuous coil of black-and-white-striped ribbon, with a feathered hat the size of the Super Bowl. "Okay, you're still the Most Beautiful," Rocher commented. "But Audrey is right up there."

As a crowd of snobby, impossibly refined royal friends and relatives watched the race, no one cheered or perspired or got wasted. But then Audrey forgot everything Professor Higgins had been teaching her and she stuck her fingers in her mouth, whis-tled and yowled at a horse to "Move your bloomin' arse!"

"That's the danger right there," said Rocher. "That's what you have to watch out for. You have to prove to everybody that even after you pretty much had sex with Prince Gregory at the museum, you're really a proper young lady. And you know how you're gonna do that?"

"Yeah?"

"You're gonna call up Prince Gregory's secretary and get an extra ticket. Because I'm coming with you. To make sure you don't fuck it all up."

Prince Gregory's secretary was incredibly nice about granting me a guest pass for Rocher and on the day of the race Tom Kelly came to my suite with dresses for both of us.

"Today is critical," Tom said, as Rocher and I stood in our underwear while Mrs. Chen and her staff unpacked, ironed and steamed our outfits. "Because not only will there be press and photographers but you may very well be introduced to Prince Gregory's grandmother."

"The Queen of England," Rocher whispered to me.

"I got that," I whispered back.

"But beyond all that," Tom continued, "you're going to meet someone else. Someone who will do everything she can to annihilate you."

"Oh my God," said Rocher. "He's totally right."

"Who?" I asked.

Together, Rocher and Tom uttered a name with reverence and dread, because speaking the name aloud could attract heat lightning, a plague of ravenous locusts or any number of other deeply ominous special effects.

"Lady Jessalyn Clane-Taslington," said Rocher and Tom Kelly.

"Wasn't she Prince Gregory's girlfriend?" I asked.

"Until you came along," said Rocher. "All of the magazines claim that Lady Jessalyn and the prince are pre-engaged. I mean, she's the total right choice. First of all, she's royal and she's his cousin, only far enough removed so that they won't have two-headed babies with webbed feet. And she's never made a wrong move."

"Even when she was a child," said Tom, "she'd always make sure that she was photographed near him but not too close, so it wouldn't look pushy. And she'd always be wearing white frilly dresses and little white lace gloves, with Alice in Wonderland blond hair spilling down her back."

"She's a killer," said Rocher. "When she was at college she majored in something like History of Art or Sonnet Structure, so everyone would know that she didn't want a career. And after she graduated she got jobs like assistant-teaching part-time at a pre-school, so everyone would know that she'd be a perfect mother to all of Prince Gregory's kids."

"And she never gives interviews," said Tom, "but her friends do and they've all been coached to say that 'Lady Jessalyn is deeply fond of His Royal Highness and treasures their intimate friendship.'"

"And in all of the betting pools," concluded Rocher, "she's the number one, odds-on favorite for a royal marriage."

"But it gets worse," said Tom. "So much worse. Because Lady Jessalyn isn't merely your competition. She is evil incarnate, and she'll do whatever it takes to achieve her fiendish ends. Because she is the greatest natural enemy of the Most Beautiful Woman Who Ever Lived."

"Why?" I asked.

"Because she is the Pretty Girl," said Tom and even Mrs. Chen and her assistants paused to acknowledge the truth of Tom's insight and Lady Jessalyn's potent threat.

"The Pretty Girl?" I said.

"Most women, most normal-looking women, as, for example, Rocher —" Tom began.

"Right here," said Rocher.

"When these women see Rebecca, if they're smart, they think to themselves, aha, got it, and they immediately give up. White flag. Broken sword. At your feet."

"I mean, look at you," said Rocher. "What am I gonna do?"

"But then we have someone like Lady Jessalyn," Tom went on. "Who has perfect, tiny little features and perfect posture and perfect spokesmodel-white, diligently bleached and bonded teeth and perfectly shiny blond, naturally straight, expensively and frequently colored hair. And all of her life, since birth, everyone has chorused, 'My, isn't she pretty!' and 'What a pretty little thing!' and 'She's so pretty, she's going to break hearts!' And Lady Jessalyn, especially growing up in England, where the playing field is somewhat sparse, she believed everything everyone said and she developed a certain bulldozer-like assurance and even though she was always religiously careful to behave modestly and sweetly, and to pat all of the orphans on the head, she's always known, with unswerving certainty, that she was the Pretty Girl. Daddy's favorite. The head cheerleader. The prom queen. The dream."

"Shanice Morain," said Rocher.

"And she is in fact, very pretty. Until . . ."

"Until what?" I asked.

"Until she stands next to you. And then it all comes crashing down. Because when a pretty girl is compared to a beautiful woman, she will always lose. All of a sudden she's a tad ordinary. A bit small-town. Even a touch piggy. Because there are so many pretty girls, every yearbook and local modeling school and divorce court overflows with them. The pretty girl stars on a sitcom, but the beautiful woman appears in films that set international box-office records. The pretty girl dates and even marries the surgeon or the investment banker or the tenured professor, and then, while they're making love, he murmurs the beautiful woman's name. The pretty girl is horrified when she unearths a photo of the beautiful woman, tucked beneath the tube socks in her teenage son's underwear drawer. And the pretty girl burns inside because until the beautiful woman showed up, things had been going so well. She'd been so popular. Unrivaled. Unquestioned. And Lady Jessalyn is the very prettiest of the pretty girls but in her steaming black heart, she knows that there are a lot of Lady Jessalyns. But there's only one Rebecca."

"Oh my God . . ."

"So when she sees you," said Rocher, "she is gonna unzip her head and the nastiest alien lizard you've ever seen is gonna pop out and it's gonna be pissed."

"Spitting fire," said Tom, "and torching the countryside."

"So what should I do?"

"First of all," said Rocher, "you're gonna have me there to protect you and to make sure you behave."

"And you will behave perfectly," said Tom. "You will be sweet and simple and demure. You will be the very shortest poppy in the meadow. A dandelion. A sprig. You will disarm everyone, even Lady Jessalyn. And do you know why?"

"Because you're gonna out-princess her," said Rocher.

Tom and Rocher were both so informed while I was still catching up. As fast as I could, I tried to mentally input everything they'd told me, about England and royalty and beauty. My brain was bursting and I had to ask, "Are you guys really sure I can pull this off?"

"Of course you can," said Tom. "Look at what you're wearing."

After a final adjustment to my left sleeve, Mrs. Chen made a small, satisfied noise and stepped aside so I could inspect myself in the full-length mirror. Because I'd gotten so accustomed to smoldering red, this alternate direction took my breath away.

While my dress wasn't a floor-length, hourglass snowflake like Audrey Hepburn's, it was every bit as lovingly fragile. Tom was moving toward my white dress, because I was wearing a wisp of ivory-toned satin printed with the most delicate pale pink roses, nurtured not from seeds but from passionate late-afternoon whispers, from a Victorian ghost's valentines and from the first bouquet that Adam had plucked for Eve, to let her know he was serious. The dress had a narrow, matching belt and Mrs. Chen floated a sheer chiffon wrap, in the same print, around my shoulders. If my earlier dresses had been hot-blooded foreplay, this was a sunlit embrace.

Tom had done equally well by Rocher. Her dress sported a pale blue silk bodice and a pink satin skirt, both outlined in a suggestion of navy blue satin piping. It took me a second to realize that, while Rocher's dress was formal and flattering, it was also an upscale rethinking of her Halloween princess costume and Tom had added a small conical hat with a flutter of pink net sprinkled with rhinestones. All Rocher needed was a wand and a cuddly pink baby dragon perched on her shoulder, curling its spiked tail around her neck.

"Yeah," said Rocher, admiring her reflection, "I get it. Maybe I'm not going to be a princess, so maybe I'm a chick wizard, or, no, I know just what I am. I love it. I'm a lady-in-waiting."

She faced Tom, with gratitude. No one had ever made anything just for her.

"Thank you," Rocher told Tom. "You're really good."

There was a knock at the door and Archie the perfumer's nose entered, followed a full minute later by the rest of Archie. "Good afternoon," he said as he handed Tom a small Lucite box. Tom opened it and removed a crystal column filled with a clear liquid. He shook the bottle sharply and held it up to the light: The liquid was no longer transparent but seemed to contain a miniature ecosystem. There were billowing scarlet storm clouds, roiling over crashing mini waves of merlot, and then a teeny neon lightning bolt halved the bottled sea, and something burst forth. There was now a glowing red creature, a frantic, flamelike imp, hurling itself against the sides of the bottle, eager for barbaric freedom.

"What is that?" I asked with trepidation.

"It's my very latest fragrance," said Tom. "Archie has been working on it for years."

"It's been a challenge," said Archie. "I've combined spice extracts with half notes of musk, elderberries and the pheromone released by cobras, just before they strike."

"That sounds dangerous," I said.

"You look lovely," Tom told me. "Innocent and fresh. But let's keep in mind, while you'll be defeating Lady Jessalyn you'll also be seeing Prince Gregory. And we need to keep him captivated."

"Helpless," said Archie.

"Horny," said Rocher.

Tom slid the crystal stopper from the bottle and I could swear that the fire-imp leaped into the air, fiendishly excited, and then vanished, bonding invisibly to the nearest molecules of oxygen. I sniffed the air near the bottle. "Whoa," I said. "I can smell the spices, and the berries, and maybe the cobra, but there's something else, it's not really a smell at all but it's definitely there. What is that?"

"Archie?" asked Tom.

"Vodka," said Archie, and I could swear that his nose blushed. "Just a hint."

"Oh my God," said Rocher, who was now examining the perfume's Lucite box. "Look at the name." She showed me the silvery label, which read, Intoxicated by Tom Kelly.

"Only a drop," Tom cautioned as he dabbed the stopper along my wrist. "Because it's very, oh, what's the word I'm looking for? Powerful? Stimulating? Convulsive?"

He smiled with a dark satisfaction because he was cranky from having forced himself to design two such virginal dresses.

"Effective," said Archie.

15.

By the time Rocher and I arrived at Ascot and had muscled our way through the many layers of security, I was a nervous wreck, positive that I was about to do something fatal, that I'd say something careless or shoot something out of my nose, disgrace myself and lose Prince Gregory once and for all. To bolster my Rebecca-tude I did two things. First, I thought about Selina, and all of the other people I could help as a royal. Then I stole a quick glance at an oval mirror hanging on a post outside the Royal Enclosure, for everyone's final style checks. I'd waited in a line of fellow invitees as they'd nudged food particles from their gum lines and then used the resulting spit to smooth their hair.

As I took my turn at the looking glass, Rocher snuck up behind me, clutching the vial of Intoxicated which she'd smuggled from the car.

"Just one more drop," she murmured into my ear.

"Are you sure? Tom said I should be careful."

"If this would work for me I would drink it."

Just as I was holding up my hair so Rocher could lightly dab the stopper along the back of my neck, someone bumped her and she spilled the full bottle all over me. Because I was Rebecca, the liquid disappeared instantly, without a splatter or stain and the scent didn't seem overpoweringly present.

"I'm sorry!" said Rocher. "Somebody nudged me, some jerk, I'm so sorry!"

"It's fine. No harm done. As far as I can tell."

Trumpets blared the first three notes of my mom's ringtone, for the opening of Ladies' Day. So far, the ringtone had signaled when something supernatural was about to happen; my mom was sending me a heads-up.

The Royal Enclosure was a pavilion elevated along one side of the racetrack and bounded by whitewashed fencing, with iron posts topped by rippling white silk banners, and there were bars and seating areas shielded by canvas awnings. Several hundred people were sipping cocktails, gossiping leisurely and pretending to occasionally glance at the racetrack while they were really peering over and around one another, hoping to spot a high-ranking royal and, in the best of all possible scenarios, catch the royal's eye and receive a wink, a nod, or, if God was truly smiling, a waved invitation to come closer for a chat.

The men were all dressed in what Tom Kelly had called morning attire, which meant high-waisted trousers, striped vests, tailcoats and top hats and the women were a summery, tossed fruit salad, in their Pepto-Bismol pinks, their electric mouthwash aquas and their blinding margarine yellows, with coordinated gloves, handbags and oh my God, the hats.

Rocher had told me that Ladies' Day was all about the hats and here they were; there was a whole other party going on atop every woman's head. There was a hat the size and shape of a spare truck tire slathered in peppermint stripes, there was a stack of eight graduated gift boxes, each in lime green, the shades growing more intense until the tiny uppermost gift box sprouted a silk-and-wire palm tree. There was a safety-cone-orange derby with a cobalt-and-mocha checkerboard brim, anchoring a spray of peacock feathers. There were bows as wide and stiff as skate-boards, and Himalayas of smushed taffeta, and an oval, sloping gingham platter supporting a wicker cornucopia spilling a full-sized velvet pineapple, some hand-carved wooden apples, clusters of hand-blown purple glass grapes and a few green sequined zucchinis.

I'd been pounded and bruised by the English press but these hats were an England I could love. The hats refused to behave themselves; they were exuberant and outrageous, expressing the most taboo thoughts squirreled deep within the skulls of the women wearing them. I could picture these women after they'd returned home, stroking and quieting their hats and then lowering them gently into gargantuan hatboxes to rest after a big day out.

"Here you are," said Prince Gregory, making his way through the crowd to greet us. He paused and said, "I can't quite put my finger on it, but there's something quite different about you, from the last time we were together, what could it be. . . ."

Was this my ultra-dose of Intoxicated taking effect?

"I know!" said the prince happily. "You're a national disgrace!"

"And do you know what else is interesting," I replied. "In America, Prince is a dog's name."

"You look suspiciously winsome," the prince observed, taking in my outfit.

"I'm working undercover."

"Has all of this been dreadful for you? All of the press and the yapping and the accusations?"

"I can handle it. Now that I'm having your baby."

"I beg your pardon?"

"Haven't you read the *Daily Herald*?"

"I'm so glad you're here," he said and I knew that he wanted to kiss me, which made me dizzy, from either my Intoxicated or the fact that I couldn't wait.

"And this must be the legendary Rocher," the prince said as he and I tried not to look at each other because we were determined to control ourselves as long as we were in public, where we might be photographed, and condemned.

"Your Most Royal Highness of All . . . Highnesses," said Rocher, dropping into a deep curtsy. She'd been rehearsing this move for days, adapted from her stint as a waitress/serving wench at a Medieval Merriment theme restaurant, where she'd been hired to wear a low-cut peasant blouse and serve tankards of mouth-watering mead, which had really been watered-down root beer, and to squeal when pinched by either the drooling village idiot or the humpbacked court jester.

"Thank you so much," said the prince, "but that really isn't necessary."

"You're a prince," insisted Rocher, going for an even deeper curtsy and tipping alarmingly to one side. "Get over it."

"You are the most cheering and well-dressed people for miles," said the prince. "Welcome to Ascot."

"Your Highness?" said a woman, lightly tapping the prince's elbow.

"Jessalyn!" said the prince. "You must meet two of the most brilliant people, Rebecca Randle and Rocher Bargemueller. Ladies, may I present Lady Jessalyn Clane-Taslington."

"At last," said Lady Jessalyn with surprising good humor. "But shouldn't we have pistols? Or nunchucks?"

I'd stopped reading the papers but Rocher had shown me editorial cartoons of Rebecca and Lady Jessalyn with boxing gloves or machine guns or chain saws, cursing each other as they battled and grunted over the prince. Everyone had been siding with Lady Jessalyn, calling her the Real Royal Choice, the Anti-Rebecca and Gregory's Girl. I was shocked that Lady Jessalyn had immediately brought this up and it made me like her.

"I think I have my Taser," I said, opening my purse.

"Stop it, both of you," said the prince. "And because you are both gifted, impressive and accomplished young women, I will offer you only my deepest respect and insist on some form of mud wrestling." As Lady Jessalyn and I exchanged a nod and each went for one of the prince's arms, to wrench them off, the prince caught sight of his secretary beckoning urgently to him. "Right back," the prince told us. "Please don't begin scratching and biting until I return."

As Prince Gregory left us, Lady Jessalyn said, "You really are unbearably attractive. I'd so hoped it was all about lighting."

"It's a hoax," I said. "There's a strange teenage girl from Missouri hiding inside me, pulling my strings and replacing my batteries. I'm just a sort of parade float."

"And I just can't stand that you're both being so normal and grown-up about all this," said Rocher, not bothering to conceal her disappointment. "It's gross. It's boring."

"It is," agreed Lady Jessalyn. "But you know, I think we both have Prince Gregory's best interests at heart. And I'm delighted that he's found someone like you, to push him toward more good works, with the burn unit and the museum. And he's said that you've come up with a massive list of additional causes and countries and organizations."

"Thank you so much," I said, genuinely grateful. I was ashamed of myself for having listened to Rocher and Tom Kelly and I became huffy and political. How come everyone, especially other women, are so eager for a cat fight? Maybe I'd also misjudged Shanice Morain, maybe she was every bit as good-hearted as Lady Jessalyn, and we could've been friends.

From a few yards beyond Jessalyn's head, Prince Gregory waved to me. Tom Kelly had said that I might be meeting the prince's grandmother and I glimpsed a sliver of her in the distance, standing in a roped-off area. I recognized her profile, capped with stiffly curled silver hair and a hat like a magenta brocade carburetor, clustered with burgundy silk roses and sheaves of golden sequined wheat.

"Oh my God," hissed Rocher right in my ear. "That's *her*. The Queen. Of all *England*. And he wants you to meet her. That's *really good*."

As I steeled myself for an introduction to my possible future grandmother-in-law, I caught a few words of ongoing chatter between Lady Jessalyn and Rocher.

"So you went out with him for all those years," Rocher was saying. "And now you're like totally okay with giving him up?"

"Oh, my dear — what was your name again? Roquefort? Crochet?"

My face twitched, because the morning was taking a screeching turn.

"Rocher. It's a French chocolate. A premium chocolate."

"Of course. Isn't that fascinating. Do you have siblings? Perhaps Snickers and Baby Ruth?"

"Excuse me, Lady Jessalyn, and Rocher . . . ," I began, with my attention split between their bickering and the prince's increasingly demanding wave.

"Ladies," said Lady Jessalyn, "I don't believe you quite understand. I'm not giving up anyone."

"And I don't think you've been paying attention," said Rocher, "but Prince Gregory is all about Rebecca. I mean, he's going to marry her."

"Rocher?" I said, frantically shaking my head no!

"Your friend," said Lady Jessalyn to Rocher, but indicating me, "is indeed very beautiful. But no one seems to know anything about her. She's appeared out of thin air, with no family and no real accomplishments. I mean, really — who is she?"

That knocked the wind out of me, because everything Lady Jessalyn had just said was true.

"Rebecca's my friend," said Rocher, "that's who she is. And she's gonna be on the cover of *Vogue* and she's in the new Renn Hightower movie."

"Playing a prostitute, I believe," said Lady Jessalyn. "Possibly from experience."

"What did you say?"

Rocher was now yanking off her borrowed garnet earrings, which wasn't a good sign. I couldn't understand why she and Lady Jessalyn had moved to their battle stations so fully and so quickly. Then I saw that they were both taking deep breaths and snorting and heaving. They were inhaling my full bottle of Intoxicated and the scent was making them cocky and aggressive, like rival gang members staking out an urban schoolyard, spoiling for a bloodbath.

"I said that if your friend thinks that Prince Gregory will respond to some overdone, overblown, almost actress," said Lady Jessalyn, "then I hope she's booked a flight home."

"My friend is staying right here," said Rocher, kicking off her shoes. "Because she's going to be a princess!"

"A princess?" said Lady Jessalyn. "On what godforsaken, polluted planet? I mean, look at her hat!"

Lady Jessalyn was right. Tom Kelly hadn't been able to bring himself to create something appropriately gaudy — he was too strict. So I was wearing a prim, tasteful, minimal pillbox, covered in the same print as my dress. My hat was chic and stylish but I couldn't compete with Lady Jessalyn. She was wearing a nubby ice blue bouclé suit with a short skirt emphasizing her toned thighs and sleek calves, but her hat was her trump card: It was an ice blue bouclé pirate ship in full sail, with a crew of white crepe de chine orchids, and rigging made from ropes of seed pearls.

There was a wood-grained crewelwork ship's wheel and a pyramid of adorable butterscotch corduroy barrels of whiskey on deck, while an elaborately hand-beaded Jolly Roger flew from a bamboo mast and a brave, yellow silk daffodil walked a burlap plank.

"Rebecca's hat is just fine," Rocher insisted to Lady Jessalyn. "But what happened to you? You look like a family of Smurfs jumped on your head and started having sex with a roll of toilet paper."

"Please," I said. "Please stop, both of you!"

"Stop what?" asked Rocher. "Do you want me to stop standing up to this total slut?"

"Or would you like me to stop speaking my mind," asked Lady Jessalyn, "to this tattered storybook gnome?"

"No," I told both of them. "Please stop breathing!"

A menacing circle of party guests was forming around us, and everyone was taking in deep draughts of my perfume and reeling and knocking belligerently into whoever was standing behind them. Titled, elderly gentlemen were unbuttoning their high starched collars, balling up their waistcoats and dropping them onto the ground, while their distinguished, frail and ordinarily teetotaling wives were guzzling champagne from the bottle and groping the waiters.

"Rebecca Randle will never marry Prince Gregory," Lady Jessalyn decreed, her hands on her hips, thrusting out her chest, which made her triple strand of pearls bounce. "And not just because she's nothing and nobody. It is a legal impossibility, because Rebecca Randle is . . ."

The crowd was pumping its collective fists in the air and chanting, "WOOF! WOOF! WOOF!" like rowdy frat boys at a kegger. A duke had stripped to his boxers and three Swedish countesses were soaking one another's dresses with pitchers of water.

"What is she, Lady J?" hooted a Lord Somebody, who was wavering atop the shoulders of a Lebanese billionaire, who'd knotted someone's discarded pantyhose around his forehead, the legs flapping like the ears of a soused bunny.

"She can't marry the prince," said Lady Jessalyn, holding both fists high over her head in triumph, "because she's an American!"

"OOOO . . . ," said the crowd before lurching toward Rocher for her rebuttal.

"And what have you got to say about that?" demanded a woman who, while still in her wheelchair, had removed her skirt and was using it to fan her vibrantly floral panties.

"I'm sorry," said Rocher, in a tight, calm, precise tone, "but I've Googled this issue and while it might be an obstacle if Rebecca were, say, divorced or a convicted felon, England has no legal objection to an American marrying into the Royal Family. But Lady Jessalyn can never possibly marry Prince Gregory and become his princess, because of a single, insurmountable, moral and ethical barrier."

I'd never heard Rocher use any of these words before; my Intoxicated had twisted her into a crusading District Attorney on one of her favorite TV crime shows, making her dramatic closing remarks to a riveted jury.

"Why not?" asked Lady Jessalyn, outraged and teetering, her eyes unnaturally wide and blazing. "Why can't I marry Prince Gregory?"

"Because, and I am sorry to mention this," said Rocher. "And I do wish you only the very best. But, and let me phrase this in layman's terms . . ."

Layman's terms? Rocher?

"Lady Jessalyn, you will never become a princess, because you are such an unbelievable fucking CUNT!!!"

As Rocher reached for Lady Jessalyn's hat, Lady Jessalyn grabbed a fistful of Rocher's hair. As they tumbled to the ground, clawing and cursing, the crowd detonated, chanting, "GO! GO! GO!" as everyone began placing bets, rooting for their favorite and shoving one another merrily. As the security staff waded into the fray, attempting to remove Rocher's teeth from Lady Jessalyn's ankle, and Lady Jessalyn's fingers from around Rocher's throat, I caught sight of Prince Gregory's head, and his grand-mother's, as they were being swiftly spirited away, along with my future.

At the hotel, I gave Rocher a tray of cupcakes along with five sleeping pills and sent her off to her room, because I needed to be alone and because she wouldn't stop apologizing and offering to slice off various body parts as a show of remorse.

Soon my Ascot dress lay heaped on the floor while the rest of me huddled under the covers with all of the curtains and blackout drapes drawn. I'd turned off my phone and I'd asked the front desk to screen any ticking packages, Molotov cocktails or irate English people waving machetes. So when someone began pounding on my door I assumed it was Rocher until a gruff voice barked, "Scotland Yard, Miss Randle! Please allow entrance!"

Oh my God — I was going to be arrested. I was going to be held justifiably responsible for the Ascot riot and if I was lucky I'd only get cuffed and deported, or if the Royal Family was choosing to press charges, I'd do time. I fleetingly wondered if English jails looked more like the boarding schools in English movies, where there might be rackety plumbing but at least everyone would wear those jaunty striped scarves. As the knocking grew more insistent, I thought about knotting sheets together and shimmying down the side of the building but people only do that in cheeseball

American movies, so I grabbed a red silk kimono and took a quick scan in the mirror of the squashed and creased Becky, knowing it would be a calm and exquisite Rebecca facing the officers. And I prayed that her beauty might hypnotize them, but since the police would be English, I knew that Rebecca's tall-poppy splendor would only triple her jail time. Finally, I just accepted my fate and opened the door.

"If you'll please come with us at once," said one of eight uniformed men; given the Ascot triage, they'd probably been anticipating a struggle.

"Can I put some clothes on?"

"As quickly as possible."

I tried to find an appropriately somber and law-abiding outfit but all I had was a closetful of Tom Kellys, so I opted to be booked and fingerprinted in style, in my original red dress, because at least I'd take the world's most fabulous mug shot. The officers marched me to the elevator, which surprisingly rose, because there was undoubtedly a police helicopter waiting to chopper me out to some barren island hellhole where the thieves and murderers would alternate between knifing me and grilling me about Jate Mallow.

The elevator opened onto a midnight picnic. The roof's industrial air-conditioning units, ductwork and chimneys were draped with white twinkle lights and there were brass planters with rose bushes and tall, swaying ferns. Someone was standing a few yards off. He swiveled and I saw that it was Prince Gregory, in jeans and a white dinner jacket. He told the police, "Thank you so much, gentlemen. If you could please guard the exits and see that we're not disturbed, I'd be so grateful."

I was beyond confused. Why had the prince commandeered the rooftop and what was the deal with the dinner jacket and why, now that I noticed, were there silver candelabra with tall, flickering white candles standing on the tar paper beside the flowering planters?

"I'm so sorry we couldn't spend more time together at the races today," said the prince. "But sadly, and I'm not certain if you're aware of this, but a pair of crude American interlopers caused a hellish mess and were forcibly ejected."

"I had no idea," I replied, tentatively playing along. "I hope they didn't annoy Lady Jessalyn."

"I believe she's resting comfortably."

The prince led me to a round table draped with a heavy white linen cloth and set with an assortment of crystal stemware and china bearing his royal crest. He offered me a gilded bamboo chair and sat opposite me.

"I hope you don't mind but I've taken the liberty of ordering a light supper for the two of us."

"Thank you, that's great. But I've just got one question and I hope you won't be offended."

"Yes?"

"What are we doing?"

As the prince signaled for a nearby waiter to pour the champagne, he said, "Well, we really didn't get a chance to chat this afternoon."

"Because my best friend got into a fistfight with your girlfriend and it turned into an all-out drunken war."

"Which I must confess, I enjoyed immeasurably. So many stellar hats utterly destroyed. And do you know, until today, I'd never seen my great-aunt Estelle in just a bra and a smile, running out onto the track and dragging a jockey from the saddle, while joyously shouting, 'I'd like to ride you, you adorable little red-hot pepper!'"

Because the afternoon had been so upsetting, I was determined not to laugh as the prince continued: "And then Great-Aunt

Estelle covered that poor squirming jockey with those great, slurpy open-mouthed kisses."

I nodded and as my mouth began to twitch from not laughing, the prince asked, "Oh wait, I'm not certain — do you recall the last thing she said?"

I shook my head no, whipping my skull back and forth.

"Are you sure? Please, I'm desperate; you must help me remember it."

"I think," I said, taking a deep breath to retain my composure, "I think she said something like, 'I'm going to munch on one of your tiny little legs.'"

The prince agreed, and then, after a few more seconds of mutual, polite nodding, we both totally lost it and began pounding the table with helpless, sobbing laughter as the silent waiter struggled not to join in. Each time the prince and I tried to stop laughing and to behave decently by holding our breath and clamping our eyes shut, there'd be a second of silence and then we'd both lose control until we were panting and crawling on the ground.

"Did you see the Duke of Gloucester" — the prince gasped — "exposing himself to his mother and pointing to his penis and yelling, 'You made this! Was this the best you could do?'"

Finally, we laughed ourselves out because our stomachs were hurting and we couldn't breathe.

"I'm sorry," I said, pulling myself back up onto my chair. "I'm really, really sorry about all of it."

"No you're not," said the prince, which set us both off again until the only way we could stop laughing was to put our heads down on the table and not look at each other.

"But sadly," the prince admitted, "the rest of the country refuses to be amused."

"And now everyone hates me even more, for so many totally good reasons."

"Well," said the prince, "not everyone."

"You are being way too nice."

"And you, even after the Battle of Ascot, and now crawling on your belly, you remain compulsively lovely."

We looked at each other and neither of us could speak because we were so embarrassed and so deliriously happy, because now we knew that we'd not only liked kissing each other at the museum, but we both laughed at the same awful things. And for a second I did something truly insane: I completely forgot that we were the prince and Rebecca. I'd never been so comfortable around a guy before and so I allowed myself to believe that the moment was just what it felt like, which was a really fun date.

But then I reminded myself about Tom Kelly and my deadline and I forced myself to be practical, asking, "So what are we going to do?"

"First," said the prince, who was also pulling himself together, "we're going to have lobster bisque. And then we might stroll a few yards to the parapet, because I enjoy saying 'parapet,' and then we will survey the city and I will helpfully indicate the more trenchant landmarks, including Trafalgar Square, the Tate Museum and the soon-to-be-available homes of our most recently indicted public figures. And then I thought we might dance."

The prince turned and a row of rented footlights illuminated an eight-piece orchestra that began playing something that sounded familiar because it included the notes of my mom's ringtone, and then I remembered why my mom had downloaded that particular tune. It was the Love Theme from *Under the Tree*. It was a sweeping, way-too-goopy melody, the kind of song you could never get out of your head no matter how hard you tried; it was a song composed for kazoos and elevators and weddings held in turnpike steakhouses. It had been my mom's favorite song ever and even though it was the musical equivalent of a red velvet cupcake frosted with pink buttercream and those chalky little hearts that read "Kiss Me" and "Be Mine," just at this moment, I loved it, because I knew that the prince's generosity, and his eyes, and especially the orchestra would have made my mother swoon. Everything was in fact unbearably perfect, in an irresistibly Oscar-night sort of way, except for one significant detail I couldn't help bringing up.

"This is all pretty damn impressive," I said. "Even for a prince. But — what about tomorrow?"

"You mean, tomorrow, when the nation rises as one and demands your head on either a spike or a platter or hanging from a branch, as a piñata? The tomorrow when everyone insists that I return to the far more sedate and well-bred and only lightly bruised arms of Lady Jessalyn? Are you referring to that particular tomorrow?"

"Yes. And if we're both being honest there's something else I should ask you."

I was ashamed of myself for coming within a thousand miles of the word "honest," but there was something that Becky and Rebecca and whoever else I was, there was something we all needed to know.

"Do you love Lady Jessalyn?"

The prince looked away and my heart sank. Maybe I was just an American interlude; maybe we'd just been having fun, before he'd return to the serious business of choosing a bride. But then he faced me.

"I'm glad you've asked. Because, you see, I'm fond of Jessalyn. I've known her since I was a child. Whenever I turn around, there she is. And we've been friends, even when I've encouraged her to travel and to see other people and I've defended her when one of the papers gave her that dreadful nickname."

"Which nickname?"

"The Prettiest Pitbull."

We exchanged a meaningful stare in which we both promised not to start laughing again.

"But — do you love her?"

"I wanted to love her, because she'd be such a good idea and because it would make her so happy and because I once saw her laptop, and she'd Photoshopped different crowns onto pictures of herself."

This was exactly what Tom Kelly and Rocher had predicted, but come on, I wasn't any better than Lady Jessalyn. I was plotting to marry the prince with just as much drive and determination.

"But no, I don't love her. And now life has surprised me. Which brings us right back to tomorrow."

"And?"

"And from where I sit, we've got only one real chance, one final hope of salvaging the situation." The prince was looking right at me and I'm not sure why but I could swear that he was trying to somehow look beyond Rebecca's beauty, because it was so extreme. Her beauty was a barrier and he wanted to make sure that he broke through so that I'd believe what he was about to say.

"Tomorrow I'm being flown, in secret, for reasons of military security, on a goodwill visit to our troops in Afghanistan. And I'd like you to come with me."

16.

I assume you've seen the papers," said Tom Kelly at 5:00 A.M. the next morning, after I'd been summoned to his town house. I nodded, although, on Rocher's advice, I'd only skimmed the headlines and the tweets and the blogs and the more boldface words on the picket signs outside our hotel. I'd tried to avoid the terms "Ascot fiasco," "massive criminal charges," "wretched, rancid Rebecca" and "HO GO HOME!!!" Rocher had pointed out that Lady Jessalyn, even in the photos where she was missing her hat, a sleeve and a shoe, had managed to pose at an angle, with her palms placed over her hips, to look as thin as possible.

"And you understand that today," said Tom, "and this trip, are your very last chance? Not just at marrying Prince Gregory but most likely at remaining Rebecca?"

"I know."

"And you realize that the odds of your pulling this off are slim to none?"

"Got it."

Satisfied, Tom raised a hand and Mrs. Chen entered, pushing a gleaming chrome rack holding my outfit for Afghanistan. I'd been pretty sure that my life couldn't plunge any further down the toilet but I'd been wrong. Really wrong. Seriously wrong. So wrong.

"No," I said, squinting, because the garment was singeing my retinas. "No, I . . . I can't."

"Excuse me?" said Tom.

"I can't wear this. I know it's beautifully designed and sewn and I know you're a genius and I'm an ignorant mess, but are you out of your mind?"

Hanging on the rack was a tailored military jumpsuit with fringed epaulets, multiple pleated pockets and shiny red buttons embossed with Tom's initials. The jumpsuit itself was made from an eye-blistering, oversized camouflage print of huge, overlapping, amoeba-like blobs in throbbing shades of scarlet, hot pink and magenta, and it was accessorized with red patent leather spike-heeled combat boots, a matching wide red patent leather belt and a perky red wool beret, pinned with a large, silvery Tom Kelly logo. There was also a boxy, battlefield-ready purse in a red, pink and magenta leopard-skin pattern and, crisscrossed over the jumpsuit's chest, from shoulder to waist, there were bandoliers of what were either hundreds of Tom Kelly Hot Combat lipsticks or runway-perfect, gotta-have-em glossy red bullets.

The outfit may have been Tom's idea of a uniform but it would only camouflage me if I was dropped behind enemy lines into a card shop on Valentine's Day.

"If I wear that," I said, "people will shoot at me. People should shoot at me. I'll look like a clown at a gay kid's birthday party."

"Rebecca," said Tom, "I believe we have an agreement. That, if you wish to remain Rebecca, you will wear what I tell you to wear. And do everything I say."

I mentally ran through my options: I didn't have any. I stared at Tom, hoping he'd cackle and shout, "Kidding!" but he didn't. As Mrs. Chen zipped and buckled and buttoned me into the jumpsuit, she handed me a bayonet with the handle stitched in red calfskin and the blade etched with the words "Tom Kelly." It could only be used to slash other designers.

"But . . . but . . . ," I sputtered, still hoping for a reprieve.

"It's so . . . not Tom Kelly. It's so over the top. Why are you making me wear this?"

"Because people have accused me, at times, of playing it safe. Of sticking to clean lines and simple silhouettes. Well, I'm going to prove that I can step outside my comfort zone and still create a sensual and flattering look. And not only is the camouflage print a classic, it will disguise any bloodstains. So please put down the bayonet and stop pointing it at me. Mrs. Chen, show her where it's supposed to go. Yes, in that hidden pocket on the thigh. Perfect."

When Prince Gregory first saw me at dawn on a private airstrip outside London, his face didn't move. I could see his mind ticking off possible explanations for what I was wearing although the only reasonable answer was that all of my other clothes had been stolen and I'd been forced to borrow a costume from an especially garish musical about Che Guevara's showgirl sister, Tiffany-Kelli Guevara. Because the prince was the kindest man I'd ever met and because his parents had raised him to be polite and because he didn't know how to begin even discussing my jumpsuit, he didn't say anything except, "Good morning — I'm so glad you're here."

We were flown in an unmarked, private 747 on a ten-hour flight to a secure airstrip outside Kabul, the Afghan capital. Then we were moved onto a smaller military plane for a two-hour hop to a remote base that housed troops from both England and America. The prince had served in the English military and while he hadn't been allowed onto any battlefields, he was respected by all of the officers and soldiers we were introduced to, especially because he was fluent in all sorts of soccer and rugby scores that left me blank. I tried to fold in on myself and become as inconspicuous and obedient as possible so that no one would notice what I was wearing, which was like trying to hide hundreds of torrid red helium balloons by asking, "What hundreds of torrid red helium balloons?" So far everyone had been very nice and a female recruit had suppressed her laughter, although she had asked me if Tom Kelly had started his own army.

"Are you all right? Hanging in?" said the prince over the grinding roar of the military plane's engines. I knew I'd become spoiled because I found myself longing for the billion-dollar hush and the cuddly cashmere bolsters of Jate Mallow's borrowed jet but I suspected that it wasn't a good time to whimper, "But aren't there any magazines?"

"I'm fine," I told the prince, although my stomach knew I was lying. "What exactly do you need me to do?"

"You'll need to become two things: every man's dream girl and every woman's best friend. It was my mother's specialty — the charm assault. Once she brought me with her on one of those puddle jumpers in the Congo. She was wearing jeans and a T-shirt with the logo of a relief organization, and I watched her as she spoke with a tribal warlord. She was asking him to allow a shipment of food and medical supplies to reach a remote village. And she worked her magic but I remember noticing that, tucked into the waistband of his pants, the warlord had a gun."

"Your mother was fearless," I said, and then I got very quiet, because the prince's story had made it clear that we were on a plane headed for an extremely dangerous and deeply foreign part of the world. I'd been experiencing all sorts of high life but I'd never been so far, not just from Missouri, but from safety.

"Are you scared?" the prince asked gently.

"Yes."

"So am I. I mean, we'll be surrounded by security, we're completely coddled, but we will be meeting a great many very brave people in a very difficult region."

"But — you've done this before."

"And I'm always scared. I'm scared that people will laugh at me, which they have every right to do. And I'm scared that they'll call me a brat and a tourist, which they also have every right to do."

It had never occurred to me that someone in the prince's position would ever be scared of anything and I wondered if, just maybe, we weren't all that different. Maybe on some level everyone's just a Becky, trying to be a Rebecca.

"Oh, and while we're here," the prince added, "if you can, I'd also like you to end global warming, promote gender equality and erase thousands of years of religious and ethnic strife."

"I can do that."

"Are you sure?"

"That's why I wore the beret."

Then the prince leaned forward and took my hand.

"You're going to be great," he said and he was suddenly so sincere and so deeply concerned with my happiness that I wanted to hug him or cry or throw myself out of the plane without a parachute but mostly, I wanted to make the prince proud of me.

Our transport was met by only a small contingent of officers since Prince Gregory had requested as little royal deference as possible. As I was introduced, everyone was welcoming and it dawned on me that despite far-reaching, Internet-driven snipe these people had better things to do than either be aware of my existence, or hate me.

"Welcome to Her Majesty's Base K-51, Ms. Randle," said a lieutenant in properly sand-colored camouflage gear and a helmet. "Good to have you. I'm sure our troops will be very happy to see you."

"Thank you so much," I said, trying not to sound pathetically grateful for his good manners.

"And I'm loving the boots."

We were shown just a fraction of the base because the prince had to remain under heavy guard at all times and we were quickly ushered into a block-long canvas tent draped with netting, which served as a mess hall. There were rows of battered folding chairs and wobbly cafeteria-style tables and the prince and I were installed behind a central food-service station to dish out soup, mashed potatoes and bread onto the dented metal trays of the soldiers who were beginning to straggle into the tent. A line formed and I suspected that the soldiers were more interested in a decent meal than in gabbing with royalty or whoever I was.

"Good to meet you," said Prince Gregory, expertly scanning the name tag of the first soldier to take his place in line. "Private Krenley. I'm Greg. Where are you from?"

Prince Gregory asked each recruit for his or her hometown and how long they'd been in the service and in Afghanistan. The prince had been conducting these mini interviews since childhood but the effort and his interest in the details of the soldiers' lives wasn't rote and he didn't seem to be congratulating himself on reaching out to lesser mortals. He'd mastered the most accomplished form of celebrity; he looked each soldier in the eye and picked up on details which led to further, personalized questions. I paid attention to the prince's example and I tried to make sure that my friendliness wasn't fleeting or phony as I met Private Drew Hemplers, from Maryland, Colonel Colin Stannard, from Sussex, and Sergeant Stacey Craddow, from Butte, Montana.

I didn't see who was next in line because my steel ladle had become embedded in the vat of mashed potatoes and I was jiggling it. "I'm sorry," I said without looking up. "I'll be right with you."

"Take your time, ma'am," said the next soldier and when I jerked the ladle free, before I could read his name tag, he said, "I'm Cal."

It was Cal Malstrup and I knew that he was from East Trawley, Missouri. I'd heard that he'd enlisted and here he was, in uniform, with his head of once center-parted, dishwater blond hair all but shaved. Like many very young soldiers he resembled an angelic serial killer, all nose and ears and sunburn.

"Ma'am, I hope this doesn't sound rude or outta line," he said, "but you sure are, well, I don't think the word 'pretty' even begins to cover it. Or even 'beautiful.' You're like the final frontier."

I was both terror-stricken and ecstatic. I was sure that Cal would recognize me and part of me wanted him to. I hadn't seen him since our graduation ceremony in the East Trawley High School auditorium, where he'd sat with his arm around Shanice, who'd partially unzipped her black robe so everyone could see her lacy pink camisole and her lacy pink cleavage and she'd tilted her mortarboard to one side, as if it were a fun, new hat thing that she'd bought to wear while playing miniature golf or for going to the Jamesburg Shopping Plaza with her friends to buy more fun hats. When I'd marched down the center aisle, holding my rolled-up diploma, Cal had looked away and then, I think, nodded at me, imperceptibly. I'd kept my black robe zipped all the way up and I'd worn my mortarboard centered and low so I'd looked, according to Rocher, like I was graduating from the nerd academy and applying to night school in pest control.

"Thank you, soldier," I told Cal, in the mess hall. "I'm Rebecca Randle."

"Really? That's so weird, 'cause back home, I knew a girl named Becky Randle, just like you. Only, whoa, I mean, she wasn't anything like you."

"Was she your girlfriend?"

"Oh no. I mean, we almost went to a dance once and she was nice and all but we were more, like, just hangin' out. You know, not hookin' up or anything."

"Was she pretty?"

"Becky? I . . . well, I guess she was okay looking but I mean, she wasn't the sort of girl where that's the first thing you'd say about her, you know?"

I inhaled sharply. I felt even worse than when I'd first heard that Cal was taking Shanice to prom and more hurt than when I'd been rated "nada special" on Pretty Or Shitty? I'd thought that Rebecca would be my armor, my emotional Kevlar vest, so that I'd never have to feel that bad or that small or that completely obliterated ever again.

I wanted to smash my ladle over Cal's head and scream at him. I wanted Becky's head to shoot out of my mouth and give Cal a heart attack. I wanted to make him crawl and apologize; I wanted Rebecca to stand, with her arm around Becky's shoulders, and inform Cal that Becky was smart and pretty and popular and that he didn't deserve her. And then I wanted Becky to give Cal a well rehearsed, high-minded lecture on how to treat people and about how looks and popularity and family money shouldn't mean anything and about how Shanice was personally responsible for the attacks on the World Trade Center.

Why did Cal's approval and his romantic attraction mean so much to me? I knew that he wasn't the only person who'd describe Becky Randle as mild and faceless, as a girl who kept her head down and succeeded at not being noticed. And now I was Rebecca, the most beautiful woman in the world, and Cal was right where I thought I'd always wanted him, standing in front of me and all but pawing the ground with lust. So what was I after? Respect? Justice? Worship? No. Because he'd known Becky and now he'd met Rebecca, I wanted Cal to do the impossible. I wanted him to stop me from going crazy. I wanted him to do what I couldn't because I wanted him to tell me who I really was.

"Rebecca?" said Prince Gregory, nudging me with his elbow as I'd begun to hold up the line.

"Ma'am?" asked Cal. "Are you okay?"

As I struggled to answer that question, a blast shook the tent, jarring the ground, and for the next few seconds, from beneath and around every flap of canvas, huge choking gusts of sand began to billow in. There were sounds of whistling mortars and machine-gun stutters, which made everyone dive for cover and lunge for their weapons, except for the people who'd already been hit and who'd crashed against the tables, clutching suddenly blood-drenched limbs.

A team of insurgents, I later learned, had highjacked a military van, loaded it with bombs and used a suicide volunteer to drive the van into the base's main gate, blowing it to bits. At least twelve heavily armed Taliban had followed this blast onto the base, to exactly where they knew the prince would be. Which was how I found myself standing at the center of what had once been a busy mess hall and was now just tottering metal supports and splintering wooden poles, some of them on fire, attached to charred bits of canvas. Through the smoke and the gunfire and the shouting in several languages, I could see that Prince Gregory was sprawled on the ground beside me, barely conscious and bleeding from a chest wound. As I knelt, an insurgent wearing fatigues with his head and face shrouded in fabric came running toward me, taking aim with his automatic weapon.

Three elements took simultaneous control of my mind and body. First, the stunt training, which I had practiced on *High Profile*, swung into gear, as if we were reshooting a more dangerous and action-heavy climax to the movie. This was coupled with my fierce protectiveness toward Prince Gregory, and not just because he was a wounded, moaning fellow human being; I became furiously English and superhumanly proud of the crown, which I would never surrender or allow to be tarnished by some terrorist lunatic. And most critically, Tom Kelly's formfitting and ridiculous camouflage jumpsuit had come to very active and invaluable life as the clashingly colorful fabric began gripping and guiding my arms and legs and making me, if not invincible, then at the very least, dressed to kill.

The strangest thing of all was this: I'd never felt so much like myself. I felt like I'd begun to assemble everything I'd been learning, and that Tom Kelly and I had become a team. I knew exactly what I had to do and, with the help of my jumpsuit and my newly acquired fearlessness, I might just be able to do it. It was as if Rebecca had told me, "You're ready," and given me a thumbs-up and stepped back.

I grabbed what was left of a wooden tent pole, yanking it from its base of poured concrete. As the terrorist came at me, he howled something and I knew that he was insulting me because I was a useless woman and a godless American and because even though I was fairly covered up, he could still see my face, along with the American flag earrings composed of pavé diamonds, sapphires and rubies, which Tom had insisted on "for a polished look."

As in any Billy Seth Bellowitch—helmed climactic on-screen battle sequence, time slowed and an invisible yet suspense-pounding digital clock appeared in the lower right-hand corner of my life, complete with a deafeningly rhythmic Euro-electro-pop soundtrack, based on my mom's ringtone. I saw the shrouded head of the terrorist bearing down on me, now yelling soundlessly. As an imaginary handheld cameraman circled me, I swung the jagged length of tent pole, first back around for momentum and then right into the side of the terrorist's head, connecting with an unbelievably satisfying, augmented crack, as if I were slamming a baseball bat into a melon with a microphone inside and hitting the whole thing out high over the bleachers and into the parking lot.

While the terrorist's head remained sort of attached, his neck snapped and hinged, and as his scarf fell away, his face betrayed surprise and his thought-bubble read, "But she's only a girl, in a really out-there jumpsuit! I didn't see that coming!" Then, as his features torqued into a final mask of hate, he slumped to the ground. As I took a breath, the fallen terrorist, like any freshly whacked monster, rose back up onto his unsteady feet, with his head wagging across his chest, and he pulled a revolver from his worn leather belt and pointed it at me. As he began, in one final, vengeful spasm, to squeeze the trigger, I spun three hundred and sixty degrees and kicked the gun out of his grasp, sending it arcing yards away, where it landed inside the tin pot of mashed potatoes that was now rolling in the dirt.

Then, just as I thought he'd run out of weapons, the terrorist reached into his sweat-soaked shirt and revealed a grenade. As he began pulling the pin using the teeth from his pendulum-like head, my sleeve wrenched my arm toward my thigh, where my hand came to rest against my Tom Kelly signature bayonet, tucked snugly within its designated pocket. My fingers closed around the handle, the jumpsuit raised my arm and the bayonet flew into the terrorist's palm and he dropped the grenade, with the pin remaining in place. Then the terrorist gave up and as he was dragged away, all I could think was, I guess I'm not in Missouri anymore. And I can take care of myself. And I can take care of Prince Gregory.

"Whoa . . . ," said Cal, peering out from behind the chaos of tables and chairs where he'd been flung by the initial blast. As he wobbled to his feet and watched as I cradled the gasping prince, Cal murmured, "Man, you are incredible." And to this day I'm not sure if I just thought it or if I said it out loud but I sent Cal the message, "Tell Shanice."

Even before the base had been fully resecured and the prince had been moved under heavy guard to a hospital unit, the video of my face-off with the terrorist, mostly from Cal's cell phone and also available in a remixed rap version, had been viewed and downloaded all around the world and I had become, depending on which tabloid you read, or which BBC or CNN anchor was reporting, "Princess Rambo," "The Gorgeous Guerilla" or throughout England, "Our Rebecca." I was being hailed as a selfless civilian hero, as Prince Gregory's ideal bride and as a role model for young girls everywhere. As the coverage and congratulations washed over me, I asked myself, would the reaction have been the same if, say, Cal had saved the prince? Sure, he would've been gushed over and invited for brief segments on every morning show, where he would've insisted that he was just doing his job and he'd have been offered a ghostwritten book deal and maybe the chance to appear, after a grooming makeover, as the centerpiece of a dating show, but he would've become a footnote, a wartime anecdote, the kid who rescued the king. But I became something greater: the world's most charismatic, heroic female pinup since Saint Joan and the best-dressed warrior since Wonder Woman. Everywhere I turned, a little girl or her mother or a patriotic stripper was wearing a knockoff of my Tom Kelly red camouflage-print jumpsuit, which gave Tom enormous satisfaction even as he groused, "And I'm not making a dime."

I was flown back to London with Prince Gregory on a jet outfitted with enough medical equipment and personnel to service a midsized city. A bullet had passed through Prince Gregory's shoulder and while his injuries weren't life threatening, he was being kept immobilized and sedated. As I held his hand he looked up into my eyes and asked, "Darling, why did you shoot me?"

"You know why."

"From what I've been told, after I was knocked unconscious, you seem to have disabled several thousand bloodthirsty infidels."

"They were trying to cut in line, for the chili."

"All right, what I'm going to say next will become quite sloppy, so let's both look in opposite directions, shall we?"

"Ready."

"You've saved my life. And there are no words. And I think that you really are the most wonderful girl."

"Because I saved your life?"

"What is it that you Americans always say — *hello*? Yes, I think you're wonderful because you saved me, but even before that I suspected something about you. Something quite strange."

"What? Why?"

"I suspected that you weren't just improbably beautiful. From that first moment at the children's hospital, you seemed obstinate. It was as if you were wrestling with your beauty and wary of it. You were demanding that I treat you as, oh, what's that awful expression, a human being. A very difficult sort of human being."

"And?"

"And I found that so annoying. And exciting. And then, as I've watched you, as you've dealt with so much, with the museum and the press and your friend Rocher, you've been so impressive. But beyond that, mysterious. And deeply private. And I keep thinking that I wouldn't mind spending the rest of my life trying to figure out just who you are. Because I love you."

I had two reactions. First, I couldn't speak. Maybe not for the rest of my life. I'd become determined to marry Prince Gregory so I could help people, but now he loved me. And he was brave enough, or drugged and delirious enough, to tell me. I knew that my mom had loved me and I knew that Rocher did and they meant everything to me, but I'd never let myself believe that someday, someone else, someone who wasn't a friend or a relative, but a guy, would love me. I didn't think I was important enough or interesting enough, or, okay, fine, pretty enough, for a guy to even notice me.

But my second thought crashed into the first: Who did Prince Gregory love? Becky or Rebecca? He'd picked up on a split and it intrigued him. But what would happen if he ever found out the truth? Would he even believe it? Would he feel foolish and disgusted and betrayed? Would he hate me if I hadn't always been beautiful? Would it matter? And how much?

"Darling?" said the prince, trying to vainly raise his injured arm and snap his fingers to grab my attention. He'd just said something else, which had zipped right past me because I'd been too lost in my own demented inner Q&A session.

"I'm sorry, what?"

"I'm sure that you'd like time to think it over and you might not even be at all interested and who could blame you? But could you at least offer, perhaps, a hint? A crumb? You could blink once for 'yes,' twice for 'absolutely not, you asshole,' and three times for 'I wish I hadn't saved you.' But please: Will you at least consider marrying me?"

Oh my God. The prince had proposed to me and I'd missed it. It was like I'd stepped out to get some Raisinets and a medium Diet Coke during the movie's climax, and there'd been an incredibly long line at the snack bar.

I was about to do the right thing, to warn Prince Gregory, to see if I could even begin diagramming the situation, to say, "I want to marry you more than anything but here's why I can't, there are these three dresses, right . . . ," but I stopped. Because he was looking at me with such helpless, impossible, only mildly sedated love, and I couldn't bear to hurt him and all I wanted was for him to keep looking at me that way forever or even for just a few more seconds. Because maybe Rebecca was used to having so many men, and especially Prince Gregory, look at her like that, but no one had ever looked at Becky with that kind of love.

"Of course I'll marry you," I said.

"Because you love me?"

"Because I really want to upset Lady Jessalyn."

"We were meant to be together. Because you're a terrible person."

I wanted to say, "You have no idea," but the prince had managed to prop himself up onto his good elbow and he had shut his eyes and was leaning toward me. I leaned forward and just as our lips were about to meet, he paused.

"But, darling?" he said. "Before the announcement and the ceremony and all of that hideousness, there's only one obstacle. You've got to do me the most enormous favor. And I'm sure that everything will go swimmingly, it's mostly a formality, but it is necessary for, you know, the future of the commonwealth."

"No, I'm sorry, but I'm not going to help you pee. Call a nurse."

"No, no, it's not that, although you are shockingly selfish. But before we can marry, you must meet my grandmother and ask for her blessing."

"Your grandmother?"

He sighed. "You know, the Queen."

17.

O kay, now pay attention, because this is really important," said Rocher once I was back in my hotel suite. Rocher had been so thrilled by Prince Gregory's marriage proposal that she'd completely forgotten her role in my earlier downfall and she was back on board as my foremost advisor on all things royal. "I've done all sorts of research but I can't totally get her. She's been Queen for, like, sixty years, since she was fourteen, and as far as I can tell she's always looked exactly the same. She wears really bright colors and carries these huge pocketbooks, which are coordinated with her outfits; they look like she's got a cinder block in them, in case she needs to take a swing at someone. Her husband is dead, Princess Alicia is gone and Gregory's her heir to the throne. Some people love her because she's like all old-school and dignified and frumpy and other people think she's scary, like they forgot to put a cushion on her throne so her butt's been aching for sixty years and she's never gonna smile at anyone except her seventy-two dogs."

"She does not have seventy-two dogs!"

"Almost! They're her favorite things! Some people say that she loves those dogs more than her family or even the whole country! So when you go to see her, that's gonna be the biggest deal of all, if you want to get her okay to marry Prince Gregory. If you want to become a princess you've got to be really nice to the fucking dogs."

"She's right," said Tom Kelly in my suite the next day as he and Mrs. Chen fiddled with my presentation outfit. "The dogs are key. I was thinking of sewing bits of liver into the hem of this dress."

"What?"

"Or mixing you a fragrance called In Heat by Tom Kelly. But here's what I've come up with. Most girls, when they're meeting their in-laws, they tend to dress down to seem modest and conservative and they end up looking like they're making a court appearance, after they've been arrested for getting drunk and plowing their minivan into a busload of schoolchildren."

"Okay . . . ," I said, because after the success of the camouflage jumpsuit, I wasn't about to question Tom's logic or finesse.

"But I think the Queen would see right through that. I think you need to make a statement."

My dress was made of heavy, stiff white duchesse satin, splattered with the most extreme abstract print I'd ever seen. It was as if Tom had backed me against a wall, shut his eyes and used a wide housepainter's brush to fling screaming red enamel across my torso and then used a stick to add wild, jagged slashes of jet black. There was a short, matching collarless 'jacket with sleeves that stopped and flared in the middle of my forearms to display armloads of chunky red-lacquered bracelets and I was issued one glossy red satin high heel and its mate in black suede. My purse was a circular vinyl box covered in a mammoth red-and-black houndstooth check and my hat was a black comb with three long, savage red feathers arcing over my head, like a fountain of nail polish. Mrs. Chen's final addition was a pair of short white satin gloves with the fingers dipped in more wet-look red, as if I'd just been called away from performing open-heart surgery.

"It's defiant," said Tom, "and I think she might go for it. God knows she loves color and this is a dress that says, 'Baby, we both know that when you die, I'm gonna be the Queen.'"

Drake drove me to Buckingham Palace for an afternoon tea that Prince Gregory wasn't allowed to attend. "She wants one-on-one," the prince had told me, "and remember, they have a metal detector."

While I wasn't carrying any contraband, I did worry that my outfit might set off, at the very least, the palace's sprinkler system.

Drake had been instructed to leave me at the elaborate iron-work front gates, where the Beefeaters stood guard in their brass-buttoned red coats and those tall hats that look like mutant pinecones. These sentries allowed me to pass and then I had to walk across the wide, reddish gravel forecourt all by myself. The palace loomed ahead, with three intimidating stories of lime-stone and fluted columns and row after row of high, paned windows; I felt like I was being marched into the police head-quarters of some communist regime for waterboarding and interrogation. I caught a flicker of movement at one of the dark-ened, draped windows, as if someone was either checking me out or taking aim through the sight of a high-powered weapon.

Once inside the palace I was greeted by a woman who intro-duced herself as "Lady Veronica Arnstelt-Bowen, Ranking Secretary to Her Majesty." Lady Veronica was wearing a fuzzy woolen suit that wasn't gray or pink or cream, yet included all of these colors, as if a few dozen kittens and a visiting Easter chick had crawled all over her and settled in for a mass nap. And while Lady Veronica's smile was steady I knew that I'd been instantly judged and that whatever Lady Veronica's assessment might be, it had been copyedited, fact-checked and filed in a small cement room lit by bare bulbs in the subbasement of her brain. Lady Veronica was most likely in her fifties and she hadn't undergone any cosmetic procedures except for a hint of almost medicinal beige lipstick and two barely blended circles of rouge, like inflamed mosquito bites. Her face was rigid with diligence and dignity, which are English Botox.

Lady Veronica took me through a mile of high-ceilinged corridors, all lined with many sizes of ancestral portraits of people who looked as if they'd never approved of being alive. We passed rooms overstuffed with chintz-slipcovered sofas and wing chairs, all with deep, sighing indentations, and there were acres of mahogany paneling and threadbare oriental carpets. So far the palace wasn't some sort of feudal castle in a horror movie, with crusty suits of armor guarding stone walls. It felt more like God's country house, if God were an Englishman with plenty of housekeepers, a harpsichord or three and a fondness for crackled ceramic dog figurines. One room was filled by a gallery of dog portraits, with Labradors and Dobermans and rottweilers standing alert beside fences, snoozing across hearths or decked out in lace ruffs, powdered wigs and plumed velvet hats, using their paws to raise delicate handkerchiefs to their wet noses.

We reached a library where the double-height walls were lined with tiers of bookshelves fronted with golden chicken wire; there was a narrow catwalk midway up, running around all four walls. Expensively comfortable antique furniture, what Rocher would call "you know, real grandma stuff" was arranged in at least five separate groupings with a central family of armchairs and couches facing a white marble fireplace carved with marble vines, cherubs and animals, all climbing to the room's coffered ceiling, which was inset with layers of moldings and gilded and painted crests. The room would have outraged Tom Kelly because floating in the shafts of sunlight from the high, stained glass windows, there was dust.

"Your Majesty?" said Lady Veronica. "I have Rebecca Randle."

The Queen rose from a tufted, high-backed, green leather armchair by the fireplace. As she stood, the carpet near her feet came to life, because eight small dogs had been dozing at her feet. These were the corgis, which were the weirdest dogs I'd ever seen, each with the tiny, alert ears of a fox, the sleek snout of a collie, the body of a long-haired beagle and the stunted tootsie-roll legs of a dachshund. They were sniffing the air busily, as if something in the atmosphere might allow them to grow taller and wider. As with short men, they were hypersensitive, straining and adorable and I wanted to pick each of them up. But, as with short men, I knew they'd be offended.

"Good afternoon," said Queen Catherine. "So pleased to meet you."

The dogs, in unison, let out an ominous, low growl and while they didn't lunge they all leaned toward me, with only their stubby little legs preventing an attack.

"Hush," said the Queen, and then, to me, "I was speaking to the dogs."

As Rocher had directed, I curtsied, which gave me a second to size up the situation. By now I'd met tons of celebrities and almost none of them came even close to matching their magazine covers or baseball cards or ads for vitamin-infused bottled water. Queen Catherine, however, looked exactly and only like herself and I wanted to pull out a five-pound note and hold it up to her face just to check, and marvel at, the similarity and the Queen's lack of vanity. She'd refused to have her nation's money Photoshopped.

Her face was both sharp and sweet, like an efficient yet maternal postmistress in an ad for some new overnight shipping service. She wore oversized, pinkish eyeglass frames and a carefully applied coat of baby-pink makeup, more powdered sugar than concealing mask. Her lips were the shiny cherry red of a Life Saver and her hair had been shellacked into a glistening, untouched snow bank. But what really wowed me was her outfit: She was wearing thick opaque stockings in the mature-shopper shade called nude, a pleated gray, just-below-the-knee cashmere skirt and a silk blouse with tufted shoulders, billowing prairie-pirate sleeves ending in wide gauntlet-style cuffs fastened with ten mother-of-pearl buttons apiece and, at the neck, a bow so full and cheery that it belonged on one of those holiday wreaths that fills an entire front door. The bonus was the color. The Queen's blouse was a vibrant black, which set off the different sizes, from half-dollars to Frisbees, of happily Crayola, rainbow polka dots. The Queen looked like the most wished-for birthday gift or a blue morning sky dancing with jubilant hot-air balloons and before I could help myself, I blurted out, "You look fantastic!"

"As do you," replied the Queen. "It's dreadful, isn't it — so many people are afraid of color."

I almost went for a high five or a fist bump in support of bold color but the dogs revved up their growling so I kept my distance. I was about to say, "I like your house," but I knew it would sound dumb and then I didn't know what to say, because meeting the Queen of England to discuss my potential marriage to her grandson was something that no one, not even Rocher, had really prepped me for.

"Your Majesty," I began, settling for being as open and truthful as I could, "thank you so much for agreeing to see me. . . ."

"Of course I would see you," said the Queen, gesturing for me to take a seat opposite her on a bottle green tufted leather sofa with rolled arms. "You have saved my grandson's life, for which I am profoundly grateful."

"He's worth saving."

"Much of the time."

As she said this the Queen smiled and I could see her resemblance to Prince Gregory.

"And now that he's on the mend," the Queen continued, "I take it he wishes to marry you."

As she said this, all the dogs yipped in outrage, a canine Hallelujah Chorus of high-pitched protest. I wasn't sure if the Queen had discreetly signaled them or if the dogs had been following our conversation, but either way, they weren't pleased and they weren't about to shut up.

"Pups!" the Queen commanded in a firm, louder tone, silencing her pets. "I'm sorry, but they've been extremely concerned."

"About Prince Gregory getting married?"

"Of course. You see, these are corgis, which are the most highly intuitive mammals next to man, although in my opinion, their speculations are far more accurate. They shredded my last undersecretary's shoe, which led me to demand a thorough investigation of her past and my representatives discovered that she had in fact forged several checks on my household accounts. I have spoken with our prime minister about including corgis in our nation's judicial system although he's been sadly reluctant."

I was about to jabber about how much I loved dogs and to ask the corgis' names but I knew I wouldn't be fooling them. I'd sound like I was pretending to be interested in someone's bratty children by asking them which grades they were in and whether they liked their teachers.

"Pups," said the Queen and the dogs formed a half circle around her, like dutiful students on a field trip. "Of course Gregory wishes to marry Miss Randle. She is an extremely beautiful and accomplished young woman."

One of the dogs began to whine and the Queen addressed her. "I beg your pardon, Natalie, but acting in a film can indeed be considered an accomplishment. Of sorts."

The Queen lowered her teacup onto its saucer and placed the

saucer on a side table. The initial friendly, getting-acquainted portion of our meeting had ended.

"I shall ask you three questions. And if we are satisfied with your responses . . ." She and the corgis exchanged a righteous nod, as judge and jury. "Then we shall offer our blessing and wish you only the greatest and most lasting happiness in your marriage to Gregory. If, however, your answers are unsatisfying or incorrect . . ."

All of those beady little eyes, including the Queen's, glared at me. "Then today, after you leave the palace, you will never see my grandson, or England, ever again. Not a note, not a phone call, there will be absolutely no further communication between you of any kind, let alone a wedding. Are we understood?"

"Yes."

"First question."

One of the corgis began to whimper and the Queen told him, "No, Patrick, you may not ask the first question. She won't understand you. Not with that lisp." The corgi sat down, disgruntled but silent.

"First question: Which person have you loved most in your life? And do not name my grandson, that's too easy."

I swear I didn't imagine this but the corgis all lowered their heads and rolled their eyes. Only English dogs are capable of sarcasm.

"My mother."

"Why?"

"Because she was my mom, and because she didn't have an easy life. She came from nothing and when she got pregnant my father left her and never came back. And she worked at three jobs, from 6:00 A.M. till midnight, until she gained too much weight and had to go on disability."

"She did?"

"But before all of that, she had another life and she was unbelievably beautiful. And it must have been hard for her to give that up but she never felt sorry for herself, or whined or even talked about it. And she always made sure that I had clothes and food and a roof over my head. I'm still not sure what happened to her but I loved her more than anything. She was the best person."

"You're correct. Because, you see, I knew your mother."

The Queen of England knew my mother? Did the Queen own a trailer? "How? How did you know my mom?"

"Question Number Two."

I was flustered but if the Queen was forging ahead I must've done okay with Question Number One.

"If you should marry Prince Gregory you will become a Princess Royal. At some point, if and when the mood strikes me, I shall die. And you will become Queen. Which royal figure do you most admire and hope to emulate? And don't say Queen Catherine, because I wasn't born yesterday. Although I do have lovely skin." The corgis began obligingly licking the Queen's smooth pink hands. "I feel that corgi saliva is the finest emollient."

"Okay . . ."

"Which royal figure?"

"Princess Alicia."

"Why?"

"Because she was beautiful but she knew that wasn't enough. Because she used her beauty to make good things happen. Because she was smart and strong and opinionated and . . ."

"Stop. Please. I know just which adjective you're reaching for."

"Headstrong? Fierce? Generous?"

"Irritating."

"Excuse me?"

"You've only known the public Alicia. I was her mother. As a child, she was willful and fretful and thoroughly obnoxious; she wouldn't sit still, not for a moment. She'd go missing for hours, and we'd find her at the stables, renaming all of the horses in honor of her favorite mass murderers, or on the street, asking passersby if they'd like to purchase one of my handbags, which she claimed were ideal for smuggling infants out of the country. And when she was a teenager I thought she'd have to be hand-cuffed and manacled, so she wouldn't keep running off with some dreadful boy to purchase drug paraphernalia and knickers printed with crude portraits of me, which she'd reveal from beneath the skirt of her school uniform. It wasn't until years later that she took hold of herself and found some direction in life. And even then she was terribly vain, she'd ask, 'Mummy, am I too tall, are my shoulders too hulking, are my ankles too thick?' Which they were. But she could look marvelous and she knew how to put herself together or, more precisely, she knew whom to ask for guidance. And that was how we both came to know your mother."

"How?"

"There was a designer, named —"

"Tom Kelly?"

"Don't interrupt. Yes, Tom Kelly, an American, and he arrived in London to open some enormous boutique, a flagship. And Alicia was thrilled beyond all measure, as she adored Tom Kelly. She thought he was so handsome and she'd clip his advertise-ments and tape them to her mirror."

"So how did you meet Tom? And my mother?"

"Alicia convinced Mr. Kelly to open his shop with a gala ben-efit, raising funds to inoculate millions of children in Africa. And Mr. Kelly agreed, provided that Alicia would put in an appearance, although, of course, Alicia would have happily cooked those needy children into a steaming broth, for an oppor-tunity to meet Tom Kelly. So off she went and at the gala, Tom introduced her to a lovely young woman, whose face appeared on all of the packaging. Her name was Roberta Randle."

Almost no one had ever used my mother's proper name. In East Trawley she'd been Robbie Randle or even Robbie Jo.

"Well, the two girls hit it off, like a house on fire. Alicia dragged Roberta back to the palace for a girls' sleepover. They were up all night, chattering away about clothes and Tom Kelly and astrology and about which film stars were, I believe their word was, 'hunk-tastic.' They became inseparable and soon Roberta had met Prince Edgar, Alicia's husband, and their children. They called her Aunt Robbie."

This couldn't be true. Yes, like just about everyone, my mom had been obsessed with Princess Alicia and she'd filled shelves of scrapbooks with the most obscure details of the princess's life, and she'd encouraged me to appreciate Alicia's every good deed, one-shoulder Grecian gown and disarmingly shy smile. My mom had known Alicia's favorite treat — a thick, chocolate-frosted English cookie called a digestive — and the entire playlist of pop hits that Alicia had preferred while working out on her elliptical trainer. But I'd always assumed that my mom had acquired this intimate information from magazines and from the tell-all books written by Alicia's servants and distant cousins, within weeks after her death.

"Together, your mother and my daughter convinced Tom Kelly to use his success and his shops to support worthwhile projects around the world. Your mother had been with Alicia, in Kenya, on the day she died. She was supposed to share the same flight for their return to London. But instead Tom Kelly rang your mother and he summoned her back to the States. There was some sort of emergency. And so she stayed behind to board a more direct flight."

"So what you're saying is, my mother might've died, along with Alicia? If Tom hadn't called her?"

"Oh, I'm not blaming Tom Kelly or anyone else. Alicia's plane went down due to the worst weather and a freak electrical storm. It was no one's fault."

But had Tom known something? Or had a premonition? Had he saved my mother's life, or had he been implicated in Alicia's death?

"When Alicia died I was, as one might expect, bereft. Yes, she could be self-dramatizing and silly and she was always after me to exercise and to drink the most repellent protein shakes but as you've said, with all things considered, she was a wonderful girl. And she would have become at the very least, a truly original Queen of England."

The color had drained from the Queen's face and she looked away. The corgis bunched at her feet, nuzzling her ankles. I wanted to ask a thousand more questions, about my mother and Alicia and Tom Kelly, but I couldn't. From what Gregory had told me, the Queen almost never discussed his mother.

"She can't," he'd said. "She misses her too terribly. And she has no idea what to do with that."

"But that was all a very long time ago," said the Queen quietly. "And your second answer is acceptable."

"But, and I promise, I won't ask you anything else — how did you know that Roberta Randle was my mother?"

"I didn't. Of course, Scotland Yard has thoroughly researched your entire existence and found almost nothing. It's as if until a few short months ago, you didn't exist. But I'd been shown photographs of you and I'd noted a resemblance and when you walked in, I knew. I felt it. You had to be Roberta's daughter. You couldn't be anyone else."

"But . . ."

"Question Number Three. For, what is that expression? For all the marbles. You marry Prince Gregory. You become Queen. Years pass. Despite your lasting and affectionate union, one morning you receive a tearful phone call from a close friend. And you discover that your beloved husband, King Gregory, is cheating on you. Who knows why? Who can say? Your beauty might have begun to fade imperceptibly. Perhaps your popularity exceeds his own. He's growing older and knows it and requires a diversion. Whatever the cause, there it is. In your lap."

The corgis were eyeing me smugly, as if they'd known about the affair months before I did. If they had eyebrows, they were arching them.

"What do you do?"

I couldn't answer, because my mind was still on my mother and her friendship with Alicia. My mother had hated talking about Alicia's death; when we'd watched that TV documentary about Alicia and the narrator had reached Alicia's final days, my mom had shut off the set before being confronted with the expected map of the rough African terrain where the plane had gone down and the close-ups of the smoking wreckage. "It was just so sad," my mom had said, "and so unfair. Alicia was just getting started. There was so much more she wanted to do." Then my mom had shut her eyes and whispered, more to herself than to me, "But people die. Everyone dies. That's how it works." Was that why my mom had run away from her life with Tom Kelly? Had she felt guilty because she hadn't flown on Alicia's doomed jet? Was that why she'd left me Tom's phone number, so I could fulfill not her own goals, but Alicia's? And make payment on some sort of cosmic debt?

"Take your time. But we need your response."

"Well, um, I guess there's a few different ways to look at it. I mean, I could become really sophisticated and ignore the whole situation and assume that it's just a meaningless whatever and that if I wait, it will take care of itself."

"Yes, that is a possible solution. And is that your answer?"

"Or, or, I could confront the king and tell him that while our marriage is over, we should stay together, for the sake of the country. I'm sure that other royal couples have handled things that way, they figure out their priorities and then they lead separate lives."

"That is not an uncommon choice, and is that your answer?"

"My answer is . . ."

One of the corgis yapped and another corgi nipped the Queen lightly on her shin.

"Sheila?" asked the Queen. "What is your problem? Oh, oh, of course, thank you. How thoughtless of me. Bless you. Wait just a moment," the Queen said to me. "I'd almost entirely forgotten but Sheila and Teddy have reminded me. It's been so many years."

The Queen went to a nearby cabinet, opened the chicken-wire doors and slid out a small flat box that had been wedged between books. She handed me the box, which had the Tom Kelly logo. Inside I found a sterling silver picture frame with a photo of Princess Alicia and my young mother standing on either side of Tom Kelly, who had his arms around the waists of both women. Tom was in a tux and both women were wearing red, although not identical, Tom Kelly gowns. The trio was standing in front of the tall silver doors of what had been Tom's just-opened London store and everyone in the picture looked so terrific and they were all laughing. It was such a joyous and carefree photo but then I began to think about what had happened next, within a few months' time: The princess had died on a flight my mother might've shared. My father had left, leaving my mom pregnant and alone. And my mother's life had collapsed around her. I'd always been hard-nosed and I'd tried never to think about my dad, because I hadn't wanted to betray my mother. But now I wasn't imagining some faceless, unknown deadbeat. I was thinking about Tom Kelly.

Whenever the idea had surfaced, the remote notion that Tom Kelly might be my father, I'd shut down every last brain cell and banished any ounce of curiosity. Because while, sure, the timeline made sense, I couldn't believe it was possible. I refused to believe it. Because if Tom had been involved with my mother, why had he left her and never tried to contact her? Had she told him she was pregnant? Was that why he'd cut her off? With a child, had she no longer been an asset to the Tom Kelly brand? And were all men like Tom Kelly? Were they all faithless and ice-hearted and never to be trusted? Did they all secretly long to be rich, successful bastards who didn't care about anything but the survival of their empires, no matter who was trampled in the process?

"Your answer? If you discovered that our darling Gregory was unfaithful?"

"I would wait until he was sound asleep and then I would grab a rusty hunting knife and I would carve out his heart and serve it to him for breakfast, with hash browns and real maple syrup. And then I'd put on a clown suit with big shoes and one of those cardboard party hats with the elastic under the chin and then I would sing the national anthem and eat an entire box of Mallomars while I tap-danced on his grave."

There was a pause as the Queen looked to her corgis, and vice versa. There was instantaneous and positive agreement.

"Welcome to the family!" said the Queen, who stood and opened her arms, as the corgis ran to me and jumped on my legs, begging to be kissed and cuddled. While the Queen and I were embracing I thought, I'm hugging the Queen of England. I didn't have to remind myself to take notes, because I was pretty sure I'd remember everything.

Prince Gregory was waiting for me outside the palace gates, leaning against a low-slung, battered convertible: a forest green MG two-seater with chrome detailing, a burnished rosewood dashboard and the top down.

"Get in, and don't ask any questions."

As the prince drove in silence, I could tell that he was deep into a Renn Hightower, international-man-of-mystery fantasy and that he especially loved manfully cranking the stick shift, as if we were being pursued in a high-speed chase by any number of speeding black cars with ninjas hanging out the windows and blasting us with bazookas. We pulled into a private lot just outside the Tower of London, where the parking spaces were marked with stenciled crowns.

"Come on," said the prince as he hoisted himself out of the car, a Hightower move which would've worked if the prince hadn't caught his heel on the door handle and fallen headlong, cursing, to the pavement.

"Are you okay?" I asked.

"I meant to do that. Ordinarily I'm extremely suave. I hate you."

"I know," I said soothingly.

The prince took my hand and led me through a back entrance and into the Tower, using keys and touch pads to open a series of doors. He took me up a stairway, climbing five flights and passing a final security desk, where a uniformed guard opened a last heavy, brushed steel door that had one of those complicated, oversized locking mechanisms involving a wheel and a lever, which I'd only seen in photos of impenetrable Swiss vaults.

"You first," said the prince, propelling me into a large, darkened chamber with only glints of light bouncing off glass cases.

"Can we turn on the lights?"

"Not yet. I have something to tell you and for right now, I like that I can't see you."

"Why?"

"Because you're so — distracting. You must've noticed it all your life. People have enormous trouble speaking to you directly, because they're so caught up in your eyes and your mouth and your hair. Just sitting and smiling you're still — overpowering."

"I'm so sorry."

"I'm not complaining, I'm just — trying to cope with it. Every time we meet, I want to close my eyes so we can simply talk to each other and laugh and carry on. So I can just enjoy being with you."

"And so I can forget you're a prince."

"Precisely."

"Could you maybe use a different accent?"

"Shut up, I'm being serious, at least for me. Because this is rather nice, isn't it? All this darkness?"

I couldn't tell where the prince was standing. He was nearby but if I held out my hand I wasn't sure I'd reach him. I felt as if we were cat burglars in black turtlenecks keeping our voices down, or two kids daring each other to step inside the haunted mansion.

"I do love you," said the prince's voice.

"Wait — are you talking to me?"

"Stop it. What I wanted to say was that I love, I suppose, all of you. And not just the bits that get photographed eighty million times a day. Although, of course, those bits are perfectly acceptable."

"Can I ask you something? When the lights come on, are you going to be wearing just a rubber apron and a goalie mask?"

"You are revolting."

"I'm sorry!"

"Now I need a different mask."

"A goalie is fine."

"I've brought you here because from all reports, my grandmother now adores you, and the corgis agree, except for Sheila, who hates everyone. But you've cleared the final hurdle. And now there's something I'd like to show you."

"You're scaring me."

"Good. Because I've told you that I love you. And most important, I've told you in the dark. And now it's time for you to make your selection."

"My selection? Of what?"

The prince activated some hidden control panel, and very gradually, throughout the room, small, deliberate spotlights began to glow and I saw that I was surrounded by glass cases containing crowns, tiaras, swords, scepters and an assortment of crosses, medallions and royal orders, all studded with precious gems and displayed against velvet. It was a moment from a pirate movie where the toothless brigands enter a cave and whoop and kill each other over a legendary stolen fortune, made up primarily of coins, goblets and Egyptian statues of cats, all spilling from treasure chests and spray-painted bright gold. Even Madame Ponelle would be speechless.

"The Crown Jewels," said the prince, "and I don't know why, but every time I say that I feel I should be unzipping my fly."

"Oh my God."

"Of course, all the best stuff was melted down in 1649 by Oliver Cromwell, who wasn't fond of the monarchy. These pieces are all practically brand-new, it's really more of a yard sale."

"Do you sort of technically, own all of this?"

"Legally it belongs to both my family and the nation but we're allowed to borrow whatever we like, for coronations and jubilees and, of course, drunken nude jogs through Kensington Park."

"But why did you bring me here?"

"Because you require a wedding ring."

I stood perfectly still. When the prince had proposed to me and when he'd sent me to meet the Queen, that had all been a major deal. But this was serious and I grabbed the corner of a display case to steady myself. I remembered the small velvet box in my mom's trailer holding the scrap of envelope scrawled with Tom Kelly's phone number; that box had been designed to hold a ring. I could feel my mother smiling as what must've been her deathbed scheme neared completion. I also remembered how Rocher would drag me into the Dreamaire Precious-4-Less jewelry store at our strip mall, where she'd rate all the rings. "See, that one's barely a chip, so the guy would be either broke or a cheap jerk and this one's sort of medium-sized, like it's a decent starter ring, for a first marriage. But look at that rock — that's what Shanice Morain has her eye on. But she'll probably end up with a cubic zirconia and she'll tell everyone it's real, until she goes swimming and it melts."

"What are you talking about?" I asked the prince. "Am I supposed to pick something out? Do you want me to, I don't know, browse?"

"Yes. You can take your pick. I considered selecting something myself but I want this to be your choice."

I was torn between asking for a shopping bag, pointing to every case and saying, "I'll take that one and that one, and oh, that one over there, with the platinum setting, as a backup," and wanting to throw up my hands and say, "I can't," and running back down the stairs. Even for Rebecca, cruising the Crown Jewels was a leap. But then I heard those familiar few notes of music from *Under the Tree*, as if they were being played on a shepherd's flute on a distant mountaintop, drawing me toward a smaller case in a corner.

"Okay, you don't have to do this, because this is all too much and it's ridiculous, but right there, that is a very beautiful ring."

The ring was a simple gold band with a heart-shaped sapphire flanked by pearls. It wasn't the largest ring or the showiest and the heart shape was corny, but that was why I liked it. It was the prize in a maharajah's box of Cracker Jacks and it reminded me of my mom.

"That was my mother's ring. An excellent choice."

For a second, I wondered if the prince was going to unlock the case, but I knew that wouldn't be necessary because when the time came, the ring would fit and I pictured my mom and Alicia high-fiving each other, as if they'd been guiding my life together from some otherworldly war room.

"And I've also been thinking about something else," said the prince, "because our life together is always going to be fairly insane. There will always be so many other people surrounding us and so many demands on our time and so much to do. So I want there to be something that's only for us. A sort of secret code. And so I've been wondering if, whenever we're alone, if I might call you Becky."

I fainted. No, I didn't, but I almost did. I wasn't just going to marry Prince Gregory and I wasn't just going to wear his mother's ring. He'd gone a step further. And so I did something equally or even more dangerous, something I had no business doing, something strictly forbidden, but I did it anyway. I dared to think, he must really love me.

And when the prince leaned toward me for a kiss, I shut my eyes and we were once again swallowed by all of that impossibly romantic, priceless royal darkness.

18.

Six months later, my *Vogue* cover began to sell out on newsstands world-wide. The issue went through fifty additional printings, the most in the magazine's history, as the twelve pages of the soon-to-be Princess Rebecca were devoured and dissected and defaced at every hairstylist's salon, dentist's office and book-chain espresso bar, and there were videos of cardio rooms where every woman, on every treadmill, stationary bicycle and stairstepper were all reading my *Vogue*. Women clamored for everything I wore but Tom Kelly refused to manufacture a duplicate of my original red dress. Although, of course, the dress had already been knocked off in a range of cheaper fabrics, which only made Tom giggle as he watched a newscast of sweet sixteens and bat mitzvahs and quinceañeras in Bali and Kiev and East Orange, New Jersey, where so many females, at every age and social level, were primped out in some approximation of Tom's work.

"Look at that," Tom crowed. "Every girl on earth wants to be you."

Two weeks before my wedding, the studio rushed the release of *High Profile* into thousands of theaters with shows around the clock. The London premiere became, thanks to Prince Gregory, a benefit for Selina's burn unit and we auctioned the international rights to the most desirable photo, which was a shot of me standing in between the prince and Jate Mallow.

Tom Kelly told me that he hated designing red-carpet gowns. "Have you ever watched those award shows? Those women look like a dessert cart stacked with rotting parfaits." But for the premiere he forced himself to create a strapless, second-skin, Tom Kelly sensation, with one opera glove beaded with the Union Jack and the other with the Stars and Stripes; I was a one-woman international peacekeeping mission.

After the red-carpet apocalypse and the screening and the gala and the more elite after-party and the scarily exclusive after-after-party, I was alone in the back of my limo with Jate, as Drake kept the tinted windows sealed for our return to the hotel.

"You're a star, baby," Jate declared, waving an invisible cigar and speaking in a gravelly, leering drone.

"But, Jate," I asked, because it was 4:00 A.M. and we were like war buddies, sharing one last beer at a local hangout, "I was there with Gregory. Doesn't it ever get to you, that you can't go to these things, that you can't go anywhere, with your boyfriend?" I wasn't positive that Jate had a boyfriend because even with me, he was cagey about his private life. I understood the need for any scrap of privacy at Jate's level of fame because, just like me, he was compartmentalized.

"Oh, sweetheart," he said, "sure, it would be nice to bring someone along for the ride. And once in a while, although I have to be excruciatingly careful, I do find a guy who can . . . go with the flow. But all of this, this stuff, the fame stuff, the everything stuff, it hit me when I was so young, even younger than you. And I let it happen, because I'd wanted it so badly. And I didn't want anything, including my sex life, to get in the way. And I know that's selfish and horrible and maybe someday I'll meet someone and I'll wake up and I'll become a great role model for gay kids everywhere, who'll think I'm some creepy old dude, because by then I'll be thirty-one."

"I think that would be great! You should do it!"

"But, Rebecca, and you must already know this. Or you will very soon. When you want the sort of things, the sort of life, and the degree of fame, that we want, and you go for it, and you get it, for as long as it lasts — there's always a price."

"Like what?"

"There's a trade-off. A sacrifice. The world says, here you go, on a platter, you're rich and you're famous, and if you ever get bummed out, or psychotic, or even just a little antsy, here's what you do: You open the window of your Tokyo hotel suite and you just bathe in it, in the shrieking and the sobbing and the 'I love you so much!' from all of those thousands of wonderful fifteen-year-old Japanese girls, holding the life-sized cardboard cutouts of you over their heads. And in exchange for that, and, of course, for the opportunity to make great, meaningful art with the world's most creative minds . . ."

Now he was grinning.

"You make a deal. You surrender something. You say, fine, here, take my private life. Or my family. Or my sanity. And so, Rebecca?"

He was looking right at me with the same puzzled, scientific curiosity of Dr. Barry and Seeley Burckhardt, the people who'd gotten a little too close and had maybe caught a flicker of Becky peering out from somewhere deep within Rebecca's wide-set, emerald, too-flawless eyes.

"Be ready."

I turned away and noticed that along the back of Drake's neck and reaching onto his jaw, there was an almost invisible white scar, which must have been a remnant of the vicious beating he'd received, the price he'd paid, after he'd fallen in love.

"Okay. Okay. Okay." Rocher and I were standing in a side room at Westminster Abbey minutes before my wedding, and Rocher kept repeating "okay" to calm herself down as she treasured her reflection in a wall of mirrors installed for the occasion. All of the room's oak paneling and gothic plasterwork had been hidden beneath twelve-foot-high mirrored panels, so we were inside a diamond or an impromptu dance studio or a carnival fun house, surrounded by stacks of worn-out hymnals and a few broken lecterns.

For the past two weeks, London had shut down, or burst, as every shop window had been crammed with images of Gregory and me and every streetlamp had fluttered with a banner announcing our approaching nuptials and every souvenir kiosk had bristled with Gregory-and-Rebecca commemorative miniature porcelain tea sets, hand-painted key chains and plastic dinner plates featuring our heads shoved close together, our foreheads touching as Princess Alicia blessed us from above, riding a heavenly cloud. There were also cheap, yellow-fringed satin pillow shams silk-screened with one of the many official portraits of the two of us standing side by side, with the prince wearing a kilt in his family tartan; there were snow globes in which tiny plastic figures of Gregory and me waltzed on a jerkily spinning disk while a music box microchip played "God Save the Queen"; there were cardboard fans with my profile on one side and Gregory's on the reverse, stuck atop a wooden tongue depressor; and there were vinyl change purses, bottle openers, toffee tins, bamboo backscratchers and poured resin paperweights, all with portraits and the date of the upcoming ceremony. There was also an infinite selection of oversized T-shirts ranging from a pastel fantasy of the two of us kissing politely, in which we both looked Asian, to a pornographic variation, in which the two of us had sex in many explicit positions, with the overall caption "50 Ways To Screw England."

Rocher had stockpiled multiples of every item she could find. "You'll thank me later," she'd say, whirling an acetate scarf — printed in Sri Lanka — with a collage of The Prince and The Pretty, as we'd been dubbed, on horseback, strolling through a rose garden, seated on matching thrones and swimming hand in hand deep underwater, with matching mermaid and merman tails.

Rocher and I had traveled to Westminster in a gilded coach drawn by a team of eight white stallions, cantering proudly beneath headdresses of high white plumes. Rocher, who was my sole brides-maid, had sat opposite me. I wasn't yet wearing my wedding dress, which was too cumbersome to be stuffed into the coach. As we were trotted through the streets, all of which had been closed off for the day, we waved to the cheering, ruddy-cheeked crowds, filled with elderly folks seated on aluminum folding stools and the smallest children whistling and clapping from atop their parents' shoulders. I locked eyes with one particular toddler who was at most three years old. He was staring at me and waving in that wan, unsure way children have and I could tell he was disap-pointed that I wasn't a baby panda or a monkey, wearing a tasseled ceremonial hat.

Since saving Gregory's life I'd won the nation's heartfelt approval. A task force of hackers and private investigators and smuthounds had combed through every moment of Rebecca's life and had dug up exactly nothing. Rebecca's official bio said that she'd been born in America, that she'd completed high school and that she was an orphan. As always, Rebecca's uncanny beauty filled in the rest; her face was all anyone needed to know. Rebecca had hypnotized the world into a global bliss-out and she was on her way to becoming beloved. Because she was a commoner, she gave girls everywhere hope and because she looked like Rebecca, she gave guys everywhere, if not hope, at least someone to visualize while they were having sex with girls everywhere.

It had taken Rocher and me the better part of an hour to reach Westminster and another two hours to dress for the ceremony itself. Now Rocher was inspecting herself, her eyes misting, because Tom Kelly had proven his supernatural supremacy by becoming the first designer in recorded history to come up with a truly flattering bridesmaid dress. Rocher was wearing a gown of deep cobalt blue velvet embroidered with twenty-four-karat gold thread in a harlequin tracery, with a real pearl nestled in coils of more golden thread at each corner of the pattern. The dress had an ermine collar and madrigal sleeves flowing almost to the floor. Her headpiece was based on a portrait of a Flemish noblewoman and Rocher's vivid red hair was braided with ropes of pearls and velvet ribbons. "I look like a fucking goddamned fairy tale," said Rocher as she reached for her reflection. "I look like a fairy tale that's so magical no one's even heard of it yet, like I'm Merlin's little sister or Snow White's American pen pal. You have got to promise me, you have to make sure it happens, no matter what, I want to be *buried* in this dress."

"Do you like it?" asked Tom Kelly, who was leaning against one of the mirrored walls wearing the morning clothes he'd had hand-tailored to his personal slimness. Even in his vest and tailcoat Tom managed to look as if he was lounging and waiting for a delivery of sex, drugs, cash or all three.

"I don't care if you are Satan himself," Rocher declared. "You are my fucking hero."

Anselmo insisted on helping me into my hopelessly fragile shoes, molded entirely of white lace, which he'd crafted himself.

"Suitable for Cinderella," he said.

"And far more appealing than glass," said Tom. "I've never understood the glass slipper concept. It sounds cold and uncomfortable and who wants to see a human foot, even a foot as lovely as Rebecca's, encased in an aquarium?"

Madame Ponelle provided a pair of diamond earrings, worked as rosettes. "These were a wedding night gift from King Louis XVI to Marie Antoinette," she said as I put them on. "She later wore them in prison, to remind herself of more romantic moments."

Archie had blended a one-of-a-kind fragrance titled Always Rebecca to be used, Archie said, "Just by you and on this day only." The bottle was white glass, shaped like a calla lily and the scent combined, Archie reported, "only white flowers — the gardenia, for joy, the white chrysanthemum, for truth, and lily of the valley, which some say was born from Eve's tears upon being forced to leave the garden. And, of course, the white rose, a symbol of both England and purity."

The perfume was delectably feminine but not cloying or prissy. "Jesus," said Rocher, sniffing my wrist. "That's exactly the way people think you smell."

"And now, Rocher, and everyone?" said Tom to his incomparable team, including Mrs. Chen and her ten lab-coated assistants, who'd been toiling under eighteen-hour-a-day lockdown, stitching and altering and beading. "If you could all just step outside, I'd like a word with Rebecca, in private."

"I'm real sorry," Rocher told me as she glided past, every inch the medieval sorceress. "But I just have to say it: No one's gonna be looking at you."

Before leaving, Mrs. Chen and her staff took a moment to admire their own handiwork. This was a rare event as Mrs. Chen and her assistants were ordinarily both far too modest and far too strict to call attention to themselves. But now, as they allowed themselves to gaze at me, each woman placed her hand over her heart.

"When we see you, in your gown," Mrs. Chen explained, "we are seeing our lives and our raw, bleeding fingertips and the sacrifice of a generation of silkworms." She turned to Tom and offered her highest praise. "Not bad."

Then Mrs. Chen did something equally unexpected. She approached me, took me gently by the shoulders and kissed my cheek.

Once everyone was gone, Tom switched off the lights and the room plunged into absolute blackness. Then, and I felt this before I saw it, a ray of late-morning sun crept, like a laser, from a tiny round window in the room's high domed ceiling. This pure white light was aimed directly at me, as if a midnight search party had found its quarry, namely Rebecca, in her white Tom Kelly dress.

I hadn't been one of those little girls who'd spent every waking moment, and all of her dreams, planning her wedding. That was my mom. She'd made me go out by myself and step into local doctors' waiting rooms and pretend to be looking for her, just so I could slip tattered copies of year-old bridal magazines into my backpack. She'd use a Magic Marker to slash Xs across the gowns which she'd deemed tacky or skimpy or "just a whole mess of white chiffon crapola." She'd say that "the perfect gown makes you look as if God made it for you, because He wants you to be happy." Once, before I'd known better, I'd asked her what she'd worn when she'd married my dad and she'd said, "I had so many pretty dresses, but we never got that far. And that's why I'm still picking one out."

And now here I was, bathed in a biblical glow, as if I were about to be raptured into the hereafter, or some Olympian Bridal Hall of Fame. Tom had challenged himself; he'd vowed to show the world that he could make Rebecca Randle even more beautiful.

He hated fuss and flounces so my gown was architectural, a modern cathedral, and while it was constructed from miles of the finest, most flawless matte ivory satin, it seemed to be spun entirely of light. Tom knew that my wedding gown would undoubtedly become the most photographed, downloaded, podcast, copied, longed-for and loathed dress ever; he knew that for decades to come, pregnant teenagers and 6'11" transvestites, along with many bookcases of don't-touch collector's dolls displayed under glass domes would be wearing some version of this gown. As I saw myself in the mirror, I finally understood weddings on a gut level. A wedding is the day when every woman gets to be Rebecca Randle.

As I watched myself, my face left the mirror, because I was starting to leave the floor. I was rising, as the endless yards of my train unfolded and began to reproduce. I can't say that I was flying but my dress was. I held out my arms, spinning, as the room was filled with a whirlwind of delicately twisting white silk, forming ribbony highways and pleated clouds, which were occupied by angels, sewn entirely of the most decadently gossamer white linen, with white chiffon wings. There were flocks of white taffeta doves with taffeta-covered buttons for eyes, swooping past drifting, somersaulting feathers crafted from thousands, no, millions of the tiniest white crystal beads, as the ancient bells of the Abbey tolled with my mom's ringtone. I started laughing from sheer delight, because thanks to Tom Kelly, I'd ascended into bridal heaven.

And then just as gracefully, I slowly returned to earth and my white lace shoes touched the floor as the angels and the doves and the fantasy yardage withdrew.

"Do you love him?" asked Tom from the outlying darkness.

"What?"

"You heard me. Prince Gregory: Do you love him?"

"Of course I love him."

"Stop looking at yourself. I know that you're feeling pretty cocky because you're getting married on the very last day of our agreement. Within minutes, according to your calculations, you'll be home free. Rebecca forever. But if you remember, I said that you had one year to fall in love and get married. Which aren't necessarily the same thing. So right now, look me in the eye and convince me, beyond a shadow of a doubt, and then I'll be proud to walk you down the aisle and I'll never ask again."

He flipped the switch and the lights blinded me as the glare bounced from one mirror to the next, making any escape, hesitation or lie impossible. When my vision cleared Tom was standing directly in front of me, two feet away. He wasn't sneering or teasing me; his face was more open, and less certain of every last detail, than I'd ever seen. For the first time Tom was asking me a question he didn't already know the answer to.

I noticed one additional development. In shadowing me around the world and supplying me with one ensemble after another, Tom had spent a considerable amount of time outside his compound and the effort was unmistakable. While he still looked impossibly young, a certain fatigue, and maybe the most minuscule creases, had appeared on his face. Time was running out, for both of us.

"Do you love him?"

"I love everything about him. I love that he could be so stuck up and snotty but he isn't. I love that he's offhand and funny and that he puts everyone he meets at ease. I love his hair and his eyes and the way, even when he's all dressed up, everything looks a little bit off, like right before he leaves his house, he jumps up and down a few times."

"You haven't answered the question."

"I'm nineteen years old! Isn't Prince Gregory who I'm supposed to be with? Isn't he what you wanted for me?"

"I wanted to make a point. I wanted to show you what was available to you. How far you could go."

"Exactly! And here I am! And I've done everything you've said, I wore the red dress and now I'm wearing the white one! And I'll be able to use all of this, I'll be able to use Rebecca, to try and help people!"

"And your mother would be very proud. But I made her a promise."

"What promise?"

"I told her, before you were born, that whatever happened in your mother's life or mine, that I would find you. And look after you. And she thanked me and she made only one demand, there was only one thing she insisted upon. She said that if I could, if there was any possible route, that I had to make sure that you fell in love."

"I don't believe you! Why are you telling me this, right now? There are thousands of people outside that door waiting for me! I have to get married!"

"No you don't. Even if Prince Gregory is wonderful and even if he's going to become the king of England and even if you're determined to become Princess Alicia and Gandhi and Eleanor Roosevelt all rolled into one, you can't marry a man you don't love. I won't let you. I won't allow it. Because, yes, for a year now, you've worn red and you've learned something about life, in all its vivid and often bloodcurdling spectacle. And now you're in white, which demands the purity of truth, particularly on your wedding day. So I'll ask you one last time and I'll know if you're lying, just the way your mother would know. Do you love him?"

This was the question I hadn't allowed myself to consider for a very simple reason. If I loved Prince Gregory then I'd have to ask myself: Who did he love? And who was he marrying? Me, or Rebecca?

I pictured Prince Gregory, who was by now waiting at the altar. Was any love I had for him tainted, or made impossible, by the way we'd met? Was whatever love I felt for him every bit as concocted as Rebecca? If I was being ruthlessly honest — did I love him at all? Or did I only love what he could do for me and the access he represented? Did I just love the image of the two of us dropping by the sick and the needy for a quick photo op and maybe a tribal hoedown? Did I love that he was a prince and that he was rich and good-looking and that he met all of my other top-of-the-wedding-cake specifications? Was I using the prince on every conceivable level but most especially, so I could remain Rebecca?

While I was trying so hard to be furiously clear-eyed, Prince Gregory kept sneaking into my brain and making his breezy, I-couldn't-care-less, oh-stop-it way into my heart. Some romantic dam burst and I was brimming with all the emotion I'd been guarding against, and buckets more. For a second I forgot that Rebecca had ever existed and there was only Prince Gregory meeting Becky, meeting me, and kissing me and proposing to me and making me laugh. While I was growing up I'd dreamed about falling in love but all of my ideas had come from my mom's favorite movies, where love had always been, as she'd liked to say, "sad and beautiful."

But now I knew exactly what falling in love was because I knew that love wasn't a choice, or a decision. Love was the thing you can't help. The thing that might never be returned. The thing that would probably destroy you, as it had destroyed Drake and my mom. Being Rebecca was the opposite of falling in love because Rebecca was safe. Rebecca knew that pretty much everyone was in love with her so her response was beside the point. Nobody would ever be worthy of Rebecca; she was a fortress. When you're the Most Beautiful Woman Who Ever Lived, all you can do is bask in the deafening applause and the colossal envy and the warehouses of fan portraits, executed in oil and jelly beans and human hair, and then head home by yourself, exhausted from being all that and more, on such an impossible, paranormal, disconnected scale.

But I wasn't Rebecca. I was Becky and I'd made a terrible mistake. And there was nothing I could do about it except own up to it and muddle through. As soon as I answered Tom's question I'd know that for the rest of my life, Becky would be an onlooker, a third wheel, an eternal spinster, watching Prince Gregory be in love with Rebecca. I guess I'd known it all along, that being Rebecca was my job and it was a lifetime position. The best I could hope for were scraps. I'd be allowed to ask Rebecca, if I caught her in the right mood, what it was like to be married to Prince Gregory. My heartbreak would be this: While Rebecca was married to the prince and eventually, the king, I would be secretly in love with Gregory, the guy I'd never really met and who'd never know I existed. And whenever he called me Becky, I would die a little more because my own name, my real name, would become a dagger. Did I love Gregory? I looked Tom Kelly right in the eye, as if I were strapped into the electric chair and Tom controlled the current.

"Yes."

"Becky?" said Rocher. I hadn't known that she'd returned or that she'd been staring at me, with her head cocked to one side.

"I'm fine," I said. "I'm ready. Everything's going to be perfect. Tell them, tell everyone that we can get started."

"Becky?"

"What?"

"Um, Becky, I don't know how to say this, but . . ."

"What?"

Rocher, tongue-tied, took me by the shoulders, so we were facing one of the mirrored panels, standing side by side. "Look," she said.

"What? What am I looking at?"

As I focused on our joint reflection, I knew why Rocher hadn't been able to speak. Because I was looking at two girls, Becky and Rocher, from East Trawley, Missouri, both grotesquely overdressed and clutching each other. Rebecca was nowhere to be found or more exactly, she was nowhere to be seen.

My thoughts splintered in every direction, like a chandelier that had come crashing to the floor. This was a trick, a brain spasm, a Tom Kelly prank.

"Tom?" I said, but I knew he wasn't there. I hadn't seen him leave but I also knew that sending Rocher out to drag him back would be impossible. When Tom Kelly left a room he wasn't about to change his mind. I tried frantically to remember everything he'd said; he'd told me that if he believed me, he'd happily walk me down the aisle. And I'd told the truth, I'd confessed that I loved Prince Gregory.

"Becky?" said Rocher. "Where's Tom Kelly? Did he do something to you? Is he pissed at you? What's going on?"

Had I been warned by my accessories? Cinderella's dreams had imploded at midnight and my perfume was distilled from Eve's sobs as she was driven into the wilderness. And as for my earrings — had I been cursed by the doomed Marie Antoinette?

I went back to the mirror, determined to will the necessary change, to force Tom's magic to reassert itself. *I am Rebecca Randle*, I told myself. *I have to be Rebecca Randle.* I'm about to get married to Prince Gregory and I need to be camera-ready and

cathedral-ready and before-the-eyes-of-God-ready. I AM
REBECCA RANDLE.

"Becky?" said Rocher in a hoarse whisper.

"Rebecca?" asked Lady Veronica Arnstelt-Bowen, the Queen's
secretary, stepping into the room. Lady Veronica had been overseeing every aspect of the wedding and before she could catch
sight of me, of whoever I was, I flung my veil over my face and the
many layers of pearl-encrusted Alençon lace fell from the veil's
headpiece to my waist.

"Come along now," said Lady Veronica. While she'd never
liked me, she was set on masterminding an epic and punctual
ceremony. Stalling or stammering or begging for a bathroom
break were out of the question. I could hear the music begin from
inside the cathedral, not yet the traditional wedding march, but
a royal processional arranged for a pipe organ, twelve mandolins,
fifteen trumpets and a massed choir, including thirty boy sopra-
nos selected by competition from across the country.

"It's time," said Lady Veronica, and with a nod of her head, the
side room was flooded with security personnel relaying com-
mands into their headpieces, and other formally dressed staff
members, each with a white rose at their lapel or breast — the
Ravishing Rebecca — bred in bulk for my wedding. One of these
smiling staffers handed Rocher her bouquet, a middle-earth
cluster of foxglove, lilies and thistle wrapped with trailing ribbons. As she was led away, Rocher wrenched her head around,
shooting me a helplessly supportive look, promising that while we
were both scheduled for the guillotine she was praying that her
own neck might shatter the blade, so my next-in-line death would
at least be delayed.

"My dear?" said Lady Veronica as the security team held the
door open and lined the outer hallway so my journey to the altar
would be undisturbed. Beneath my veil, I opened my mouth to

say something, but what? "I'm not exactly sure who I am under all this lace, but hey, let's give it a shot"?

With Lady Veronica and two of her undersecretaries holding my train aloft, we made our way to the rear of the cathedral and the center aisle. Tom Kelly was waiting because I'd asked him to serve as, maybe not my father, but as a close friend of my family, and to give me away. At the time, a month earlier, this had seemed not only a heartfelt but a necessary gesture, because without Tom's magic I'd never have met Prince Gregory and I'd never be standing at the back of Westminster Abbey, drowning in white satin and white-knuckled fear. I searched Tom's face for some hint of explanation or guidance. What was going on? Did he think I'd lied about loving Prince Gregory? And if that was the case why was he still participating in the wedding? Had he turned me back into Becky for only a few short seconds so I might say good-bye to my earlier self? Had he just wanted to remind me of where I'd come from and how much I owed him?

Or was Tom Kelly, as I'd secretly suspected, the devil himself? Jate Mallow had warned me that all great fame and success came with a price, so had Tom just presented me with an itemized bill for his services? Tom had created me and if he was Satan he would take his greatest delight in crushing me as well. Because that's what the devil does, he demonstrates what's possible and then, just as happiness seems within reach, he fiddles with the brake linings on the honeymoon car or wraps the umbilical cord around the unborn baby's throat or he takes a nobody from nowhere and shazams her into Rebecca, or maybe not.

Tom's expression was, of course, impenetrable. He was Dr. Frankenstein, urging his monster into the world just to see what might happen and who might get hurt. He offered me his arm and as two thousand guests, along with five billion other people from all over the world watching via TV and Internet hookups, turned to enjoy us, we began our deliberate, rhythmic march to the altar.

Back in East Trawley, I'd wanted a bigger life and now here I was, leading a life greater and more terrifying than anything I could have imagined. As Tom and I made our way down the aisle, I tried not to focus on the world-renowned faces and the mammoth jewels and the storybook's worth of royal titles we were passing, on the pew after pew of international movie stars and beribboned viscounts and esteemed prime ministers and emperors, all of them looking at me, looking at Rebecca, with only Tom and Rocher aware of the potential catastrophe, the worldwide insanity that was only seconds away.

I'm fine, I'm fine, everything's going to be fine, I started repeating to myself, as if all I needed was a new mantra, but my brain began shouting, NO IT'S NOT! NO IT'S NOT!

And now I saw, seated between a retired BBC commentator and, oh my God, the vice president of the United States, there was Dr. Barry, from the burn unit at the children's hospital.

Dr. Barry was studying me with the same intense curiosity as when we were first introduced. Now, as she watched me barreling toward the altar she suddenly smiled, with the giddy satisfaction of a safecracker as the final tumblers click into place. WHAT DID YOU SEE? my brain howled at her, WHO DID YOU SEE?

We came even with the Royal Family in the very first pew. Prince Edgar, Gregory's father, turned to watch me. He was slightly balding and even taller than his son and for the first time since I'd known him, he looked almost hopeful. Gregory had explained to me that his father had never really recovered from Alicia's death, and about how his son's engagement had reminded him that romance was still possible. "I'm sorry," my brain whispered to him, "I'm so sorry! I'm a liar, I'm a lie, and I'm sorry!"

Right next to Prince Edgar were two armloads of jumbo, buttery yellow silk daisies on green satin stems, and beneath this raucous garden of a hat was the Queen. As I pulled up beside her, the Queen turned to me and her smile was so wide and benevolent that for a heartbeat, I froze, because how could I betray this woman who'd put so much faith in me and who was relying on me to continue her legacy? HATE ME! KILL ME! HELP ME!

Then the Queen faced forward, toward my future. Prince Gregory was standing at the altar, gazing at me with such unguarded joy that he almost didn't seem English. Beside him was the Archbishop of Canterbury in his high, stiff white cope and his gaudy golden vestments.

Rocher was opposite the prince and Prince Jasper, Gregory's younger brother, who was serving as best man. Jasper was a scrawnier, loopier, out-of-it version of Gregory and mixed with the altar's incense, I smelled weed. While Gregory had forced Jasper to remove his earbuds for the ceremony, they were still visible, barely tucked behind his lapels and his hands were folded in front of him. I was later told that at precisely this moment he was tweeting "Big white dress, must be bride" to his millions of followers.

Tom Kelly brought me up the carpeted steps and placed me across from Prince Gregory. I stared frantically at Tom for any hint of either reassurance or gloating, even a wink would mean something. But he was serenely self-satisfied, as if whatever was about to happen was just what he'd had in mind all along.

As Rocher knelt and adroitly arranged my gown, I made a fatal mistake. I faced out and I took in the entire cathedral and the full congregation in a single wide shot. I gasped because, while I'd rehearsed the ceremony earlier, the pews had been empty and the lighting dim. Now I was trembling, encased in white and good intentions, before what was either the world's wealthiest and most big-name fan club or what might quickly become the world's wealthiest and most big-name lynch mob.

The archbishop nodded, which was the signal for me to delicately but decisively sweep the veil from my face so that the vows might begin. I was shaking uncontrollably but my gown was so massive, and its understructure so rigid, that no one could tell: My dress was holding me together and upright. Like anyone with their toes on the last inch of a cliff and trying not to look down at the knife-edged rocks and the churning sea and the circling sharks, I prayed, to God and the universe and to Tom Kelly's better nature, if he had one, but most of all, I prayed to my mother. As the months had passed I'd begun to know her more completely. I still wasn't certain about everything she'd been through or how she'd ended up on the couch in our trailer, but I knew what I'd always known — she had loved me. And she'd left Tom Kelly's phone number for me to find. So whatever was about to happen, she'd wished it. Mom, I told her, I love you right back and no matter what happens next I always will and everyone's watching and the archbishop is scowling impatiently and Prince Gregory looks trusting but a little unsure and even Jasper has half opened his eyes and picked up on my hesitation and if Rocher holds her breath for one more second she's going to pass out, so here goes whatever and by whatever I mean here goes everything and by everything I mean my life.

Using both hands, as I'd practiced, I lifted my veil in a single graceful swoop, until the yards of lace fell away from my face and swept down my back. With my now unimpaired vision I saw Prince Gregory, as his features twisted into equal parts horror, confusion and terrible loss.

"Who . . . who are you?" he said, but he didn't sound angry or disgusted. It was worse, because his voice had grown hollow, as all of his happiness evaporated, as if someone's thumb and forefinger had snuffed out a candle.

Here was the harshest truth: If being beautiful meant being loved, then I wasn't beautiful, not anymore. I was Becky, and I'd never felt so ugly.

BECKY

19.

Because I was facing away from the congregation, only Prince Gregory, the archbishop and Rocher were immediately aware of the catastrophic switch and Prince Jasper, of course, didn't notice anything. Within seconds, Rocher leaped forward and jammed one foot onto my train and used both of her hands to rip away the yards of satin. She hissed, "Run!" and grabbed me by my waist and we both took off, high-jumping over the altar, sending a few altar boys sprawling to the floor and then we hurtled down a rear hallway. For a few brief moments we had shock and chaos on our side, so no one tackled or shot us and all we knew for sure was, don't look back.

With Rocher in the lead we sprinted down the hallway, passing offices, choir rehearsal rooms and private chapels, shredding more of our Tom Kelly originals as we ran. We burst through a fire door and out into the alley behind the Abbey where we threw what was left of our gowns behind a Dumpster. Rocher had snatched two pairs of worn, stained custodial coveralls from hooks in the hall and we dove into them. Rocher howled "Taxi!" and we leaped aboard and sped off as we began to hear the police sirens, along with the news crews and the bewildered crowds in mounting uproar.

"Have you heard what happened?" our cab driver asked

breathlessly. "It's all over the radio! She's gone! That girl, that American, she's jilted our Greg!"

Before Rocher and I had even cleared the Abbey, first-responding entrepreneurs had registered the following domain names, among so many others: RebeccaTRUTH.com, Hardcore weddingfacts.net and www.weknowwhathappened.org, where they promoted such theories as the Queen changing her mind about having such a bumpkin for a daughter-in-law and hocking her own grandmother's best tiara to bribe Rebecca into taking a hike; Rebecca experiencing a disfiguring malfunction with her tanning mist on the morning of the wedding, leaving her unphotograph-ably orange and splotchy; and Rebecca, at the last second, being summoned back to her home planet by the Venusian high command, in preparation for the full-scale draining of Earth's water supply.

Later that day Prince Gregory and his family issued a brief statement apologizing to the nation and insisting that they held "no rancor toward Rebecca Randle, only a deep sympathy for her youthful turmoil." The prince then asked for the entire matter to become "closed and respectfully private."

This was, of course, impossible. Rebecca had not only aban-doned Prince Gregory at the altar, she'd vanished. She'd left behind a Tom Kelly wardrobe and disappeared into the ether, along with her American bridesmaid with the odd first name, causing the chocolate company, Ferrero Rocher, to strenuously deny any connection to either of the young women, proclaiming in a commercial that "Ferrero Rocher is always in love."

Because, prior to her almost wedding, so little had been known about Rebecca, the media now concentrated on her meteoric rise from total obscurity to top-selling *Vogue* cover girl and her equally stratospheric movie debut. By jilting a prince, she'd become even more improbable. It was as if on the happily-ever-after page of her fairy tale, Rebecca had spontaneously combusted in order to preserve her beauty forever at its dewiest, most adored and most scandalous peak.

Jate Mallow, naturally, was kept under round-the-clock surveillance, because so many people, with no other explanation at hand, decided that Rebecca had ditched Prince Gregory in favor of Hollywood royalty. Everyone enlisted in either Team Jate or Team Gregory and the online justifications included "Jate loved her more!" "Jate was going to attempt suicide!" and my personal favorite, "Right before the ceremony Rebecca found out that Prince Gregory is gay!" Jate did nothing to combat these rumors and he was sometimes photographed leaning pensively against his Harley, parked on a lonely Los Angeles hilltop, as if he were heartsick over Rebecca or maybe meeting her, heavily disguised, at 4:00 A.M. When he was asked about the woman who was now known as The Runaway Princess, The Outlaw Bride and The Invisible Girl, Jate would only comment, with a crack in his voice, "Wherever Rebecca is I just hope she's happy."

All of this international tabloid frenzy had only just ignited when, late on the evening of my canceled wedding, I sat beside Rocher on a hastily booked flight out of London, in coach. Since I was Becky, no one gave me a second glance and in the airport bathroom, Rocher had dyed her hair, along with her eyebrows, a thick, toneless black, so she resembled a goth Groucho Marx.

"Look at that," Rocher murmured, nudging me as we watched the footage of ourselves leaping over the altar which was being endlessly replayed on every video screen and handheld device. "Those girls are crazy!" Rocher said loudly, for the benefit of our seatmates. "I bet they ran all the way to France!"

As I sat there in the 3:00 A.M. darkness, lit only by the reading bulbs of the few passengers who, like me, weren't about to get any sleep, I tried not to think about anything at all, to erase Rebecca forever and to treat the entire episode as a psychotic break. But it wasn't any use. First and foremost I blamed myself, because I'd said yes to Tom Kelly's proposal and I'd worn the dresses, and even if I'd never trusted him, I'd done everything Tom had commanded. At first I'd told myself it was all meaningless because Tom was deluded and could never deliver on his absurd promises. But even back then, before my transformation, pre-Rebecca, I hadn't just been humoring a nutcase, because like anyone who's ever whooshed the fuzz off a dandelion or tossed a penny into a chlorinated water feature at the mall or shut their eyes and blown out the candles on a birthday cake in a single breath, I'd wanted the wish, Tom's bargain, to come true. I'd wanted to become the most beautiful woman on earth, although back then, I hadn't had the slightest idea of what that might feel like and lead to. I'd thought that being beautiful might be like getting a really terrific haircut or finding a well-fitting pair of jeans or just feeling less like the plainest, most forgettable, least-likely-to-be-kissed sort of person. But for me, becoming beautiful had been like waking up behind the wheel of a Ferrari that had just been dropped out of a plane somewhere over the Atlantic and trying to remember my name.

I tried to hate Tom Kelly, to curse him as he'd cursed me, to invent a punishment as bizarre as the one I was experiencing. But I couldn't, because more than wanting to kill him as painfully and publicly as possible, I wanted to grill him, to finally get some answers. Why had he done it, all of it? Why had he made me so beautiful and encouraged my adventures and my marriage, only to trash everything? Did he hate me, did he hate beautiful women, or all women, or the possibility of love, or my mother? What had she done to him? Was I his revenge?

Every thought arrived at my mother. Why had she sent me to

Tom? What had she hoped for? Had Tom perverted her deathbed dream of seeing her daughter gorgeous and happy and in love?

But none of these questions could ever be answered. My mother was gone, the Queen of England and her snarling corgis had every right to hate me and I prayed with all my heart that I would never see Tom Kelly again. I told myself that I'd been granted an impossible, supernatural opportunity and that it had been insane fun while it lasted and I'd seen the world and I'd fallen in love and you know what, Becky Randle from East Trawley, Missouri? You're sitting in coach, where you belong and you're lucky to be there. Get over it. Stop wallowing. You're young, you're healthy, you're safe and nobody likes a whiner, especially a whiner whose most recent activities are preempting every top-rated sitcom, every major sporting event and the president's State of the Union address.

I wasn't beautiful, I wasn't going to marry the guy I loved and I was never going to become the Queen of England; as Rocher liked to say, boo-fucking-hoo. I was torn between heartbroken sobs and giggling like an idiot, because I couldn't believe that these were my problems. I was almost convinced that I'd be fine, but then I saw Prince Gregory's face on the cell phone of someone two rows in front of me. Then I did something I had no right to do. I tried to stop and to sit up straight and to not let Rocher or anyone else see what was happening, but the tears began coursing down my face and onto my T-shirt and seat belt. I was crying because I loved Gregory so much and because no matter what might happen to me, for the rest of my life, I'd never be able to tell him about it and make him laugh and hear his wisecracks and feel his arms around me once he'd run out of wisecracks. Even when I'd been mad at him, if he was acting childish or crabby, I'd loved watching him. I'd loved the idea of the two of us, figuring out our lives together. And I'd loved having someone who'd loved me right back, even in my red camouflage-print jumpsuit. Someone who'd called me Becky.

But that wasn't really why I was crying or it wasn't the only reason. I'd probably never stop crying because I'd fallen in love with a great guy and I'd hurt him, maybe as deeply as anyone can hurt someone else. I'd lied to him and Rebecca had been the worst category of lie, because she, or it, had been so deliberate. And Gregory would never know that whoever I was, my love for him had never been part of the lie.

I knew that I was going to have to bury that love more deeply than any other memory of my year as Rebecca or I wouldn't be able to take another breath. I began to understand my mother on a more visceral and grown-up level because whatever had happened to her, I knew exactly why she'd retreated and why she'd hidden herself away. Whoever my father was, she had loved him and he had left. And the only way she'd been able to deal with that had been to stay very still and very alone and to never answer any questions. And now I felt even worse, because I'd badgered her about my father. I hadn't known what it meant to fall in love and then lose everything.

I knew that I couldn't head back to East Trawley, because my mother's trailer had been hauled away months ago and sold for scrap. The Super Shop-A-Lot had closed and as Rocher had said, "We've already been rejected and bummed out in Missouri." So we spent two days in a motel near the New York airport, where we came across the previous guest's nail parings and pubic hairs underneath our flat, slimy pillows. We went online and offered ourselves as roommates to a pair of girls who described themselves as "stars of tomorrow today" in their listing. The apartment was up five flights in a decrepit building in the part of Manhattan called Hell's Kitchen. The building had started its life as a brownstone but the facade had been repeatedly resurfaced, as if some chugging machine had swallowed gallons of stucco and vomited all over it. There were rats scurrying across the stairwells and the hallways looked like they'd been scrubbed down with raw sewage.

The two girls who lived in the apartment both claimed to be nineteen but they were most likely in their late twenties or older; Rocher and I really were nineteen and we looked like their little sisters. They introduced themselves as Aimee Cheviot and Suzanne Morgyn Reed, although later, after checking their phone and utility bills, Rocher and I saw that their real names were Amy Farn and Susan Durkheimer, but I was in no position to snub anyone for manufacturing a new name and personality.

"So hi hi hi hi hi," said Aimee as we settled onto Aimee's aunt Renee's donated sleeper sofa in the cramped living room of the two-room apartment. Aimee and Suzanne had laid claim to the bedroom and if we met with their approval, Rocher and I would be bunking together on the sleeper sofa, which was upholstered in what seemed to be the skin of a really unpopular teenage boy and which wasn't a treat even to sit on because the inner mechanism was broken and the hidden, barely folded-up mattress was attempting to lurch its way to freedom.

"So we're both aspiring actresses," said Suzanne. "I'm from Tampa and Aimee's from Teaneck."

"Not 'aspiring,'" Aimee corrected. "We agreed not to say that anymore, because even if we aren't, at the moment right now, working in any of the artistic or commercial mediums, we're still doing scene work and learning audition monologues, which makes us actresses. You have to own it, you have to say, 'I am a whatever.' Although, of course, I'm really a leading lady—type category, while Suzanne is more of a, like, still totally attractive and sexually viable character person."

I decided that Aimee was the leading lady because she was taller, with wider hips and probably more than one nose job. Like many people who have plastic surgery, Aimee had gone too far and her nose now resembled a tiny wad of tip-tilted chewing gum stuck dead center in her face. Aimee also had dark, waist-length hair and she'd used a curling wand to mold cylindrical corkscrews, so she came off as either an octopus wearing too much blush or an old-time telephone switchboard operator wrestling with clusters of dangling wires. Suzanne was shorter and rounder, with hair the color of a semi-successful tooth bleaching razored into a frenetic shag, so if you only saw her in passing, you'd think her head was glued with a haystack of forgotten Post-its. They were both members of a comedy improv troupe that posted its skits on YouTube, where the only comment any of the videos had received was "Are you all guys?"

"Oh my God, before we, like, decide if we're all gonna do this," said Suzanne, standing abruptly and holding out her arms with her palms raised like a belligerent traffic cop, "you guys have gotta tell me right this second and this is a total deal breaker: What do you think about Rebecca Randle?"

"Well, uh . . . ," I said, "I haven't really been following the whole thing. . . ."

"WHAT?" said Aimee, as deeply offended as if I'd insulted the Bill of Rights or her chances of being cast as a recurring gorgeous forensic crime-lab specialist on a locally shot procedural. "What is WRONG with you? See, I think that Rebecca is a truly tragic and romantic figure and a great role for me."

"It is so a great role for you," said Suzanne. "I mean, you're a brunette."

"Here's what I think happened," said Aimee, leaning forward as if she possessed privileged information and the room might be bugged. "I think that Rebecca was totally and deeply in love with Prince Gregory, I mean enduringly in love, like she would cut off her arm for him and say, 'Here's my arm,' right? But I heard that just before the ceremony, like fifteen seconds before, there was this aide, like, a royal underperson, and he handed Rebecca a phone with a video of the prince doing it the night before with that English supermodel, you know, the one who did crystal meth but still has her own line of yoga wear? So Rebecca sees the video and she just snaps, and then she was, like, reaching out to the prince and telling him, 'I love you but I can't marry you, not till you get your shit together and stop fucking supermodels who take drugs and do yoga, because that is just not what yoga is all about.' And so Rebecca was all heartbroken and heartsick and heart . . . heart . . ."

"Heart shat on," suggested Suzanne, who was by now so committed to Aimee's story that she was miming all the participants and sobbing.

"Heart shat on," said Aimee, "and so she ripped off her wedding gown and ran away and now she's in this Buddhist spa somewhere. Don't you think that's what happened? I do, I mean, at least that's how I'm gonna play her, when they make a movie about the whole thing."

"Rebecca was messy but special," said Suzanne. "And I mean, Aimee is incredible at both of those things."

By completely and instantly agreeing with Aimee and Suzanne about everything and by solemnly swearing that the people who said that Rebecca Randle was a crazy bitch were just jealous and evil and wrong, we managed to sign a lease that entitled us to the sleeper sofa, and half a shelf in the mold-encrusted student-sized refrigerator that stood in a corner of the living room beside a toaster oven sitting on the floor, defining an area that Aimee and Suzanne referred to as the kitchen. It was weird because while I'd grown up in a trailer that hadn't been any larger or nicer than this roach-happy apartment, my year as Rebecca had turned both me and Rocher into secret snobs.

"We have to get jobs and get out of here," Rocher whispered forcefully to me on our first night using the partially unfolded sleeper sofa. We knew that Aimee and Suzanne were in for the night because, after using the bathroom down the hall, they'd both crossed through the living room. Suzanne had been wearing her basketball-hoop-sized wire retainer and Aimee had spread three strips of cloudy, crinkle-edged hair-set tape across the bridge of her nose, so that her old nose wouldn't grow back.

"This place is so filthy," I told Rocher, "but do you remember our bathroom in London?" This memory caused the two of us to moan with such violent, passionate nostalgia that the next day Suzanne asked us if we were, "You know, not that it matters, I mean, I would have no problem playing, like, someone's beautiful but feisty lesbian daughter on a soap, but are you two, you know, together?" Rocher and I denied any same-sex attraction, not because we minded being mistaken for lesbians but because we dreaded the idea of Suzanne using us for research.

The next morning Rocher and I were hired on the spot, without even much of a job interview, as cashiers, by the manager of the Valu-Brite drugstore just a few blocks from our new address. Valu-Brite was a national chain and every Valu-Brite was pretty much the same, especially the merciless fluorescent lighting, which always made the stores feel as if the lights had been bumped all the way up, to spot shoplifters and deliberately abandoned children. The stores sold everything from budget cosmetics and hair-care products to adult diapers, cat litter, singing Christmas stockings, home pregnancy tests and every brand of cookie, cracker and chip. Everything was vacuum-sealed and labeled in the brightest colors and there were always stacks of partially unpacked cardboard cartons clogging the aisles, left unattended by clerks who were on their breaks or on the run from their underage girlfriends.

Rocher and I began working at the Valu-Brite on West 48th Street that afternoon, right after we'd been issued Day-Glo purple vests with other peoples' name tags still attached; "Let's just use their names," said Rocher, "it'll be fine, because you know they're probably dead." Rocher was installed at a register to my left and on my other side was Vivian, a veteran cashier who glanced at the two of us and grunted, "New bitches on the block. You better be watchin' your behinds."

Vivian was four feet eleven inches of undiluted spite and swagger. She was muscled and wiry and she wore only a tight wifebeater under her vest, exposing the tattoo that covered her left shoulder of a laughing clown with a hatchet buried in his forehead. Vivian's eyeliner was tattooed on and she had a heavy iron cross dangling from an ear, but people mostly noticed the thick five-inch pointed metal spike, the base of which was embedded beneath the skin at the top of Vivian's shaved head. The spike made Vivian look like either a heavy-metal unicorn or an Aryan Nation ringtoss game.

There were plenty of customers so Rocher and I were busy, although the line at Vivian's register was always the longest, as she practiced a deeply personal business technique. Vivian would weigh each item in her hand and she'd inspect the product from all angles and then, while still ignoring her customer, she'd make loud comments directly to the item, such as, "This bitch is buyin' pantyhose, I guess she's got herself a date, or maybe she's gonna stroll on over to the supermarket and shove some ground chuck right down under that control-top panel and walk herself back outside. Either way she's gonna have herself one fine night." After holding extended, skeptical chats with the entire contents of a shopper's wire basket, Vivian would finally advance to the next person in line and a new set of brand-name friends. "This dude is gettin' all up with, now what is this damn thing, a Fleet enema? What's he gonna do, clean himself out for the holidays, so he can stick his damn Christmas tree up his butt? He could save himself some serious money by just climbin' into the tub and standin' on his head, and stickin' the faucet up his no-no hole. And he could just hold it all in and then shoot himself right up to Mars, like an ass-tronaut."

At one point, because I was working faster, Vivian turned her head slightly toward me and said, "You're lookin' at my spike, aintcha? You're wonderin' if it hurt when I got it stuck in there. Damn right it hurt! It hurt damn good!" That was when an impatient customer made the mistake of saying to Vivian: "Miss, oh Miss?" in a huffy, pretending-to-be-polite way. "I'm on lunch and I have to get back so could you please just ring me up, please?" Vivian looked at the woman, at which point all of the other customers, waiting on all three lines, crouched down to avoid whatever Vivian was about to spit or throw.

Instead Vivian removed a magazine from the woman's shopping basket and got acquainted with the cover story. "Runaway Rebecca, the Disappearing Princess," said Vivian, noting a fuzzy photo of me from behind, snapped by a security camera in Westminster Abbey's back hallway. Every cover on every magazine in the racks by the registers was devoted to Rebecca, her wedding fracas and the ongoing mystery of her current whereabouts. There were also Special Issues, the sorts of one-time-only almanacs which most often follow a presidential election or the early, substance abuse—related death of a revered pop star or sex goddess. The very latest Special Issues, with their "Collector's Edition" medallions, included a Rebecca Report, a 101 No-Show-Weddings-Palooza, documenting the rash of worldwide, copycat jiltings that had mimicked Rebecca's example, with lurid photos of weeping, discarded brides and drunken, suicidal grooms, and *Where in the World Is Rebecca Randle?*, a three-hundred-page, triple-priced, photo-heavy guide to all things Rebecca.

"Ya wanna know about that Rebecca bitch?" Vivian asked the entire store, holding aloft her customer's magazine, which promised a "First Exclusive Post-Wedding Interview with Rebecca!!!" "Ya wanna know the super-duper-secret, only-I-can-tell-you inside poopedy-poop about where she's been hidin' herself at?"

The store became very quiet as at least twenty people, including Rocher and me, waited for Vivian's inside information. Vivian's unshakable confidence made me wonder if she knew details even I wasn't aware of.

"I *am* Rebecca Randle!" declared Vivian. "I got myself put under a magical spell, but then right before that royal weddin', the crazy witch-bitch reversed herself and when I was liftin' up my weddin' veil, that Prince Gregory, he's goin' all, 'What?' and then he's looking all surprised and shit and then he's sayin', 'Shee-it! Vivian? Is that you?'"

Everyone burst into uproarious laughter, accompanied by supportive shouts of "You got that right!" "That's who he shoulda married!" and "The Princess Vivian! Rulin' the Valu-Brite!"

"You know what I really think?" Vivian continued, warming to her subject, with her audience in thrall. "I think that Rebecca bitch ain't even that pretty. I saw her movie and I seen her in all of them magazines and I'm just thinkin', huh. I know a million bitches a whole lot prettier than that little look-at-me—my-shit-don't-stink pissy-pants bitch-hole."

"She was not a bitch-hole," said Rocher from behind her own register. I recognized her dangerous tone, from so many school-yard brawls, not to mention the Royal Enclosure at Ascot.

"Maybe she was a bitch-hole," I said, hoping to sound impartial. "Or maybe she wasn't, but who really cares, right?"

"No man, I just gotta say it, it's been itchin' at me like somethin' that would make me shave the affected area," said Vivian. "That bitch-hole had everything, she had, like, stylists and hair people and her own signature trademarked fuckin' butt-spray, she's gettin' herself in the movies and doin' the nasty with Jate Mallow, who is one fine-lookin' piece of man-meat, and then she's gonna be the motherfuckin' Queen of the whole damn England! And she just walks away! She runs away! And she leaves her man cryin' where everybody can see! I think she's just a selfish, spoiled, scaredy-ass little bug-up-her-butt bitch!"

"You take that back . . . ," said Rocher, slamming the drawer to her register closed. "You didn't know her. You didn't know what she was going through."

"Oh, and you did, little missy new-bitch at the Valu-Brite?" said Vivian, who now slammed her own register shut.

"Girls, ladies, Valu-Brite employees," I said desperately, trying to defuse or at least contain the situation. "It doesn't matter, Rebecca Randle is gone and she's not coming back and nobody knows anything, so it's all guesswork, right? And hey, look at this, it's really interesting," I insisted, grabbing another tabloid from the rack and opening it to a non-Rebecca-related story. "How about this woman in Pennsylvania who married her own grandson and gave birth to three sets of conjoined twins? Isn't that amazing?"

But I was too late, because Rocher and Vivian were now both inches away from me, on either side, puffing out their chests. Rocher was wielding the metal tool that stamped "Valu-Brite X-tra Valu!" adhesive stickers onto sale items and Vivian had peeled off her press-on fingernails, which had been airbrushed with happy yellow smiley faces, and replaced them with longer, sharpened metal talons airbrushed with ravenous hammerhead sharks.

"I'm glad that Rebecca bitch-hole didn't marry that prince!" shouted Vivian. "He should marry himself somethin' special, not some ugly-ass Rebecca pig-butt! She don't deserve to be no Queen! That Prince Gregory, he's a fine hunka man chunk, even if he's a little pasty and vanilla bean! But that Rebecca bitch don't love him! She only love Re-bitch-a!"

"Fuck you!" howled Rocher as the crowd, thrilled to be witnessing such a boisterous lunchtime smackdown, began to chant, "FIGHT! FIGHT! FIGHT!"

"Oh yeah?" said Vivian, reaching over my left shoulder and under my right arm, trying to grab, slap or stab Rocher. "Ain't nobody gonna love that bitch, not no time never! She don't deserve to be loved!"

"What . . . did . . . you . . . say?" I asked. I could take the insults and the smears but Vivian hadn't merely touched a nerve, she'd yanked on it with both hands and started to braid it into a pain pretzel.

"I'm just sayin' . . . ," said Vivian, her smile now stretching wide and mean because she'd located her true rival. "I'm just sayin' that Rebecca Randle, wherever she is, she is gonna die alone and nobody's gonna care. And I bet she knows it."

I felt like after swinging a sledgehammer and slamming it into my stomach, Vivian was now gleefully Rollerblading through the store, looping my intestines around the pyramids of avalanche-fresh mouthwash and ultimate-strength, power-propulsion laxatives. I let loose with something midway between a samurai shriek and the anguished, moonlit cry of a wounded animal with her paw caught in a rusty iron trap.

"AAAACHHHAAKKKKWAIII!!!" I bellowed as I grabbed Vivian's spike and tried to slam her head into the register, but she managed to dig her talons into my cheeks, leaving deep and blood-gushing grooves as she yelled, "Rebecca's gonna die alone in a mudhole, ho-bag!"

Fifteen minutes later, after the police had come and gone and Rocher and I had both been fired and our cashiers' vests revoked, we sat on a high step of the broad outdoor staircase that climbed over the half-price ticket booth in Times Square. This Plexiglas stairway to nowhere was illuminated from within, so it glowed a throbbing red beneath our legs. There were thousands of tourists clogging the sidewalks, with families stooped from their layered shopping bags, like pack mules from Düsseldorf and Umbria and Boise, and there were hundreds of people seated on the steps around us, taking a breather or deciphering a subway map or scarfing their sushi from plastic trays as their overexcited children scampered up and down the pulsating steps.

As Rocher and I tried to cope with everything that had happened to us and with how far we'd fallen, I saw the largest sign in the whole area, hanging directly across from where we were sitting, only it was mounted on the umpteenth floor of a skyscraper many blocks away. The sign was so huge that every inch of it was blazingly visible and because it was one of those LED video screens, the projected images were concocted from zillions of tiny flashing lights, so it was like sitting in my mom's trailer watching TV along with a few hundred thousand guests. Rebecca's smiling, impossibly gorgeous face appeared on the screen in a photo from the *Vogue* shoot. And even though the shoot had occurred only a little over a year earlier all I could think was, look at her, she's so young. Then, beginning as a microdot and hurtling and blossoming forward, like a comet bursting through the earth's atmosphere, until it covered Rebecca's face and filled the entire mammoth screen, there was a vibrating red question mark.

Something buzzed inside my backpack and when I dug around, I found my mom's phone, although I hadn't heard her ringtone, which made sense, because nothing romantic or magical was ever going to happen to me again. I opened the phone but no one was calling. I checked my mom's address book but there were only a few names, including my grandparents, a woman my mom had worked with behind the counter at a fast-food place, Princess Alicia and Tom Kelly. Everyone on the list, except Tom, was dead.

Rocher was staring at me.

"What?"

"It's just, I don't know," she said, still staring. "I was just about getting used to you being Rebecca. And when we'd talk, it almost seemed normal, like, of course I'm friends with Rebecca Randle. But now . . ."

"Now what? Now that I'm just me again, it sucks?"

"No, no, it's not that, it's just — okay, when you were around Jate or the prince or the Queen, you got that jolt, didn't you? That sort of buzz that people get when they're standing next to a famous person, or even more, when the famous person is talking to them? It's like a contact high, right? It's like, when I was around Rebecca, I felt like — anything was possible."

I couldn't get angry at Rocher because I knew just what she meant. If standing next to Rebecca had been a thrill then standing inside her had been pure adrenaline. Being Rebecca had been its own extreme sport, so how could I blame Rocher for missing the rush?

"It's just weird," she said, like someone who'd woken up to an empty house on Christmas morning.

Things were getting desperate. Rocher and I couldn't find work, and Aimee and Suzanne were impatient about the rent and the utility bill. "I mean, there are a lot of people who would kill for this apartment," Aimee sniffed and I wanted to ask her how many people had been killed *in* the apartment, but I knew that Rocher and I had to come up with some money fast, because I didn't want to find out what the next lower rung might be below Aimee and Suzanne's sleeper sofa.

I'd try anything, so when I came across a job listing for an assistant concierge position at the Royal Criterion Hotel, I called the personnel director and said that I was Claire Ridgefield of Ridgefield Employment Options and that I was sending over a Becky Randle, who'd be perfect for the job. I name-dropped Rebecca's favorite European hotels as references and insisted, sort-of truthfully, that Becky had only just returned to the States and was entertaining multiple offers. In order to appear as grown-up and professional as possible I sweet-talked Aimee into lending me the tailored gray gabardine suit she wore to any audition for the role of an Ivy League lawyer, a Wall Street honcho or the still-warm corpse of an Ivy League lawyer or a Wall Street honcho, partially hidden in a culvert. Aimee said that she usually wore the jacket without a blouse because "I want to look super-educated but still totally hot."

To save the subway fare, I hiked the thirty blocks to the Royal Criterion in Rocher's look-of-leather navy pumps, inhaling bus exhaust, getting a puddle of filthy, day-old rainwater splashed in my face by a passing cab and attracting the following comment from a homeless woman: "Oh, honey, did somebody steal your real clothes?"

The Royal Criterion was the city's most glamorously staid hotel. It dated from the early 1900s, but it had been sumptuously refurbished by its current Saudi owners at a price tag of over a billion dollars, which had ensured cutting-edge WiFi access, fail-safe security precautions and a five-star French-Baltic fusion restaurant. I stood across the street from the hotel, admiring the thirty stories of Italian marble, heavy silk window treatments and the array of international flags billowing over the grand main entrance. Would Rebecca have stayed here, I wondered, or would she have opted for something equally pricey, but more trendy and architecturally of-the-moment, somewhere downtown? I almost could've asked her, because Rebecca's face was taunting me from a nearby newsstand, a movie ad shrink-wrapped over an entire crosstown bus and a dramatic black-and-white photo in the window of one of the hotel's street-level shops where Rebecca's long neck was draped with enough freshwater pearls to buy Rocher and me a house in the suburbs with five bedrooms, all with walk-in closets, a four-car garage and a great room with a river-rock fireplace.

Rebecca was beginning to seem less like a memory and more entirely fictional — had she really existed? All I knew for sure was that Rebecca's feet hadn't ached because she'd never had to squeeze them into borrowed shoes, and she'd never had to worry about whether she'd combed all of the petrifying pigeon crap out of her hair, and whether applying toothpaste to a seriously recurring chin-zit ever really helps. But I was Becky, so I straightened Aimee's skirt, with its safety-pinned waistband and Scotch-taped hem, and I ordered myself to suck it up. Then I crossed the street and smiled at the uniformed doorman as if we were already devoted colleagues, while he ignored me completely.

Since no one was rushing to help me, I shouldered my way through the heavy bronze revolving door. It was like entering the most stately, hushed bank, where, instead of storing the rich people's fortunes, they stored the rich people themselves.

As I crossed the geometrically inlaid marble floor, I saw that there was some sort of bottleneck at the reception desk, which was a long marble-topped counter set within a gilded archway. There were five outraged, impatiently snorting guests, some toting hand luggage and others draped in fur, all standing in line and not liking it one bit. For rich people, even a half-second's waiting period, especially in public, was an arrow to the heart and a possible socialist plot. Some of these people were already barking into their phones and jabbing at their BlackBerries, berating distant underlings and spouses for booking them into such an incompetent, bush league, nickel-and-dime establishment. The head concierge was standing behind the counter, overseeing three assistants, each more flummoxed and near tears than the next.

"I'm so sorry!" wailed one of the concierge's assistants, a twenty-something man wiping his sweating palms across the pockets of his maroon Royal Criterion blazer. He kept poking frantically at his keyboard, as if the system could be prodded, or, if necessary, sucker-punched into behaving itself. "It's totally frozen, it's dead, I've never seen anything like this! I can't verify anything, I don't know who anyone is, it's a nightmare!"

"Stop whimpering, Kevin," said a female assistant, a much tougher number in her own pressed and lint-free blazer, with her hair yanked into a rigid blond ponytail. "Don't be such a girl."

Watching the now openly cursing and threatening guests, I also noticed the door that might get me behind the counter and I made my move swiftly and unobtrusively. I elbowed aside another assistant until I was standing beside, according to his polished brass nameplate, ELDIN TALDECOTT, CONCIERGE. He was a narrow, unruffled man who, I imagined, had never permitted himself to leave his nearby rent-stabilized, frighteningly uncluttered one-bedroom apartment without making sure he was scrubbed, shaved, combed and deodorized, and dressed in something that had spent most of its life traveling to or from a plastic dry-cleaning bag. He was a born concierge, someone who received a quietly yet richly orgasmic satisfaction from neatness, order and level-headed problem solving, particularly in the face of rampant hysteria.

"Good morning, Mr. Taldecott," I began in a low, respectful and helpful tone. "I see that our first guests are Lord and Lady Netton-Bashmere of East Chittenden, in town for the Winter Antiques Show." I'd met this elderly, tottering couple on several occasions: at a palace tea, a cocktail party and my rehearsal dinner, as they were cousins of Prince Gregory, and Lady Veronica had briefed me on their eccentricities, their medications and their world-class horde of Victorian trivets and toleware trays.

"Welcome to the Royal Criterion, your Lord and Ladyships," I continued. "Your suite will be ready momentarily and the hotel would be so grateful if you would enjoy a complimentary cocktail in our lounge. That will be a scotch-and-water, no rocks, for his Lordship, and a spearmint, not peppermint, schnapps for her Ladyship, I believe. And while you're relaxing and enjoying a complimentary assortment of scones, tarts and toast points, you might also inspect our supply of catalogues from both the Winter Show at the Armory as well as similar upcoming events in St. Petersburg, Madrid and Basel. We can also provide the monograph to the Cooper-Hewitt Museum's current exhibition of late-Regency-period trivets and cache-pots in brass, painted tin and papier-mâché."

"You know I can't resist papier-mâché," said Lady Netton-Bashmere, quivering at the thought of a decorative flowerpot decoupaged with butterflies and marigolds. I knew about the Armory show because I'd seen a poster for it on my trek uptown; I'd also passed the Cooper-Hewitt Museum where there had been banners silk-screened with the title "A Proper Parlor" and pen-and-ink sketches of teapots, flatware and fingerbowls.

"And while it is far too early for even a decent whiskey," said Lord Netton-Bashmere, "I believe that, under such trying circumstances, I shall make an exception." I knew that the keys to Lord Netton-Bashmere's cooperation were his alcoholism and the word "complimentary." As Rebecca, I'd learned that rich people crave freebies more than anyone. I'd seen billionaires shove their children aside to grab two additional goody bags at a film premiere, each bag rattling with just a few perfume samples, a promotional coaster and a soundtrack CD.

"Who are you?" Mr. Taldecott whispered to me as Kevin and Trish, the severely ponytailed sorority nazi, led the royals off to the lounge.

"Becky Randle," I replied with a professional directness, and then, more brightly, "And here is Ms. Helen Flain, of the Danx-Talman Investment Group. Welcome to the Royal Criterion, Ms. Flain. In just a few moments we will have access to all global markets in our Financial and Media Center on the third floor. And meanwhile there are branches of both Cartier and Van Cleef in our lower lobby promenade, and once your suite is ready, you'll find the minibar stocked with a selection of cranberry and peach yogurts along with family-sized bags of plain, peanut and almond M&M'S."

"Thank you," said Ms. Flain, "and I shouldn't mention this, but . . ."

"You will find the Girl Scout Thin Mints on the night table beside your bed along with three fresh boxes of doughnut holes in honey-glazed, coconut and maple stripe."

Ms. Flain was the vice president of her firm, which Prince Gregory had been leaning on to donate the financing for malaria nets in Zimbabwe. Two months ago she'd discovered that her husband, who was the CEO of Danx-Talman, had sent over three hundred pleading, sexually explicit, unreturned texts to Rebecca, which had emphasized increasingly lucrative offers for her preferably used panties. Ms. Flain was considering either a divorce or some major reconciliatory jewelry and she was also a binge eater, with a weakness for airport crap. When Prince Gregory and I had lunched with the Flains, Helen had only picked at her salad but there had been an almost empty package of soft-baked chocolate-chunk cookies tucked into her Hermès shoulder bag beside three cream-filled crullers.

As Ms. Flain wandered off to check on the current value of her husband's portfolio to guide her in choosing a diamond tennis bracelet and maybe a matching eternity ring, Mr. Taldecott asked me, "How did you know all of that and what are you doing here?"

"I'm a smart girl, I'm applying for a job as one of your assistants, and you'd better send Kevin over to Dunkin' Donuts right away."

"Roche, I just went for it," I said later that night when we were under the sleeper sofa's torn and hemorrhaging polyester quilt. "Here's why I got the job: It's like the whole time Rebecca was being a movie star and falling in love and almost becoming a princess, I was watching everything. It's like I was filing everything away, like I was Rebecca's secretary. And it all just came pouring out, everything I'd been learning about rich people and royalty and hotels. I've become an expert in everything I'll never be able to afford."

"It's like, you went to the University of Rebecca, instead of that two-week manicure school in Jamesburg."

"Exactly!"

"Excush me!" shouted Suzanne from her bedroom, although her words were slurred because her corrective dental headgear was in place. "I'm trying to get shum shleep, I have a callback tomorrow, for a commershul! I'm thish girl with cold shores who pullsh her turtleneck over her fash! So could you pleash shut the hell up!"

20.

Even without references or a resume, I quickly became Mr. Taldecott's most valuable resource at the Royal Criterion. Thanks to my mother's decades of scrapbooking and my time as Rebecca, I was like one of those idiot savants who, if you mention any date in history, can automatically supply the day of the week, except that I had an infallible memory for the lives of royalty and anyone from the fashion or movie industries, along with a working knowledge of the dermabrasions, hushed-up abortions and beverage preferences of the mega-rich. I was constantly astonishing Mr. Taldecott by hovering at his side and murmuring, "She'll need extra pillows, because she just had three ribs removed so she could wear a bikini," "He likes Asian prostitutes who'll spit in his face" and "The parents are cokeheads and their older child likes to chew on electrical wiring until he passes out, but they're all really nice."

"Becky," said Mr. Taldecott, who'd called me into his small private office after I'd been working at the hotel for five months. The office was a cross between a pharaoh's crypt and a universal lost and found; the walls were lined from floor to ceiling with plywood shelving, holding every possible item — no matter how obscure — a guest might request, including newspapers from countries that had only existed for a few days, hand towels so hypoallergenic that they were delivered in freeze-dried pouches, condoms in every variety from cinnamon-scented sheepskin to triple-extra-wide with a reservoir tip, along with hearing-aid batteries, folding canes, temporary teeth, eyelash curlers, travel irons, mini-sizes of every known shampoo and a basket of what I at first thought were tennis balls and pepper mills, but which turned out to be sex toys.

"I don't know who you are," Mr. Taldecott continued, "or why you're so phenomenally informed, but you've impressed me beyond measure."

"Thank you so much, but I told you, while my mom was pregnant, she read a lot of magazines."

"Perhaps. But you also have a gift for service, for anticipating a guest's needs. And you wrangle even the most offensive requests with modesty and discretion."

I'd learned how to do all of this when I'd been Rebecca because I'd picked up on how the world worked. People who were born rich often never appreciated their own good luck and could become helpless because they always assumed that someone would be trailing them to pick up, launder and return their discarded socks, and to remember their PIN numbers and raise their children. Sometimes these heirs and heiresses weren't being snooty, they just didn't know any better. And self-made people who'd worked their way up from nothing could be especially generous because they remembered where they came from, or monumentally unpleasant because they were out for revenge. At the Royal Criterion I was professionally nice to everyone but I'd smile more sincerely at the people who looked me in the eye as they said thank you or who remembered my name, or even both my names. I tried to recall if Rebecca had ever carried on like the people whom Mr. Taldecott referred to as Challenges and whom the assistants called, among ourselves, RTAs, for Raging Total Assholes.

"Becky, at the hotel, as you know, it will ordinarily take an assistant concierge at least five years of unblemished employment, without a single day's absence, even to be considered for advancement to the position of deputy concierge."

There were, at any given time, eight assistant concierges working in shifts and only two deputies. If Mr. Taldecott was either ill or absent, neither of which had ever occurred during his thirty-one years at the hotel, one of the deputies would assume his duties. I suspected that Mr. Taldecott pictured himself dying while behind the front desk, of a silent, tidy stroke, which would permit him to slump graciously out of sight while one of the deputies stepped artfully over his body and asked the next guest, "How may I be of assistance?" The deputies were also the only employees, aside from Mr. Taldecott, who were authorized to interact with the most valued and powerful guests.

"Becky, in all my years of service, I've never come across anyone with your natural abilities. And so, if you continue to perform at this remarkable level, by the end of the year I will consider advancing you to the rank of Second Deputy."

I was stunned because aside from having worked behind the registers at the Super Shop-A-Lot and the Valu-Brite and having been the Most Beautiful Woman Who Ever Lived, I'd never really held a job let alone done something that anyone thought I was good at. As my days at the hotel continued I found that Rebecca had taught me many useful things, but mostly I drew on her confidence. Because while I no longer owned her staggering physical assets or her wardrobe, I always remembered how she'd walk into a room or onto a soundstage or the deck of a yacht, as if she had every right to be there, and as if she knew what she was doing. So sometimes, when Mr. Taldecott sent me on an impossible errand, like when I had to knock on the door of an eighty-million-dollar-a-year NFL quarterback's room, after a neighboring guest had reported a horse's whinny, a wailing baby and gunshots, I'd tell myself, I can handle this, because I am Rebecca Randle, sort of.

Rocher had also been hired, subbing on street corners all over town, at the portable pegboard walls and rickety card tables that sold five-dollar fake cashmere scarves and imitation designer-label purses, along with knitted hats and printed rayon shawls, all stitched by child laborers in Third World countries. These rolling and folding merchandise marts were almost never licensed and could be assembled or collapsed in seconds to avoid citations and arrests. Most of the men and women who staffed these stands were incredibly hardworking illegal immigrants, who lived eighteen to a room in the outer boroughs, but who sometimes had to abandon their goods to avoid getting deported. This was when Marcus, the guy who controlled over fifty of the stands, would text Rocher, so she could show up, protect the bogus pashminas, and woo Bible study groups from Akron and bridal parties in town for the weekend from Kyoto into purchasing, hopefully in bulk, "glamorous boutique-type items with a real Fifth Avenue look," either for themselves, "because you never do anything nice just for you," or for "that special someone back home, who'll just die for these 100 percent cashmere-style earmuffs." Marcus loved Rocher because not only was she a born salesperson, she also liked working outdoors, she was fast on her feet and she probably wouldn't get deported back to Missouri.

I wasn't on duty when Jate Mallow checked into the Royal Criterion one Tuesday at 4:00 A.M. under an assumed name. The Rebecca madness had finally been eclipsed when Jate had fallen in love, and a paparazzi using a zoom lens had sold both the stills and the video of Jate lying in his lover's arms and having sex on what Jate had been guaranteed was a secluded and off-limits private beach in Tangier. Although at first Jate's people had scoffed and insisted that all of the pictures were fakes, the lover had soon sold his own "shockingly exclusive" story to both a tabloid and a publisher, and Jate had been undeniably outed.

Jate had a new movie called *Death Tracker*, which took place in the future after the planet had been decimated by a nuclear war. The radioactive fallout had created mutants, and Jate played a bounty hunter who captured these creatures, until his rugged, gun-for-hire character fell in love with a beautiful female half vampire. The film was set to open in two days, and it was planned as the first chapter of a projected trilogy, so the studio was frantic. Jate had been besieged by every news show, talk show, magazine and gay rights organization; these various factions wanted Jate to either announce his sexuality, in an upbeat, what's-the-big-deal-duh-I'm-gay cover story, or confide that he was entering an intensive, two-week program of Christian rehabilitative therapy to "correct the problem." Jate had responded to all of these offers, the online meltdown and the unauthorized sale of his sex tape, which the packaging called "An XXX Date with Jate," by vanishing from the face of the earth.

When Mr. Taldecott told me that a Mr. Wibblewort had checked into suite 1718 and was not to be disturbed under any circumstances, I said, and not as a question, "It's Jate Mallow," because Wally Wibblewort had been the name of the pet cockatiel which had cooed from Jate's shoulder on *Jackie + Jate*. Mr. Taldecott was no longer surprised by my psychic gifts regarding celebrities and he nodded as I compiled a list of Jate's favorite Sun-Brawny bronzer, lip-plumping Tangy Lime ChapStick and a product called Head Scum, which was guaranteed to give the user "thick, pungent, swamp-stylin' hair."

From glancing at Mr. Taldecott's encrypted, most confidential hotel log, I saw that Jate hadn't left his suite for three days and had refused all letters, calls and packages. I knew that if I got caught trying to contact Jate personally on hotel property, I'd be fired on the spot. But Jate had been so good to me and he was having a really rough time, so I had to do something. I knew what it was like to be riding ridiculously high and then to have everything come crashing down. And besides, if I couldn't come up with a way to help Jate Mallow, Rocher and my mom would never forgive me.

I studied the hotel log and I found out exactly when Mr. Taldecott would be off duty. Then I swapped shifts with another assistant and right after my work hours ended at 2:00 A.M., I snuck up to the seventeenth floor and used my pass card to enter Jate's suite.

"Mr. Wibblewort?" I said, stepping into the darkened rooms. I could hear distant dialogue from a TV, so I made my way through the front parlor, which was ordinarily the image of a formal reception room at a Tuscan villa. But now the heavy red-and-green-striped damask draperies were duct-taped shut, obliterating the high, mullioned windows that would have overlooked Central Park. The deep, down-filled damask sofas were buried beneath mounds of unwashed clothing and stacks of barely touched room-service meals. A lamp was overturned, and there were opened wine bottles balanced precariously along the edges of a desk. Even though the entire hotel was non-smoking, every surface held soda cans that had been used as makeshift ash trays and there was a thick haze in the dank air, as if Jate's suite had become a Los Angeles overpass at rush hour.

Using my foot I nudged aside a discarded leather jacket embroidered with the *Death Tracker* logo, and I approached the bedroom. The door was being held open by a never-worn cashmere sweater with the tags dangling, which had been shoved under the door itself. The light from the flat-screen TV, beaming from within an armoire, barely illuminated Jate, who was slumped in the king-sized bed beneath a heap of bedding. Jate was hovering somewhere between being drunk and stoned, and being theatrically drunk and stoned, with one arm flung across his eyes as he leaned against the quilted headboard. He was ignoring an episode of a syndicated medical show, where Dr. Whoever was helping a single mom cope with her Lyme disease by assuring her that having Lyme disease didn't make her a bad person. What worried me as the most genuine hint of Jate's anguish was that his hair, which was ordinarily so time-consumingly and radiantly spiked and awry, was now truly and dejectedly messy. It was, in fact, lifeless and limp, it was hair that had lost the urge to swirl. And if Jate didn't care about his hair anymore, then he was in real danger.

"Mr. Mallow?" I began.

Jate grunted, lowering his flung arm slightly to prove that his eyes were resolutely shut. Then he said, "Look at her. That chick on TV. She's all upset because she's got Lyme disease." He opened his eyes and looked right at me, shouting, "I wish I had fucking LYME DISEASE!"

"Mr. Mallow, do you need anything?"

"What? Do I what? Oh my God, are you a reporter? Did you sneak in here? How did you find me? I'm calling security!"

"No, no, please don't!" I said as Jate fumbled for the phone. "It's fine, I'm with the hotel! I'm Becky Randle!"

"Becky Randle?" said Jate, holding the phone in midair. "Like Rebecca Randle?"

"No relation."

"Too bad. 'Cause that's just what I'm doing."

"What?"

"I'm pulling a fucking REBECCA RANDLE!"

"What do you mean?"

"What do I mean? Haven't you been out there? In the world? Haven't you watched TV or checked out, oh, I don't know, a few billion magazine covers and I Hate Jate websites and fan tweets and fan sites and fan blogs? Look at me! I'm Jate fucking Mallow! The big Hollywood homo!"

"Okay . . ."

"Okay? OKAY? It is not OKAY!"

"But there are plenty of gay actors. And lots of them have come out and everybody's fine with it."

"EXCUSE ME? I'm a LEADING MAN! Those other actors, they're all supporting or old or funny or talented. I'm a MOVIE STAR! And I've got a flick coming out this weekend, where I'm a bounty hunter from the future and in two weeks I'm supposed to start shooting another movie, where I play a fucking MARINE!"

"But — they repealed that law, so now people can be gay in the Marines. . . ."

"I know, but not in the MOVIES! So I'm gone! I'm outta here! Just like Rebecca Randle!"

Waving the remote, Jate shut off the TV and resumed disappearing by whomping the covers over his head. Only a few drooping stalks of his once-fabled hair remained visible, like a retreating militia.

"Mr. Mallow?" I said, moving tentatively toward the bed.

"Jate," he said, his voice muffled by the covers.

"I knew Rebecca Randle, I mean, not well, but she was often a guest at the hotel and I would assist her with theater tickets and plane reservations. And do you know what Ms. Randle and I talked about? All the time? For hours?" Jate's head lump rose a few inches, from curiosity, because no one loves gossip more than a movie star.

"You."

"Me?" asked the muffled heap.

"Of course. She adored you. She thought that you were so

handsome and so smart and such a great actor, and she said that she owed all of her success to you."

The lump jerked from side to side, as a modest, no, no.

"And I knew that she was right about you because she knew you personally, and I could always tell that you weren't just, you know, a legendary star and an inspiration to people all over the world but that you were also a really decent human being. I mean, I just knew it because — I'm your biggest fan."

I waited, unsure if I'd played the wrong card and if the lump was panicking at being trapped in a bunkerlike hotel suite with a deranged stalker.

But then after a few suspenseful seconds, Jate's eyes and then most of his face appeared, with his fingertips clutching the top sheet. It was like a puppet show, starring the increasingly hopeful head of Jate Mallow.

"You are?" he asked, as if I was his only fan left in the world.

"Oh, yes! When I was growing up I cut out hundreds of pictures of you and I made this huge collage over a whole wall of my bedroom. And when you got that frosted perm, with the tight ringlets, I got one too."

"You did? I wasn't sure about it at first, 'cause a perm is really hard to pull off, and maintain. Especially with any sort of humidity."

"Totally. And then two weeks ago, I heard that you were gay."

Jate went pale and without his touching it, his hair seemed to cringe in fear and he began to dip back under the covers.

"And at first I was so confused and I didn't know if it was true or not."

"But then?" asked Jate, his voice cracking.

"But then I thought, he's still Jate. He's still unbelievably gorgeous and famous and generous and a really good guy. And I thought, sure, fine, maybe some idiots are gonna have Jate hate just because you're gay and they're not gonna go see your movies. But then I thought, in your new movie, the one that's opening this weekend, you meet a mutant girl from the future, who's a vampire on her mother's side, right? And you fall in love, even though humans and vampires are supposed to hate each other, right?"

"Yes, because that's the whole point of the movie, it's like, even though I've been assigned to round up her relatives and keep them in partial sunlight, I realize that the daughter is also still human. And so together we protect the last remaining medical researcher on earth, who has the formula that allows vampires to live on contaminated water and bark."

"And so it all works out! And you prove that there are all kinds of love. And so maybe when people, even straight guys, when they go to see *Death Tracker*, maybe they'll understand all of that."

There was a pause and then Jate said, "You are so full of it."

"Find out. Don't be like Rebecca Randle. Don't run away. Give the world a chance. I mean, what's your choice? Do you just want to hide in here forever? What if you got up and maybe took a shower and air-dried your hair and scrunched in some of that fantastic new scrunching gel, called Pus Muss, and you went outside?"

Jate looked down at his hands and I saw that he was now completely and maybe far too sober. "I know what you mean," he said, "but I'm not even sure if it matters. Because do you want to know something? The most insane part of all of this? The kicker?"

"What?"

"That guy? On the beach? The one in all the photos and the video? The guy who sold me out? I . . . I loved him. Or I thought I did. He was this rich kid, he'd worked as an assistant art director on one of my movies, and we weren't together for all that long, but we were having such a great time and I just thought, fuck it. I mean, I know I'm Jate Mallow and I should know better, but do you remember how on my TV show, I'd always be meeting someone and we'd hold hands and make out? Well I just thought, what if, for once in my life, I really did that. What if for once I didn't call my manager or a private investigator to check the guy out and I didn't make him sign a confidentiality agreement. What if I just went for it."

"So you did?"

"Yes. And for a little bit, for those few weeks, it was wonderful. Because you know what's so great about falling in love?"

"What?"

"I stopped thinking about myself. When you're a star, it's so easy to forget about everything but your career and your image and the money, and how to keep it all going. But for at least a little while, I thought about someone else. And all I wanted to do was to make him happy."

I knew just what Jate was talking about because I still thought about Gregory all the time.

"But here's the problem. And I don't know if you'll be able to understand this, but for almost my whole life, I've felt like I was two different people. And I was always so scared that if the world found out who I really was, that no one would like me. Does that make any sense?"

"Yes," I said quietly. "It makes perfect sense. And it sounds like it would drive you crazy."

"Becky?" said Jate. "I still don't really know who you are but — you seem really sweet. And smart, about all of this."

"I just . . . I just work here."

"Have you ever been in love?"

As I was about to answer, my phone went off.

It was Rocher. "Becky, I know it's really late and I'm so sorry but they wouldn't even let me have my one phone call for hours and I don't know what to do and Beck — I'm in jail."

21.

Rocher had been arrested during a sweep of street vendors in Midtown and while all of her coworkers had run, she'd loyally stood beside her folding table stocked with fake Tom Kelly sunglasses and those dorky Peruvian hats with the knitted balls dangling from the earflaps, which only look good on bicycle messengers. "I stayed because I'd just gotten everything perfectly folded and arranged by color," Rocher explained. She didn't have a phone number for Marcus, her boss, because he'd always contacted her and blocked his own information, and now the police were holding her at the precinct on West 52nd Street.

When I got there the sergeant at the front desk wouldn't let me see Rocher and he told me that the department wanted to make an example of her, and that bail had been set at twenty thousand dollars. "Maybe your little friend thinks it's just about selling those crappy Peruvian hippie hats," said the sergeant, "but it's about the law. How do we know that every time your buddy makes five bucks off some fake Tom Kelly purse, that half of that money doesn't go right back to the terrorists?"

I was only making an entry-level paycheck at the Royal Criterion so Rocher and I could barely scrape together each month's rent. I'd run through my tiny East Trawley savings and all of Rebecca's money had been spent while I was still Rebecca. Because I'd been so beautiful, and because I was going to marry

Prince Gregory, I'd assumed that money would never be an issue; my face had been my bank account.

I knew that there was just one way I could pull together twenty grand because I only knew one person who'd have that kind of cash on hand. And he was the last person on earth I wanted to see: Tom Kelly. But Rocher was in police custody and I had no other prospects so I told myself, just brace yourself. And I wouldn't be begging because Tom Kelly owed me.

I took a cab over to Tom's compound and all the gates swung open. I had the cab drop me out on the pier inside the white graveled courtyard, where Drake was waiting. As he paid my cab fare and led me inside the glass pavilion, he said, "It's good to see you. Tom told me not to worry but I've been thinking about you a lot."

"Why does anyone ever listen to Tom Kelly?" I asked, although I knew I shouldn't blame Drake for his employer's evil.

"Rebecca," said Lila, meeting me in the lobby. As always she was sleekly and forbiddingly dressed — today, in a sleeveless white linen sheath outlined in black piping.

"It's Becky," I said, correcting her. "And I need to see Tom, right away."

As Lila brought me into the black glass elevator, I could tell that she wanted to say something but she was hesitating.

"What?" I said. "What is it? And please, whatever you do, don't try to make excuses or explain Tom's behavior. Because I swear, I will punch you."

"There are no excuses," Lila said. "And I'm not going to tell you that everything that happened is for the best. Because why would you believe me?"

As I watched Lila, with her flawless chignon and her infinitesimal waistline, I wondered: I knew she was devoted to Tom, and that she was probably in love with him, but what else did he have on her? Had she robbed a bank, was he supporting her family, what could explain his hold over her?

"Why?" I finally asked. "Why do you stay with him?"

Lila smiled, because she wasn't about to reveal anything. "Free clothes," she said.

When the elevator doors parted, I saw Tom seated on one of the low black leather couches near the blue flames of the glass fireplace. He was wearing a fitted denim work shirt, unbuttoned halfway and partially tucked into the faded jeans that hung off his hips, for a Hamptons cowboy lankiness. It was as if he'd done nothing but lounge, tended to by his slavish staff, ever since I'd met him. And because he'd returned to his compound, to his black-and-white garden of hatefulness, he looked better than ever. He was about to greet me, but I cut him off.

"I need twenty thousand dollars right now," I said as I crossed the miles of glossy white flooring. I stopped ten feet away from Tom because I didn't want to be anywhere near him. "Rocher is in jail and I have to bail her out. And you owe me."

"I owe you?"

"Don't. Don't even try. Don't even start."

I didn't run at him or kick him or slap him and I didn't start sobbing and falling apart and here's why: because I couldn't complain. Tom had promised to make me the most beautiful woman on earth and he'd delivered. He'd offered me the world and I'd grabbed it. My only problem was I'd cheated. I'd cut in line. As Tom had always told me, beauty is unfair, it's sheer genetic roulette, but I'd hacked the system.

But there was another, completely legitimate reason for my fury at Tom Kelly. I had fallen in love and I'd told him about it and he hadn't believed me. He'd denied the only absolute truth of my year as Rebecca. And that was the one thing I could never forgive.

"I just have one question," I said and then I waited a beat, so I could be as simple and direct as possible. "Why?"

"Why did I make you beautiful or why did I stop?"

"Both."

"Because I promised your mother."

"You promised her what? To transform me? And then burn me to the ground?"

"I'll give you all the money you need, on one condition."

"What? What do I have to do?"

"Trust me."

"Trust you?"

"Yes. And do you know why?"

I exploded. I couldn't strategize or keep a tight lid on my rage for one second longer. I just lost it, like an unmanageable, spitting-and-biting four-year-old, high from too much sugar and not enough sleep. "Why? WHY? I'm supposed to ask WHY I should trust you, you pure evil, satanic, piss-headed . . . evil . . . gross . . . repulsive . . . evil . . . fart-faced   evil . . . nowhere-near-as-good looking as you-think-you-are . . . fuck-headed shit-nosed fuck-faced fuckwad . . . why? WHY? WHY???"

Tom laughed at my kindergarten diatribe, although his laughter didn't sound cruel or spiteful, but that couldn't be, since Tom Kelly was the most cruel and spiteful creature who'd ever lived. Being cruel and spiteful was probably his skincare regimen; being cruel and spiteful kept him looking so ungodly young and so smug and inappropriately happy.

"Here's why you should trust me," Tom said. "You should trust me because — you have one dress left."

Then Lila appeared with an envelope of cash, which believe me, I counted. Then I let Drake drive me to the precinct house, where I bailed out my best friend.

Later that afternoon, just when I thought my day couldn't get any more impossible, as I was standing behind the reception counter at the Royal Criterion, a new guest arrived, with her mincing, jabbering and demanding entourage: Lady Jessalyn Clane-Taslington and her closest buddies, Annabelle, Tinsy and Bims. After Westminster Abbey, Lady Jessalyn had felt it her duty, subtly at first, to begin comforting the scorned and unmoored Prince Gregory, and her brief calls, her emails of sensitive quotations from Buddhist scholars and her heartfelt, handwritten notes offering only "honest friendship" had soon reestablished her in first position of the Princess Preakness.

I knew all of this because the Royal Criterion's newsstand stocked all of the oversized English glossies with their upbeat, sunshiny titles like *Cheerio!*, *First Up!* and *Have At It!* These weren't gossipy, vindictive, smut-hungry tabloids but full-color celebrations of all that was right and good with the Royal Family. I'd tried not to read them but from the cover lines, and from Lady Jessalyn's increasingly large and prominently positioned photos, I was aware that she'd been one of "five hundred intimate guests" at a Buckingham Palace Christmas tree—lighting ceremony, that she'd been spotted giving Prince Gregory a genteel, supportive, sisterly hug at a rock concert promoting international literacy, and that, only a month earlier, both she and the prince had been the guests of a Greek shipping trillionaire on board the trillionaire's tri-level yacht, which housed two helicopters, a bowling alley and a putting green, for a quiet sail around uninhabited islands in the Aegean. A telephoto lens had captured the prince with his long legs dangling from the stern of the yacht, as Lady Jessalyn with her lithe, tan, bikini-clad body had stood nobly behind him, her glinting, predatory eyes obscured by oversized white-framed sunglasses as she'd placed a blameless, cautiously soothing hand on the prince's troubled shoulder.

"Good afternoon, Your Ladyship," I said through gritted teeth as my one-time nemesis burbled up to the counter, leading her gaggle of friends, who were all vying for maid of honor. "Annabelle, stop picking your teeth," Lady Jessalyn was saying, "I told you not to have that sesame mini-bagel, and Tinsy, I'm sorry, and I say this as a friend, but even though we're in the States that doesn't mean you should attempt turquoise, you look like an enormous bottle of dishwashing liquid, and, Bims, please bring me my smaller Vuitton case, no, the lavender one, with the crest, because I need to speak with this girl about a safe-deposit box. Hello, I'm sure you have a name and I do hope our rooms are ready, we've been through absolute torment at the airport — they insisted that Luella remain in her little carrying cage, even though I told them repeatedly that she was drugged to the gills."

"I'm sorry," I said, "which one of you is Luella?"

"Luella is Lady Jessalyn's teacup poodle," Annabelle informed me, holding up the wire carrier; the tiny animal inside was near comatose but its glassy eyes were pleading for either freedom or death, anything to get away from Lady Jessalyn and her nattering cronies.

"Everything is in order, Your Ladyship," I said, handing Lady Jessalyn a packet of electronic keycards, minibar keys and invitations. "We're delighted to see you and we're so pleased that you've chosen the Royal Criterion."

"Of course you are."

"You should really give us our rooms for free," sniffed Tinsy. "We really do dress the place up."

"We should at the very least receive complimentary Pilates sessions and seaweed wraps," declared Bims.

"I'll see what I can do," I said evenly while I imagined all of them at the bottom of the Atlantic, with stinging jellyfish and electric eels attached to their screaming faces.

As half the hotel's bellmen hefted Lady Jessalyn's matched luggage and began to escort the group to their many suites, Lady Jessalyn turned and shot me a harsh, quizzical look.

"Do I know you?" she asked.

"I don't believe so," I said. "I'm fairly new on staff, but if there's anything I can do to make your stay more pleasant, please don't hesitate to ask."

"I won't!" she trilled, and then, to her chums, without lowering her voice, "Americans! Simply besotted with royalty! They're all such impossible suck-ups!"

"Oh my God," said Rocher, later that evening at the apartment as we were digging into Hunan takeout. I'd brought enough for Aimee and Suzanne as well, because while they'd both insisted that they were sticking to strict macrobiotic diets in anticipation of being cast as teenage gymnasts, they didn't consider poaching food from Rocher and me to be a form of eating.

"So Lady Jessalyn is staying at your hotel," said Suzanne, craning her neck to maneuver a power suck from the straw of my milk shake.

"I love her," said Aimee. "I mean, she's so pretty, I think she's almost as pretty as Rebecca Randle."

"Oh, please," insisted Rocher. "Lady Jessalyn looks like something Rebecca Randle would flush down the toilet after Mexican food." Rocher was always on my side, but my bailing her out had made her reach for poetry.

"I read that Lady Jessalyn and Prince Gregory are totally back together," confided Aimee, as if the royals had sworn her to secrecy. "It's like, she's always been there for him and she's been so good and kind and understanding about Rebecca dumping him. Although some people say that Lady Jessalyn poisoned Rebecca, by hiding radioactive isotopes in her wedding bouquet and that's why she went psycho and ran away and that Rebecca's in a private clinic somewhere, and she's glowing this, like, lime green."

"And I bet that Lady Jessalyn is going to marry Prince Gregory," added Suzanne. "Especially after the whole Rebecca thing, people say that he's come to his senses and that he's ready to love again and that he realizes that Lady Jessalyn was always the right choice. And on Crowntown.com, where they handicap all of the candidates, Lady Jessalyn just pulled ahead of that Swedish girl, the Olympic skier, because one of her breast implants just exploded due to cabin pressure on a flight from Gstaad. And the papers say that Lady Jessalyn claims she's only in town for the international dog show, but that she's really here because Prince Gregory flies in tomorrow to speak at the United Nations. And I heard that during his speech, about England supporting the global initiative on clean energy, you know, like being all brown and everything . . ."

"All green," corrected Aimee.

"Whatever, all I know is that during the speech, I bet he's gonna announce his engagement. You know, so that people will pay attention to the clean energy part. What is clean energy, anyway? I mean, when I'm onstage, I try to be really focused and centered and in the moment, so maybe I'm, like, giving off tons of clean energy."

"What?" I said, because all I'd heard was the part about Prince Gregory's possible engagement.

"It's gonna be fine," Rocher assured me on the sleeper sofa at 2:00 A.M. "Aimee and Suzanne are full of shit. Although I bet Aimee could win that whole fucking dog show, if there's a category for dogs who should get their facial moles removed."

"It's a BEAUTY MARK," said Aimee from behind the closed door of her bedroom.

22.

The next morning in the employee locker room at the Royal Criterion, as I was getting ready for my shift, I knew that if I wanted to avoid a wrist-slitting breakdown or a drug-and-tequila-fueled rampage through the hotel lobby, I had to decide exactly how I felt about Prince Gregory moving on with his life and very possibly moving directly toward Lady Jessalyn.

What did I want the prince to do? Should he stay single forever and grow increasingly gaunt and hollow-eyed as he languished and longed for Rebecca and secretly for Becky, until he died tragically young with the words, "Where are they?" on his parched and pining lips? That sounded just fine. But if I still had any true feelings for the prince then I should really wish him only the best, although if he had to marry someone else he deserved so much better than Lady Jessalyn. He deserved someone who really appreciated him, someone who would know just when to make fun of him and someone who'd help him to be the best prince ever. But now I was drowning again in a vision of the two of us together and I had to stop doing that, I had to become strict about any sort of daydreams or memories or me-and-the-prince moments.

I looked at myself in the square, unframed mirror glued to the back of my locker door and I told myself, stop it. You are Becky, you will always be Becky, Rebecca is long gone and that's that. But as I continued to stare at myself I began seeing flashes of Rebecca, as if she were teasing me or reaching out from another dimension.

"No!" I said out loud as I slammed the locker shut, because I was pretty sure that this was how bona fide, straitjacket-worthy mental illnesses began. I'm fine, I decided, and it doesn't matter what I think about Prince Gregory, not anymore and if I'm alone forever, well, lots of people are alone. My mom had been alone and she'd never griped about it.

So in honor of my mom and her selflessness, I ran a gluey lint roller over my blazer, used a rubber band to pull my hair back into a neat ponytail, spritzed my tongue with my ever-present, pocket-sized, meeting-people-is-my-business breath spray, gave my hands a thorough coating of Santine, the Ultimate Strength Antibacterial Germ Slayer, left the locker room and stepped into position behind the reception counter beside Mr. Taldecott, who, with a quick side-long glance, noted that my wardrobe was in order and that I smelled reasonably antiseptic. And then I looked directly into the eyes of Prince Gregory, who'd only just arrived at the hotel, with a far smaller and much better behaved retinue than Lady Jessalyn.

"Good morning, Your Highness," I said without missing a beat in the warm, welcoming, mechanically modulated voice of a customer-service recording.

"Good morning," said Prince Gregory, not taking his eyes off mine as I silently screamed at him, no, I'm not that insane girl from the altar! We've never met before! And the name tag on my lapel doesn't read "R. Randle"!

"Welcome to the Royal Criterion, Your Highness," said Mr. Taldecott. "It's so good to have you with us again and your suite has been prepared."

"Thank you so much," said Prince Gregory as Mr. Taldecott handed the prince's secretary a packet of keycards along with the stacks of schedules and briefings that had already arrived from the United Nations. As the prince was led away, he kept making half-turns and scratching his neck, as if he was about to ask a question but wasn't sure what he wanted to know.

"What is he doing here?" I asked Mr. Taldecott as soon as the prince was out of earshot. "Why didn't you tell me he was staying at the hotel?"

"The prince travels under several assumed names to protect his privacy," Mr. Taldecott replied. I'd been so distracted by having both Jate Mallow and Lady Jessalyn on site that it hadn't occurred to me that Prince Gregory might also be a Royal Criterion regular. "You had no need to be aware of his arrival," Mr. Taldecott informed me. "We can't be too careful about unwanted publicity, particularly for our most cherished guests."

"But . . . but . . ."

"Becky? What's the trouble? I will be dealing with Prince Gregory myself as I always have."

Mr. Taldecott's phone rang. He listened, said, "Right away," and told me, "Prince Gregory has requested a carafe of ice water. And he's asked that you bring it to him personally."

"Me?"

"He asked for the young lady at the front desk."

"Maybe he meant Trish. . . ."

"Trish isn't here. He meant you, quite specifically."

"And he wants me to bring it to him now?"

"Yes. Have you ever met Prince Gregory or any member of his staff?"

"Of course not. Don't be ridiculous."

"Then get busy. Suite 2812."

"Do I have to go?"

"If you wish to continue working here."

"Of course," I said. "I'm sorry, I'm just a little nervous because he's a prince and all. I'll be fine. And I'm on my way."

Mr. Taldecott nodded frostily, because this was the first time I'd ever questioned any of my tasks. I nodded back and headed for the hotel kitchen. The second I was out of Mr. Taldecott's sight, I veered to the left, down a side hallway and out of the building, striding purposefully, as if I knew where I was going in case I was seen by any other hotel employee.

Once I'd left the hotel I realized that I hadn't taken a breath since the prince had shown up and I wasn't about to resume breathing anytime soon. I kept walking faster and then I ran until, without waiting for the traffic light to change, I raced across Fifth Avenue as cars honked, a bus driver slammed on his brakes, and a cabbie yelled, "Crazy fucking bitch!" I barely heard any of this because I was already on the other side of the street, sprinting along the sidewalk and then hoisting myself over a low granite wall and into Central Park.

I kept running blindly, not toward any destination, but just away — from the hotel and Mr. Taldecott and especially Prince Gregory and his ice water. I overtook joggers and teams of bicycle riders in matching spandex outfits and I vaulted over strollers being pushed by outraged nannies. All I knew was that I couldn't stop or something, most likely my life, would catch up with me and grind me into dust.

I headed into a more rustic corner of the park, clambering atop one prehistoric boulder after another, surprising a pair of hooky-playing teenage lovers and then a low-level drug deal. I kept moving until I reached a grove. I twisted and shoved my way between the birches and pines, ripping long scratches into my face and hands until I found a deserted clearing and, winded and flailing, I fell to the ground, first on my side, and then rolling onto my back, smearing myself with grass and leaves along with crumpled candy wrappers and something I hoped was a deflated balloon from a children's birthday party.

Shit, I thought, as I stared up at the cloudless blue sky and then blocked out the bright sun with my hand. I couldn't face anything, especially not a balmy April day, not right now. Shit shit shit shit shit. Until that moment I'd never considered how useful the word "shit" was; if I could just keep repeating "shit" for the rest of my life, as a single run-on sentence, I'd be fine. I'd be safe. I'd just lie on the ground and get covered by the seasons, by the rotting leaves and the frozen drifts and the year-round grit, until I became a small hill, a part of the landscape which only the occasional drunken vagrant would overhear mumbling "Shit shit shit shit shit . . ."

But my favorite word abandoned me even as I was determined to think about nothing, which never works, because a blank mind is an invitation to truth.

I had seen Prince Gregory. He had seen me. He'd known it was me. Or he'd known it was that terrible girl who'd replaced Rebecca at the altar.

If I had any guts at all, any decency, I would run right back to the hotel and face the music, which would be a dirge. I would own up to everything I'd done and I'd deliver a mealymouthed apology, which would solve nothing. But I couldn't even do that because I was a hopeless, disgusting, career coward and because I couldn't bear the thought of seeing the prince again and having him regard me with such well-deserved contempt.

I had to leave New York; I had to keep running, maybe all the way back to East Trawley or to some other East Trawley, to someplace where I could stash myself for the rest of my days. I had to become my mother. Maybe she'd hoped I could escape her fate, but no such luck; I wouldn't be running away, I'd be completing a circle. I had to find a shack or a tent or a trailer, I had to become a complete nonperson, someone entirely off the grid, a blank space on the census form, so Prince Gregory would never be able to hunt me down.

I sat up. I would sneak back to the apartment and shove my stuff into my backpack. Then, after scrounging up whatever cash was around, I'd get to the bus station. I thought about texting Mr. Taldecott and inventing some family emergency, but I knew it would be better just to never show up for work and to let him hate me. I wasn't sure if I'd tell Rocher what had happened or where I was headed, especially because I wasn't sure myself. All I wanted was to become as imaginary and untraceable and nonexistent as Rebecca.

I took the stairs of our apartment building two at a time. I remembered that Aimee was out at one of her many classes; today was the seminar where she was developing a one-woman show based on her own life. Suzanne was off polishing her audition technique with a woman who charged a lot to yell at her clients and to teach them to yell at themselves; this woman had self-published a paperback guide called *Be Your Own Bully*. For a second I envied Aimee and Suzanne because at least they knew what they wanted and they were working hard and who knows, maybe someday one of them might get a job as an actress and she would've earned it. I hadn't earned anything and now karma was cackling with vengeful glee.

I shoved open the door and there was Rocher, who was supposed to be out searching for a new job.

"Um, Becky . . . ," she began.

"Rocher, I'm really sorry, but I can't talk and I can't really explain anything but I'm getting out of here, I mean, out of the city, out of everywhere. . . ."

"Becks . . ."

"I know, I'm sorry, I should be here to help you with your court case but please, I'll try to dig up some more money and send it to you, but I have to go. . . ."

"BECKY."

Rocher stepped aside and standing a few feet behind her was Prince Gregory.

23.

One phone call to Mr. Taldecott had given the prince my address.

"Oh my God," I said and I didn't know if I was more shocked to see the prince or to see the prince standing in front of Aimee's aunt Renee's sleeper sofa. "I'm sorry about your carafe of ice water. . . ."

"Don't," he said. "Stop it. Don't you dare."

"Um, I'm gonna go, maybe into the other room . . . ," said Rocher, edging toward the bedroom.

"OUT!" said the prince to Rocher, who ran for the front door. On her way she caught my eye and waggled her arms helplessly and I made an "It's fine, just go" gesture and she left.

After the front door shut the prince and I stood staring at each other, in silence.

"The last time I saw you," said the prince, "you were standing directly across from me before the high altar at Westminster Abbey, on what was supposed to be my wedding day. You had replaced the woman I loved and then you ran off with your friend, and you both disappeared, seemingly forever. I have spent the entire last year of my life hating you beyond all measure. I have hated you with a passion and a rage I didn't know I was capable of. I have spent every waking moment plotting your extended and agonizing torture and this was my plan: I wouldn't just force you to reveal what had happened to Rebecca and why, oh no — I wanted you to suffer. I wanted you to writhe in torment until you begged for death. I wanted your eyes to pop out and your ears to spin and your fingers to drop off one by one. . . ."

"Got it," I said. "Got the picture."

"You are despicable. You are repugnant. You are immoral, amoral and lower than hyena vomit. You are hyena vomit festering with typhoid and gonococcus and thousands of squirming, brainless white maggots. . . ."

"Agreed. Moving on."

"So if you don't want me to fetch the burning coals, the rusty ice-pick and the ball-peen hammer, then you are going to tell me one thing. You are going to answer one simple question and you are going to tell me the truth. Or I swear to God I will strangle you with my bare hands and then I will hurl your lifeless body from the rooftop, where it will land directly in front of an ice cream truck and the driver will use what's left of your gall bladder to create a repulsive new flavor called Apple Strawberry Compulsive Liar Swirl."

He'd said all of this on a single, propulsive, merciless breath, barely pausing for my objections and now he needed a moment to refill his lungs and to prepare for an even more satisfyingly ferocious reading of his final words, which he'd clearly reworked over many drafts and memorized. His righteous fury gathered in his curling toes and rocketed upward, causing tremors and quivers, finally attaining full Baptist preacher Judgment-Day's-a-comin' glory in his flaring nostrils, his bulging eyeballs and his outraged hair.

Then all of this powerful and well-rehearsed wrath left the prince's body as he slumped, and became the most heartbreaking figure. He was a young guy in love and that love had been taken from him and he didn't understand anything, and he was scared that he never would. His words came out in a yearning whisper and they not only tore me to pieces, they made me love him even more as he asked: "Who are you?"

My life, in all of its unlikely monstrosity, didn't flash before my eyes. Instead I saw, as if in skywriting or engraved on granite tablets, every possible, screw-loose, potential answer to the prince's completely sensible question. I could tell him that Rebecca had been a hologram that I'd projected with my mind. I could say that Rebecca had been my fraternal twin sister who'd died of an undiagnosed heart ailment on her way to the wedding and that with her last breath, she'd asked me to take her place. Maybe Rebecca was me if I parted my hair differently — see? Rebecca was an angel sent to earth to marry the prince but at the last second she'd been reassigned, due to a clerical mix-up, to a prince in another country. If you squinted and spun around hundreds of times really fast, I looked just like Rebecca, once she'd pulled a pair of pantyhose over her head.

But — Prince Gregory's face. I couldn't add one more second of lies and muddle and evasion to his misery. Rebecca, or me, or the two of us working together in unholy concert, had committed a crime. We'd loved him and then without a word of explanation or apology, we'd left. I owed him. And all I could offer was the truth.

In a feverish, unstoppable geyser of words, I told him everything. I told him about my mom's death and my discovery of the mysterious phone number. I told him about my earliest trip to New York and about Tom Kelly's impossible offer. And then I told him about the three dresses and about how everything Tom had promised had come true, and about the *Vogue* shoot and Jate Mallow and about how after our visit to the burn unit, a royal marriage had become my goal. From that point on, he knew most of the story, until I reached the side room at Westminster, where Tom Kelly had asked me if I loved Prince Gregory.

"And what did you say?" asked the prince.

"I said yes."

"And then?"

"And then Tom Kelly turned me back into Becky Randle from East Trawley and I knew, from the look on your face, that I had to run and hide and that there would never be, as long as I lived, any way for me to apologize to you and to everyone else, for becoming Rebecca and then for turning back into me."

I was about to say "I'm sorry," but the words caught in my throat. How dare I say them, as if they could make any difference? As if the prince had believed a single word I'd said? Instead, because the floor had refused to open, allowing me to free fall into hell or more specifically, into the hell reserved for people who don't just tell lies but who live them, I just stood there. Shaking.

Prince Gregory was staring at me, and, if anything, he looked even more furious and more confused and more utterly lost. He looked as if he were trying to stop his brain from tumbling out of his skull and rolling across the floor, coming to rest at the webbed plastic tote bag that held a stack of Aimee's headshots, the pictures of her that had been so airbrushed that she didn't even have a nose, just two tiny black nostril-dots. Abruptly, the prince turned away toward the bedroom door, which had one of those shiny, erasable memo boards hanging on it, in bright yellow with jolly ladybugs and fat bumblebees wagging their antennae beneath the printed heading, "What's the Buzz, Honey?" There was a long-dried-up Magic Marker knotted to a strand of frayed orange yarn, which was anchored to the board with a thumbtack. Just as suddenly the prince turned back to face me.

"Do you know something?" he said. "That is exactly what I thought had happened."

"What?"

"Sit," he told me. "Sit on that . . . mucus-colored, hump-backed thing." As he spoke I remembered how nice he smelled and how his neckties were always yanked to one side but I warned myself to stop thinking about any of that and I dutifully sat on the sleeper sofa, which wasn't easy; I slid into a corner.

"Here's the terrible problem," said Prince Gregory, swaying and tugging at his hair the way passengers hold on to a subway strap to steady themselves. "The problem is — I believe you."

"You do?"

"And that's a problem because . . ." He began speaking more spontaneously, against his better judgment and with more of his natural kindness. "I suppose it's because I'm a prince. Which is already so absurd and outlandish. And which means that I'm supposed to be the hero of a fairy tale. When I was a child I assumed that fairy tales, that all of those ridiculous stories, were true, because after all, I lived in a castle and there were crowns and scepters and orbs lying about. And whenever the stories mentioned a Prince Charming or a Good Prince So-and-So, I'd assumed they were talking about me. Or, if the prince was awkward or bedraggled or had a limp, about my brother. It all just seemed to follow. But as I grew older I found that I certainly wasn't a hero and that armor and chain mail looked extremely uncomfortable and that if I wanted to wear a crown to school my parents would laugh at me. And, the way everyone does, I realized that fairy tales never come true. Or more precisely, I learned that regarding life as a fairy tale would require only the very blackest sense of humor."

"I don't understand. . . ."

"Because in real life, fairy tales always end badly. My mother was absolutely the most caring and beautiful princess. She was a storybook creature who deserved to glide through life, bouncing around in sparkling carriages and consulting with blue jays and bunnies and casting inspirational smiles upon her adoring subjects. But instead she died quite horribly, at a very young age. Which was when it dawned on me that everything I'd been told, every story and fantasy and film that begins with the opening of some enormous, hand-lettered book and the words, 'Once upon a time,' was a complete and utter crock."

"I'm so sorry. . . ."

"And then just when I'd become used to the fact that fairy tales were total rubbish and should be outlawed, I meet the most absurdly beautiful woman. And she seemed truly enchanted because she even had a sense of humor. At first I resisted. Rebecca was too beautiful, too entertaining, too onto herself, too ideal. Everything came too easily to her. I wondered if she'd been planted as some sort of sleeper beauty by a foreign government, to win my confidence, convert me to some fundamentalist belief system and then urge me to blow up Big Ben. I said to myself, this is impossible. I can't be falling in love with a woman who seems, above all else, like perfect casting."

"I know. . . ."

"But then it got even worse, everything became even more unfathomable, because just as I was prepared to dismiss Rebecca as a sort of Technicolor-fueled, Disney-backed, German-engineered mirage, she proved herself. She made me laugh and she saved my life and God help us all, she even survived tea with my grandmother and those wretched little dogs. But beyond all that, there was a rightness. A connection. When I was agitated or unsure, she'd say something unexpected and I'd feel so much better."

He bit his lip, because he wasn't usually this direct and this exposed. But he was determined to be completely honest:

"She made me feel that I wasn't alone."

I wanted to reach out and touch his cheek, to reassure him, to tell him that I'd felt exactly the same way, but I didn't dare.

"And then on my wedding day, it happened again. The lesson of my mother's death. Because my bride, my sparkling fairy-tale soul mate, didn't show up. And I blamed myself for allowing it to happen, for imagining that such mythical happiness was ever remotely possible. Because, yes, Rebecca was impossibly beautiful. But she was also impossibly herself. And I didn't deserve her."

"That's not true!"

"That's what I came up with. All I could think, the only conclusion that made any sense, was that Rebecca had realized, at the very last second, and I'm just going to say it, because goddamnit, I'm entitled to, she'd realized that I wasn't her prince. And I didn't blame her, not one ounce, because I'm dim and I'm selfish and because marriage to me would have become a living hell, of waving maniacally from dusty balconies and cutting ribbons to open car parks and trying to remain awake and attentive while choral groups of small children stood three feet away and sang droning folk songs in the original Gaelic. I decided that Rebecca simply couldn't find a way to tell me that she'd changed her mind and that she'd come to her senses and that she didn't love me. Or that she didn't love me enough."

"But she did!"

"But we couldn't discuss it, any of it, her doubts or her fears, because we were always inundated by so much fuss and by so many pairs of Greg-and-Becks souvenir kneesocks. So ultimately I couldn't fault Rebecca. Because I knew in my heart that she hadn't been kidnapped or drugged or waylaid. She hadn't vanished — she'd fled."

I wished that the prince was still cursing at me and threatening to electrocute me because that had been easier than watching his despair. I shut my eyes painfully tight and for the millionth time, I tried to pray Rebecca back into existence because maybe she could set things right. But I also knew that even if somehow

Rebecca could return, it would be even crueler to everyone but especially to Prince Gregory. I'd be taunting him and proving even more definitively that he'd fallen in love with a cardboard cutout, that he'd been punked as publicly and sneeringly as possible.

So I opened my eyes and I asked, "And now?"

"And now, and now, I wish there was some fairy-tale handbook, some large print, ye-olde-magick-for-dummies. I wish I knew how the story ends because I wish that's all it was — a story. But instead I'm the most useless sort of prince; I'm just an idiot with a closetful of extremely uncomfortable formal clothing and a trunkful of extremely impressive engraved stationery for writing notes of abject apology to everyone. And I have no idea what to do, because after everything you've told me and after the fact that I've chosen to believe it, I'm still left with only one very real question."

"Which question?"

"Who are you?"

I was every bit as lost as Prince Gregory. I'd managed to explain Rebecca and her disappearance and he'd bought it. And he'd just asked me the one question I'd never been able to get anywhere near answering. I wondered if anyone, even under far less freakish circumstances, could ever successfully and convincingly answer that question.

I stood and walked to the cheap, plastic-framed, round drugstore mirror that Aimee and Suzanne had hung at eye level right beside the front door. I looked at myself and I saw a very young woman, someone who was only just beginning to look like herself. Someone who had been terribly hurt but whose features now held at least a hint of hard-won self-knowledge and therefore exhibited at least a glimmer of confidence and maybe even a certain strength, around the eyes and the jaw.

I turned away from the mirror, which was a really good idea, because mirrors lie. This mirror had told both Aimee and

Suzanne that they were glamorous stars-of-tomorrow and it had convinced Rocher to get her nose pierced and if I kept asking it to tell me everything, or anything, it would make me want to kill myself, or get cheekbone implants, or slam my fist into its snickering, unreliable, glittering surface. Mirrors are more dangerous than guns or cars or crystal meth, because they're cheap, readily available and everyone's addicted.

"Asking someone who they are," I told Prince Gregory, "is never a fair question. Because the only honest answer for anyone is 'When I find out, I'll let you know.' But I loved being Rebecca. It was like flying, because I knew it wasn't possible but I was doing it anyway. And even then I knew it was cheating. But I'm not sorry. And I have no idea who or what you fell in love with. But I do know one thing, for beyond certain: Rebecca didn't love you."

"I know that. . . ."

"I did."

"I hope you guys folded up the fucking sleeper sofa," barked Aimee, barreling through the front door. "Because my one-woman-show class didn't go very well. I did my whole show about my life and then there was a critique and the teacher said that I should use someone else's life."

After dumping her many shoulder bags, most of them silk-screened with the logos of not-for-profit theater companies, and her plastic grocery sacks filled with I-didn't-get-the-part comfort snacks all around the room, Aimee began chugging from a carton of soy milk and caught sight of Prince Gregory. I hoped that as an actress, Aimee would remember this moment in detail because it was the only time I'd ever seen anyone actually perform an unpremeditated spit take, as the soy milk blasted from Aimee's mouth, spewing all over the prince.

"What the hell . . . ," Aimee began, wiping her mouth with her hand. "Oh my God. OH MY GOD."

"I'm so sorry," said Prince Gregory, reaching for a paper towel and delicately dabbing at his dripping jacket. "I'm intruding, I was just leaving. . . ."

"Are you HIM?" said Aimee as if she'd just run into Jesus in the marketplace a few days after Easter. "Are you PRINCE GREGORY? Of ENGLAND?"

"Yes I am and I'm so sorry to be trespassing in your . . . lovely . . . home. . . ."

Then for the second time in under a minute, Aimee looked like she'd been struck by the most thrillingly joyous lightning.

"Oh my God," said Aimee. "Are you here because I got the part? In the cable movie about your wedding? I mean, I told my agent to submit me but he keeps saying that he hasn't heard back and I thought that maybe they were going for a star, you know, instead of a real actress, but oh my God! Did you come here to tell me that I have the lead? Are there cameras here? Are you like the guy who shows up with one of those six-foot-long checks and huge bunches of balloons, when someone wins the lottery?"

"I've told you people not to leave the fucking front door open," growled Suzanne, appearing in her audition costume for the role of a stressed-out young mom in an ad for nerve-calming, chamomile-scented air freshener; this meant that Suzanne was wearing a beige pantsuit and toting a grimy plastic baby doll in a carrier on her chest. "People come in and steal things, we have valuables, there's the sleeper sofa and that really nice watch my father gave me when I lost the first three pounds at fat camp. . . ."

She spotted the prince.

"No," said Suzanne. "NO! No FUCKING WAY."

"But it's true!" yelped Aimee, grabbing Suzanne in a triumphant bear hug. "I'm gonna be Rebecca Randle!!!"

24.

Prince Gregory ended up hugging Aimee and Suzanne, and then he auto-graphed the women's headshots. "Write, 'To my favorite actress in the whole world,'" said Aimee, "and on Suzanne's put something else." Then he convinced them that he wasn't associ-ated in any way with the upcoming cable movie on his life, to be called *Prince of Pain*.

When a disappointed Aimee asked what he was doing in their apartment talking to me, the prince explained, "Becky works at my hotel and I'd asked her about sleeper sofas." This seemed to cover it and the prince left. As the door swung shut, he paused. He was puzzled and unsure and still completely at sea, but no longer furious.

I didn't go after him because there wasn't anything left for me to say. Instead, I took my backpack and told the girls that I was headed off to work. Once I hit the street I began walking down Eighth Avenue toward the Port Authority Bus Terminal. As I angled my way through the locals and the tourists and all of those girls texting while holding oversized cups of coffee a few inches out in front of themselves, like crucifixes warding off possible boyfriends who didn't make enough money, I began to feel a cer-tain lightness. I had talked to the prince and I'd told him exactly how I felt so I'd never have to brood and torment myself over what it might be like to see him again as Becky. I'd behaved in a truthful and straightforward manner and so I now had what the afternoon talk shows liked to call "closure." Closure was what the victims of spousal abuse or tornadoes or bad hair-coloring sessions always said that they wanted, sometimes along with cash settlements and, of course, appearances on afternoon talk shows. And like all of those once-suffering people I was now just fine, because whatever had happened between the prince and me, and between Rebecca and the world, it was all properly finished. I couldn't say that I felt happy but I was definitely relieved.

I became aware that I was being followed by a limo. The car pulled up beside me and the rear window rolled down.

"Get in," said Tom Kelly from the backseat. Drake was driving.

"Why?" I asked. "I mean, I'm sorry, but I don't have your money. I'll pay you back once I get another job."

"Just get in. I have something to tell you and then we'll drive you to the bus station. It's always important to arrive at the Port Authority in style."

I got into the car. Since I'd said good-bye to the prince I might as well say good-bye to Tom Kelly and then I'd be completely free, with ultra-supermax-economy-sized closure, because I'd never have to see either one of them again.

"You're so much stronger than your mother," said Tom, getting right to the point as the car stopped at a red light. "Your mother was almost as beautiful as Rebecca but the problem was, she didn't have your grit. Or your curiosity. Or your knack for self-preservation."

"And?" I said impatiently, because the bus station was only a few blocks away and because I was sure that Tom knew I'd just had it out with Prince Gregory, because Tom always knew everything and he was here to gloat.

"So stop feeling sorry for yourself and all of your little boyfriend troubles and pay attention. After I discovered your mother and after she'd moved to New York, everything happened very fast. She was offered money, movies, marriages — you know the drill. And while she was incredibly excited by all of it, she was also scared to death. Because unlike you, your mother was, at heart and forever, a very small-town girl. I think that's why, until I spotted her on that street corner, she'd never really known how stunning she was. The idea of admitting to or capitalizing on her beauty would have seemed vain and sinful. And far too tempting."

Which did sound like my mom. Which was why I kept listening.

"Sometimes I would practically yell at her — it's your shot! Make a move! Say yes, to everything! But unless I was with her she could become paralyzed. Painfully shy. No matter where we went, all over the world, she could never quite accept, or believe, that this was her life. Or that she deserved any of it. We'd be invited to some fabulous party at someone's Florentine palazzo and I'd find her in our hotel room, curled up in her T-shirt and sweatpants, watching a TV show about polar bears. And she'd look up at me and say, 'I can't go to the party. I won't know what to say. Everyone will think that I'm just some stupid model.'"

"So how did you deal with it? Did you just scream at her until she did what you wanted? Until she knuckled under?"

"No."

"So what did you do?"

"I loved her."

I didn't believe him — Tom Kelly couldn't love anyone. It wasn't possible.

"You exploited her. You took a teenager and put her picture everywhere, all over the world. And probably the second she started gaining weight you sent her right back to where she came from."

Tom was looking at me as if he was thinking about opening the car door, shoving me out onto the pavement and then asking Drake to back the car over my head. Instead, he smiled.

"I know you might think that," he said. "But that isn't what happened. You see, I wasn't one of those people who work incredibly hard and build an empire and then realize that it's all hollow and that money can't buy happiness. Because money can buy anything and happiness comes when you drive whatever you've bought or wear it out dancing or when you turn the air-conditioning all the way up and then open the French doors to the wraparound terrace, just for the sheer thrill of wasting electricity. What's great about having money is never having to worry about money, never having to ask yourself, can I afford dessert, can I pay off the loan shark, can I make it to the end of the month without living on the street. I loved being successful and seeing my name on the rear pocket of everyone's jeans and on the waistbands of their underwear. It was so satisfying. I once slept with a woman who, before I'd met her, she'd had the Tom Kelly logo tattooed along her inner thigh because, as she told me in her adorable French accent, 'I want to 'ave everyzing be Tom Kellee.'

"But early on I'd been a bit like your mother, a bit afraid of ever glancing up from the grindstone. With every step forward, with every new collection that blew out of the stores, with every magazine cover proclaiming me the hot new whatever, I knew that it all became that much more precarious and that it could all be taken away overnight. I'd seen it happen to so many other people — they'd believe their own press, they'd get stoned once too often, they'd miss too many deadlines and boom, they were calling me and asking if I could hire them, off the books, to design my budget housewares for the big-box stores. And maybe that's why I married Lila."

"Wait, hold on, what did you just say? You married Lila?"

"She was my receptionist and my fit model, from when I was first starting out. She knew where I'd come from and how hard I'd worked. Lila had seen me shaking and sweating over the tiniest details, over a collar not lying flat or a trade paper review that called my swimwear line 'acceptable'; she knew me better than anyone. She kept me sane."

I'd always wondered about Lila and her endless loyalty to Tom. But — marriage?

"We lasted less than a year. We were much better as friends. Co-conspirators. Because as I think Lila was aware, from very early on, I wasn't really the sort of person whom anyone should marry."

"You mean because you were — gay?"

"Oh, sweetheart," said Tom, laughing. "After all this time, even after Jate Mallow, you're still such a nice girl. You can't even imagine what I was. I was young and good-looking and I was doing great, and almost nobody ever gets all three. And so I took full advantage. Anyone I wanted, I had. Men, women, every possible combination. Have you ever found yourself, at 4:00 A.M., under a full moon, out of your mind on hashish laced ever so gently with angel dust, in a tent in the Sahara having sex with an entire nomadic tribe?"

"No . . ."

"It's amazing and you don't have to call anyone the next day because they're gone."

"You made that whole thing up!"

"I so love how you said that, you were appalled, but you still weren't sure it wasn't true. Because believe me it was, and beyond. But all I'm saying is, I enjoyed myself. I wanted to see how far I could take things, in business, in sex, in every possible direction. But when I met your mother it wasn't that she made me feel old or ashamed or depraved. She was just . . . the most open-hearted girl I'd ever met. She wasn't innocent because I don't believe that anyone over three months old is ever innocent, but she was . . ."

"She wanted everyone else to be happy," I said. "She never thought about herself, not for a second. Sometimes, a lot of times, I wanted to shake some sense into her but I never would because I knew she'd just agree with me. It was like because she was so sweet and because she wanted to be a good person all the time, she couldn't figure out how to live in the world. Where everyone wasn't like her."

"Yes," Tom agreed. "And I'd never met anyone like that. And so I loved her. I'm not saying that we ever could've been married and I'm not saying that she wasn't more than a little crazy but for a very few months, we had the best time. We did whatever she wanted to do, things that no decent New Yorker ever does, at least not without cocaine and irony. We went to the observation deck of the Empire State Building and we'd go to see the worst movies, these hideous romantic comedies starring actresses with unnaturally toned biceps and we watched home shopping. And I say this with only the greatest affection, but your mother had no taste."

I couldn't argue. Our trailer had been infested with those polyester fleece blankets with sleeves and my mom had tended a herd of those brown ceramic animals that grow clover instead of fur.

"And so what happened?" I asked. I was stunned at how much Tom was telling me after so many months of refusal. Maybe I was pressing my luck but it was now or never. "Did you break up? My mom would never tell me anything about her life — did she catch you with someone else? Did you get bored and dump her?"

I was being vicious, even though I could tell that Tom had genuinely loved my mom. But I'd seen how Tom could turn on people and I didn't know if anyone had been off-limits.

"No, that isn't what happened. Maybe it would have but we didn't have all that much time together."

"Why not?"

"Because I got sick."

Tom was still smiling as he continued his story. "I was just about to launch the biggest campaign of my career. Every major city, every market. London, Tokyo, Sydney, you name it. We were really going to establish the brand as a global power. I was going to be Mao and Stalin and Evita, only so much bigger, because I understood sneakers. And your mother was so excited because we'd be together. It was going to be a sort of honeymoon."

"Until . . . ?"

"Until the week before we were set to leave. I'd been coughing, a few aches, nothing more than that. But before I left I had a complete physical. And I was diagnosed with a truly repulsive disease and there wasn't any treatment, let alone a cure. Not yet. And I'd seen so many people die shockingly fast, in agony. And so I called a meeting, with Brant Coffield. Because I trusted him."

"I met him on the street outside Seeley Burckhardt's studio. . . ."

"Yes. And we both agreed that if people knew I was sick, the Tom Kelly brand would be hopelessly tainted and everything would collapse."

"Because you were sick?"

"Because the disease was so awful and because it was sexually transmitted and because the Tom Kelly brand was all about sex. And because when a seven-year-old got sick from a blood transfusion in Iowa, his neighbors burned his family's house down. And because people were scared shitless, and scared, ignorant people would stop buying Tom Kelly jeans. I wasn't about to let that happen. And so I called your mother, who was in Africa, with Alicia. I said that I had something to tell her, in confidence. And I asked her to come home."

"So she did," I said, "which meant that she wasn't on the plane with the princess, when it crashed."

"Yes. But by the time your mother got back, she'd heard about Alicia and she could barely speak. And so I felt even worse, because of what I was about to say."

"But you told her? That you were sick?"

"Yes. As calmly as I could. I think that's what I hated more than anything else, almost more than being sick — telling people. And watching their faces crumple. And feeling their pity mixed with their horror. But your mother, well, this was why I loved her. Because when I told her that I was sick, she didn't cry or fling herself on me or start jabbering on about how it wasn't fair or about how I'd survive, I'd be a special case, an exception. And she didn't start in about going to India and being healed through chanting and brown rice and wearing sacred crystals around my neck on a leather thong. She just said, 'Oh, Tom,' and then she kissed me."

"But . . ."

"I know what you're thinking and, yes, I made sure she was tested and thank God, she was healthy. And then I retired. I stayed in the compound with only my inner circle. I didn't see anyone and sure, I had access to the most advanced and expensive and discreet medical care, which amounted to zero. There was nothing remotely effective. Soon I'd lost half my body weight, I was covered with lesions and I was all but blind."

"Oh my God . . ."

"Which was a blessing, because of my vanity. I knew what I looked like and what I was starting to become and all I wanted was absolute privacy. I was not going to let the world watch Tom Kelly shrivel and rot. Because I was a very superficial guy and because I wouldn't give my enemies the satisfaction."

"Your enemies?"

"Please. You've met me. But my friends, and especially your mother, they understood. Your mom would sit with me and feed me, although I was barely eating anything, and she'd make sure I had pillows and fresh flowers and sometimes she'd read to me. Fashion magazines."

"But . . ."

"She would describe them to me, what the models were wearing, so I could make bitchy remarks. But I kept getting worse and I wasn't able to walk and I became incredibly obnoxious and disagreeable, even for me. I couldn't stand having so little control over even the tiniest things, like brushing my teeth or moving from the couch to a chair. And your mother, even though she'd never talk about it, she was devastated. She'd decided that all of it, my illness and Alicia's death, and the plight of the migrant workers in Albania, she thought it was all her fault."

"Of course."

"And then, because she couldn't hide it anymore, she told me she was going to have a baby. My baby."

I didn't say anything. I couldn't. All I could think about was that photo Queen Catherine had given me, of my mother and Tom and Alicia, when they were all so young and gorgeous and happy. In the photo my mother had most likely already been pregnant.

"That's right, Becky. As you've always suspected. You're the luckiest girl alive."

Tom's eyes sparkled, as if he was delivering the most delectable punch line and enjoying himself thoroughly.

"You're my finest product. You're a Tom Kelly original."

I sank into the supple black leather of the backseat, like a fly ball landing in God's catcher's mitt. I'm not sure why but the first thing I thought about was a scene from one of the Star Wars movies with Darth Vader, the guy in the black plastic helmet that makes him sound like a heaving humidifier and who's the embodiment of all human evil. I flashed on the part where Darth tells young Luke Skywalker, the blond, noble, Jedi-warrior-in-training, that he's his real father. Once Luke has fully digested this information, in one of the later sequels, the father and child have a climactic laser duel.

"I know just what you're thinking," said Tom. "You're reaching for your lightsaber."

Sure, it was true that months earlier I'd wondered if Tom could possibly be my father but I'd avoided the whole concept. It wasn't just that I thought Tom was gay, it was more that he didn't seem like he'd ever be anyone's dad. He just wasn't interested enough, or equipped, to carpool or help with homework or attend a parent-teacher conference. But then until I'd first come to New York I never would've pictured my mother as a gorgeous face filling half the acreage in Times Square. And now all I could think about was that billboard, the one with Tom and my mother, glowing on that sun-washed Greek island: Those were my parents.

"So my mom, when she told you she was pregnant — how did you feel?"

"Well, like I said, I was already pretty out of it but, honestly, I felt surprised and then — delighted. Amused. The whole idea of Tom Kelly as a father seemed so unlikely and that's why I liked it. And I liked that I wasn't just leaving a company behind, a brand. And then, of course for just a second, I hated you. Passionately. Because having a child and becoming a father, it made me feel so old."

"But you were dying!"

"Fine, but I still didn't want you spitting up on my cashmere or having people look at me and think, isn't that sweet, he's settling down. But then I hoped you'd be a girl. Because if you were a boy and you grew up to be really good-looking I'd feel competitive. But if you were a girl I'd know just what to do."

"What? What would you have done?"

"Everything. If things had been different, we all could've been in the ads together. The sexy Tom Kelly clan, in moody black and white, posed in slouchy cotton sweaters on a sand dune, admiring the sea or sprawled on a mountaintop in matching parkas, with fabulous ski goggles shoved onto our foreheads or hanging around our necks."

"But what if I'd rebelled? What if I'd hated you and everything you stood for? What if I'd become a surgeon or joined the Peace Corps or worn other labels?"

"Foster care."

"But then what happened? How did you get better?"

"I didn't."

"What do you mean? Look at you!" As always, Tom was handsome, youthful and athletic. The real word for Tom Kelly was vigilant. He refused to age or gain an unnecessary ounce or to look anything other than effortlessly, devastatingly, unapproachably great.

"I never got better. I died."

"What?"

"Almost twenty years ago. At the compound. I knew it was happening and all I wanted was as much morphine as I could get. Your mother was with me. And I was satisfied that the company was intact. Which meant that in a way, as far as the rest of the world was concerned, Tom Kelly would never die. Not as long as anyone was wearing sunglasses or cologne or simple, modern, twelve-hundred-dollar A-line skirts."

"You . . . you're dead?"

"Yes. And stop looking so dumbfounded, this isn't your first brush with, what shall we call it, the supernatural? Rebecca would certainly understand."

"But . . . but . . ."

"Stop it. Becky, look at me. And I'm not being presumptuous, only accurate. My face. My body. My enviably thick head of hair. Did you really think that God, or whoever is behind all this, would really let Tom Kelly go to waste? Without a fight?"

He was almost laughing, not just at my slack-jawed disbelief but at the sheer insanity of what he'd just told me. Could it be true, any of it? All of it? Tom Kelly was sitting right there, a few feet away. And he didn't look like a man in his seventies or barely his thirties.

"On the day that I died, just before the drugs made me completely unreachable, your mother made a request. No, she made a nonnegotiable demand."

"What? What did she want?"

"Well, it wasn't money, because I'd offered her a fortune, so she'd be taken care of. But she wouldn't accept it, not a penny. She said that wasn't the point."

"So what did she ask for?"

"She couldn't save Alicia, or me, but her baby, our child, was going to be protected. She became this rampaging lioness and she told me, 'I don't know where you're going or if there's a next step, for anyone. But you're this baby's father. And you have to help her in any way you can, to make sure that she's not like me. I don't want her to be afraid of anything. I want her to know that she can take on the world. But most of all, I want her to fall in love, with someone wonderful, and I want that person to love her right back, no matter what she looks like. You have to guarantee that our baby, once she grows up, you have to make sure that she falls in love, for all the right reasons.'"

"So what did you say?"

"I promised to try. I said I'd do what I could. Your mother was fragile and I wanted to make sure that she could handle my death. So I promised her your life."

"I'm not sure she believed you."

"Which is probably why she ran right back to, what was it called? East Trawley. Where she could hide and keep you safe. And that's most likely why she gained so much weight. So she'd never be recognized and have to answer questions, about me, and you. And also because after her time as a model, she was undoubtedly very hungry."

"But she kept that phone number. Your phone number."

"Your mother also believed in knocking on wood or in the case of your trailer, wood laminate. She was also convinced that space aliens had landed on earth millions of years ago and married Mormons."

"But when I showed up, at the compound, why didn't you just tell me? About you and my mom? About all of this?"

"Because you wouldn't have believed a word of it. And because that wasn't what I'd promised your mother. I had to equip you for the world. I had to show you what was possible and how things work. I had to let you make all of your mother's mistakes and learn from them. I had to make you three dresses. Because if you hadn't worn them, if you hadn't become Rebecca, you'd still be back behind the cash register, at the Shop-A-Lot."

"The *Super* Shop-A-Lot."

"So sorry. And you never would've met Alicia's son. And fallen in love."

"With a man who hates my guts. And I don't blame him. Because that's where your plan backfired. Because he fell in love with Rebecca."

"Did he? Drake?"

25.

From the front seat, Drake activated a video screen that flipped down from the car's ceiling. The screen was carrying live coverage of Prince Gregory's speech at the United Nations. The prince was wearing one of his slightly ill-fitting, navy blue worsted suits, and his hair looked like he'd just fallen out of bed and onto a broken comb. He was working his boyish, neck-scratching, what-am-I-doing-up-here charm. He was being respectful enough to come off as a well-tutored royal and squinty and casual enough to melt teenage hearts. He was addressing the full international membership in support of an eco-sensitive global initiative.

". . . And surely, a commonsense approach to clean energy and green living is something, and perhaps all, that every nation can agree on."

He looked up from the teleprompter as if he'd done his duty, pleased his family and his homeland and was ready to veer off-road onto more what-the-hell terrain.

"And while I personally support the research and development of myriad sources of renewable energy, I can't say that I find any of them all that terribly interesting. I mean, we've got solar, wind, methane, everyone in China patting their heads at the same time to power the Hong Kong skyline — who really cares?"

Once their earpieces had transmitted a translation, there was an audible, disconcerted buzz from many of the delegates, who were mystified and secretly entertained by the prince's cavalier attitude.

"I mean, here I am, yakking off at the United Nations and you're all thinking, ah, yes, another willfully rumpled, vaguely well-meaning, undoubtedly inbred and brain-damaged royal, young Prince Potato Head. And, of course, you're correct, but today I do have something genuinely important and of true global impact on my tiny, regal, genetically hopeless mini mind. Because against the strongest of odds, I have done something unspeakable. I have done something which many of you, in all of your equally nonsensical native tongues, may also be guilty of. I have done something I feel required to confess, for the simple reason that I'm on television and that is what one does. Because ladies and gentlemen of the world, I have fallen in love."

Oh my God, I thought, he's going to do it, he's going to propose to Lady Jessalyn on live TV. And while I knew I should be happy for Prince Gregory and even for Lady Jessalyn, all I could think about was how much I hated anyone who'd ever been in love.

"Turn this shit off," I said.

"Never," said Tom Kelly. "Just keep watching."

"I can't," I said, and I opened the car door and stepped out into the stalled gridlock of Times Square traffic.

"Becky!" said Tom from his window. "You have to see this! Trust me!"

"Trust you?"

"I'm your father!"

I couldn't even begin to respond to what Tom had just said and besides, I was distracted by the enormous crowd that was now pin-drop silent, overflowing Times Square and staring up at the same huge LED screen that I'd been watching a few months ago, when I'd seen Rebecca's face obliterated by a fiery red question mark. The screen was now broadcasting the prince's proposal.

"And there's a bizarre dimension to my announcement," the prince was saying, "especially for those of you with vivid tabloid memories. Because I have fallen in love with the most marvelous person and her name is . . ."

I tried to run but the crowd had grown so jam-packed that I couldn't move to escape this ultimate moment of worldwide humiliation.

"Oh, I'll just blurt it right out," said Prince Gregory. "Her name is Becky Randle. And yes, I know that sounds just like the woman who, as a very few of you might dimly recall, left me high and dry and sobbing at the altar. But this is a very different Becky Randle. A Becky Randle who has a far firmer grasp on both reality and my heart. And clearly, I am willing to risk a second, fully webcast, interplanetary disgrace. I may very well become the hero of a bleak comic fairy tale, entitled 'The Idiot Prince Who Kept Getting Dumped.' I am risking the manufacture of inflatable, full-sized rubber clowns, printed with my face and designed to be punched again and again, yet always returning to a moronically eager, upright position. Because right now, here at the center of this supremely august and dignified assembly, I would like to ask the following question. . . ."

I was craning my neck to catch every inch of the prince's face and every single word, as I battled all urges toward hope and wonder and jumping up and down and screaming.

"Becky Randle," said the prince, looking directly into the camera with an expression that managed to combine abject hopelessness and desperate belief. "Will you marry me?"

As the prince bowed and left the podium, all of the delegates began laughing, then applauding and then cheering, and this response was amplified by all of the people filling Times Square, with the addition of celebratory car horns, hooting office workers hanging from skyscraper windows and the especially victorious shrieking of single women, fueling a mass roar, which when measured later in the day, topped the decibels recorded on the previous New Year's Eve. As thousands of newscasters from all over the world began dissecting the timing, content and sincerity of the prince's proposal, I was clawing through the mob to try and reach Tom Kelly's limo. But even though the traffic was still a parking lot, the limo had vanished or managed a crosstown escape, or maybe flown off.

As the crowd hubbubed over the prince's speech and questioned his mental state, more than one person demanded to know, "Who the fuck is Becky Randle?" But within seconds everyone was back to sightseeing and nibbling giant pretzels and hunting for miniature souvenir license plates from their home states as I was shunted off to a side street, where I was backed into a corner between a parking garage and a large, family-style restaurant specializing in tube steak and cheesecake.

I knew that I should be over the moon about the prince's proposal but instead I felt worse than I had at any point since I'd left Westminster Abbey. How can I marry Prince Gregory, I asked myself, I'm just some nothing, some distant runner-up, some impossible fluke from Missouri. What if I can't handle becoming a royal? Gregory had put all his faith in me and what if I let him down? What if I messed up everything all over again?

I began walking purposefully toward the Port Authority Bus Terminal and an appropriate and welcome oblivion. As I waited for the light to change at an intersection, I was standing beside the plate-glass windows of an electronics outlet, the kind of store which, on its opening day, ten years earlier, had posted banners proclaiming, GOING OUT OF BUSINESS!!!, EVERYTHING MUST GO!!! and NO REASONABLE OFFER REFUSED!!! The windows were stacked with flat screens and the very latest must-have phones and tablets, with every monitor tuned to a highly rated, late-afternoon women's talk show, which was too popular to ever be preempted, even by a surprise royal marriage proposal. The hostess of the show was a big-bosomed, universally revered, epically relatable woman, and one of my mother's greatest addictions.

The most forceful aspect of this show was the lighting, which was so blindingly generous that it made every guest appear lovingly unlined and rested, which was why at first I didn't recognize that the hostess was deep into a searchingly heartfelt one-on-one with Jate Mallow. The flattering glare made Jate look like a twelve-year-old, as if the show was a rerun from the heyday of *Jackie + Jate*. As the hostess tilted sympathetically forward, Jate was telling her about the moment when he'd first known he was gay.

"I was, like, five years old," Jate was saying. "And I remember reading a Spider-Man comic and thinking, whoa, Spider-Man is in really good shape."

"Did you think that Spider-Man was gay?" asked the hostess supportively.

"I hoped so," Jate replied. "But then, and I just have to say it, I dumped him for Aquaman, maybe because Aquaman was more naked. I guess in a way, I wanted Spider-Man and Aquaman to fight it out over me."

"I love it!" exclaimed the hostess as the studio audience applauded, which they tended to do every time a guest paused. "But, Jate," the hostess continued, "aren't you worried, now that you've told the world you're gay, that audiences won't accept you as a leading man? That you won't get to make any more of those terrific Renn Hightower movies?"

"Well, I'll admit it, at first I was scared out of my mind," Jate confessed as the camera cut to an Idaho homemaker and her mother in the studio audience, nodding ruefully, as if they were also major male movie stars coming out on national television. "But then I met this amazing girl at my hotel," said Jate. "I think she was a chambermaid or a waitress or something. And she was a fan."

Jate was getting choked up, so the hostess took his hand.

"And I told her that I'd been trapped in a lie and that I felt like I was two different people. And she said that she totally understood."

"Wow," said the hostess, "that must've been some smart chambermaid."

"She was," Jate agreed, "because she convinced me that just maybe, if I was honest about everything, that people might understand."

The women in the studio audience were now passing around boxes of Kleenex.

"Because you know what?" Jate continued. "Everything I have — the movies and the worship and the houses and the cars, none of it means anything."

There was a pause, as the camera located an audience member, a plump, sweet-faced dog groomer from Milwaukee, looking puzzled by Jate's last remark.

"Unless I also have the right to fall in love!"

The audience was silent. Had Jate crossed a line? Everyone looked to the hostess for guidance.

"God bless America!" crowed the hostess, who was very big on affirmations and lightbulb moments and happy endings. She opened her arms as if she were the worldwide audience for Renn Hightower films, and she gave Jate a mighty, record-breaking-box-office hug as the Idaho homemaker yelled, "We love you, Jate!" and another woman, not to be outdone, yanked her husband to his feet and called out, "Take him, Jate!"

I turned away from the set and the store window and against all of my knee-jerk, hard-earned caution, I thought, if Prince

Gregory, who was probably the most publicly jilted man in recorded history, can propose to me after charting the half-life of radioactive waste at the UN, and if Jate Mallow can risk something even more important than his life, by which I meant his career, if they could both manage to be so fearless in the face of being condemned by world leaders and by the eleven-year-olds who might post seriously cutting remarks on their Facebook pages, then maybe I'd better step up to the plate.

I thought about my parents, as a couple, about my mom and Tom Kelly, and how they'd come through for me. Like so many moms and dads, they'd wanted what was best for their kid and they'd been relentless in helping me to find happiness. Only unlike other moms and dads, they'd managed to provide their most heartfelt and powerful support after they were dead. If I had known that much love, love that had defied, well, just about everything, then maybe I was worthy, or at least prepared, to become a princess and maybe someday, no, I couldn't even think about someday. Because I still had to give Prince Gregory my answer.

"There you are!" yelled Rocher, snapping me out of my Times Square reverie. "I've been looking all over! What the fuck are you doing, just standing there? Prince Gregory asked you a question! Go find him!"

26.

Once I got to the Royal Criterion, Mr. Taldecott was behind the counter and not pleased, telling me, "Ms. Randle, I am sorely disappointed with you on several counts. First of all, you were asked to provide a guest with a carafe of ice water and you did not. Secondly, I fear that you have wasted your many months of training and you may in fact never become a deputy concierge. And finally, and this defies all understanding, why are you standing here when His Royal Highness is expecting you?" Mr. Taldecott burst recklessly into his version of orgiastic pleasure, which involved the almost microscopic upward curl of the very farthest corners of his lips as he murmured, "As you are no longer on duty, you may run."

As I bolted from the elevator out onto the twentieth floor, there were bodyguards holding open the door to the Royal Suite. I cannonballed inside to find Prince Gregory standing in the grand parlor before a full-length oil portrait of his grandmother, stone-faced in her coronation robes, crown and scepter. I skidded to a halt a few feet away, as if I were a cartoon coyote kicking up a whirlwind of red clay and dust.

"Why?" I asked, or really, demanded. "Why did you ask me to marry you?"

"Because I love you."

"Do you love me, or Rebecca?"

"You."

"Good answer. But what would you do if Rebecca came back, right this second? Would you beg her to stay?"

"Yes. And then once we had reached the altar, I'd abandon her and leave her a voice mail of me laughing maniacally, to teach her a lesson."

"Very nice. So if I say yes, then we'll really get married and everything?"

"Yes. But only if you stop asking ridiculous questions and if you promise to stop changing into other people."

"Deal. But I just have one more ridiculous question. Why do you love me and not Rebecca?"

"Because Rebecca was perfect in every way. Which made her just the skimpiest bit inhuman. I know that unthinkably beautiful people are now a protected species, and so I really shouldn't say this, but Rebecca was too beautiful. It was daunting. She was astounding, but she didn't need anything, or anyone. There were no raw edges. But what she had, and I told her this when I proposed, was mystery. I knew that there was something else, or as things turned out, someone else, lurking beneath that flawless exterior. And after you and I spoke at that horrid little apartment, something clicked. Something became clear. Because as I thought about it I realized — you're Rebecca's soul."

"I'm her soul?"

"Yes. You're everything that wasn't perfect. You're the part that's angry and funny and unsure. The part which I might not worship but which I can understand. The part which can't be photographed. The part that needs me. No, you're not Rebecca, thank God."

He smiled with delight, as if he'd finally solved a puzzle so that his life could make sense. "You're Becky."

When he said that, I gasped. I wanted to kiss him, but we'd both been through an awful lot and I needed to be absolutely sure about just what was going on.

"Wait," I said. "So you're saying that you proposed to me because I'm a mess and I'm a person and because we need each other, while Rebecca was — something else? I get it, I follow you, but I'm also thinking, is the bullshit getting a little deep in here?"

"Yes, it is. You've caught me. And so fine, I will come clean, and I will tell you the absolutely true and naked reason why I want to marry you and only you, and not Rebecca."

"Why?"

"Because when I'm with you, I'm the pretty one."

I walked over, reached out to take Prince Gregory in my arms and instead I punched him really hard in the stomach. Punching a prince was deeply satisfying because almost no one ever gets to do it. Then, once he'd stopped moaning and stood upright, I kissed him for a very long time, while his grandmother watched approvingly. Like those Ideal Females at the British Museum, the portrait seemed to have changed its expression, as if beneath her sumptuous robes the Queen had slipped into comfortable shoes or maybe bare feet, and she was sighing with satisfaction.

Later that night, just before Gregory and I made love, I was apprehensive.

"I've never done this before," I told the prince as I joined him, naked, on what he loved calling his king-sized bed.

"When you say that do you mean that you've never made love, or that you've never made love to such an inspiring, well-endowed, impossibly sensuous prince and humanitarian?"

"Oh, no, I've had sex with your brother."

"Did I deserve that? Really?"

"I'm scared. I'm from Missouri."

"So you're scared because we're not related? No, I'm sorry! Don't hit me again! I take it back!"

Before either of us could say anything else, I kissed him, and after that everything went well, really well, for the following reasons: I loved Gregory, and that included his body and his surprising shyness and the fact that he was really hot for me. I may even have been his fantasy commoner. But beyond all that I was ecstatic because thanks to Rocher's advice, Rebecca had never had sex with Gregory. There was no way I could've lived up to that. No one could. The idea of following Rebecca, particularly in bed, was so overwhelming that I got stupid and afterward, as Gregory and I were lying in each other's arms, I asked, "So do you wish that had happened with Rebecca?"

"Oh, yes," said the prince. "Of course. Absolutely. Don't you? I mean, do you remember what she looked like? Who she was? Wouldn't you rather have had sex with Rebecca than with me?"

"Okay, we both know that I have to punch you again. You have three seconds to pick a body part. One . . ."

The prince leaped out of bed, and I laughed as I swore silently that I'd never ask a question like that again, not just because no one could ever compete with Rebecca but because comparing myself to myself would only give me an existential headache.

"You know," said Prince Gregory, climbing back into bed and reaching for me, "this really is a full-service hotel."

27.

The next morning I went back to the apartment to pack my things for my return to England and to analyze everything with Rocher. "So now you know who your dad was," she said. "But I guess, if you'd known sooner it would've made a big difference. Especially since you probably would've gotten a humongous discount on everything."

"Roche, I know that you've been through a lot, but will you come with me? To London? To help me with everything?"

"I would love to but I'm still out on bail. I can't go anywhere. I mean, you're gonna be a princess and I'm gonna be in jail for selling bogus earmuffs to nurses from Wisconsin."

"But I asked Gregory if we could use his lawyers. I mean, they got his brother off after he got caught selling weed to the Vienna Boys Choir, so I bet they can help you. And he said sure."

"Oh my God. I love rich people. And royalty are the best because they're rich people who can't be fired. But, Beck?"

"Yeah?"

"I have to tell you something, because it's been eating me up, and because I'm a terrible person. But I just have to say it and just sort of get it out there, so you can hate me."

"Roche?"

"Okay, I know that, before, I loved being around Rebecca, because she made me feel special, like she was my permanent guest pass to the best party ever, and because I knew that when I died, people would say, 'Rocher must've been pretty amazing, because she was Rebecca Randle's best friend.' And when you were Rebecca and the prince fell in love with you, I just thought, perfect. Duh. I mean, who wouldn't fall in love with Rebecca?"

"And now?"

"And now — I'm glad that she's gone."

"You are?"

"Because now that the prince is in love with you, I mean, with normal, regular Becky you, with the you I grew up with, it's just better. Because now I sort of feel like maybe, someone could fall in love with me."

That was when Aimee and Suzanne returned from their latest class. They took one look at me and howled, "WE HATE YOU!!!"

"I'm sorry," I said. "I didn't plan for any of this to happen and I'll keep paying our half of the rent until you can find someone."

"I can't believe that Prince Gregory is marrying you," said Aimee, staring at me in total disbelief. "And no offense, but are you pregnant?"

"No . . ."

"Was there, like, a raffle or something?" asked Suzanne. "I mean, we like you and everything, you're fine, but Prince Gregory?"

"Okay, here's what I think happened," announced Aimee. "I think that the prince was still totally heartsick over Rebecca Randle, it was like the tipping point of his life and he's never gonna really recover. So he decided that to protect himself and to make sure that his heart would never get broken like that ever again, he decided to marry someone who was the total opposite of Rebecca in every way."

"Okay . . . ," I said.

"No offense. He just wanted someone who was, you know, simple. And good-hearted. And so he was staying at the Royal Criterion and he saw you behind the desk and he said, that's it. That's her. That's the safest choice in the world. I'm gonna marry that little assistant concierge mouse."

"Aimee?" said Rocher.

"That *wonderful* little assistant concierge mouse! And when he asked you to marry him, how could you possibly refuse? Even though you barely knew him. And, in a way, that makes the whole thing even more romantic. It's like, if it was a movie it would be called *The Prince and* . . ."

"*The Prince and the Peon*?" suggested Suzanne.

"No, it would be called *The Prince and That*," Aimee said, pointing to me. "Am I right? Is that how it happened? I mean, I'm really good at this, at figuring out psychological motivations. So is that how it happened?"

I knew I couldn't tell Aimee and Suzanne anything even approaching the truth and because it would give both of the girls hope, and satisfaction, I smiled and said, "Yes. That's exactly right. Are you psychic? You're incredible."

"Good save," said Rocher after Aimee and Suzanne had bustled into their bedroom, trying to decide which of them should play me in the revised cable movie. "I mean, maybe you should do it," Aimee informed Suzanne. "Because if it's Becky it's really more of a character part."

"But I just thought of something," said Rocher. "What about the third dress? The last one?"

I'd already shoved most of my T-shirts and jeans into my backpack, and just as Rocher asked her question I was prying open the door to the one narrow closet that Rocher and I had been allowed to use. The door had been repainted so many times that it stuck and Aimee and Suzanne had filled the lower regions of the closet

with cartons of clippings from their high school drama club pro-
ductions, their old tap shoes and a stash of self-help paperbacks
with titles like *Listening to Your Stomach*, *Sing Yourself Thin* and *Stop
Chafing Today!*

I'd left my down-filled vest hanging on the closet's crossbar
but it had been replaced by a silvery-gray garment bag printed,
across a wide diagonal band, with the shadowy Tom Kelly logo. I
unzipped the bag to find the simplest black dress, a cap-sleeved
shift in a weightless blend of finely spun silk and wool. At the
bottom of the bag, from Anselmo, there was a pair of classic
pumps in the most supple black leather, along with a single strand
of rare black pearls, from Madame Ponelle.

"Put it all on," urged Rocher.

It was the sort of dress that looked like nothing on the hanger
but once I was wearing it, I felt the wicked embrace of couture. My
body sighed, as if it had come home after months in scratchy,
shapeless acetate and denim. For a second I panicked, and I
checked the full-length mirror on the back of the closet door to
see if Rebecca had returned, but there was only Becky, wearing a
dress that would cost half a year's paychecks.

"What do I look like?" I asked Rocher.

"You look like you," Rocher decided. "Only I guess, more
grown-up. It's like there's always something creepy about anyone
our age wearing a black dress, unless they're being like a goth
or Vampira, for Halloween or whatever. A dress like that just
looks too fancy or too serious or something. But I don't know,
it looks right. It doesn't look like you stole it or borrowed it or like
you're wearing your mom's clothes. It looks like it's your dress.
Like you've earned the right to wear it."

In a pocket hidden within a seam, Archie had left a tiny perfume bottle shaped like a black crystal lily and labeled TOM

KELLY'S FAREWELL. As I opened the bottle and inhaled, I was confused, because there was no scent at all.

"But what do you think it means?" I asked Rocher.

"Ask Tom Kelly."

Wearing the dress, I took a cab over to Tom Kelly's compound. I could've taken the subway but I told myself that a Tom Kelly original demanded a taxi. I had the driver leave me on the highway beside the first barrier of chain-link fence, which was now coated with rust; chunks of the fence were missing, or bulging, or sliced and corroded and gaping inward, as if someone had stomped on them.

I found the entry where the gates had always parted for Drake's limo but now the security cameras were dangling and disabled. By turning sideways I slipped through the gap where the gates had once meshed and headed out onto the pier.

The outer walls of the block-long warehouse had once been artfully and expensively weathered but now they were dilapidated, with jagged holes where the metal had worn thin and layer upon layer of story-high, looping, spray-painted graffiti. I wondered if all of this extremely realistic decay was an art piece Tom had commissioned, but that didn't feel right because Tom hated age and grit.

"Hello?" I called out. "Drake? Lila?"

There was no response, so I circled the building until I came to an opening at least eight yards wide. A corrugated iron panel was lying on the ground nearby. Stepping over some crumbling cinder blocks and a pile of empty, crushed beer cans and the shards of broken wine jugs, I made my way inside the building itself.

Tom Kelly's compound was gone. It hadn't been changed, or re-thought, or downsized — it wasn't there. In the few days since I'd last come by to borrow the cash for Rocher's bail, the pavilion had vanished, or moved on. There were no layers of glass, no ghostly lobby, no core of workrooms and guest quarters, no undying black-and-white garden, and no evidence of Tom's lavish, arctic greeting zone with its soaring glass fireplace. The warehouse's interior was echoing and empty and looked as if it had been that way for many years. There were a few halfhearted clumps of the white gravel that had once been so meticulously raked and furrowed, but otherwise there were only cracked concrete slabs, tufts of valiant, scraggly weeds and a small orchard of those hardy urban trees that take root in any abandoned building, nurtured by puddles of gasoline and gusts of bus exhaust. The debris was illuminated by shafts of grayish-white sunlight streaming from the gaps in the building's rotted roof, and a pigeon squawked and flew out.

"There's been nothing here, for almost twenty years," said a voice, and Brant Coffield, Tom Kelly's business partner, stepped out of the gloom and stood a few feet away in a camel-colored cashmere topcoat, with the raw light glinting off his highly polished wing-tip shoes.

"After Tom died, I thought about keeping everything just the way it was, as a sort of memorial," said Brant, "or a museum. But I knew that people would get suspicious. And Tom and I had made a deal: He'd wanted everyone to believe that he was still alive, that he'd live forever. So I let people think that Tom was always out of the country or at his house in New Mexico. I said that he was tired of this place. Bored to tears."

"Did they believe you?"

"Of course. Pretty soon I didn't even have to start the rumors, they'd just spring up, from all over the world. People would claim that they'd seen Tom meditating at some mountaintop ashram in Nepal or scuba diving with a hot Australian lifeguard along the Great Barrier Reef or sketching outside a tent pitched on a glacier in Greenland. As long as he never showed up, people would believe anything."

"And you knew my mother?"

"Yes. She was so beautiful, just heart-stopping, but she had something else. She was the only person, male or female, who could make Tom, not relax, or even behave himself, but she could make him, I suppose the only word is — happy. She delighted him. He once told me, 'This girl, she knows exactly who I am, she knows that I'm the most cunningly constructed pile of horseshit known to man. And she loves me anyway. And I still can't figure out what's wrong with her.'"

"What happened to everyone else? What about Lila?"

"Lila needed Tom more than anyone. So when he died, she couldn't function. Your mother tried so hard to comfort her, but two weeks later Lila killed herself. Pills. She left a note, it was mostly just random words and cross-outs, but there was one complete sentence: 'I don't know what to wear.'"

"Jesus . . ."

"Your mother found the body. And she left the next day. I didn't blame her. All of those deaths, Tom, and Alicia, and then Lila. And your mother was still so young."

"And Drake?"

"Drake was lucky. Tom had left him money and a beach house. So Drake lived to a ripe old age. He died a few weeks ago. Natural causes."

"But how did all of this happen? What allowed it? Or who? I mean, do you think it was God?"

"I don't know and I don't think we'll find out, until we get there, to wherever, although I'm sure that wherever Tom ended up, things are very exclusive."

"Of course. He'd never go to heaven, unless there was a VIP room."

"But I do have a theory. I think I know who might be behind everything. Someone like God or Allah or Buddha, one of that crowd."

"Who?"

"Mrs. Chen."

I smiled. Maybe he was right. Mrs. Chen had been aloof but very good at her job, and she'd been the only person Tom had listened to. Maybe Mrs. Chen had designed Tom himself and Rebecca and the rest of us. Maybe only Mrs. Chen had the necessary skills to create not just some extraordinary dresses, but so many far less chic human beings, for a far-ranging Fall collection. Or maybe, like Lila and my mom and me, Mrs. Chen had worked for Tom, and the larger answers lay elsewhere. But I did know this: If my red dress had embodied, as Tom had told me, the sometimes violent, occasionally cinematic and always vivid spectacle of life itself, and if my white wedding gown had called for truth, especially in matters of the heart, then my black dress was definitely this season's uniform for an elegant lesson in loss and grief and acceptance.

When my mom died I'd been heartsick, but even more, I'd felt angry and frustrated. I hadn't understood why she'd hated doctors, and why she'd found refuge in sour-cream-and-chives-flavored corn chips and orange soda and old TV shows, but most of all, I'd felt that my mom had let herself die and that she hadn't even put up a fight. But now I was even more amazed — at how long she'd held on, and at her cheerfulness, and at her belief in the ultimate goodness of the universe. I almost loved her more now that I knew the details of her own breakneck joyride outside East Trawley. For such a reluctant person, she'd dared so much, and just like me, she'd fallen in love with someone she never would've met in the canned goods aisle of the Super Shop-A-Lot.

"But what about you?" I asked Brant. "Why did you keep Tom's secret, for all of those years?"

"A deal's a deal. And Tom was right, his plan was good for business. But when I saw him that day, oh my God. I had missed him so very much. I'd even missed fighting with him."

"And when you saw Rebecca?"

"I saw your mother."

"But just now, how did you recognize me? I mean, come on — things have changed."

"You're right. Rebecca was quite something. She was pure Tom Kelly, showing off. But while Rebecca was extraordinary, I mean, simply staggering . . ."

"I remember."

"You're not bad yourself. You look just like your parents. I'd have known you anywhere. And they'd be so proud of you."

I could feel myself blushing, as if a teacher had just awarded me an A-plus and five gold stars on my final exam. I loved what Brant had told me but I also knew that, well, he was a friend of the family.

That was when it occurred to me to investigate my square, quilted black kidskin purse with the silver clasp worked with Tom's initials. Inside I found the latest issue of *Vogue*, which fell open to a full-page ad with a radiant color photo of my mom and Tom Kelly, standing with their arms around me. We were wearing Tom Kelly T-shirts and unlike Tom's usually disdainful models we were all grinning ear to ear, as if we were sharing the very best secret. We were on a white-sand beach with the bluest ocean and the ad was for a new perfume in a heart-shaped bottle, called Forever by Tom Kelly.

The ad made me start to cry and smile at the same time. Then I heard my mom's ringtone, for what I was pretty sure would be the last time, coming from inside my purse.

I answered the phone. It was Tom.

"We have to go," he said. "But there's someone who'd like to talk to you."

"Becky?" said my mom's voice.

"Mom?"

"We love you, sweetie."

Before I could say anything, she was gone, forever. But I knew that I'd been so lucky to have a mom like her, and I also knew that wherever she and Tom were hanging out, the cell phone service was incredible.

HER ROYAL HIGHNESS

Epilogue

I have now been the Queen of England for almost fifteen years and if you believe the online polls and my husband and at least one of my children, I'm doing pretty well at my job. And my life has become bigger and more rewarding than anything I'd ever dreamed.

Of course after Gregory and I were first engaged, everyone, meaning the English press, was irate and suspicious. The consensus was that Prince Gregory, on a drunken binge, had picked up some drab American hotel employee, renamed her in honor of his great lost love and had then disastrously decided to Do the Right Thing. My name had been the source of international consternation, no matter how often the palace liaison had explained that I was, at most, an extremely distant cousin of Rebecca Randle's and that I preferred being called Becky and that no, neither the prince nor his fiancée nor any other human being had heard from Rebecca.

Rocher had ended up solving everything with a highly rated, in-depth interview on an American network newsmagazine. She'd watched this program for years, so she'd known what she was doing.

"Yes, I knew Rebecca, and Becky is my best friend," Rocher had begun, while seated on a white marble bench in a picturesque rose garden, wearing an earnest aqua pantsuit, with her hair in a tidy braid. She'd been the image of a fresh-faced, perhaps Amish, girl being truthful. "Rebecca was so lovely, like a beautiful butterfly. She was devoted to Prince Gregory, but she felt a higher calling. She was summoned. I'm not saying that she's in a convent, in a distant land, heavily veiled and using another name, like Sister Silencia Pax Serena, and that she's not allowed any contact with the secular world, but who can say?

"As for Becky, well, she's the best. She's a hard little worker and when she was four years old and we would play with our Barbie dolls, her Barbie would always visit the broken toys and the spoiled food left out on the counter and anyone who was sad. And I remember thinking, Becky should grow up and become a registered nurse. Or a princess."

When she was asked if Becky and the prince were in love, Rocher had grown misty, gently placing her hand over her heart.

"I only hope that someday, I can find a love as deep and as lasting, with someone as handsome as Prince Gregory, with a built-in pool and a hot tub."

After I'd accepted Gregory's proposal I'd flown to London, where I'd been introduced to Queen Catherine in the palace library. "But we've met before, haven't we?" she'd said. I'd always trusted the Queen so I'd replied, "Yes we have. For a while I was Rebecca Randle, but then Tom Kelly returned from the dead and changed me back into Becky, and Gregory and I are both fine with it."

The Queen had taken a prolonged sip of tea and leaned back in her chair as the corgis looked to her. "We thought so," she'd concluded and the dogs had happily charged at me, demanding to be petted and nuzzled. Gregory and I had been married in a simple, private ceremony in a reception room at the palace, with only the prince's immediate family and Rocher in attendance. I'd worn a Tom Kelly wedding dress that I'd bought off the rack.

Queen Catherine had died three years later, and because Gregory's father, Prince Edgar, wasn't a blood relation, the crown had passed to Gregory. Queen Catherine had left a proclamation that had been read into the record at Parliament, stating that her grandson, "If he applies himself, will become a more than acceptable King" and that her granddaughter-in-law, Becky, "has the makings of a really number one Queen." Of course I'd had to abandon my American citizenship but I was considered a humble yet welcome bridge between the two nations. I became what one tabloid had headlined, "Queen Becky and Why Not?"

Gregory and I had then produced two children, a son, whom we named Thomas, because I knew how much it would've embarrassed Tom Kelly to become a grandfather, and our daughter, Roberta, for my mom. Prince Thomas, who's now twelve, still adores me and whenever his father scolds him for running through the palace halls or for eating with his fingers, Thomas likes to claim, "I can't help myself, it's the Missouri." Robbie is only four, but she's already a heartbreaker and I'm not sure how I feel about that. Maybe someday I'll warn her about the hazards of beauty, just so she can ignore and pity me. In the meantime, she's stubborn and she likes to throw things. She's not being haughty or entitled, she just likes to throw things.

After my wedding I'd appointed Rocher as my secretary. Since then she's run my life and encouraged me to wear a down-filled vest with my crown for at least one of my official coronation portraits. Rocher has now been married three times that I know of, first to a bartender she met at my wedding reception, then to a Brazilian soccer player and who can blame her, and finally to the Earl of Lownesderry, who's squat and sputtering but who lets Rocher introduce him using an exaggerated backwoods drawl to tell people, "And y'all, this here is Earl."

Being the Queen of England is, of course, exhausting and yes, I make sure that my staff glues thick felt pads along the interior bands of all my crowns and tiaras, because otherwise I get deep, painfully reddened indentations across my forehead and behind my ears. But together Gregory and I have been able to do some good, and Dr. Barry now oversees five new burn units across England, along with outposts in South Africa, Indonesia and India. I've spent time with Selina, who, thanks to countless reconstructive surgeries, now uses a wheelchair and has graduated from Oxford with a degree in a form of mathematics I can't even pronounce. Her face is still a mass of scar tissue and she sometimes wears a hat with a veil. "I don't do it to spare people the sight of me," she's explained. "I wear it because I get so tired of seeing everyone trying to arrange their own faces into appropriately compassionate expressions. I sometimes wish that just like me, nobody had a face, just so we could all stop wasting so much time worrying about what we look like, and what other people look like, and how we measure up."

Which brings us to Rebecca. I have to admit that occasionally, when I see another Exciting Exclusive on her purported whereabouts, I forget what I know and I think, oh, wouldn't it be amazing if they actually found her! I wonder what she looks like now? Then I catch myself but still, I find myself missing her, as if she'd been an entirely independent person. Some nights I'll stumble across Rebecca in a showing of *High Profile* on late-night cable. I'm glad there's an irrefutable record of Rebecca's beauty so that when someone asks, "I don't get it, what was so special about her?" they can take a look.

Every so often I catch Gregory, when he's asleep in bed or dozing on a convenient couch, murmuring, "Rebecca, Rebecca . . ." But so far, it's always turned out that he's been secretly wide awake, so that he can laugh uproariously at my vanity. Despite this I still love him, which is why at those moments when I don't feel like making love I pass him the remote and say, "Oh, just watch *High Profile* and do it yourself."

As the years go by I'm more and more aware of what I really look like. I'm remarkably similar to Queen Catherine. I'm not hideous but I'm not even remotely beautiful. People, especially the English people, approve of me because, as many school-children have tended to put it, I'm "a regular sort of person," like someone they might find themselves standing behind at a grocery store checkout. But because I'm the Queen, I secretly believe that there's an additional dimension to my neighborly appeal and I like to consider myself majestically ordinary. I also feel that my profile looks very distinguished on all the souvenir shot glasses and tea towels.

I wish with all my heart that my kids could've known their grandparents, but mostly I'm grateful for my own unorthodox upbringing. I've decided that my mother, for my first eighteen years, taught me how to be good and then Tom Kelly taught me everything else. Since he'd only been given a year, Tom had packed in as much tough-love fathering as possible. He hadn't been a conventional dad but that didn't matter so much. You can learn a lot from three dresses.

And when I'm feeling glum, because Gregory's away or because my daughter's just hurled her full glass of milk at my head, or just because time is passing, I like to scroll through the annual East Trawley High School online newsletter, which gets mass-emailed by Shanice Morain, who's on her second marriage and who cohosts her own Christian Soul-Support and Teen Prayer Variety Hour on local TV and who's been appointed our class secretary. In the current Alumni Notes section I read that Katelynn Streedmore has just been named the head dietitian at the Jamesburg Assisted Care Facility, that Cal Malstrup and his wife Chelsea Marie have just welcomed their fifth bundle of joy, whom they've christened Blake-Jorlinda Malstrup, and that Becky Randle is still the Queen of England.

ACKNOWLEDGMENTS

I would like to thank my editor, Rachel Griffiths, for her inspiring enthusiasm, her pitch-perfect insight, and for making this book so much better, and shorter. I am also endlessly grateful to everyone at Scholastic for making me feel so welcome, including Lori Benton, Ellie Berger, Stacy Lellos, Bess Braswell, Leslie Garych, Sheila Marie Everett, Tracy Van Straaten, David Levithan, Kelly Ashton, Rachael Hicks, Elizabeth Parisi, Annette Hughes, Elizabeth Whiting, Corrine Van Natta, Alan Smagler, Jacqueline Rubin and everyone in the sales department, Lizette Serrano, Candace Greene, Catherine Sisco, and Emily Morrow.

I would also like to thank David Kuhn and his terrific staff for making sure this book found such an ideal home.

For their patience, humor and support, I am hopelessly indebted to Jay Holman, Todd Ruff, Patrick Herold, Susan Morrison, Claudia Shear, Christopher Ashley, Harriet Harris, Peter Bartlett, Dana Ivey, Jamie Krone, Scott Berlinger, Robert Wyatt, Kim Beaty, Adrienne Halpern, Allison Silver, Marea Adams, David Colman, Albert Mellinkoff, Dan Jinks, Candida Scott Piel, Andre Bishop, David Remnick, Scott Rudin, and for friendship and wisdom on all things royal, William Ivey Long. I'd also like to thank Robert Bookman for his many years of advice and dedication.

Finally I must, as always, thank John Raftis, for putting up with so much, for making my life possible, and for baking the very best brownies, from scratch and otherwise.

In my opinion, all of the people mentioned above, and anyone who has read this book, are all impossibly gorgeous.